NICKLE BRICKLE'BEE
IN THE HEART OF
EARTHWORKS

STERLING NIXON

The final approval for this literary material is granted by the author.

First printing

All characters appearing in this work are fictitious. Any resemblance to real persons, living or dead, is purely coincidental.

ISBN: 978-1-951780-06-7 (Trade paperback)
ISBN: 978-1-951780-16-6 (Hardcover)
ISBN: 978-1-951780-07-4 (eBook)

Printed in the United States of America

Sterling Nixon

Dedicated to Arnica, Adelaide, Conner, Eden, Hunter, Isaac, Jack, Jane, Jordan, Johnathan, Madeline, Rosie, and Talon

NICKLE BRICKLE'BEE
IN THE HEART OF
EARTHWORKS

Prologue

The Death of Hector

Between the last night of the old year and the first day of the new one, a man named Hector lay dying on his bed. He had blue eyes that twinkled in the weak light of the room. Long silver hair flowed from the old man's head and crowded in around him, almost as if he was swimming in it. It was not his strange sickness that was finally finishing him, nor was it old age catching up. This man was, in fact, as healthy as a four-hundred-year-old man should be.

But his time had run out. The three wisest scholars of EarthWorks knew this end would come, they even planned on it, but now as it was happening, none of them felt prepared. And so a host of Healers were summoned to the bedside of Hector, each one doing the best they knew how, yet each one failing in their own right. After their many attempts, they were sent away like a flock of disappointed school children.

Instead of sending for his closest friends to replace the Healers' presence, Hector sent for his closest enemies—his great-great-great-great-grandchildren, who, by the way, were not that great. There were five of them—all of them thirsty for the power they thought they deserved.

Jane Hawthorne was the first to arrive, or so she thought. She stepped into the small windowless room and peered into the darkness. When her eyes finally adjusted, she sat next to her great great great great grandfather's side, patting the old man's hand. Jane Hawthorne was tall and slender. She could have easily been athletic, but a lifetime of book reading prevented it. She was smart and ambitious—or so said the whispers in the dark. From the top of her head, a nest of black hair twisted down in worm-like curls until it reached her neck.

"Oh, great Hector, it is I, Hawthorne, your firstborn granddaughter and the first to arrive here this night—"

Before Jane Hawthorne could finish, a large man exploded through the small front door. The sudden entrance was so forceful that it snapped one of the hinges and sent it swinging to the side. The man stood in the doorway, his barreled chest puffed up like a threatened lion. His arms were thick and leathery; his eyebrows were bushy and unkempt. It took a moment for the large man's eyes to adjust to the dimness of the room, moments longer for his small brain to register the scene. "Hector, it is I, Brutus. I hope I'm not too late—"

"Be quiet, fool," Jane hissed. "He sleeps."

"He does not sleep," answered a third voice. Another man stepped out of the shadows, revealing a well-built frame with a set of sharp eyes. The man was not as tall as the other two, but he seemed twice as sure-footed. A large scar dripped down the man's left eyebrow until it reached the bottom of his chin. It had been a horrific wound when it was first inflicted, but now, it was nothing more than a purple reminder of a horrible past. "He was in the midst of conversation when you came in, Jane."

"Locke?"

"Yes," the dark figured replied.

"What are you doing here?"

"I would ask you the same question," Locke said as he took another step forward, "but I already know the answer. You came to see if it was your poison that finally finished the old man off."

"It's not like you're any better than the rest of us, or have you forgotten your sins as easily as you remember mine."

"I am not perfect, I'll readily admit it, but I at least learn from my mistakes."

Before Jane Hawthorne could reply, another man galloped into the quickly shrinking room. This man was dressed differently than all the rest, having a mix of colors on him that were so bright it forced the other three to squint. Hobbes was short and chubby. He had a fat nose and a smile that was as contagious as the flu. The man had been drinking, there was no doubt about it; how much he had been drinking became the question on everyone's mind.

Jane Hawthorne straightened up. "Hobbes, you intoxicated wretch, how in the world did you find the right place?"

"I was looking for a urinal—so you tell me if I found the right place."

"Well, this is no urinal," Brutus barked. "And if you turn it into one, I'll rip your arms off and force you to clean up the mess."

Jane Hawthorne arched her eyebrows and rubbed her forehead. "How will *he* be able to clean it up if he has no arms?"

Brutus' only response was a blank stare.

Hobbes weaved back and forth through the room on his wobbly legs. "Why aren't the rest of you as drunk as me? The old man is finally dead; it's time to celebrate! He must have made the Selection."

"He's not dead," Jane Hawthorne hissed.

"He can hear you," Locke added.

"Well, I hope he can," Hobbes said as he gave a slight bow towards Hector.

The other three individuals rolled their eyes.

"What?" Hobbes shrugged. "All of you wanted him gone more than me, and now that he lies on his death bed, you pretend that you did not? Liars! Hypocrites! Wolves are more loyal than you three."

Jane cleared her throat. "Actually, wolves are very loyal creatures."

Hobbes frowned. "What? What do you know; I'm the one who's drunk!"

Just then, the door slowly slid open, revealing a man clothed in one of the blackest robes ever made. The color was so dark that it seemed to carry the very essence of the night sky. From the middle of the hood, two large eyes peered out, watching each of the others with care. The already dark room turned even darker as the figure stepped forward, a loud clanking sound followed with each step. The man stopped mid-stride and looked at everyone in turn. "Well, is the old crank dead?"

"No," Locke replied.

"Not quite yet," Jane Hawthorne added.

"I hope he will be soon," said Hobbes.

Dante put a cold hand on Hobbes, who could not help but shiver. "So anxious, my festive fiend. And why do you think he will Select you after everything you have done?"

Hobbes shrugged the hand from his shoulder. "I have done the least evil of any of us—everyone knows that. While the rest of you have plotted and pretended civility, I at least did not play the part of a hypocrite. Hector knows I hate him; he knows I don't trust him.

If I'm guilty of anything, it's of a truthful heart and the courage to speak my mind."

Locke cleared his throat as Hobbes mentioned the word "courage."

The colorful man turned around and faced the noise. "All of you are crazy—including you, Locke. Do you think you can fool Hector into believing that you have changed? Do you think he can't peer into your soul and see the Demon within? You can't trick the old man for he is *the wisest fool of us all*—don't you remember? For he knows all."

Dante let out a long slow breath, which sounded like a violent wind being squeezed through a narrow crack. "If he is as wise as you say, then he already knows why we are here. Let's be done with this business."

The five figures turned their gaze back towards the broken body of Hector.

"You can't kill me, Dante, not even now," Hector whispered. "But don't worry, I won't be alive much longer; there's no need to add my blood to your already bloody hands. Come closer, all of you. I wish to share with you the most powerful secret I have ever carried."

The others pressed in all at once, pushing each other for a closer position to Hector. Hobbes elbowed Locke, who in turn, shoved Brutus. It became a pushing match for the space around the bed. Soon they were so close to Hector that the old man became stifled by the stale breath that came at him from five directions.

"Don't stand that close," Hector said. "Give me a little more room than that. I won't Select one of you based on how close you are to me when I die."

"Then how will you Select one of us?" Brutus asked in his sluggish voice.

Hector closed his eyes and took in a deep breath. His body then went very still. Moments passed. Jane Hawthorne gave a slight yawn. Then Hobbes yawned. It was only a moment later before another one was yawning, and then another. The yawning became contagious and skipped around the room to each one in turn.

Locke tried to glue his mouth shut, but a yawn forced its way out. He tried to pretend like he was opening his mouth to talk, but the others were not fooled. "Maybe he's fallen asleep."

"Maybe he's dead," Brutus added.

Jane Hawthorne shook her head. "He can't die until he's made the Selection—you know that, or at least you should."

Suddenly Hector stirred, his body gaining new life. "Silence. I need all of you to swear to me a vow of silence. Only three people know what I'm about to tell you, and after I'm gone, there will only be two. I can't tell you everything since I too am held to a sacred oath, but what I tell you now, must be held close to your hearts. You will find that in repeating these words to other people who are not present in this room, you will forget them completely. They will be lost to you as a leaf is blown free from a tree by a winter wind. If you hold to this agreement, I will impart the most important information I have ever carried."

Two of them nodded, another wiped their brow.

Locke swallowed. "What about the Selection?"

"The Selection does not matter now; I made the Selection two hundred years ago. The only thing that matters now is what I'm about to tell you."

Hobbes gave a loud laugh, one that echoed sharply off the small walls around them. "You mean you chose someone a long time ago? That's your news? That generations have been waiting for the Selection and without telling anyone—"

"Ease up," Locke said. "Let him speak."

There was a long pause before Hector finally continued. "In the exact moment of my death, a child will be born. This infant shall appear as nothing, he will be treated like he is nothing, but in his eyes, you will find the key to Everything. He will have the power to bring forth new life; he will have the power to save our people. We stand on the brink of a cliff, a precipice so high that if we fall, we will never recover. This child has the power to stop the evil wave that will soon crash against our crumbling society."

Dante shrugged. "Save us from what, old man? Our people are stronger now than they have ever been. We're not falling apart."

"Oh, Dante, you lean too much on the power of your flesh. None of your mortal strength can stop the immortal tides of darkness that will be set upon you. It will not be many more years before your only hope lies in the heart of a child. You must find this child and aid him in the task he was sent to perform."

11

"How will we know him?" Jane Hawthorne asked.

"Who cares?" Hobbes interjected. "One out of billions of babies are born and—"

"Silence," Locke hissed. "Let Hector finish." He turned his gaze back towards the old man. "How will we recognize this child?"

But Locke's question remained unanswered, for Hector, the wisest fool of all, spoke no more.

Chapter 1

The Life of Nickle Brickle'Bee

Nickle Brickle'Bee was odd—even by his own standards. When most boys were starting to get hair under their arms, Nickle started growing whiskers on his chin. By the time he was fourteen, or so he reckoned, he could grow a full beard. Doctors would have blamed it on his hormones—that is, if Nickle had ever been to a real doctor. Sometimes Nickle would just stand in front of a mirror, staring at his odd features for hours on end, trying to decide why he was so different from everyone else.

But that is not where the oddities ended, which his peers were more than eager to point out. He also stopped growing when he was six, and everyone around him quickly passed him up. He felt ambivalent towards his small size. Sometimes it was nice to be short: He permanently fit into his favorite shoes and pants, and he also received extra portions of food, almost as if everyone was trying to force-feed him more height. But unfortunately, his small size also had a downside: He permanently became the front row of every photograph he was ever in, and he could never go on any of the roller coasters that everyone talked about. He had tried all kinds of stretches and exercises, ate all types of high-protein foods and drinks, but nothing seemed to work.

Of all the things that prevented friendships the most, the color of his eyes was by far the worst. His eyes were blue around the center of the pupil, but as they progressed to the outside, they suddenly became an emerald green. The contrast was so sharp, so unique that his eyes would often send people pulling back in surprise.

Nickle Brickle'Bee could not remember anything before the age of six, and even then, it was somewhat foggy. His first real memories situated him at an orphanage in a cold, grey building. Kids were not so judgmental back then, and Nickle made friends quickly.

He read a lot, even though he was not good at it. The orphanage library was not very extensive, and it almost seemed to end before it really began. Half of the "books" were comic books; the other half consisted of outdated college books. But there was a tiny portion of books that were somewhere in between. This is where Nickle spent most of his time.

After several years in the orphanage, Nickle was sent to live with a foster family, the Gretchens. Their house was large but ill-kept. They had more dogs and cats than Nickle thought was possible—or legal. Every day, as Nickle would stroll through the lonely house, he would see a new cat or dog that he had never seen before. The Gretchens rarely spoke to Nickle, and when they did, it was usually about his feelings. They were horribly afraid of trampling on his feelings, almost as if Nickle's emotions were more important than Nickle himself. Frequently, Mrs. Gretchen would apologize for no apparent reason at all.

"We're so sorry," she would constantly say. "So sorry that you aren't feeling as good as you should."

The one nice thing about the Gretchen's house was a library that offered a more extensive selection of books. These books had real stories in them—ones that made you think long after the last pages were read. He would spend hours in the library, reading and re-reading everything he came across. Months passed and still, Nickle did not feel like he knew his foster parents any better than he knew the enigmatic man that dropped mail into the house at three o'clock every day.

At first, Nickle ignored the mound of letters that began to stack up by the door, that is, until they started tipping over. One day as he passed by the entrance, he happened to take a look at a few of the top envelopes. All of them had been marked with an odd phrase that was in blood-red ink: LEGAL ACTION HAS BEEN TAKEN.

The longer Nickle stayed, the less he saw of the Gretchens until one day, he never saw them again. A few days later, two men with black ties showed up and took him to a new home, one that had a bright red door and blue curtains.

This family had a little daughter who insisted on being called Susan B. Worthhall, even though her name was Kerri Livingston. They, at least, appeared to be a functional family. Mr. Livingston enrolled Nickle in Karate a few days after he had arrived. On the ride over to the Dojo, Mr. Livingston explained to Nickle that his small size would make him a prime target for "muggers."

This, unfortunately, was the only piece of advice Mr. Livingston gave that was worth listening to. Within the first five minutes of being in the Dojo, Nickle found himself thrown up against a bathroom locker by two large kids dressed in Karate attire. Nickle was not sure how he did it or if it was even him, but the next moment the two kids were rolling on the floor in pain.

The rest of the Karate lesson was not so bad—that is, until Mr. Livingston had to come early to pick up Nickle. The two large kids had told on Nickle, saying that he had jumped them while they were in the bathroom. The Sensei called all three boys into a small office and stared at them separately for several minutes—Nickle was half the size of one of the two kids. The Sensei did not believe a word of the other two boys, but that did not matter to Mr. Livingston, who was sure it was all Nickle's fault.

It was not many days after that incident before Nickle was sent to another family—the Creshaws. The Creshaws enjoyed two things more than anything: first, their plasma television, which they loved so tenderly they nicknamed it "Old Skip." Nickle thought the reasoning behind the name "Skip" was because the Creshaws "skipped" everything else so they could have more time with the TV. Second, they loved seafood. If it was not the main course in every meal, it was most assuredly the topic of discussion. Mr. Creshaw had once worked on a fishing boat named the Navigator. While at sea, he had eaten anything and everything that could even remotely be called a fish. He had been hospitalized several times because of what he ate, but through his efforts alone, scientists learned loads about non-edible fish and their effects on the nervous system.

It was actually through Mr. Creshaw's fishing exploits that he met Mrs. Creshaw. Several months after Nickle had arrived, and during commercials of prime-time television, Mr. Creshaw related the romantic story in detail, which involved a sinking ship, a roguish rescue, and six orders of oysters. Between the detailed descriptions of fish guts and the Creshaws' first kiss, Nickle began to feel queasy. Just before the story finished, he felt his fishy dinner swimming up his throat.

Ten minutes later, Nickle was rushed to the hospital. His arms were shivering while the rest of his body was sweating. After several hours in the emergency room, the doctor came out with the prognosis, "Nickle is deathly allergic to shellfish."

The Creshaws wept for days.

A few weeks later, Nickle was moved to a different family—the Darengers.

On the first day there, Mr. Darenger sat Nickle down in his home office. "It's good to meet you, Nickle Brickle'Bee—that's an interesting name. Where does it come from?"

Nickle swallowed hard. "...Don't know, Mr. Darenger, I was very young when they gave it to me."

"Hmmm...," Mr. Darenger scratched his head. "It doesn't sound Swedish or French. Maybe Danish? I will have to look into it. Well, that doesn't matter. Call me John, all the kids do."

"Are they all your kids, Mr....I mean, John?"

"Some of them are, but not all of them. Mrs. Darenger and I take in a lot of kids and do what we can for them. We built this farm to facilitate as many as we could. Now, I have only one major rule here: never lie. If you do something foolish, you'll get in trouble, but if you lie about it, you'll find yourself with much bigger problems. Can you live by that, Nickle?"

"Yes...John."

John was a handsome man, although premature wrinkles were showing up just beneath his eyes. He had short brown hair that was stylishly messy. Every morning, John would wake up at first light, run four miles, lift weights, and work out his abs before breakfast. Most of the older kids followed the same routine.

At eight every morning, the whole family gathered for breakfast, which was always prepared by Mrs. Darenger. Every meal was served buffet style. It was all delicious, from the crispy, honey-smoked bacon to the weird toast the kids called "camel's eye" to the warm blueberry muffins. The oldest kids were always assigned to eat next to the younger ones, and Nickle found himself paired with a hulking ten-year-old. Even though Nickle was several years older, the kid was several inches taller.

"My name is Brian."

Nickle gave a slight nod and rubbed his light beard. "I'm Nickle."

"So how old are you?"

"Don't know, really. Probably fourteen, maybe thirteen."

"How come you don't know?"

"No one has ever told me."

"How come you can grow a beard already?"

"Why can't you grow one?"

Brian rubbed his face thoughtfully. "I don't know. No one has ever asked me that. How did you get one?"

"I rubbed hot sauce on my face," Nickle said as he took a big bite of sausage. The topic of his beard had always been a source of amusement to his peers, and so Nickle always had a response ready. Sometimes he said the beard grew best after an application of syrup or garlic. It was one of the few things he said that occasionally got a laugh or two.

"And that worked?"

"Depends on the face. It worked on me."

"Why would anyone want a beard anyway?"

"Hey, you asked me. I was just answering."

After breakfast, the kids excitedly left the house and walked over to a massive structure that was in the backyard. They filed into a side room that had dozens of dirt-covered cubbies and rows of coat racks. As the children entered the room, they began fishing out and putting on overalls. By the time Nickle arrived in the changing room, the only pair of overalls not claimed by the throng of screaming children was three sizes too big. He put it on anyway, hoping that his broad shoulders would compensate for the saggy bottom. He had to walk slowly to keep from tripping, but even at the sluggish pace, he almost fell twice. The kids made a long line as they headed through another set of foggy glass doors that opened up into a gigantic room. Nickle was the last one to enter.

The moment he went through the door, he knew that this place was something special. The smell of coarse dirt and water-soaked air hit his nose.

John walked through the glass doors. "There you are, Nickle. Come here. I've got something to show you." He grabbed Nickle by the arm and pulled him through a third set of glass doors. The air suddenly became even more moist and warm, almost as if they had just stepped into a bathroom after someone had taken a hot shower.

It was so thick that Nickle found himself gagging for breath. "What is this place?"

"This is a nursery."

In every direction that Nickle faced, he could see nothing but a stretch of greenery. There were thousands of plants, from bushes to trees to multi-colored flowers to large vines that hung from the ceiling. Many of the plants were on large tables that were placed in perfect rows. Just above these plants was an elaborate system of pipes and tubes that moved water and fertilizer throughout the whole building. In the middle of the structure there was a gigantic tree with a trunk that was ten feet in diameter. The tree stretched up to the top of the building where it suddenly stopped. Large vines hung from the top of the branches and sunk into the ground, almost like they were roots.

As they walked, John pointed to his right. "These are Encyclia Citrina. They have waxy flowers that smell like lemons." Then he pointed to the left, "Those tube-like flowers are called Clivia Caulesens. They are a rare plant that only blooms every three or four years. Do you see those red ones behind it? Those are Protea Compacta; they have a furry center." He stopped in front of a flower that had purple petals hanging down from a bushy middle. "This is a Passiflora Aragorn, and it was grown by Brian—that young boy you were sitting next to at breakfast. I feel sorry for the poor kid. He hasn't adjusted well since being here. Just this morning, I caught him trying to spread hot sauce all over his face. Poor guy."

Nickle turned pale as guilt knotted in his chest. For a few brief moments, he began to wonder if he was in trouble. *"I've told that joke at least a dozen times before, and no one actually tried to put something on their face. But, if Brian did, would that really be my fault?"*

"Nickle," John repeated.

Nickle looked up, his attention being pulled from his thoughts. "I was just joking."

John arched his eyebrows in question.

Nickle shrugged as he realized that John had continued to talk and was now speaking about something completely different. "I must have been daydreaming."

John smiled. "Come on. What I want to show you is over here." They passed a jumble of kids as they continued to walk deeper into the greenhouse.

John nodded to all of them. "Good job Robert. Remember to water the roots and not the leaves; they can get sick if you water the leaves. Excellent idea to repot that Bluebeard shrub, Megan; I was wondering when someone would get around to it. Jane, did you check the soil pH? You might not need to add more lime if the soil is not acidic."

With Nickle still at his side, John climbed a set of stairs that wrapped around the central, gigantic tree. "This tree is the heart of the nursery and is as rare as they come. As a young boy, my father and I went on a search for these trees—we only found four of them. I was able to cultivate one of the seeds and bring it back here, where it became the first plant of the nursery. It grew for a few years, but then started to die. It was not until fifteen years ago, while I was out on safari, that this thing really started taking off."

"It's amazing."

John stopped and looked at the branches. "Yeah, it is, but that's only half of what I wanted to show you." He walked another ten feet onto a catwalk towards a small planter. "This one is yours."

"My what?"

"Your responsibility."

"What is it?"

"A planter. It's empty now, but soon, with your care, this box will be full of plants." John handed Nickle a bag of seeds. "Whether these seeds grow and bloom, or wilt and die, will depend on you."

"What are they?"

"They are Laelia Furfuracea. When they are well cared for, their flowers bloom a bright purple; if they are not, they are usually a light yellow."

"What do I do to take care of them?"

"I'll teach you. We have a lesson every day at 11 o'clock. You'll learn everything from how to fertilize and check a plant's pH to how to make sure you're not overwatering."

Nickle looked from the seed bag to the planter and then back to the bag. "I've never done this before. I'll probably kill them."

"Maybe, but I think not. You're a smart kid, and I'll be helping you the whole time. All of the kids here started just like you, but most of them now have a greener thumb than me."

"A green thumb?"

John gave an affectionate smile. "Just an expression."

Nickle sighed deeply and looked around. Just a few feet farther down the metallic catwalk, there was another planter with a gigantic plant. It had a considerable stalk that climbed up to an enormous bud. The bud was light green and sickly looking—most of the edges were brown or black.

Nickle pointed to it. "What's that?"

John's shoulders lowered. "That's my failure; that's a Titan Arum. It's the world's largest blooming flower, growing up to eight feet and weighing in around two hundred pounds. It took six years of care for the flower to reach the blooming stage, and now that it's there, it just won't bloom. When it does bloom, it has a large white center that smells like rotting flesh, which attracts flesh flies that pollinate it. But don't worry about that plant; I don't think she'll be with us much longer. Here, let me help you plant those seeds."

Chapter 2

The Doppelganger

Nickle was not sure how it happened, or even if he agreed to do it, but within a few days, he found himself waking up at 6 o'clock every morning and running with John. There was a mess of kids that ran with John, all of them between the ages of 10 and 16. Nickle hated running. To him, it was like watching the nature channel in slow motion.

Slowly, ever so slowly, he pushed his body along, heaving with deep breaths as the other kids left him far in the dust. He imagined himself as some little caterpillar, eking across the pavement in the morning sun.

As Nickle was finishing his first lap, a motley group of kids approached him as they were coming back from their second. Nickle recognized a few of them. As they passed, he could feel their stares, feel the way they looked at his light beard and discolored eyes. A few of them even snickered as they jogged. Nickle did not give it much thought, however. He was used to kids staring.

After running, Nickle ate breakfast and returned to his planter in the nursery. He did not know why, but for some reason, he was excited to see his plants. It had been only a few days since he planted them, but already they were three inches tall, which did not seem possible—even to Nickle, who knew next to nothing about plants.

He attached his hose to the rack above and opened a water valve. Nickle looked around, making sure that no one was watching. He leaned in closer to a plant until he was only inches away. Then he put his finger in the dirt, pinching it as delicately as he possibly could. Nickle's mouth started to water as he placed the soil on his tongue. The taste was rich and creamy, almost like an Oreo milkshake. It made him thirsty.

"You need lots of water today," Nickle whispered as he pulled

21

the hose in closer. He released the valve and carefully sprayed the base of the plant, which seemed to eagerly suck in the moisture. After several moments of watering the first plant, Nickle moved to the second. He tasted the soil—it was like a saltine cracker.

"Hmmm…your soil is slightly acidic. How about a little mixture of lime and water?" Nickle applied the correct dosage and moved to the next plant. This soil tasted different, almost like a mix of burned onions.

"I'm not sure what that means, but I'm sure water will help."

Nickle continued to go to each plant, tasting the soil as he went. Each one wanted something different, and he did his best to comply with their wishes. Just as he was finishing up, someone put a heavy hand on his shoulder.

"Nickle."

Nickle turned around to see John's muscular frame.

"I thought that was you. You skipped right through lunch; I was worried. What have you been doing?"

Nickle turned towards his plants. "Just working on my green thumb."

John smiled. "That's good. I'm glad to see you've taken to gardening." There was an awkward pause as the large man pulled a bucket closer and sat down. "How do you like it so far?"

Nickle shrugged his shoulders. "Not bad."

"How have the other kids been treating you?"

"Good."

John gave a slight laugh. "You're a pretty brave kid."

"John," Nickle said quickly. "There's something I've got to tell you."

John frowned. "What's wrong?"

"I told Brian that my beard grew after I smeared hot sauce on my face. I say that joke all the time, but I didn't think anyone would actually try it."

John laughed, his frown disappearing. "I'm sure you didn't mean for him to try it." He pulled in closer, his eyebrows arching with concern. "What are you so worried about?"

"I just really like it here…with the plants and everything," Nickle said quickly. "I don't want you to be mad at me."

John shook his head. "No harm done. But maybe that joke is

one that we should—" Suddenly, he stopped talking; he almost stopped breathing. "Whose plants are these?"

"Mine. We planted them on my first day."

"Those are close to three inches tall. Are you sure they're yours?"

"They should be."

John pulled his face closer to the plants, touching one of them gently with his hands. "This is a Laelia Furfuracea."

"Yeah, that's what we planted, isn't it?"

"How's this possible?"

"I know. I can't believe how big they are already."

"I don't think you understand, Nickle. These plants can't be this big. What did you add to the soil?"

"Same stuff everyone uses: fertilizer, water, lime—"

"—I can't believe this," John whispered. "This is amazing. Can I take one of these plants? I need to run some tests."

"Sure."

John grabbed a shovel and a small pot. As gently as he could, he started reaching for one of the plants.

"Wait," Nickle said, "not that one…that one gets lonely…."

John raised his eyebrows slightly. "Ok, what about this one?"

Nickle nodded. "That one works."

John stood, brushing dirt from his pants. "Thank you, Nickle. Oh, by the way, you've got a bit of dirt at the corner of your mouth."

"Oh, right. Thanks."

As John was disappearing down the stairs, he gave Nickle a thumbs up. "Good talk, Nickle. I'll get back to you soon about your plant."

Nickle went back to work on the rest of the plants, each one seemed to take longer than the last. Finally, after all the watering was done, he sat down on a bucket. His fingers were numb from the water, and his shoulders were sore from stretching back and forth along the planter. As he sat there, thinking about the last few days, he happened to look to his right. There sat the wilting Titan Arum.

Nickle stood and slowly approached the plant. He did not know why, but for some reason, he felt a reverence for it. Once he reached the plant's side, he put a dirty hand on the base of the plant. The soil for the Titan Arum was a composition of the finest dirt that

Nickle had ever seen. It had everything that a plant could possibly want, including an automated watering device that knew precisely when the plant was thirsty.

"Why aren't you blooming?" Nickle whispered. He dragged his hand through the dirt, feeling the texture of the soil. It gave off a rich smell that tickled Nickle's nose. He took a pinch of the earth and put it on his tongue.

"He's eating dirt," a voice yelled.

Nickle turned towards the voice to see the pale and unpleasant face of a boy he did not recognize.

The boy continued. "Did you see him? He was eating dirt!"

Nickle stood up and brushed his hands together. "No, I wasn't."

"I saw you."

Nickle took a step forward. "That's crazy. Who eats dirt?"

"Don't lie," another boy said. "I saw you too."

"What are you talking about?"

The boy ignored the question. "Why are you eating dirt?"

Nickle laughed nervously. A large weight of embarrassment trickled down his throat until it settled in his stomach. "I was smelling the dirt not—"

Suddenly a voice from a loudspeaker interrupted. "It's time for dinner. Everyone wash up."

The pale-faced boy gave off a sharp laugh. "I guess you can stay here because you've already eaten."

The other boy laughed.

Nickle stared at the other kids, unsure of what to say. He was trying to think of something witty, but all his comebacks had disappeared from his mind—so had his confidence. The only thing he could do was stare at the two boys, hoping they would interpret his gaze as being intimidating rather than indecisive.

One of the kids, a tall, skinny boy, threw his head back in laughter. "Look at him! He can't think of anything to say! What a loser."

"What's wrong," the other kid chimed in, "you forget how to speak?"

"What an idiot!"

"You're one to talk," came a low voice from behind the two

boys. All eyes turned towards the source of the noise. It was a boy named Jason Burntworth.

Jason stepped closer to one of the larger boys. "Jeremy, just two days ago, you wore your shirt inside-out for half the day, and when someone finally told you about it, you nearly broke down in tears. And then when you did come back, supposedly after you had fixed your shirt, you were wearing it backwards."

Jason turned towards the other kid. "And you, Handel. You can't even spell your name the same way twice in a row. Look at the knot you tie your shoes with. I'd suggest buying Velcro shoes, but you'd probably manage to mess that up just as badly."

Jeremy and Handel stiffened, their mouths slightly open.

"Well, you two better get off to dinner," Jason said with a wave of his hand. "Go on. Get outta here."

The two boys locked eyes with Jason, sizing him up. Suddenly, Jason lunged forward, slamming his foot into the metal floor. The noise, coupled with the movement, sent the two boys running down the metallic stairs.

Jason laughed as the boys disappeared. "They're never as tough as they seem." Once the boys were gone, he turned his attention back to Nickle. "Punks. When I first got here, everyone made fun of them. Now, here they are picking on the new guy."

"Thanks," Nickle replied. "I'm good at coming up with comebacks, but it's usually a day after I need them. While in the moment, I can barely think of my name, let alone something witty to say."

"Forget about those kids," Jason replied as he stuck out a hand to Nickle. "My name is Jason, Jason Burntworth." Nickle took the kid's hand and shook it. Jason was only slightly taller than Nickle and had a broader chest. He had a dark complexion that complemented his brown eyes. His face was narrow and seemingly chiseled from stone. He was a messy eater, as Nickle quickly observed. At the end of almost every meal, he would either end up with a goatee of ketchup or a mustache of Kool-Aid. It was hard to take anyone seriously when they were sporting a red mustache. Nickle had to stifle a laugh when he first looked at Jason, who was now wearing an odd combination of the two.

"My name is—"

"—Nickle Brickle'Bee," Jason interjected. "Yeah, I know who

you are. Let's get something to eat before all of the good stuff is gone. Come on." Jason led the way down the stairs, Nickle quickly followed. Once they reached the outer doors, Jason nodded towards the house. "Don't worry about that lanky kid. He's been acting like that lately."

"I'm not."

"He's bigger than you."

"That just means he's easier to spot when he comes charging towards me."

Jason laughed. "Where did you grow up?"

"All over. What about you? How old are you?"

"Ten."

Nickle shook his head. "No way. You seem older than ten. If I had to guess, I'd say that you were about my age."

"That's because I use a rejuvenating cream on my face every day."

Now it was Nickle's turn to laugh. "So how long have you been here?"

"Just a couple of weeks, but it feels like months. This place is a lot different from where I'm from."

"Where are you from?"

"It's a long story. I'll tell you later."

Dinner was oddly quiet that night. Besides some small conversation between Nickle and Jason, no one seemed to laugh too loudly or talk too much. If someone did talk, it was all in whispers, almost as if they were in the middle of church. Nickle had the sinking suspicion that they were whispering about him.

As Nickle was halfway through his food, odd ideas started bubbling up in his mind. Every thought that came to him eventually formed into the large bulky shape of the Titan Arum. Its weathered bud appeared in Nickle's mind, whispering to him. It was like a thousand small voices that poked and prodded his brain.

Before anyone was finished, Nickle grabbed his plate, scraped off the food he did not eat—which was mostly peas—and headed back towards the nursery. He was halfway there when a bush just right of the large greenhouse suddenly shook. At first, he ignored the noise and pushed on, but the closer he got to the nursery, the more violent the bush began to shake. Soon it became a constant, unremitting thrashing that sent dozens of leaves flicking through the air.

Nickle stopped. "Who's there?"

The bush stopped shaking. "I'm just a bush."

Nickle rolled his hands into two fists. "Who's there? What's your name? It's too late for you to be out here."

"And what about you? Isn't it past your bedtime too?" The voice was odd and accented.

Nickle slowly approached, trying to peer around the leaves of the bush. "I forgot something in the nursery."

"And what was that?"

Nickle sidestepped to his right. Something about the stranger's voice sounded so familiar. "How do I know you?"

"You see me every day."

Nickle sidestepped again. He could see the intruder crouching against the nursery wall. "Where do I see you?"

"Every time you look in a mirror—"

Nickle leaped in, grabbing his opponent around the shoulders. The intruder did little to resist, and soon Nickle had him around the waist. With a massive breath of air, Nickle threw the intruder to the ground. The crash did not have quite the effect he had hoped. Instead of seeing the scared face of his opponent, as he suspected, he could see nothing but an old tattered coat that had been stuffed with some sort of pillow.

A boy revealed himself from behind another bush. "That's it! You tell that old coat! Give him all you've got."

Nickle turned and faced the voice, his hands ready to fight, but as soon as the boy's face came into full view, Nickle relaxed his fists. The boy wore a white shirt and leather pants. He had a thin beard, a roundish nose, and two eyes that had circles of green and blue in them.

"Don't be shocked," the boy replied. "It's always easier if the person does not panic or ask stupid questions."

Nickle took a step back. "What are you?"

"Already, you're beginning with the stupid questions. You might never know why I'm here; you might never see me again. If I attempted even the smallest explanation, it would just confuse you."

Nickle felt his face. "You look just like me."

The other boy began walking around Nickle, inspecting him as if he was some sort of relic. "Yes, I do. They did good work tonight. Most of the time, it's some rookie Cennarian that's assigned the task of the Changing. I usually end up with a few missing toes or fingers, which is a detail that most of these Piddlers tend to notice."

"What are you doing here?"

"I can't answer that."

"Why not?"

The boy pulled out a fist-sized Frisbee from a pocket. "Against regulation."

Nickle stepped forward. "What do you have in your hand?"

"This is a Rune."

Nickle swallowed. "A...Rune? What is a Rune? Is it dangerous?"

"Your questions aren't important."

"I think that last question was."

The boy laughed. "I knew there was something different about you—you've got a sense of humor, although it's buried deep beneath your dirty little hands. Maybe you don't belong here after all."

"What do you—"

"—Here, catch." The boy threw the Rune towards Nickle, who snatched it out of the air. As soon as he caught it, he regretted it. The disc began to hum like an idling car. He tried to drop it, but it would not let go; it grabbed him and stuck to his palm, almost like it was melting into his skin. Light began to pulse from the disc. It became stronger and stronger, sending glowing rays that reflected off the ground and the nursery wall. It was so overpowering that Nickle could not see anything around him. Moments later, the light shot into the dirt. The earth shook and sputtered, sending a ripple that set off the neighbor's car alarm. In the distance, dogs began barking.

Nickle swallowed. "What is this?"

"It's your ticket down."

"To where?"

"Save your questions," the boy yelled.

The earth began to shake more and more. Each time it moved, it cracked like lightning. Nickle's legs felt like jelly. His whole body twisted and turned. As the noise became more constant, the ground beneath Nickle started to split open. It was just a small hole at first, but soon it stretched out until it was six feet in diameter. Nickle was hovering in the air, his body seemingly unaffected by gravity. The thunder became more constant until it was one thick sound.

Suddenly, the noise stopped, and the light disappeared.

Nickle's body was held in the air for a second longer before he was hurtled into the darkness below.

Chapter 3

The Cogs of Hurn

Nickle's face rippled in the wind. Every time he opened his mouth to yell, he could feel his cheeks slapping against his teeth in quick succession. He still held the disc in his hand, which occasionally gave off a faint blue light; instead of trying to shake it from his grip—like he did before—he now held onto it as if his life depended on it. After several moments of falling, he began to lose all sense of direction. He shivered and shook his head, trying to shake off the feeling of vertigo.

He could see nothing but dirt. From what he could tell, the circular tunnel seemed to have no end. He squinted his eyes, trying to see into the blackness below, but this only made his vision blurry.

On and on, he fell. He tried counting the seconds, but he kept losing track after a hundred. It could have been hours or just minutes, but finally, the air started to change. A warm wind hit his chest, which seemingly slowed his fall. He looked at the walls around him and noticed that they were not blurring past as they did before. Far below, he could see people walking around. He was still so high above them, they seemed like ants. He drew closer and closer until, suddenly, he belly-flopped onto a stone floor.

His chest hit first, followed by his head. The air was instantly pushed out of his body. It took a couple of agonizing seconds before his lungs were able to work correctly.

While he struggled for air, two sets of hands grabbed him by the armpits. "Why didn't you put your feet out in front of you? You could've broken a rib."

Nickle could only pick out a few words—the rest was a muffled blur. He was barely aware of people all around him talking, barely aware that he was being dragged across the ground. He was not sure how long he was out or where he even was, but when he first opened his eyes, his mind immediately rejected his surroundings. After blinking as many times as he was old, he realized he was not dreaming.

All around him were miniature women and men with braided hair and beards. Some were dressed in medieval battle armor, others were clad in leather, and still, others who wore kilts with white baggy shirts. The room Nickle was in was the biggest he had ever seen. It was carved from a smooth stone. The walls stretched up until they became an elegant dome high above. Large Nordic letters lined the room, occasionally glowing with an amber-brown or a light green.

Along the walls and in almost every direction were statues of fully armored, bearded men and brawny women. As Nickle watched them, he noticed that their chests heaved back and forth with breath; a few of them were even bouncing weapons in their hands, almost as if they were looking for a fight. As Nickle looked up at one of the statues, the stone figure furrowed its brow and stared back, gritting its teeth.

He was pulled to his feet by a squat woman. "And what is your name?"

"Nickle…Brickle'Bee."

The woman pulled out a flat piece of rock and began drawing on it using her finger. "Nickle Brickle'Bee, eh? Here you are. Ooh, you'll be heading off to the Cogs of Hurn. Your case must be a special one."

Nickle did not want to sound rude, but he could not help himself. "Why do you have an accent? What kind of people are you?"

The woman pulled her head back and put a hand on an axe that was at her side. "What do you mean 'you'?"

"What are you?"

"Same as you—or at least I think."

Nickle squinted. "What am I then?"

"Confused," the woman replied.

"What are you?"

"Not confused."

Nickle shook his head impatiently. "Why are all of you as short as me?"

This phrase did not seem to have the effect that he was hoping. Silence fell across the big room as every face within close proximity turned Nickle's direction. In the distance, a tray of dishes crashed.

From all around, axes were being drawn and teeth clenched. A group of a dozen or so stepped closer to Nickle, sizing him up.

Nickle frowned. "I think there's been a mistake." He leaned into the closest man and whispered, "I don't know where I am, or who all of you are. I don't know why I'm down here."

"Mistake, boy!" The largest of the bearded men yelled as he stepped forward, pushing a few of the others out of the way as he did. "Yes, there's been a mistake, but you just made it."

Nickle swallowed. "I apologize. I'm sorry."

"Down here, lad, we follow the rules and regulations. And the first rule you have to learn is never to call a Dwarf short—that sort of thing will get your head severed."

"What?" Nickle's voice squeaked. "Easy now. I don't want trouble."

The man stepped forward. In his hands bounced a massive axe that was as thick as a book and sharp as a razor blade. "Oh, don't worry, this won't be any trouble at all."

"I'm sorry."

"Close your eyes, lad."

Nickle closed them, but only slightly. "Just wait a second. Are we sure this is the best idea?"

The Dwarf did not seem to be listening. Instead, he pulled back his axe, ready to strike. "Don't worry. This will only take a second." As the axe came forward, the bearded man yelled. A moment later, Nickle felt something cold hit the back of his neck. He fell forward and grabbed the wound with his fingers, screaming as he collapsed to the ground.

For a few brief seconds, Nickle was almost positive that his head had been removed from his body. He slowly reached up to his neck, where he thought he would find nothing but a stub. After his fingers reached his hairline, they tentatively continued on. With a sigh of relief, he realized his head was not missing. Nickle suddenly became aware of the laughter that was all around him. A rush of embarrassment flushed through his body as he realized how stupid he must have looked, crumpled on the floor, screaming like an infant.

"Thornhead!"

The man with the axe turned. "Who calls?"

A large man with thick forearms stepped forward. He was taller than the bearded people around him, much taller. A scar hopped from the man's right ear to his left eye, traveling in a wicked and purpled "L." The man was undoubtedly a warrior. Neatly cut and carefully trimmed black hair marched around his mouth and covered his chin. It was barren in places—to allow small scars fresh air—but it so completed his presence, it looked as if he had been born with it. Along his arms were dozens of old purpled wounds. The scars were so course that they looked like roots, grown over years of farming on the battlefield. He was calm, except for his eyes, which darted from left to right. He was wearing blue armor that was slightly dented and worn. Collectively, his presence demanded attention, and respectfully, it was entirely given. "What are you Dwarves doing? Why are you pestering one of the Fallen?"

"You watch your tongue Locke, mind breaker. This area is under our control, not yours. The Tri'Ark doesn't control any of the Dwarf outposts that are still near the surface."

"You might be Chief Warlord of the Dwarves, but I'm one of the Holders of the Five Seats, and I've been placed in charge of the new recruits by order of the Tri'Ark."

"New recruits!" Thornhead laughed. "This boy won't pass the scrutiny of the Cogs of Hurn, nor does he deserve to be down here. It's against regulation for a watered-down version of a Dwarf to be enlisted by the Tri'Ark."

"That regulation has been absolved and is no longer your concern."

"You're right," Thornhead hissed. "It's not—yet."

Locke smiled and laughed. "You power-hungry dirt-digger."

Thornhead matched his smile. "You brain-numbing Scathian." He then turned back to Nickle. "You're lucky that old Locke got a litl' bit of mercy still left in him. Watch your tongue next time."

The crowd dispersed, leaving the confused Nickle in the middle.

The Scathian walked up to the boy. "My name is Locke."

"What sort of creature is Thornhead?"

"He's a Dwarf, same as you—or so they say." Locke dropped his tough demeanor ever so slightly and nodded towards a distant door. "Follow me. I'll explain it on the way to the Cogs of Hurn."

"What are the Cogs of Hurn?"

"They are the Dwarf senate. They consist of the oldest, most talented group of Dwarves ever assembled—at least, they're supposed to be. I don't put much stock in what they say, but that's the way it has been done in the Dwarf Quarter for the last two hundred years."

"And what are they going to decide?"

"If there's enough Dwarf in you to consider you a Dwarf."

"I thought you just said I *was* a Dwarf."

"Well," Locke replied, "you look like one."

"Is it because I can grow a beard?"

"Most Dwarves start growing a beard at age six—you didn't see hair until you were ten, or so they say."

"Who are 'they'?"

"The spies that have been watching you."

"Dwarves have been watching me?"

"Just one Dwarf has been watching you, and that wasn't until recently. Before you moved to the Darengers, you were being watched by a group of Thieftians."

As they spoke, a man on top of a horse appeared, a thick sword in his hands. "Hail, Locke, Holder of one of the Five Seats. Is this the Dwarf I'm sent to protect?"

As Nickle stared more at this newcomer, he began to realize that this was not just an ordinary man on top of a horse. He had, in fact, the lower body of a steed and the upper of a man. His Human form was sharply defined with muscles that covered every inch of his body. His nose was flat and wide.

Locke nodded. "One and the same, and just in time. This boy only has been down here a few minutes, and he's already had a run-in with Thornhead."

"Thornhead is more bark than bite."

Locke gestured to his side. "This is Nickle Brickle'Bee."

The horseman bowed. "My name is Edward. Most everyone calls me Ed."

"Ed?" Nickle smirked.

Edward sheathed his sword. "Is there something about my name you find funny?"

"It's just...you're part horse, and you talk, and your name is Ed."

The giant warrior flexed his muscles and tightened his jaw.

"And what of it?"

Nickle's face turned serious. "Nothing. Nothing at all is funny about that." The air turned awkward. Nickle scratched his shoulder and looked around. "So you're a Centaur, eh?"

"That's the name the Piddlers have for us. We call ourselves Cennarians after the old language."

"I find it hard to believe that—"

"—we actually exist," Edward said with a grin. "Yes, I know, but we've existed longer than humans, longer than any creature if our legends are to be believed."

Locke sighed. "There's much that Piddlers don't understand about the world—especially what's beneath them—but there's too much to explain and not enough time to do it." Locke gestured towards a large set of golden doors. "This is the entrance to the Cogs of Hurn. If you run into trouble, Edward will make sure you get out alive."

"What do I do?"

Locke furrowed his brow. "You pull on the handle and walk inside."

"No, I know how to operate the door. But what do I do when I'm inside? Why do I need someone to protect me? Are they going to ask me questions?"

Locke shrugged. "There isn't really...a set way that the Cogs of Hurn decide something. Maybe they will, maybe they won't. But either way, go in there with confidence and your head held high."

"And what if I don't want to do this?"

"In this matter, I'm sorry to say, you don't have a choice," Locke kneeled. "Once the Cogs of Hurn issues a Summons, you are compelled to answer. Be honest with them; be honest with yourself. But, for your sake and mine, don't call any of them 'short.'"

Nickle nodded.

"Don't worry. Ed will be waiting right outside the door if you get into trouble. Get in there; you'll do fine."

With a nod, Nickle tentatively approached the entrance. He finally reached a large doorknob and tugged on it until it opened, revealing a long stone hallway. Along the walls were large, carved depictions of Dwarf warriors. As Nickle stepped farther into the entrance, torches lit up along the way. He could hear noise ahead of him; it sounded like a boxing match. The closer he got to the room, the louder the noise became. At the end of the tunnel, he found himself in a large room that had eight walls and a massive dome. In each corner, there was a giant statue of a grim-looking warrior.

But it was not the room that surprised Nickle; it was the two figures in the middle. Two Dwarves were locked in combat, both of them bloodied and bruised from battle. They wore rags that were wrapped around their thick fingers. Despite the strain on both their faces, neither one seemed ready to yield. The room was filled with laugher and random cheering.

"Hold it!" shouted a voice to the right. "Hold everything! The boy is here."

This sudden announcement distracted one of the fighters, giving the other a clear shot to his chin. The Dwarf was struck hard and fast, sending him flying backward; as he hit the ground, a golden tooth popped out of his mouth and flipped through the air towards Nickle. The boy caught it just as it was about to pass him by.

The room filled with applause, almost as if this was a planned spectacle. Nickle did not know if he should take a bow or not; fortunately, he was not given too much time to think about it.

The warrior that lost his tooth righted himself and walked over to Nickle, patting him on the shoulder. "Thanks, lad." Using a thick set of fingers, the Dwarf stuck the tooth back into his mouth, where it locked into place. He pulled Nickle into the center of the room, "Here's the boy. Did I not tell you he would be here on time?"

Some in the crowd booed while others cheered.

A high-pitched voice cut through the noise. "Quiet, everyone. Quiet. As the elected Consul of the Cogs of Hurn, I call this meeting to rotation. All arise." The Dwarves slowly arose, almost as if this was the greatest inconvenience. The voice continued, "With the Imperial Mandate of 212, which was supported by seventy-five votes to sixty, all those of Dwarf descent are hereby subject to the call and command of the four Dwarf Lords. The Cogs of Hurn, with the oversight of the Tri'Ark, has now been entrusted with finding and educating those of Dwarf descent of their duties. In light of the World Devolution act of 209, Dwarves have been summoned to return to the earth from whence they came—"

"Do we have to read this every time?" a gruff voice asked.

The Consul continued, acting as if she had not heard. "It is our duty to study a…Mr. Nickle Brickle'Bee…to see if his blood belongs to the people of Hurn. I will moderate this session, and if there are any more outbursts, Mr. Dangerfield, I'll have you dragged out, and your vote absolved. Mr. Brickle'Bee, please come to the center of the room."

Nickle swallowed as all eyes rested on him.

"He's slightly taller than normal," said a gruff voice.

A younger Dwarf cleared her throat. "That doesn't mean anything. My father was a finger's length bigger than this lad, and he was a pure-bred Dwarf."

"Or so your grandmother claimed," whispered a voice in the back. The room filled with scattered laughter.

"Who said that?"

"What color are his eyes?"

"I think they're blue, or maybe green."

"Dwarves always have brown eyes—even if they are a watered-down version."

"So, is he a Dwarf?"

"He can grow a full beard."

"So can Humans."

"But not by the time they're fourteen."

"But most Dwarves have a full beard by age seven. This boy has had a late start."

The Consul cleared her throat. "What do the Runes say, Pontifex?"

All eyes turned towards a grey-haired Dwarf that was seated in the back row. The old codger was so filthy that he looked more like a pile of dirt than he did a Dwarf. One of the Dwarves nudged the Pontifex in the side.

The old Dwarf stood up. "Present."

The Consul shook her head. "Pontifex Greggory McDooble, you have been entrusted with the high office of Pontifex, and since you alone control the Runes of Prophecy, please try to stay awake."

The Pontifex nodded.

"Well, Pontifex, what do the Runes say?"

"Oh, oh," McDooble coughed. "They say that the surface will be sunny today with a high of 95 degrees—"

"No, what do they say about the boy."

"Boy? Boy? I'm no boy. I'm over seven thousand years old—"

"Tell us about Nickle Brickle'Bee."

The Pontifex was silent for a moment before he spoke again. "I was a Legate in the Great War. I fought against the Vamps of Nordum—I am no boy."

"Tell us about *the* boy."

"The boy…the boy," the Pontifex raised his eyebrows. "Oh, that boy. What did you say his name was?"

"Nickle Brickle'Bee."

The old man wrinkled his nose and sat up in his chair. A cloud of dust followed as he stood. Nickle was unsure if anyone else saw it, but he could have sworn the old Dwarf gave him a wink. The old codger pointed a shaky finger towards Nickle. "Yes, that is the boy. Bless Hurn's belt, that is the boy."

"What do the Runes say?"

"They only say one thing about Nickle Brickle'Bee: He isn't not a Dwarf."

"That means he's a Dwarf, right?" the Consul asked.

"I did not say that."

A larger and fully armored Dwarf on the front row stood up. "Oh, let's just punch the lad in the face and see if he can take a hit like a Dwarf. That's the best way to find out if he is suited to live down here anyway."

"What if you hurt the boy? Wonder if you kill the lad?"

"Then, we know he's not a Dwarf."

Another Dwarf stood up on the opposite side of the room. "How about I hit *you* in the face and let's see how well you take it."

"Come on then, you mangy, bearded pup. But be sure you say your goodbyes before you do."

Before either of the Dwarves could step forward, the Consul's weary voice interrupted. "We will not have another fight in here—that would be our fourth of the day. Sit down, both of you. We are not a bunch of drunken brawlers. This is the Cogs of Hurn, not a street show."

A Dwarf with a thick red beard nodded. "Aye, let's get this vote on the way. It's time to eat, and I'm so hungry my stomach is about to leap of out my body and start chewing on the stone floor."

The Consul stood up. "I don't think we have all the facts. We haven't talked about the boy's history with magic or his physical strength. We have no idea what the boy is capable of, or if he's capable of anything."

"Well, if he can get this assembly to call a vote, then he is certainly more capable than the rest of us. Listen, the Runes of Prophecy have spoken—sort of. They say he's a Dwarf; the old man is just reading them backward. I vote for conscription."

"I think the old Dwarf is reading them just fine; I don't think Mr. Brickle'Bee is a Dwarf."

"We need more time to discuss it, Dangerfield," the Consul insisted.

"I second Dangerfield's vote. He's not a Dwarf."

"Yes, he's certainly not a Dwarf."

"We already have too many of these half-breeds messing everything up as it is. We don't need another one."

"He doesn't belong here. His world is with the Piddlers on the surface."

"Yeah, that's right."

Nickle felt something rising in his stomach. He had watched the Dwarves debate his future long enough. "Don't I get a say in all this?"

"No," the Consul said quickly.

Before Nickle hardly knew anything about this new world, it already felt like it was being taken away from him—just as every foster parent he had known, just as every friend he had ever made. "I don't know who I am. I don't know anything about your world, but I can tell you now that they don't want me on the surface."

"Quiet, Mr. Brickle'Bee," the Consul ordered.

"I've never asked for anything from anybody," Nickle replied. "I've never expected anything more than what I've earned. But there has to be a way I can prove myself."

"That is not how things are done," Dangerfield yelled.

The Consul clenched her jaw, her frustration finally overflowing. "Dangerfield, your vote has been absolved. And you, Mr. Nickle Brickle'Bee, are to remain silent unless questioned."

"I'm sorry," Nickle said.

"Look at how weak he is," Dangerfield added. "I bet he wouldn't last a day in Tortugan."

"You don't even know me," Nickle whispered.

"That's it," the Consul roared. "Guards, escort Dangerfield out of here! And take that half-breed with you. We'll make this determination without any more interruptions from either of you."

Nickle looked up, his face rising to meet the eyes of the Consul. "I might not be a Dwarf, but I'm not weak—"

Nickle would have continued, but two giant Dwarves in bulky armor approached his sides. They had large axes on their backs and smaller throwing axes on their belts. Even on Nickle's most impetuous days, he would not want to anger these guards.

The Consul finally regained her composure, "Thank you, Brickle'Bee. We have all we need from you. We will let you know soon if you'll be conscripted. Please find your way out of here."

Nickle opened his mouth to say more, but one glance at the two warriors at his sides, and he knew it would all be in vain. Without another word, he followed the warriors to the end of the long hall. They stopped just short of the entrance, allowing Nickle to walk out alone.

Ed was there waiting, his face set in a deep frown. "That was quicker than normal."

Nickle shrugged. "I guess it didn't take long for them to size me up."

Ed tightened his jaw, afraid to ask his next question. "And how did they vote?"

Nickle frowned. "It was good to meet you Ed, but I doubt I'll ever be seeing you again. I appreciate you protecting me. I better get back to the surface."

Ed opened his mouth to speak, but no words came out. He tried again, but again there was nothing but silence. Finally, he nodded resolutely, "Follow me. I'll take you to the airshaft that will send you back to the surface."

Chapter 4

The Conscription

Nickle Brickle'Bee shot out of the earth like lint from a dryer, his legs kicking wildly as he did. The wind was knocked clean out of him as he landed on his back. Despite it being the early hours of the day, he could see stars just outside his reach, flashing and disappearing as he stared up at the sky. He shook his head and leaned on his elbow for support. *"I must have been down there the whole night."* He could see Mr. and Mrs. Darenger cooking breakfast, a group of boys coming back from a morning run, and the large greenhouse and its misty windows.

Nickle stood up and began walking towards the house, but he did not get very far before he heard a voice behind him.

"Hey, Brickle'Bee."

Nickle quickly turned around. "Yeah. Who's there?"

"It's your substitute." A small boy revealed himself from behind some bushes.

Nickle forgot all about the look-alike after he had been swallowed by the earth, but now as he saw him, the memory came rushing back. "What are you doing hiding again?"

"These people are crazy."

"What do you mean? What are you talking about?"

"Hey, I'm just warning you."

"What did you do?"

"Just be careful—that's what I'm saying. And if they ask you about the living room, just tell them it was like that when you got there. Just tell them it wasn't you."

Nickle frowned. "It wasn't me."

"I know that, and you know that, but a lot of people in the house don't know that."

"I didn't do anything."

"That's the spirit. Deny even if they pry—that's my motto."

Nickle glanced back at the house, straining his neck so he could better see the temperament of Mr. Darenger. "I need you to come with me. They'll never believe I didn't do it." But as Nickle turned around again, he quickly found out he was talking to himself—this time, it was only himself. His look-alike had left him, left him to pay for his crimes. Nickle clenched his jaw.

Two seconds later, he heard John Darenger's voice coming from the house. "Nickle! I see you hiding out there. Get in here!"

Nickle obeyed, but he went as slowly as he could. When he reached Mr. Darenger, he looked up with his set of big colorful eyes, trying with all his might to eke out an ounce of compassion from John.

"What did you do to the living room?"

"I…I…," Nickle shrugged, "I honestly don't know."

"Let me remind you," John said as he led Nickle through the house.

The two walked down a hall, through the kitchen, and past the front entrance before they finally reached the living room. The room was drastically different than what it was only a night before. Instead of wood walls, the room was stone. Large pillars circled the edge of the room, giving it an ancient look. The pillars illuminated an ambient light that waxed and waned as someone approached or touched them. Along the far wall was a massive fireplace that was sprawling with precise and perfect carvings. The room was bigger and taller—a lot taller. Where the second floor should have started, the ceiling pushed higher and higher into the house. Oddly, however, this did not seem to interrupt the rooms above.

As Nickle stepped further in, the wonder only continued. On the far wall and a few steps down, there was a marble Jacuzzi, which was currently bubbling out a sweet vanilla smell. A few feet more and there was a steam room.

"I did not have anything to do with this," Nickle whispered.

"Well, it's amazing," John answered. "Handel says he saw you working on it all night."

"Handel? Who's Handel?"

"He's the tall, freckly boy. He says that once you saw him, you called him a 'filthy Piddler' and punched him in the face."

"That doesn't sound at all like me. I wouldn't punch anyone in the face—not even if they deserved it."

John kneeled next to Nickle. "Whatever you did in this room is amazing, but just because you have talent in one thing does not mean you can pick on Handel."

"Is he ok?"

John nodded slightly. "He'll be all right, but you gave him a bad black eye and a bloody nose. I've been looking for you all morning, but you keep getting away from me. Listen, I appreciate what you did for the home, but I don't think you belong here."

Nickle pulled his head back slightly. "What? I just got here."

John frowned. "I know, but we just can't have someone going around punching kids. It's not safe, especially when we have so many kids."

"John, I'll do better. I promise."

"This isn't the right place for you."

"I'm so sorry. Can I apologize to Handel?"

John shook his head. "He spent the night at the hospital. He doesn't get home until later today."

Nickle's eyes began to fill with tears. "What about my plants?"

John's voice cracked as he answered. "We'll take good care of them. This might be temporary; we don't know. Maybe we can get you back after a few weeks."

Nickle looked down, ashamed at the gathering tears. He knew John was lying. There would be no way he would be allowed to come back. He knew how the system operated—knew how state official's decisions were always based on decreasing any and all liability. After this, Nickle would likely be returning to the orphanage. At least for a time, foster families would not be an option for him.

Nickle wiped at his eyes, forcing his tears back. He made sure his voice was level before he spoke. "Can I see my plants—just one last time."

It was too much for John, who seemed torn between two splitting emotions. A tear slipped from his cheek and hit the floor. "All right, sure."

Nickle turned to go, his steps slow and methodical. He glanced back just before he reached the kitchen. "Thank you, John. You've got a good heart. I won't forget that."

John gave a weak smile. "You're a special kid, did you know that?"

"When do I leave?"

"In an hour. I'll pack your things."

"It shouldn't take you too long," Nickle jested. "I've only got one small suitcase to my name."

John laughed politely, and Nickle left the room. With his shoulders low, he walked out the back door and down the path that led to the nursery. He was slow to put on his coveralls and even slower to find his gloves. After a few minutes, he finally reached his planter. His plants shook ever so slightly as they felt Nickle's presence. But Nickle did not stop there; he continued until he was next to the Titan Arum.

He collapsed next to the large plant and covered his face with his hands. Then the tears came, unbidden and unwelcome. He only allowed two tears to escape, and he hated himself for it. One of the Dwarves had accused him of being weak, and now he seemed to have confirmed that weakness. He wiped away the tears and took a deep breath.

When he looked up, his eyes fell on the Titan Arum. "You don't belong here either, just like me."

Then something weird happened. For a split second, a memory popped in Nickle's head, almost as if it had been a segment of a dream. Nickle looked at the Titan Arum more closely. "Was that from you?"

The plant did not answer.

Nickle stretched out a hand and scooped up some dirt. "What do you know that you're not able to share?" The earth felt moist as if it had recently been watered. He looked around to make sure no one was watching. He did not know if he could stand to be teased right now. After he was sure he was alone, he put some of the dirt on the tip of his tongue. It tasted like nothing but dirt at first, but, slowly, thoughts, almost like memories, began to drift into his mind.

Nickle pulled his head away from the dirt he was holding, almost as if it had been poison. "What are you telling me?" He hesitated for a moment longer before he tasted the soil again.

There was a man. He had a sword in his hands. He was running, running from something...or to something. He was in a tunnel that stretched out for miles. The sword slowly turned into a scepter and then a sword again. The man's skin flashed purple and then back to peach. This repeated a few times until his skin turned a permanent red. Nickle did not know why, but this figure was so familiar. It was the eyes that stood out to him; they were just like Nickle's eyes, having a circle of green around a smaller circle of blue. *"Is that me?"* The perspective of the memory constantly shifted: One moment Nickle was the man, another moment he was watching the man run. As the man drew closer to what he sought, his eyes grew darker.

When the man found what he was looking for, the image turned hazy. There was a loud noise—someone was screaming—and then silence. The man finally emerged again, this time with a bandage tied around his eyes.

"Nickle," A voice called from behind, "they've decided."

Nickle was so lost in thought he did not hear the boy that was approaching from behind. "What does it mean?"

"It means you have to go now."

Nickle turned around. "What?"

It was Jason. "You've been conscripted into the Silver Army. You are to report to Hurn."

"Hurn? Conscripted? What are you talking about?"

"I'm just like you," Jason replied.

"Where's your beard?"

Jason rubbed his chin. "I swallow Rune pills every day that keep me from growing one—at least for a while."

Nickle gave a weak smile. "So, you're a Dwarf?"

"We both are." Jason handed Nickle a silver coin the size of his palm.

Nickle looked at the coin, confused by the gift. He turned it over in his hand, each side was blank. "What is this?"

"It's your debt to Hurn," Jason replied.

"My debt?"

"As a Dwarf, you owe your allegiance to the people of Hurn. To pay this debt, you must serve faithfully in the Silver Army."

"For how long?"

Jason nodded to the coin. "Until you fill both sides of that coin with your deeds or…until, you die."

"Die? Nobody said anything about dying."

Jason laughed. "You're funny. But don't make those kinds of jokes when they get here."

Nickle felt more confused the longer the conversation went on.

"They?"

"You'll see."

"I don't know if I'm cut out for the Silver Army. I didn't even know it existed until just now."

"I know it's a lot to take in," Jason said, "but you'll do fine."

"And if I don't want to go?"

"Then you stay here, and you'll never know what could have been."

Nickle concentrated on the coin in his hand, slowly flipping it over. It was just as blank on one side as it was on the other. He looked back towards the Darenger's house. He knew just inside John was packing his pitiful possessions into a broken suitcase. He knew that if he stayed here, he would have to move to some unknown situation that could be worse. As these thoughts came to him, the coin he was holding began to drift into smaller pieces. These smaller pieces broke into even smaller pieces before they seemingly disappeared into his hand.

"What did you do!" Jason yelled. "You broke it!"

"What?" Nickle asked. "I'm sorry…I was just holding it…."

Jason let out a friendly laugh. "I'm just playin'. It's supposed to do that as soon as you accept the offer. They did the same thing to me when I received my coin. It's a lot funnier on this side of the joke."

"But I didn't agree to sign up."

"You didn't have to."

"I'm still not sure if I should go."

Jason put his hand around Nickle's shoulders. "Listen, you've got a place in this world. You might not know where that is, but it's definitely not here. Give yourself a chance to find it. And don't worry. I'll be going with you."

"What happened to the coin?"

"It's part of you now, as is your sacred oath to serve the Silver Army," Jason whispered. "You'll never see it again until your last day when it is completely filled with your deeds."

"So, you're part of the army?"

Jason sighed and looked down. "I'm a Dwarf Tenderfoot, which is about half a step above nothing."

"How do you like it?"

Before Jason could answer, the glass windows on the nursery

began to vibrate. The earth was shaking. It was weak at first, but soon it started gaining in strength. Pots and plants fell haphazardly to the ground, spilling dirt and fertilizer. A window shattered. Nickle was tossed to the floor as if he was nothing more than a sheet of paper. The roof above began to crack and bend, squealing in protest.

Then the dirt started moving. It sifted out in long trails, weaving back and forth like hundreds of small snakes. The soil slithered towards the center of the room, where it collected into a mound on the floor. A wind picked up, forming into a small tornado that ravaged the gardening tools and plants, blowing some of them clear through the nursery. The dirt that was collecting in the middle was soon as tall as John and was still getting bigger. More dirt collected. It began to form into a sizeable six-sided building. Pillars shot out of the floor to support the dirt roof above; a massive set of double doors appeared.

Just as quickly as it started, everything stopped.

Nickle looked up at Jason, who was just standing there as if nothing happened.

"What was that?"

"It's a Cohort. They've come to take you."

"How come you weren't thrown around?"

"It was magic—you'll learn how to resist it."

"What do we—" Nickle began to say, but he was immediately interrupted by a deafening yell. The doors on the newly formed dirt building snapped open. A horn as rich as a symphony orchestra was blown. There was another yell, and then the sound of soldiers marching. The clamor echoed off the walls and became louder with each passing second. At the peak of the noise, a column of armored Dwarves marched out of the center building and into the nursery. They wore silver suits of armor that glistened with Runes. In their hands, they carried large axes that seemed sharp enough to cut through stone. As they marched, they pounded their axes into the large square shields they carried, which made a thunderous tremor that shook the plants around them.

Nickle's eyes went wide as the Dwarves continued to pour out.

"Halt," boomed a mighty voice. "Present arms!" The Dwarves stopped their march and yelled as they held their axes in front of them.

"Form up. Two lines." The Dwarves spread out into parallel

rows that faced opposite directions.

A Dwarf that was as broad as he was bold stepped forward. "We, the sons and daughters of Hurn, call for Nickle Brickle'Bee! We come to claim your allegiance!"

Nickle swallowed.

"Looks like our escort is here," Jason said.

"Where are we going?"

"To the Heart of EarthWorks."

Chapter 5

The Tube

Deeper and deeper, Nickle walked into the earth. He looked at his escort of one hundred armed Dwarves, all who walked with a calm and confidence Nickle felt he would never have. The armor they wore did not seem bulky or heavy, nor did it seem to hinder their movement. The Dwarves moved as freely as if they wore nothing but a thin pair of clothes. The silver-plate armor was so intricately designed with flowing symbols that it seemed more like an object of art than one of protection. Occasionally the symbols would glow a fiery red or a dark blue.

Nickle whispered out of the side of his mouth. "When do I get a set of armor?"

Jason laughed. "You've been in the Silver Army only a few seconds, and already you want your Tines."

"My Tines?"

"It's an old Dwarf word that means your 'second birth'—that is when you get your set of armor. But don't worry about your armor; it will be a good twenty-five years before you'll earn it—maybe even longer if you're not talented."

"I'll be an old man by then."

"No, you won't—not if you're a Dwarf."

"How long do we live?"

"There's not an exact age, but the average Dwarf lasts around six thousand years before they turn into dust."

"Hah. I'm gonna live to be six thousand years old?"

"Yeah," Jason replied. "That is if the Dwarf blood in you is stronger than the Human blood."

"How do you know I'm a mix?"

Jason looked surprised. "How could you not be? You've got multi-colored eyes, and your beard just set in."

"What do you mean, multi-colored eyes? What color eyes do

you have?"

"Brown. Just like every other Dwarf. Only magic-wielding Humans can have blue eyes, and only Elves have green."

"Elves?"

"Yeah, Elves—those pompous pointy-eared prats. They think they own the world and everything in it, and just because they do, does not mean they need to act like it. You'll learn to hate them, all Dwarves do."

"You're telling me that Elves are real."

"Yeah, a little too real if you ask me. I liked them much better in the folklore I learned as a kid. They're so much nicer in stories; of course, that's because they wrote them."

"What about Giants?"

Jason sighed loudly. "Listen, Nickle, I know this might be hard to take in all at once, but this world is a lot bigger than the Piddlers would have you believe. I'm sure that you're full of questions, but I promise you, they will be answered."

"What about Witches?"

Jason laughed. "You'll see."

"Well, at least tell me this: Where are we going?"

"We're going to the Administrative Quarter in EarthWorks."

"Where's that?"

"At the center of the world where the Earth is still alive. Right now, we're traveling to a Worm that will take us to New York City, where we will take the Tube."

"A Worm?"

"Don't get caught on the name. It's a machine made by Mech Dwarves that enables us to travel along the Earth's upper crust. It uses Runic magic to transfer the mass of everyone into a different sphere, which enables the travelers to float through the earth like a submarine does in water. It only works close to the surface, where the dirt can be persuaded to move out of the way. It's a lot quicker and easier to manage than the larger Dwarf Warships. It's complicated. If you ever get the chance to ask a Mech Dwarf about it, I wouldn't take it. Trust me, I did, and I was locked into a three-hour conversation with a bearded dictionary."

Nickle nodded like he knew what Jason was talking about. Every few seconds, Nickle wanted to stop Jason and ask him another question, but he resisted the temptation. By the time they reached the Worm, he had so many questions in his head that he barely noticed the small contraption on the ground.

When Jason finally pointed out their mode of transportation, Nickle laughed as if he had been joking. The Worm was small, almost too small to fit half a person in, let alone one hundred Dwarves. It looked like it only had room for a few backpacks and maybe someone's left foot.

Jason let out a long breath. "I hate this part."

Nickle cleared his throat. "I can see why."

Jason pulled Nickle back a step. "Watch the other Dwarves as they get in. It will make more sense if you see them go first."

The commanding Dwarf took the lead. "Line up! Prepare to board!"

After a few moments of armor clanking, the Dwarves were in one, single-file line. The Dwarf in front slowly put his foot into the Worm. Just as soon as he did, the foot disappeared, almost as if it had evaporated. The Dwarf tightened his teeth as he continued his plunge into the Worm. As the first Dwarf disappeared, the next one followed.

"Is it painful?"

"Not to a Dwarf," Jason replied. "We don't feel pain like Humans do."

"What about a half-Dwarf?"

Jason slapped Nickle on the back. "You'll be fine. It feels like freezing water more than anything else."

It soon was Nickle's turn. He studied the Worm for a second, gauging its size and scope. He could see nothing inside the Worm except a metallic bottom. The other Dwarves had either disappeared entirely or had shrunk so small they could not be seen.

"Just step in," Jason said. "Pretend you're stepping into a pool."

"Hurry up, Nickle," the commanding Dwarf ordered.

Nickle sighed one last time before he put his left foot in. He felt a cold chill trickling up his body. The Worm began pulling him in inch by inch. He panicked. Pushing with his right leg, he fought against the pull of the Worm. The machine stalled for a moment before it doubled in strength.

Jason ran up to the side of the Worm. "Don't fight it. It will snap you in two."

"I can't get my leg back out."

"If you want your leg to stay attached to your body, just let yourself be pulled in."

Nickle half obeyed. He put his other leg in the machine but then braced himself with his arms. "It's freezing."

"It will be done in a second. Just let go of the sides."

Nickle grunted as the Worm pulled him down to his waist. He still held on tight, refusing to be sucked in completely. The Worm once again kicked into a higher gear and began pulling twice as hard as before. He could feel his grip slipping.

"Let go, Nickle."

Whether his grip slipped or he finally obeyed, Nickle found himself sucked into the Worm. His lungs tightened as his breath was cut short. His body felt like it had just been thrown into an icy lake. Everything was so disjointed and confusing. He could see, but just barely. He drifted to the front of the Worm, where he looked around at the other Dwarves that were there. Everyone seemed more like a mist of smoke than they did a person.

Someone bumped into him. "Watch where you're going."

"Sorry," Nickle whispered.

"Someone strap that Tenderfoot down to a chair; he's running into everything."

Nickle felt someone tug on his arm.

"Come on," Jason whispered. "You'll want to sit down before we start moving."

Nickle nodded—or at least he thought he did. He felt so disconnected from his body that it was hard to know exactly what he was doing. He felt himself pulled to the side and strapped in.

The engine howled and the Worm started moving. It dug into the dirt like a corkscrew, twisting and turning with a voracious appetite. The ride was rough. Between the constant bumping and the occasional massive jolt, Nickle could feel himself getting sick. He knew he was going to throw up—he already could feel his mouth start to salivate—but he prayed that it was not before the ride was over. The next jolt, however, forced it out of him.

The vomit drifted like a floating rain cloud, threatening to unload a torrent of disaster onto whatever it collided with. The other Dwarves made a game out of it, almost like hot potato. Using the

Runes in their armor, several of them conjured a wind that sent the filthy mess spiraling around the Worm. This exchange went back and forth until it hit the roof, where it stuck like glue.

Nickle felt much better.

They stopped thirty minutes later in the basement of a large building. Just like they had shuffled into the Worm, they made a long line as they marched out.

"Don't worry about the mess," Jason said. "It happens all the time to Tenderfoots."

As Nickle walked out of the Worm, he felt himself shooting back into his body. The motion was so strong it about knocked him to his knees. He shook his head and cleared his throat, which was still burning.

"There's a drinking fountain on the top floor; that should help your throat."

"Why are we going to the top floor?"

"That's where we board the Tube."

Nickle scratched his head.

Jason slapped him on the back. "Not much is going to make sense in the next few weeks." He turned towards the captain of the Dwarves and saluted by pounding his chest. "Captain HoleSlinger, I can escort him from here."

The Captain eyed Jason carefully. "Are you sure you can manage, Tenderfoot?"

"Yes, sir."

Captain HoleSlinger took a deep breath as he considered the situation. "All right, but do you know where to take him after you get down to EarthWorks?"

"The Administrative Quarter."

The large Captain nodded. "Yeah, that's right. Once there, take him to the—"

"—the New Admissions Desk. I can manage. I've done this before."

"Well," Captain HoleSlinger grimaced, "don't get all cocky."

"Yes,   sir.   Sorry,   sir."

"Well, off with you, lad. You need to catch the next Tube if you're going to make it before nightfall."

Jason pounded his chest again, Nickle awkwardly did the same.

They both turned and headed towards a set of elevators. Just as they arrived, one of the elevators opened up, and the two boys stepped inside.

"What is this building?"

"The Chrysler building."

"Isn't that the one that has the pointy top? I've seen pictures of it before."

"Yeah. The Piddlers say that the top was an unplanned addition that enabled the builder to win the record for the tallest building. But, in reality, the metal top was added by Dwarf engineers who needed the conical shape for the construction of the Tube."

"This is a Dwarf building?"

"Yeah, sort of. It was built by Dwarves, but it's owned by Elves—those pompous fools."

They stood in silence as the elevator went straight to the top. When they reached their destination, Jason led them to a back door that was marked "Maintenance."

He pointed towards the door handle. "This is the tricky part. You have to use Runic magic to get through the door."

"What's Runic magic?"

"Remember all those symbols on the armor of those Dwarves you saw? Those are Runes. That's what empowers those Dwarves in their armor. Runes are the mainstay of Dwarf magic. You'll find that magic is as different and diverse as are the races that use it. We Dwarves are masters of Runes, and a good thing too, because they are needed to construct pretty much every building in EarthWorks."

"Will I get to learn magic?"

Jason gave Nickle a wink. "Everyone in EarthWorks knows magic. It's as common down there as reading is up here. Your first year in the Silver Army, you'll learn all sorts of Runes for battle. The year after that, they'll teach you how to use Runes to build buildings. I can't remember what they'll teach you your third year or the year after that, but for the first five years, you'll learn how to use Runes." He turned his attention back to the door. "The trick with Runic magic is drawing the correct symbol and coupling it with the right word of power." As he spoke, he traced his finger along the door. "LackNar."

The door unlocked and slid open.

Jason gestured towards the inside. "You first."

Nickle stepped into a dark circular hallway. At the other end of the hall, he could see the Tube, which at first glance, looked like an ordinary train with square windows. After studying it more closely, however, he could tell that something was definitely odd. Instead of running horizontally, the Tube was positioned vertically. Not only was the train sideways, but so were the people that were walking back and forth along the platform. It seemed like some sort of surreal V8 commercial.

"How is that possible? How can they stand on the wall and not fall down?"

Jason smiled. "The same way you're going to do it—magic. To them, that's not a wall but the floor."

"What do I do?"

"Just walk through the tunnel, and by the time you get to the other side, you'll think that the train is right-side up. Go ahead. I'll catch up."

Nickle obeyed, stepping forward as quickly as he dared. He could not sense any change in his direction, but by the time he reached the end of the hallway, he was sideways. What should have been a wall was now the floor.

Nickle touched the ground. "Amazing."

"Yeah, it is," Jason pointed with his chin towards a wall. "There's the drinking fountain. You thirsty?"

"Sure."

Jason walked with Nickle to the fountain, which was shaped like a fat Troll. "As with everything Dwarf made, there's a trick with this fountain. What's your favorite drink?"

"Water."

"Water?"

"Yeah, that's all I want right now."

"Well, that's easy enough. Just push the button and water will come out. But if you wanted something else—whatever it is—I bet you this drinking fountain can produce it."

"What about orange juice?"

Jason grinned. "That's an easy one." He reached down and tickled the Troll in the armpit, whispering as he did. The next moment, a stream of orange juice shot out of the top.

Nickle leaned in and tasted the juice. It was so fresh and sweet that he was sure that it must have been recently squeezed. "How does this work?"

"You'll have to ask a Mech Dwarf. All I know is that it does."

After Nickle drank his fill, the two boys boarded the Tube and sat on leather seats. As they did, seat belts automatically pulled them in and strapped them down. Nickle fought against it at first, but he found that he was quickly overpowered by the snake-like coils.

Jason shook his head. "You'll need to learn to control your mind better. Those seat belts won't strap you in if you don't want them to. You just need to focus your thoughts and tell them to let go. Same as that earthquake that happened in the nursery today. If you noticed, you were tossed to the ground, but it did not affect me."

"How do I do that?"

"For me—and it's different for everyone, so this might not work for you—it's like tightening your eardrums. It creates a little build-up of pressure that allows me to resist or control the magic. But don't worry about that quite yet; you'll be trained on that later."

"When?"

"In camp Tortugan—it's like a Dwarf boot camp."

"Have you been there?"

"No, not yet. I was three days too young last year, but I'll be going with you."

"How old do you have to be?"

"Fourteen."

"That seems a little young to be in the army."

Jason shook his head. "I'm hoping it will be more like a glorified football camp."

Nickle sighed, sinking back into his chair. "Man, I'm glad to find out there's a reason I'm so different."

"That reminds me. I gotta ask you. Were you really eating dirt?"

Nickle's body tensed. "Why? Is that uncommon in EarthWorks."

"Well, you're going to see a lot of creatures down there, but none of them eat dirt."

"Well...," Nickle said, his voice falling. "I'll keep that in mind."

"That's probably for the best."

Nickle paused for a moment before he asked his next question, trying to decide if it was rude or not. "Are you from the surface?"

Jason arched his eyebrows and let out a big sigh. "If you're asking me if I'm a first class Dwarf, the answer is no. I'm labeled a second-class Dwarf—but not because my parents aren't both Dwarves. My folks were sent on a scouting mission when I was born. No one is sure what happened, but I ended up being raised by a sheepherder in Brazil. After accidentally exploding a bathroom with a Runic spell, the Tri'Ark found me and took me in. I was six. Since then, I've floated between the surface and EarthWorks, like a vagabond stuck between both worlds. Dwarves born in EarthWorks don't care to visit the surface much, especially since the Weakening."

"Weakening?"

"The Weakening of the world," Jason swallowed, "that's another thing you'll learn. Things aren't as pretty as they used to be under the surface."

Someone interrupted their conversation. The voice seemed close, but as Nickle looked around, he could not see anyone.

"All aboard for departure. All aboard."

Jason gave Nickle a grin. "You're going to like this."

Nickle swallowed. "What's that?"

The voice spoke again. "Last call. Departure in twenty seconds."

Nickle felt his heart beating against his rib cage. He was not quite sure what to expect, but whatever it was, it had Jason grinning like he was paid to do it.

"10...9..."

Nickle checked his seat belt. It seemed tight, but he began to wonder if it would hold. *"What if I started resisting magic and my straps let go? What if they snap and I go flying through the car?"*

"5...4...3"

At the number 3, Nickle felt his weight pull against his seat belt, almost as if gravity had returned, and he was now on the top of a huge roller coaster. As the countdown finished, there was the sound of metal scraping somewhere behind them. Suddenly, the Tube was released.

Jason screamed and raised his arms above his head, yelling as loud as he could. "Come on Nickle, put your hands in the air!"

Owing to his height, Nickle had never been on a roller coaster that was faster than a bumper car; but now, as his cheeks flapped in the air, he was quickly making up for it. He could see the city zooming by in the window to his left. They were moving so fast that it was only seconds before the whole of New York City disappeared completely as they passed underground.

The lights went out. When they flashed back on a split second later, the tension in Nickle's seat belt was gone. It seemed that gravity had once again returned to normal.

Jason unbuckled and kicked his legs up on the nearby window sill. "Make yourself comfortable. It will be a few hours before we reach the Heart of EarthWorks."

"I'm starving. Where can I get some food?"

"Oh, yeah, that's right. You didn't eat breakfast, did you."

"How did you know that?"

"John told me."

"And what did you tell John?"

"About what?"

"About the nursery the Dwarves destroyed. About their living room, which is now like the entrance to a five-star hotel."

"The Humans are on it—that's their department. They'll send up a Scathian to change the memories so they're more like faded dreams. And I'm sure the Nursery is repaired by now—that's our specialty. As far as the living room goes, I imagine they'll convince John that their home had a makeover by one of those home improvement shows. Don't worry about him; he'll be all right."

"What's a Scathian?"

Jason leaned closer to Nickle. "Those are the top guns of the underworld; you don't want to mess with them. They're Humans, initially anyway, but they have trained their minds to the point where they can control the undisciplined minds of others. The Scathians claim that they have uncovered all the mysteries of the brain. They have their own secret society." Jason leaned even more forward as if imparting a secret. "I hear that they don't eat or sleep for months at a time, just to hone their mental powers. But it's an invite-only club, and not many ever get invited. Fewer pass their insane tests."

"Have you seen one?"

"Yeah, I've seen a few in my time, but I've never talked to one."

"I met one the day I was summoned to the Cogs of Hurn."

Jason sat up. "What? You lucky dog. I'd pay a good amount of gold dust to talk to one. I wonder if they accept Dwarves into their order." While he spoke, he pulled out a medallion from his pocket. "Here, take this. The food car should be just a few Tubes ahead of us. Get what you want—my treat."

"How do I pay?"

"Just show them the medallion."

Nickle focused his thoughts on his seatbelt unbuckling, which it did a moment later. He stood up. "Sounds easy enough."

Jason shifted in his seat. "And can you bring me back something to drink too?"

"Yeah, no problem."

Nickle walked slowly through the Tube, looking at the mix of people as he went. He saw a group of dirty looking Dwarves, all of them had long beards and weary eyes. Next to them were two Cennarians who were angrily talking about something. The next Tube had a similar mix of Cennarians and Dwarves, but this time he spotted a Satyr—or at least he thought he did. This creature had the lower body of a goat and the upper body of a muscular man. He was shorter than the surrounding Humans but about the same height as Nickle.

Nickle gave a polite nod, but the Satyr only gave a weak "bah" in response.

After seeing a dozen more creatures that Nickle could not readily identify, he finally passed into the food car. This section of the Tube was not the same size as the other cars; it was much bigger. It stretched in every direction that Nickle looked; it was like a food court in a mall. There were dozens of restaurants, all of them with long lines and impatient customers. He was not sure which line went where, but he soon found himself in one of them.

Despite the size of the lines, everything went quickly—too quickly, in fact. Before Nickle knew it, he was standing at the front of one of the lines and staring at a menu he did not entirely understand. Either every item had a different name than what people used on the surface, or he was now looking at the longest list of food he had never tried. He did recognize a few words like Spicy Fist and Bunker Box, but these items seemed like they belonged at a garage sale, not in a restaurant.

The employee behind the counter was a large Cennarian that seemed forced into an uncomfortably small hat. His name was Bill.

After a while he spoke. "Welcome to Meaters. How can we help you?"

Nickle swallowed. "What's good here?"

"Depends on what you like."

"What do you get?"

"Whatever I want."

Nickle scratched his head. "I'll have the Bunker Box."

"Do you want that Rinacon-sized?"

Nickle nodded slowly. "Yeah, Rinacon-size me."

"That's a lot of food for a little guy like you."

"Well, how do you think I'm going to get any bigger?"

"Good point."

"And I want two drinks too."

"What flavor?"

"What did the last guy get?"

"He got…Silver Slime."

Nickle shook his head. "What about Pepsi?"

"We've got that too."

"All right, Pepsi it is."

"Please put your medallion on the tablet."

Nickle grabbed the medallion that was around his neck. "What tablet?"

"The white one in front of your face."

"Oh," Nickle said, "that tablet." As he put the medallion down, a fine mist began to strip away flecks of gold. The gold trail was suspended in the air for a moment before it was sucked inside the tablet. When the last bit of gold dust vanished, Bill gave Nickle a large tray.

Nickle nervously cleared his throat. "Wow, that was quick—a little too quick. Are you sure it's cooked?"

Bill's eyebrows narrowed. "Next."

Nickle lifted the tray off the counter, grunting in surprise from the weight. He walked to the center of the room, where he had seen some empty chairs earlier. The place was packed with every sort of creature imaginable. Nickle did not have to wait long, however, before a chair and a table found him. The chair was the first thing to catch his attention. The four-legged thing galloped towards Nickle as if it was a white steed coming to his rescue. A bulky table quickly followed, and soon, Nickle was able to sit. The space was cramped at first, but as Nickle sat down, the neighboring tables seemingly stretched away until they were a reasonable distance from him. He turned his attention to his food, which was encased in a giant clam.

He felt along the seams of the clam, trying with all his strength to crack it open, but to no avail. Using a plastic knife, he found on his tray, he then tried to pry it open. He succeeded in opening the clam a crack, but the knife broke before too long. This small crack allowed the warm sweet fragrance of food to eke out and tease Nickle's nose. The food was so frustratingly close, so sweet-smelling that Nickle was tempted to grab the giant clam and smash it against the ground. Nickle found himself talking to the crustacean. "Come on, big fella. I only want the food inside, and then you can go your way. Open up. LackNar. I'm hungry. Please, open. Open says me. I own you—you must obey me." He picked up the wretched thing and shook it—still, the clam would not crack.

"Do you need help?" A voice said from behind.

It was Bill, the oversized Cennarian.

"Yeah, how do you get this open?"

"Just tell it what kind of fast food you want to eat."

"I thought I already ordered my food."

Bill shook his head. "You must be one of those Fallen Dwarves. It's not hard. Just tell your order to the clam."

Nickle turned back to the clam, his tongue rubbing the back of his teeth as he thought. "I could use some crispy fries and a double patty hamburger from In-N-Out, and a slice of pizza from King's Pizza, an Oreo milkshake from McDonald's, six cheese poppers from Chili's, two chicken wings from KFC, a few hush puppies from Long John Silvers, a large order of onion rings from that bowling alley I used to go to—"

The clam opened, revealing everything that Nickle had requested. He was now staring at the largest and most diverse collection of fast food he had ever seen. It had appeared precisely how he had pictured it; it even had the individual wrappers from each respective restaurant.

Nickle picked up a large fry, dipping it into the fry sauce that was amply provided. "I think Bunker Box might be my new favorite food."

Chapter 6

In the Heart of EarthWorks

By the time Nickle got back to his seat, Jason had fallen asleep. Nickle looked around for a spot to put down his Pepsi, but he did not see one. As he was thinking about it, a cup holder appeared in the arm of the chair, which Nickle thought was a nice touch.

The Tube teetered back and forth as they traveled, slowly rocking most of the passengers to sleep. Nickle moved to one of the windows and looked outside. There was nothing to see besides an occasional light and the everlasting wall of rock. Hours passed by, and still, Nickle stared, captivated by the view. He felt a mix of emotions that he had never felt before, like a young child trying a new flavor of ice cream. He was not quite sure how much he was going to like EarthWorks, but he was certainly glad to have Jason along for the ride.

While Nickle was gazing out the window, a sudden flash of fire streaked through the tunnel. The flame was so unexpected that he instinctively pulled away from the window. A few moments later, another burst of flames whipped the side of the Tube. It was not nearly as startling as the first flash of fire, but it certainly demanded attention. The farther they traveled, the more prevalent the flames became until the Tube was completely engulfed.

Nickle could hear a faint chanting as they passed through a solid wall of fire. Outside the window, the landscape opened up into a gigantic canyon of flames and red rock. Large fountains of lava spewed skyward, spraying the Tube with a mixture of gas and superheated liquid. Still, the Tube traveled on, as if the heat was nothing more than a gust of mild wind. From out of nowhere, a colossal rock zoomed past Nickle's window and exploded into the side of a mountain, leaving only smoke and ash. More rocks whizzed back and forth as they traveled. The farther they went, the more menacing the weather became. The cave was soon filled with lightning bolts of lava that left trails of steam as they struck the ground. In the distance, a massive volcano erupted.

In the valleys of the crimson land, there were thousands of red, Human-like creatures, all of whom moved lethargically along their various paths. From the upper backs of these creatures sprung black wings that turned darker as they moved. A few of them attempted to fly, but before they could get very far, they were sent hurtling back down to the ground.

As Nickle stared at the distant faces, he heard a loud thud from somewhere above him. He glanced up. One of the red beasts had managed to fly up to the Tube, where it now rested on a skylight, panting for breath. With inch-long fingernails, the brute scratched at the glass, trying to force its way in. Despite the creature's relentless attacks, the Tube remained unharmed.

Nickle stood up and moved closer to the creature. Its red skin changed shades with each breath it took. The deeper the breath, the darker its chest became. It was impressively muscular from the top of its shoulders down to its massive legs, which had daggers of bone protruding from its knees. From the top of the beast's head, a cluster of horns jutted out at random and sharp angles.

Then the creature locked eyes with Nickle. The exchange was as odd as it was brief. Nickle did not know why, but for the slightest moment, he felt as if he knew the creature—knew where it had come from. He even thought he knew its name.

"Baulic?" Nickle asked.

The creature's face spread wide with a wicked grin. The two stared awhile longer before the creature hissed and flipped off the Tube, disappearing completely.

Nickle let out a huge sigh. He had not realized it before, but he had been holding his breath. Moments later, the canyon of fire disappeared and the wall of rock came back into view. Nickle collapsed into his seat.

The tunnel continued for a few more minutes before it again opened up to an expansive landscape of lush forests and green fields. The land was mist-filled and distant, almost as if Nickle was viewing it through a foggy window. Despite it appearing to be mid-day, Nickle could not see where the light was coming from.

Jason suddenly stirred awake. "Do you have my drink?"

"Yeah, but the ice is probably melted."

Jason blinked his eyes twice before he could properly see. "Not down in EarthWorks. Ice doesn't melt down here until you've finished your drink."

Nickle nodded to the window. "What is this place?"

Jason took a long drag on his drink. "This is called The Land of the Beasts."

Nickle pointed outside. "What are those watery creatures down there?"

Jason sat up. "Those are Gelikos. The creature itself is actually only the size of a baseball. It has the ability to create a protective sphere of water by sucking it against its body. It uses the water to trap small creatures like ants and bugs by running over them."

"What is that creature attacking them?"

Jason leaned closer to the window. "You've got a good set of eyes for a Dwarf. I didn't even notice them. Those are called Beast'Heads. They're six-inch tall creatures that have the body of a Human but the head of an animal—like a snake or a bird. Those look like a group of Hawk'Heads. You'll see plenty of those in EarthWorks; they fancy themselves as guides and Taxi-Lator drivers."

"And what are those antlered creatures on the border of that forest?"

Jason squinted. "Wow, you really do have good eyesight. Those are Hamadryad, I think. They've got antlers like deer and bark-like skin. Their lives have something to do with the Cottonwood tree."

"How did you learn all this?"

Jason took another drag on his drink. "By Hurn's belt, I didn't learn as much as I should have. I was assigned to a Dwarf Discovery Unit. We were in charge of keeping track of certain creatures and making sure they weren't going extinct or something like that. Before too long, however, a few of the creatures filed complaints with our unit saying we were trying to enslave them. The group was disbanded not long after, leaving me with nothing but a large amount of useless information."

The Land of the Beasts stretched on for an hour longer. There were so many creatures that not even Jason could identify them all. Finally, the green landscape faded away, and the Tube entered into another rocky tunnel. A few minutes later, the Tube jolted to a stop.

Jason stretched out his arms and legs. "Welcome to EarthWorks."

As the doors opened, the two boys jumped out of their seats and exited the Tube. The platform was crowded and incredibly complicated. Its design was by far the most wretchedly designed subway station Nickle had ever seen. Just like the Tube, it was perfectly cylindrical and everywhere he looked, there were scattered exits and entrances, toll booths, and ticket stands. People were walking everywhere, including along the ceilings and walls. It seemed that to the people of EarthWorks, gravity was nothing more than a word used in myths. Food and newspaper stands cropped up in unexpected places; mostly, they floated in the air above crowded areas.

"Stay close to me," Jason yelled over the noise. "It's twice as easy to get lost in here as it is to be found."

Nickle swallowed.

Jason led the way into another room that looked exactly like the one they had just left. He began walking up a wall, towards an exit on the ceiling. Nickle felt disoriented as he walked. Between all the noise, and the sudden changes in direction, he was not sure which way was up—or even if "up" was that important to remember. They entered a long hallway, made four left turns, walked up a long flight of stairs, and finally into the center of the city.

Nickle's first impression of EarthWorks literally took his breath away. Just as he was exiting the Tube platform, a small pipe shot out a puff of green smoke that left Nickle choking for air. The city was twice as crowded as the platform below. There were hundreds of people, all mixing and moving in every direction. Dozens of food stands floated upside down above the large crowd, all of them displaying bright flashing signs and menus.

Jason pulled Nickle close. "Watch out for Goblins. If you make eye contact with them for too long, they'll spam your tongue. You'll find yourself shouting out commercials for the next several hours."

More annoying than the floating food stands were the hundreds of Goblins that flew around in Zephyrs. Attached to the bottom of each flying ship, a large banner whipped in the wind, advertising everything from various cleaning products or odor removing spells to authentic battle gear. The flags came so close to Nickle's face that he could hardly see the buildings above or the streets in front of him. When one of the pedestrians became fed up with the little green creatures and lashed out at them, the Goblins would reel back, cackling with laugher. A moment later, they would return—this time with seemingly bigger and brighter banners.

Whenever there was a gap in the air, and Nickle could see the buildings above, he felt a trickle of panic run down his spine. The buildings were as tall as any skyscraper he had seen but, unlike those on the surface, these structures were as crooked and jagged as a system of ill-conceived sewer pipes. The leaning tower of Pisa would have fit right in with the winding structures. The massive buildings sometimes wrapped around each other—almost as if they were organic. Whole skyscrapers sprouted out the sides of different structures and twisted upwards. It was difficult to tell if some buildings were considered one structure or several.

Everything was so convoluted, so confusing, that it took Nickle the longest time to realize that instead of a sky above, there was another portion of the city. Just like the Tube and the subway station below, the entire city of EarthWorks was built in an enormous sphere. All of the buildings pointed towards a globe that was precisely in the center.

Nickle cleared his throat as he pointed at the sphere. "What is that thing?"

"That is the Heart of the World!"

Nickle was seeing so many surprising things that his arching eyebrows weren't able to keep up: To his right, there was a stand that sold flying monkeys, to his left a vendor with a table full of basketball-sized elephants. There were all sorts of floating craft carrying people to their destinations; many of them looked like spiked Warships. By far, the most common mode of transportation were elevator-like cars labeled "Taxi-Lators" that zoomed through the air, carrying dozens of people in every direction and to every floor of every building.

Just in front of him, a towering Cennarian whispered an incantation and turned the contents of a large trash can into hundreds of butterflies that took to the crowded sky. A few of the insects did not make it very far before they were struck by a low flying Taxi-Lator, which turned the little insects back into trash upon impact.

As they walked along, Nickle noticed a countless variety of Beast'Heads scurried on the ground below. He saw one that had a frog's head, several more that looked like snakes, and at least a dozen others that had faces of rats. They looked so vulnerable on the ground that Nickle was scared that he might squish them. The creatures, however, were so apt at ducking and dodging the people around them, that it seemed like it was more of a game than a real danger.

Jason turned to Nickle. "This is the Tri'Ark Quarter. Be careful. It could be dangerous." As they turned down another street, the mass of goblins and street vendors disappeared. Instead, the Dwarves ran headlong into a group of Cennarians that were surrounding an immense square building. The large creatures were splashed in paint and armed with flashing protest signs.

A huge palomino Cennarian stepped up to the front—his face smeared with red paint. "We've been the footstool of the Tri'Ark too long!"

The crowd cheered.

"We will no longer be relegated to the shadows, forced to watch as the Tri'Ark mismanages and ruins the Earth. It is our time to be counted as equals; it is time that our voices are heard! We are a proud race, born from the essence of Mother Earth herself. Long before these Elves and Humans could even string sentences together, the Cennarians tamed the woods. And now, these Humans and Elves, these dirt-digging Dwarves, are killing the Earth. Well, we have had enough!"

Noise rippled through the mob of horsemen.

"We demand equality for our people!"

Again, the mob cheered.

"If we don't act now, there will be nothing worth saving later!"

Jason pulled Nickle close. "Keep your head down; we need to pass through the crowd to get to the Administrative building."

Nickle nodded.

The two Dwarves began pushing their way between the Cennarians, mumbling apologies as they went. As they walked, Cennarians all around them gritted their teeth and growled. They were almost out of the bedlam when one of the Cennarians latched on to Nickle's arm.

"Here's one of the dirty little Dwarves!"

Nickle broke the horseman's grip and continued on, pushing deeper into the crowd.

The dappled Cennarian followed. "Come back here, you rodent."

It did not take long before the horseman caught up and began stretching his hand out for the back of Nickle's shirt. Just before the Cennarian snatched him, Jason pushed Nickle out of the crowd and drew two small discs from his belt. "Back off! We're members of the Silver Army on official business. You touch us again, and I'll end your little protest with an explosion that will send your herd galloping off into the streets."

The large palomino pushed through the Cennarians. "Easy, litl' Dwarf, I just wanted to know your opinion. Are you for our freedom? Or, against it?"

Jason laughed and back-stepped out of the crowd. "I don't care one way or the other—I'm not the guy who makes the decisions—but if you take another step forward, you'll find yourself in a heap of pain."

"What?" The Cennarian laughed. "Do you have Runes in your hands? I bet those aren't even real! You're too young to know how to craft anything worthwhile. Did your mommy make those for you?"

Jason took another step back. "I don't want trouble."

The Cennarian smiled as he took one last step forward.

Jason flipped one of the discs at the Cennarian, and slammed the other into the ground. The first Rune hit the horseman square in the chest and exploded, flinging him into the air. The second Rune shot out a blue light that formed a shield. A moment later, Jason found himself the target of a dozen Transformation spells.

"Run!" Jason yelled.

Nickle did not need any prompting. As quickly as he could gather himself, he turned and bolted for the building.

The protective shield that Jason left behind absorbed seven of the bird-like projectiles before it fizzled away. With the shield gone, the Transformation spells flew through the air all around them, bouncing off the walls and pillars as they came within inches of their targets. Jason dove behind a large planter just as a phoenix-shaped spell incinerated the plant above him.

Nickle sprinted inside the building and ran headlong into a dozen armored Dwarves that were pouring out. The conflict grew louder as the Dwarves drew their axes and paired off with a few of the largest Cennarians. They exchanged a volley of spells, which cracked the front steps and sent planters flying through the air. The Dwarf armor was far superior to the magic of the Cennarians, and soon the four-legged creatures were forced to retreat.

Nickle blinked twice as he assessed the damage. Smoke and debris drifted through the air as if a bomb had been detonated. "Wow."

Jason pulled himself off the ground and shook his head. He rejoined Nickle, giving him a large wink. "It gets a little more hectic every day. Didn't I tell you things are a bit crazy down here?"

"That was amazing. How did you learn to do that?"

"Technically, I shouldn't know it—so let's just keep that between you and me. That Rune is strictly reserved for combatants. If I did it right, it should have broken the ribs of the Cennarian."

"So, who's going to clean up back there?"

"Probably a Mech Dwarf—they love fixing things. It's a different kind of magic, one that requires a talent that's similar to playing a musical instrument. It was a Mech Dwarf that was assigned to impersonate you on the surface. Come on. Let's get you registered."

The two continued down a long hallway that was alive with office furniture. They passed through two large doorways and entered into a stone area covered in Runes. Everywhere they looked, Dwarves and Humans were running through the room, carrying everything from stacks of papers to large battle axes. They continued until they reached a desk that was overflowing with thousands of sheets of paper. Behind the desk, there was a small Dwarf that wore an enormous set of eyeglasses.

Jason gave a polite nod. "Hey, Doombringer. We've come to register Nickle Brickle'Bee as a Dwarf."

The Dwarf scratched his tiny head. "Nickle Brickle'Bee, eh. Yes, I remember seeing him. I know I had his documentation around here somewhere." The squat man leaped on top of his desk with surprising agility. He began shoveling through the papers as if digging for lost treasure. The deeper the Dwarf dug, the more confusing the paperwork became. After a few moments, Doombringer stuck his hand triumphantly in the air. "Hah! Here we go. Your case has been assigned to a Human—a Mr. Shemway."

Jason took the paper. "A Human? Since when did Humans start taking on Dwarf assimilations?"

Mr. Doombringer scowled. "Since the Cogs of Hurn started drafting fourth class Dwarves. We don't have enough staff to handle every case. They've got us recalling more Dwarves than we can manage. I'm overworked and underpaid as it is…"

Jason put his hands up in defense. "Easy, Mr. Doombringer. I was just surprised, that's all."

The little Dwarf waved a finger as if it were a sword. "What are you? A Tenderfoot? And already you're questioning me. I've got more power in one of my pinkies than you do in your whole body, but look how the Silver Army has relegated me to this paper-pushing job. I once led a whole brigade against an army of Trolls, and now…."

Jason slowly pulled Nickle away from the desk. "He's been a little overworked, that's all." Once they were a good distance away, they turned and headed up a flight of stairs, which was more like an escalator than anything else. They reached the third floor and passed a dozen different offices before they arrived at a crooked door that had a pitifully small plaque next to it. The inscription on the plate was brief, "The Office of Shemway."

Someone had drawn a little arrow in between the first two words and written "tiny" with a blotchy pen. Jason nodded towards the door and Nickle entered.

The office was smaller than Nickle thought possible; it was more like a closet than anything else. If he had wanted to, he could have reached the opposite wall in three short steps.

There was an extraordinarily handsome-looking man sitting across a tiny desk. With his perfectly balanced ears, his symmetrical face, and his even eyes, he could have been a model. The man stood up. "My name is Shemway Darkfiend, pleasure to meet you."

Nickle nodded and stuck out his hand. "Nice to meet you."

Shemway did not take the hand. "Please, have a seat, both of you. You must be a new Dwarf. Nickle, there's much you must learn about EarthWorks, but the most important thing to learn is that I don't shake hands—not since the Swine Flu epidemic. And you shouldn't either."

Nickle laughed. "Swine Flu?"

Shemway mimicked Nickle's laugh for a brief moment before stopping abruptly. "Yes. But this is not the Swine Flu you've heard about—that was just a cover story. The real Swine Flu is an aggressive pathogen that was supposedly released by the Faerie Queen Titania. If one contracts it, their body morphs into a pig. If the disease is not treated quickly enough, the victim becomes permanently trapped in their new porky body. It's required the bulk of the Tri'Ark's agents to stop the spread of the sickness on the surface, and we don't want the epidemic down here, do we?"

Nickle shook his head.

Shemway gave a generous smile and clapped his hands together. "But that is not why you're here, not immediately anyway. It looks like you are to be registered as a...Dwarf, fourth class. Wow, fourth class—they're really scraping the bottom of the barrel, aren't they?"

Jason straightened up. "Shemway, we're right here. We can hear you."

Shemway winked at Jason. "Easy, little Dwarf. I know exactly what it's like to be placed in the fourth class. I myself am a fourth class Human."

Jason arched his eyebrows. "I didn't know Humans had classes."

"We do," Shemway said, "it's just based on different criteria. Mr. Nickle Brickle'Bee is considered a fourth class Dwarf because his physical traits are far removed from the typical Dwarf. Humans, on the other hand, base their class system on ability. A first class Human is someone whose magical capacities are far above average. A second class has lesser ability but is still powerful, and so forth—"

Nickle shifted in his chair. "So, you're not very good at magic?"

Shemway narrowed his eyes and puffed out his chest. "I'm excellent at magic; I'm the very best at what I do. But, I was labeled a fourth class Human because of the type of magic that I'm good at. One thing that you'll learn down here, Mr. Brickle'Bee, is that there are dozens of types of magic. Some Races are good at one—such as, the Dwarves are good with Runes, and others are good with a mix of magic."

"So, what are you good at?"

"Thieftian."

Jason laughed. "That's hardly a class of magic—that's more like a cult."

Shemway placed his elbows on his tiny desk and frowned. "Oh, is that right little Dwarf? I can assure you, you don't know anything about Thieftian magic. In the right hands, it's one of the most powerful things on this earth—more powerful than scribbling a Rune into the dirt."

Nickle looked at Shemway and then at Jason. "What is?"

Shemway leaned back in his chair. "Thieftian magic, my boy, is potion-making at its best. I can bottle liquid air and brew invisibility; I can make objects float, melt locks, and open almost any door. Have you ever seen liquid darkness? Have you ever wondered what your own death might taste like? These are just a few of a Thieftian's trade potions. No place can keep me out, and no prison could keep me in. It's sophisticated and powerful—like a bottle of 1402 Burgundy wine."

Jason leaned over to Nickle. "Thieftians either become hired assassins or legendary thieves."

Shemway clenched his jaw. "I'm not a thief, nor have I ever been an assassin. Don't pretend to know who I am, or what a Thieftian is."

Jason shrugged his shoulders. "Thieftians are hired thieves—everyone knows that."

"Perhaps. But it depends on how you define thieves," Shemway hissed, "but who do you think hires us? The very people who publicly condemn us are the ones who privately employ us. It's the 'good and honest,' such as yourself, that fill our medallions with gold dust."

There was a long pause as both Jason and Shemway stared at each other, neither one willing to turn away.

Nickle cleared his throat. "So, um, what about my paperwork?"

After another moment, Shemway turned his attention back to his desk. "Everything is in order. Here's your passport, your license, and your identification card. You're required to carry one of these things with you at all times. I'm your point of contact; if you have any problems, please come to me first."

"Can you write your telephone number down for me?"

Shemway laughed. "Boy, you do have a lot to learn. Why would anyone care to use a disease-carrying telephone? It's like sticking a toilet seat against your ear every time you use it."

"Actually, toilet seats aren't that dirty," Nickle asserted.

There was an awkward silence.

Nickle shrugged his shoulders. "What? I read it in a book."

Shemway held out a business card that had his photo on the front. "Here is my picture. If you need to call me, just tap the picture twice and say my name. Make sure you don't tap me in the eyes because it makes my vision fuzzy—I hate when people do that. The card will only work within a certain distance of EarthWorks, as all photo callers, but it should work just fine in Tortugan. Now, away with you."

Nickle stood up. "Well, that was very informative. Thank you for your time."

Shemway also stood, grinning widely as he did. "I'm glad you learned something—though I don't think your friend did." Jason scowled as Shemway continued. "You two are both to report to Tortugan by tonight. Let me walk you out."

As the two boys were leaving, Shemway called them back. "Oh, Jason, you must have dropped this." Shemway playfully dangled a gold medallion on the tips of his fingers.

Jason narrowed his eyes. "How did you get that? And how did you know my name?"

Shemway laughed. "Let me give you some advice: Only a poor man can condemn a society of thieves—and that's because they have nothing to lose. Next time you speak to a Thieftian, I suggest you guard your medallion better than you guard your tongue."

Chapter 7

The Lineage of Hurn and Lucretia

Nickle and Jason left the large building and waded through the debris that had been left by the protestors. The large open area was empty of anyone else except for two small Dwarves who were busily cleaning up the mess.

Jason was still red with anger as they entered the main street. "That arrogant Thieftian. Who does he think he is? It's so unfair how the law never touches Thieftians. They get to sneak around, stealing and doing anything they want, and still, there's not a judge from here to the surface who would convict a Thieftian."

Nickle shrugged his shoulders. "Does it matter?"

Jason rolled his eyes. "Oh, if only you knew the fun they have. Those psychos do everything from double base jumping to Taxi'Lator running, and yet, they never get into trouble."

"What's Taxi'Lator running?"

Jason's face spread wide with a grin. "That's the best thing in the world. As you've seen, the air in EarthWorks is filled with flying vehicles—especially Taxi'Lators—each one zooming to their next destination as quickly as possible. There are so many, in fact, that a Thieftian can jump from one to the next without falling. They've gotten so good at it that they never have to pay Taxi'Lators for a ride."

Nickle shook his head. "That's crazy. I don't think I could ever do that."

"I tried it once. I was doing pretty good too, but my little Dwarf legs couldn't make the big jumps. I ended up crashing into one Taxi'Lator after another until I finally landed in a dumpster. I've been afraid of heights ever since."

"I'm surprised you didn't die."

"Nah, it wasn't that bad, a few broken bones and three cracked ribs. Dwarves are a lot tougher than Humans or Elves. It only took the

Healers a few hours to patch me up. But I did end up in a mess of trouble for it. I was sentenced to one month at The FireWall."

"FireWall?"

"Do you remember that fiery place we passed through while riding the Tube? I was asleep, but I imagine you saw it."

"Yeah."

"Well, that's a prison. And to maintain the burning walls around that prison, there is a group of people called 'Wailers' that use Rote magic. Rote magic is performed by the repetition of simple magical phrases. Have you ever heard someone repeat the word 'please' a dozen times when they wanted something? Well, that's a form of Rote magic. It's not powerful when just one person repeats a phrase or a word, but when thousands of people chant it, it can create some of the most potent spells. It is the job of the 'Wailers' to sit in front of the FireWall and repeat the same phrase all day and night."

"Do they get a break for lunch?"

"Yeah," Jason nodded, "we're not barbarians. It's just like a normal job. They go to work, clock in, and then repeat everything their boss tells them to. I imagine it's very similar to a Piddler job."

"So, how did you like it?"

"I didn't do it," Jason laughed. "I kept jumbling up the words so badly that they attached me to that Dwarf Discovery Unit I told you about."

The two Dwarves once again entered the thick crowd that poured through the streets. Nickle followed as Jason led them to a Taxi'Lator that was parked in a large metal stall.

"Two, please," Jason said to a Beast'Head that was sitting in a tiny control booth. The small creature was slightly chubby for a Hawk'Head, but it did have a brilliant plumage of feathers. His voice was sharp and parrot-like.

"Where are you going?"

"To Hurn," Jason replied.

The Hawk'Head whistled. "Oh, that will be lots of dust."

Jason pulled out a medallion from around his neck. "We can pay."

"Do you want a receipt?"

Jason pulled his head back. "You guys are printing receipts now?"

"Oh, no," the Hawk'Head shrilled, "but we get in trouble if we don't ask. Now, both of you get on board. Let's go. Let's go. Get on board. Do you have luggage?"

"Just ourselves."

"I forgot my suitcase," Nickle said suddenly.

"You don't need it," Jason replied. "You're part of the Silver Army now."

The Hawk'Head climbed up to the top of the Taxi'Lator and into a small ball that was filled with clear slime. As the Hawk'Head climbed in, the walls began to vibrate. The tiny creature looked back towards the two boys and winked. "Hang on. Hang on. We'z going for a ride."

Jason gripped the bars along the wall, Nickle did the same. The next moment, their Taxi'Lator shot into the sky. Initially, Nickle thought it would be cool that the Taxi'Lator was all glass. It would give him a chance to get a bird's eye view of the whole city. As soon as they were airborne, however, he wished he could see nothing at all. The higher the vehicle flew, the more congested the air became. All sorts of vehicles were coming and going in every direction. Their Taxi-Lator swerved left and right, ducked under a bridge that did not seem to be going anywhere, and then shot straight up in the air. Almost every second, they nearly collided with vehicles that seemed to appear out of thin air. Despite the Taxi'Lator's constant change of direction, none of the riders were tossed around, as Nickle thought they would be. The vehicle had somehow maintained its original direction of gravity.

After long, tense moments, the Taxi'Lator exited the most congested part of the city and made its way towards a giant tunnel. The traffic became more orderly and regulated the farther they went. As they entered the tunnel, they passed a myriad of crooked buildings.

Suddenly, everything went black.

The Taxi'Lator hummed as it slowed to a stop.

"Hold on, everyone," the Hawk'Head squeaked. "They'll come back on."

Nickle blinked. "What happened? I can't see."

Jason's calm voice answered back. "None of us can. The lights went out."

"There are power outages in EarthWorks?"

"Yeah, it's hard to believe, isn't it? The Asrais Faeries are probably on protest again."

"Faeries?"

"Yeah, who did you think lights up EarthWorks?"

"Why are they on protest?"

"Well, the Asrais Faeries, or the light Faeries as everyone calls them, are the nicest of the Fair Folk—at least, they don't outwardly hate us. They can change from a physical form into light. Most Faeries can turn to light, but since Asrais Faeries are so much more comfortable at doing it, and they didn't charge that much initially, everyone in EarthWorks became dependent on a company called Faerie Light. But then Titania the Queen of the Faeries took over the company and the little pixy pukes have been raising their prices ever since. When the Tri'Ark doesn't pay, we have these blackouts. There are other ways to make light with magic, but it's all so much more expensive than what the Faeries charge. We never had blackouts before, but now we have them at least once a week."

"How long do they last?"

"A few minutes."

"No, no," Squeaked the Hawk'Head. The little creature had apparently moved and was now much closer. "Sometimes blackouts longer, much longer."

Jason scoffed.

"It's true! You Dwarves might not see it, but I do in the Beasts Quarter, yes. Sometimes we goes for hours without light, sometimes longer."

"That can't be," Jason scoffed. "The Tri'Ark pays everything all at once, and I'm sure the power comes back on all at once."

"It's not the Faeries that cause the blackouts—it's the Tri'Ark."

This time, even Nickle laughed.

Jason was smiling, despite neither of the other two being able to see it. "You're a bit paranoid, aren't you? What are you saying, that the Tri'Ark is out to get you?"

The Hawk'Head was obviously ruffled by this because he did not respond until the light came on a few moments later. When the lights did come on, the little creature quickly returned to the control station and hissed at the passengers. "Hang on. Hang on. We'z starting again."

They rode on in silence. The deeper they traveled into the

Tunnel, the more distinct and different the buildings became. Nickle's eyes remained glued to the window of the Taxi-Lator. The apartment buildings began to be more expansive and elaborate. Instead of chaotic and twisted structures, they became extremely orderly and well designed. It reminded Nickle of the pictures he had seen of Mayan ruins in South America, except instead of being worn and cracked with time, these buildings looked brand new. The whole demographic changed as well. Everywhere he looked, Nickle could see nothing but Dwarves. There were hundreds of them, including Dwarf children that kept tripping over their baggy clothes as they ran.

Then a low rumble hit Nickle's ears and trickled down his spine. Something deep inside of him stirred. It felt like a breath of fresh air after being cramped in a dirty laundry basket, or a splash in a cold pool on a hot day, or the tingling feeling one gets when their foot falls asleep. It was a mystical sound that waded in all around him, filling him up as if he were thirsty for it. There was simply no way Nickle could describe the noise: It was an emotion that tugged at his heart and filled his lungs with air.

Nickle swallowed. "I hear singing."

Jason smiled. "It's the Timotayin—the song of the Dwarf. You're definitely a Dwarf if you can hear it; no other creature can."

The long tunnel suddenly expanded into an enormous cave spotted with large buildings. Despite the vastness of this area, it was filled with thousands of Dwarves that were armed with pickaxes and blacksmith hammers. As the squat folk worked, their tools and voices rang in a low, resonating harmony. The singing and ringing of metal were so intertwined that it seemed impossible to separate. Even though his feet were still firmly on the floor of the Taxi'Lator, Nickle felt like he was floating.

The longer he listened, the more he began to understand. It was not so much the words that made sense to him, but the emotions that filled him. He could feel how the Dwarves were once selected to leave their ethereal homes and come to this world. They had been great princes and princesses, powerful kings and queens, but since coming to this world, they had been stripped of everything and charged to fight against an evil that they did not create. The song was not sad, but it certainly was not happy. If Nickle had to describe it in one word, he would have said "honor."

Nickle pressed his face against the Taxi-Lator glass. "What are they making?"

"Most of them are making Dwarf armor, I suppose. The Timotayin is essential to temper the armor and endue it with magic. Now you know why Tines are so expensive."

They passed by the largest contingent of Dwarves and headed over towards a collection of large buildings that looked like a series of gigantic steps. On the far side of one of the buildings, Nickle could see a dozen massive Warships. The vessels looked somewhat similar to the old frigates Piddlers had once used to sail around the world—except these ones were floating in midair and had small square sails. The ships looked fierce, having rows of spikes that ran the length of the decks and splashes of color that ran across the front.

Nickle pointed. "What are those?"

"Those are vessels from the Dwarf Armada. I've never been in one, but I hear they're so padded down with armor it's cramped. That's only a small portion of them; I imagine the rest are hidden deep inside the earth. I wonder why they're here. I've never seen them in Hurn before."

The Taxi'Lator flew past the Warships and went to the seventh floor of a large pyramid-shaped building. The doors opened. Jason nodded a "thank you" to the Hawk'Head, and then the two Dwarves walked into an elaborate room decorated like a medieval castle.

"Come on," Jason gestured with one of his hands. "I hope you're hungry."

Nickle nodded slightly and followed Jason down a flight of stairs. It was not long before they found themselves in a gigantic, octagonal banquet hall brimming with Dwarves. The room was loud with invigorating fiddle music and uncontrolled bursts of laughter.

The first thing Nickle noticed was a female Dwarf hefting a large jug above her shoulders and drinking from a spout on the front. Despite himself, Nickle could not help but stare. He was under the impression that the girls would be grizzly and tough, almost like a pack of tom-boys. They were tough, as the girl Nickle was staring at soon proved by punching another Dwarf in the face, but they were also beautiful. Most of the girls had their hair braided into elaborate twists and curls, much like the men did with their beards.

Between the loud music and dancing, the echoing laughter and the constant fistfights that broke out, Nickle felt awkward. He followed Jason closely as they made their way across the room and sat down at a circular table. Moments after they sat, they found themselves both standing again as Jason shook the hand of a gigantic Cennarian.

"Edward Thunderhoof!" Jason said with a wide grin. "I hoped you would be here. I've brought a new recruit with me. His name is Nickle Brickle'Bee."

Edward gave a quick bow. "I'm glad to see you made it, Nickle. I wasn't sure which way the Cogs of Hurn were going to vote. Obviously, they saw what I did—real potential, or so it was reported to me by Jason."

Jason nodded. "Nickle, this is Edward, most people call him Ed. He is the legendary Cennarian that rode through molten lava to rescue the inhabitants of Atlantis. He also was the most valiant warrior against the Witches of Stobbin."

"So, there *are* witches," Nickle said.

Jason continued. "This man is a legend!"

Edward gave Jason a hearty slap on the back. "You're making this old horse blush."

Nickle furrowed his brow. "What changed with the Cogs of Hurn? It looked like the vote was against me? There were only two or three of them that thought I was a real Dwarf."

"Well," Edward said as he rubbed the back of his neck, "when they called the vote, almost everyone did vote against you. The Cogs of Hurn were about to adjourn when old Thornhead burst through the doors carrying his large hammer. He gave a speech that was so forceful, so stirring that he quickly turned the votes right around."

"Thornhead?" Nickle asked. "He pretended to cut my head off—"

"Yeah, he can be a bit brisk sometimes, but as soon as he found out your name and who you were, he changed his tune immediately. He is the only reason you are down here. That reminds me, how was the trip, Jason? Any problems?"

"No, no problems at all."

Edward's face went serious. "I heard you used a Rune and sent a Cennarian flying through the air."

"Are you sure it was me?" Jason's voice cracked as he pointed to himself. "Maybe it was. I can't remember. It all seems so fuzzy now."

"Rules," Edward huffed, "as Thornhead would say, cannot be broken, especially now that you're officially in the Silver Army. You represent all of us now, and that includes me. You're one of the most talented Calligraphers, but I can't have you using unauthorized Runes. Now, I don't want to make a big deal out of this, so I'll leave it at that."

Jason straightened up and pounded his chest with his hand. "Yes, sir. I apologize—"

Edward shook his head and laughed. "I don't know how you manage it, but you always seem to find trouble."

Jason shrugged.

The Cennarian began walking away but then abruptly turned around. "Do you have your orders? Do you know where you two will be staying tonight?"

Jason nodded. "Yes, we picked them up from the Administrative Quarter from an official of the Tri'Ark."

"Good. Don't stay up too late tonight. You've got a long day ahead of you tomorrow."

Jason pounded his chest. "Yes, sir."

Nickle was about to speak when a loud thud interrupted him. The whole ambiance quickly changed as a massive, armored Dwarf entered the room from the top of a long and elegant stone stairway. The Dwarves below started slamming their fists and feet against the tables and floors, hitting them with so much force that several cups spilled.

"I know him," Nickle whispered to Jason.

"Yeah, of course you do," Jason whispered back. "Everybody knows Thornhead Back'Break, the Elected Chief Warlord of the Silver Army."

Nickle arched his eyebrows. "He's the leader of the Silver Army?"

"Yeah," Jason nodded, "at least for now."

Thornhead slowly walked down the steps, grimacing as the crowd cheered for him. When he was a few steps from the bottom, he raised his right hand dramatically in the air. "Sons of Hurn! Daughters of Lucretia! You have heard the call of the Silver Army and answered dutifully. EarthWorks is more powerful than ever, more prosperous than anyone could have hoped. We have strengthened our ties with the Humans; we have expanded our investments with the Elves. The old racial and social barriers that prevented harmony between all of our races is at an end. Each day our ties get stronger, EarthWorks becomes more stable, and our world becomes healthier.

"The construction of EarthWorks began over two hundred years ago by Dwarves more pure than most of you here. Before then, our mythical and magical races were scattered across the globe, isolated by our prejudices. Now we can speak politics with Cennarians, we can dine with Elves, visit Beast'Heads, and even have open communication with the Faeries.

"But to keep the peace, to keep the power of EarthWorks alive, we need a new generation of *obedient* Dwarf warriors. None of you are first class Dwarves, most of you aren't even second class, but all of you are somewhat Dwarves, which is the noblest of all the races. By our ingenuity, the Tri'Ark was able to reach the center of the Earth. Our Mech Dwarves built EarthWorks from the ground up. It is by exact obedience that we as Dwarves prosper. If we are to succeed, we must follow and obey every rule and regulation. The orders I give you must be followed exactly. But there's still more to build. Will you help me!"

On cue, the crowd roared their approval. The cheering was so loud that the noise carried far beyond the reaches of the building. Nickle clapped, but he was not sure why. He was not too excited to go build things. Moments later, Thornhead's grimace slackened as he joined the crowd. He started giving out hugs and shaking hands as if he was running for election. It was not much later before the fiddle picked up again, and a mass of people began to move to a lively jig. Jason excused himself, grabbed the hands of a beautiful Dwarf girl, and began to dance the best way he knew how.

In those few moments, Nickle learned two things about Jason. First, he had no fear of women, whether he was talking to the prettiest or toughest of girls; and second, he had no idea how to dance. The poor kid was so off-beat that Nickle felt embarrassed just watching him.

Nickle sat at a table and helped himself to the ample portions of food that were placed in front of him by Cennarian servers. Most of it was meat of some kind, which he readily enjoyed. The food was like nothing he had ever tasted. It was so tender, so juicy, that each bite only got him more excited for the next. Halfway through a turkey leg, a voice interrupted him. Nickle turned around, a stringy piece of meat still dangling from his lip. It was Thornhead Back'Break.

"Ah, so you be Nickle Brickle'Bee, eh?" The warrior's face was stern and rough, like a rock that had been freshly chiseled.

Nickle wiped his face with the sleeve of his shirt. "Yes, sir."

The large Dwarf stepped closer, cracking his knuckles as he did. "It's good to meet you, lad."

"Yes, it is," Nickle answered quickly. "I mean, it is good for me to meet you—again."

Thornhead's eyes burned with an emotion that Nickle could not quite figure out. "Just a few years ago, fourth class Dwarves could not even dream of coming below the surface; now, they're the majority of the new recruits. You half-breeds have changed everything. Before we started bringing you down here, our society had no reflection of the lifestyle of Piddlers; but now, you fourth class Dwarves have taken the best ideas from the surface and infused them with magic."

Nickle shyly shrugged his shoulders, unsure of how to react. "Crazy world, isn't it?"

Thornhead's jaw tightened and his eyes narrowed. The air became as tense as a rope caught in the middle of a tug-of-war. Suddenly, the large Dwarf slapped Nickle on the back, grinning broadly as he did. "And isn't it grand. Now, we've got the best of both worlds, and all because of fourth class Dwarves. Genius, pure genius."

Nickle let out a long, tense breath. "Well, I hope I can help even more."

"That's the spirit, lad. You've been in the Silver Army all of a day and already want to get your hands dirty. I'm expecting great things from you, Mr. Nickle Brickle'Bee. The true temper of a Dwarf is found in their obedience to regulation, and I think I see a lot of potential in you. We are each like a brick in a large building; if one of us fails to do our part, then the whole structure becomes weakened. Your father was the icon of obedience. He put the orders I gave him before everyone and everything else."

"You knew my father?"

For the first time since the conversation began, Thornhead broke eye contact. "Yeah, sure I did—that is, before he turned Troll."

"What?"

"Listen, lad, that's a dark tale, one that you should not be thinking about at this moment. Now is your time to live; now is your time to prove yourself. You should be focusing on the tasks ahead of you, not on the obscure details of the past. Tomorrow is your first day as a real Tenderfoot. Do your father proud—he would have wanted it that way."

Nickle furrowed his brow. He opened his mouth to speak, but he was too intimidated to make a sound. Thornhead continued. "Take care, lad. You've got your father's build, but let's see if you have his courage." With this, the large Dwarf grinned and turned around, leaving Nickle with nothing but his thoughts. He sat back down and tentatively poked at the food in front of him. What was left of his appetite seemed to have disappeared.

A few moments later, Jason collapsed in a nearby chair, sweat beading on his forehead. "I saw you talking to Thornhead. What did he say? That guy is the coolest, but most intimidating Dwarf I know. He's like a rockstar with a lighted stick of dynamite strapped to his chest. He's an awesome guy to hang around, but you never know when he might explode. He's the kind of Dwarf that could insult you, and you'd be inclined to thank him for it. He sure knows how to throw a party."

"What do you know about your parents?"

Jason shook his head and opened his mouth, but before he could answer, the light in the room disappeared. There were a few gasps as the darkness was replaced by a faint red glow. A small Dwarf suddenly appeared. So little, in fact, he made the others around him look like giants. Despite his size, his beard was just as long as all the other Dwarves and, consequently, it swept the floor as he walked. "You now know what you are, but many of you still don't know what that means.

"Dwarves are the oldest of races, born from the very hand of Freyr. When Freyr was first made a God, while he was organizing the world we now call home, he struck his hammer against his anvil so hard that it sent two sparks skidding across the land. These sparks left a trail of flames that quickly spread into a voracious fire. Before long, the giant creatures of old were caught in the flames and burned into extinction.

"When the sparks rolled to a stop, they became the first two Dwarves. They were named Hurn and Lucretia. Since they were chips from the very earth itself, they had power over the land. Where they roamed, the earth flourished and blossomed.

"But the fire still ravaged the land, gaining strength as each day passed. This fire's name became Aldrick—the Tempestuous One. Aldrick set about destroying the world and subjecting many of the smaller creatures to its unquenchable will. The more powerful Aldrick became, the more the fire spread.

"Lucretia built an anvil and armed herself with a hammer. She began making armor that could withstand the might of Aldrick. Day and night, she worked tirelessly, hammering until she began to bleed from her knuckles. Still, she persisted in her task, knowing that if she failed, the world would be destroyed. After completing the armor, she set about making an axe. This axe was no ordinary weapon, having been mixed with the finest metals and tempered with the blood from Lucretia's cracked hands. She worked so hard that when everything was finally complete, her body fell to the ground and moved no more. Her flesh became ash and drifted into the air, while her spirit seeped into the ground and became the soul of the Earth."

"Just before all hope was lost, Hurn donned the armor and grabbed Lucretia's axe. He charged headlong into the fiery pits of Aldrick, slashing at the flames that were in his way. When the two opponents finally clashed, the ground shook and groaned until it cracked down the middle. For months they were locked in combat, each one unwilling to submit to the other. But Hurn, because of his mortality, began to lose his strength. All hope faded as Hurn's movements slowed with exhaustion. Then Aldrick raised his mighty fist to strike the final blow, but just before he could, Lucretia's soul rose up from the Earth and empowered Hurn. The stout Dwarf leaped forward and grabbed Aldrick around the neck, squeezing him with all his might. The beast twisted and turned, but he could not shake the powerful Dwarf. Harder and harder Hurn pressed until the fiery creature was forced into the Dwarf's chest—forever trapped by the brave warrior's strong heart.

"And now you know where Dwarves get their fiery temper." The room filled with scattered laughter, and the small man continued. "To reward Hurn for his bravery, Freyr blessed Hurn with twenty-four children, each of them as tough as the Earth itself. The mighty god charged Hurn and his children with the task of rebuilding the devastated land. Hurn did his duty until his last day, but he still longed for Lucretia—his first true love.

"Now the task falls to you, Sons of Hurn and Daughters of Lucretia, to pick up where he left off. We Dwarves are builders. Upon our shoulders rests the whole foundation of the world. Now you know how Dwarves came to be; now you know what is expected of you."

Chapter 8

Grindlemire

Nickle and Jason were assigned to barracks "B." Like almost every Dwarf structure Nickle had seen, the barracks had eight marble walls and pillars that circled the room. At the very center of the domed roof, there was a circular skylight that radiated a kind of sunlight. Along the edges were rows of bunk beds that were six levels high. To get to the top, one had to climb up a wall that had multicolored grips. This would have been easy enough except the handholds kept changing size and position. In all, the room housed fifty Dwarves.

As the Dwarves walked in, they were each given three pairs of workout clothes, seven sets of day-to-day clothes, and two pairs of sandals. The day-to-day clothes consisted of white baggy shirts and black leather pants. They were also handed two different sets of formal wear outfits. By the time Jason and Nickle received all of their gear, only a few bunks were left. Nickle was assigned to the sixth level of the farthest bunk, which was covered in dust. Jason was assigned to the one just below that.

"I hate climbing," Jason said as he stared at the bed frame.

"It's not so bad," Nickle replied as he began his trek up.

"I don't care for heights."

As Nickle settled into his bed, he watched the last few Dwarves stumble into the room. They seemed as clueless about EarthWorks as Nickle. Besides a few awkward conversations among some of the Dwarves, the place was painfully quiet. Not long after the last Dwarf arrived, the overhead light was turned off by some unseen hand.

"Nickle, are you still awake?" Jason whispered.

Nickle shifted in his bed. "The light has only been off for half a minute—"

"So, you're still awake?"

"Yeah."

Jason let out a long sigh. "You nervous about tomorrow?"

Nickle shrugged his shoulders. "No. Not really."

"I wish I had your stomach. I'm so nervous I can't sleep."

"Why are you nervous? You at least know what you're doing down here. I bet you know more about EarthWorks than everyone else here combined. You'll do fine."

"Yeah, maybe, but what if I'm no good."

Nickle scoffed. "What are you talking about? Just today, I saw you send a Cennarian twenty feet in the air."

"Yeah, but I've heard Tortugan ain't no picnic."

"What do you mean?"

"Other Dwarves say it's pretty tough."

"Oh, great," Nickle whispered, "now you've got *me* feeling nervous."

"You'll do fine."

"What? That's the same thing I just said to you. You don't know that."

"Well, I guess we'll see."

Nickle sighed as he repositioned himself in his bed. "I guess so. Goodnight, Jason."

"You too, Nickle."

***

"Attention!"

Nickle stirred, but his eyes did not open.

"Get up before I drag your limp bodies out of your beds!"

This time the whole room became alive as Dwarves flung their bodies out of their sheets. A few Dwarves on the upper levels of the bunk beds forgot how high they were before they leaped out. The result was noisy as a dozen or so Dwarves belly-flopped onto the ground and began rolling around in pain.

"Get up you liver-loving lilies. Get used to the pain—you're gonna feel a lot more of it. You're now under my command. Each day, before I arrive, you'll wake up and stand at attention."

As Nickle began climbing down his bed, he noticed that the

giant Dwarf was a woman. She had a snub nose that flared like a trumpet. Her eyes were small and beady, almost like two buttons sown into her face. Her hair was knotted and frizzled and tied up into a bun. By far, her most distinguishing features were her thick, hairy biceps.

"My name is Cynthia Mallet, and I'm your commanding officer. Any questions?"

A tiny Dwarf in front timidly raised his hand. "Can we sleep in a little bit longer?"

Instantly, Cynthia's face knotted up into the most hideous expression imaginable. It was a few tense moments before she responded. "LINE UP! All of you! At attention. For that little smart remark, ya'll gonna pay."

As quickly as a lightning bolt strikes the ground, the Dwarves moved into rows in front of their bunks. Everyone was unsure exactly how to stand at attention, but they made up for it by attaching serious expressions to their faces.

"I want you boys in rows two deep with an arm's length separating you and the person in front of you. Your hands are to be at your side, your thumbs following the seams of your pants. Puff out your chests when you are at attention. When I come into the room, you stand at attention and salute by pounding your chest. Is that clear?"

The response was loud and disjointed. Some of the Dwarves said "yes, ma'am," while most of them said, "yes, sir."

"Oh, I see, I've got a witty bunch. Let's see how witty you are at the end of a long hike. Get dressed! You're going to sweat like you've never sweat before."

This sent everyone into a scramble for their clothes. Moments later, they were marched out of barracks "B" and into a large grass field. For the first time, Nickle was able to see the camp in full light. Tortugan was a lot bigger than he initially thought, having dozens of stone barracks that dotted the edge of the camp as well as massive free-standing pillars that had Runes carved into them. In the center of the camp was a large green field that was surrounded by an oval track. On the far side of the field, there were seven more substantial and ornately designed buildings. The biggest one was undoubtedly the cafeteria; another had the look of a gym. Despite the early hour, several Dwarf Cohorts had already assembled and were either stretching on the field or doing laps around the track. Nickle happened to catch sight of a unit full of girl Dwarves, which distracted him long enough to get him into trouble.

As they went, Cynthia yelled and screamed at each Dwarf in turn, correcting every mistake she saw. It was not long before the group began marching in perfect synchronization. Nickle quickly discovered that he was not the only one that hated running. Before they had gone very far, the kids on either side of Nickle were holding their sides and gasping for breath. For the first time in Nickle's life, he was actually the strongest runner in the group. After a few laps around a track, Cynthia marched the boys into one of the large, ornate buildings—this one was surrounded by odd-shaped bushes.

Cynthia went to the center of a large room. "Gather around me." The Dwarves complied quickly, eager to stop their brutal running regimen. Nickle was shocked as he looked at the others around him. Even though they only ran a few hundred yards, the Dwarves were all sucking in air like they had asthma—a few were even on the verge of fainting.

"Each time I hear something I don't like," Cynthia said, "you'll find yourself doing more laps. Is that understood?"

Again, the group responded with a mixture of "yes, sir" and "yes, ma'am."

Cynthia's face turned red. "It's ma'am, and if any of you maggots say differently—"

"Ah, Miss Mallet," a voice interrupted. "You brought your Cohort over early. They weren't supposed to be here for another thirty minutes."

"Well," Cynthia barked as she turned around, "they're here now." She turned her attention back to the Dwarves in front of her. "Cohort sixty-four, this is McDwindle, your High School teacher. He will be teaching you everything you need to know about things that don't really matter."

McDwindle had a long white beard that seemed to curl when he talked. The longer he spoke, the more pervasive the curls became until his face completely disappeared under a nest of hair. He then had to smooth it out before he could continue to speak. He also had a massive belt buckle that was more like a shield than a piece of apparel. Whenever he walked, his belt would scrape against his belly and make a squeaky sound.

"Follow me," McDwindle said.

Nickle leaned towards Jason and whispered. "High School teacher? Why do we need a High School teacher?"

"Silence!" Cynthia screeched. "You'll be silent until spoken to, is that clear!"

"Yes, ma'am."

"Good, I'll meet you in a few hours, after you've graduated. If I hear that any of you treated McDwindle in a less than courteous way, the whole lot of you will be running until your feet bleed." With this, Cynthia stormed off, slamming the door behind her.

McDwindle smiled. "It's nice to see Cynthia in such a good mood; usually, she's chucked one of her Tenderfoots through a window by now." The Dwarves all looked at each other, unsure if this was a jest or not. They passed into another large room that had a row of desks. On each desk were six well-used books. Some of the books were so worn they looked more like a pile of papers than a textbook.

"Everyone grab a chair," McDwindle said. "Anywhere will do." The room filled with screeching as the Dwarves all pulled out chairs and sat down. McDwindle continued. "I'm your High School teacher and will be teaching you everything that Piddlers claim to know. Now, I know what you might be thinking: 'Piddler's don't know a thing.' But you'd be wrong. They've gotten quite a few things right."

Jason sighed loudly.

McDwindle cleared his throat. "Does someone have a comment?"

Jason leaned back in his chair and raised a hand. "What do we need to learn this for? When do we start learning magic?"

"Under article seven thousand and two, you'll not be learning magic until you graduate from High School. You Dwarves will be going to the surface more than you know, and you'll need to know how Piddlers think. In my classroom, you'll learn mathematics, geography, social studies, political science, writing composition, Piddler history, and Philosophy."

"What?" Jason asked. "Piddler history? Mathematics? How long will this take?"

McDwindle frowned. "For some, it will take longer than others, for obvious reasons. But, for those of a keen mind, it won't take more than a few years off your life. Now, please open the book with the blue cover entitled *Mathematics: A Crazy Piddler Invention that Might have Some Fair Application.*"

Amidst a few groans, the Dwarves searched through their stack of books until they were able to produce the correct one.

"Please turn to page one," said McDwindle in a high-pitched voice.

As Nickle turned to the correct page, the room suddenly rippled—almost like a pond does when a drop of water falls into the middle of it. He looked up from the book and glanced around the room. Besides McDwindle suddenly smiling, everything appeared normal. He turned his attention back to the book. As he began reading the title of the first chapter, the room rippled again. Nickle continued to scan the text, ignoring everything else around him. The more he focused, the more unstable his surroundings became. Before long, he could feel his body lifting in the air, almost as if gravity had suddenly been turned off. The book began pulling him in. With each passing second, the suction became stronger and stronger. He closed his eyes just as he was pulled entirely into the book.

When he opened his eyes, he found himself in the same seat in the exact same room. Everything seemed so similar that he began to doubt if anything had changed. Mr. McDwindle began teaching basic mathematics. The longer he talked, the quicker his speech became. It was almost like a video being fast-forwarded. Soon, his movements blurred as he went back and forth across the room, scribbling and erasing mathematical equations and theorems. Despite the pace, Nickle understood it all. He could feel the information just pouring into his head as quickly as water is poured from a pitcher.

As the lessons progressed, Nickle noticed that Jason was continually getting into trouble. He was first yelled at for talking, then for making paper airplanes, then for throwing things, then for standing on his desk. The more complex the mathematics became, the more rebellious Jason seemed to be. In the middle of a geometry lesson, he set his desk on fire. When they were learning about trigonometry, he pretended to pass out.

Suddenly, Nickle felt something tug on his face. The room rippled again. The next moment, he was sitting back in the classroom.

Mr. McDwindle was still smiling broadly. "Back already? I do believe that is a record return."

Nickle squeezed his hands into fists and then let them relax. "Is this the real world?"

"Yes," McDwindle replied.

"I know calculus."

"You're supposed to."

"How long was I…in the book?"

"Ten minutes, or so, and only your mind was in the book—not your body."

"Ten minutes? It felt like I had been learning math for years."

"You have been. In fact, you've just shaved off ten years of your life."

"Ten years. I can't just give ten years of my life away; I don't have that much to give. Are you saying that I'll die ten years earlier?"

McDwindle walked up to Nickle. "Don't worry, lad. To a Dwarf, ten years is nothing. By the end of my class, you'll probably lose close to a hundred years of your life."

"Is this how we will learn magic?"

"Oh, good heavens, no," McDwindle replied. "You can't learn something like magic through books. That's like learning how to fight by watching 'Karate Kid.' No, magic is too precise, too emotionally dependent to be learned in such an archaic manner."

Nickle was about to ask another question before he was interrupted by McDwindle. "Looks like you have some time to kill; I guess that's the price to pay for being smart."

The two sat there in silence, waiting for the rest of the students to finish their books. It was another five minutes before another kid stirred and then another. Before long, everyone but Jason was back to themselves. It took another seven minutes before he finally awoke.

"Good!" McDwindle said. "We're off to a good start. Now pull out the orange book entitled *Political Science: A Study of Failed Diplomacy.*"

The class obeyed, this time with a little more eagerness. Just as the book before, Nickle found himself pulled inside and taught by McDwindle. This time the book went by even quicker, which put a smile on the teacher's face. Nickle learned the names of all sorts of presidents and politicians, all kinds of governments and laws. After political science, the students studied geography and social studies. They then read a book on Piddler history, which took the longest of any of the other books, and another on Philosophy. On and on, the learning continued.

After a few hours, McDwindle stood before the class, his beard bristling with pride. "We've got a good bunch here, I can tell. I think this is the fastest class I've ever taught. Congratulations. You've graduated from High School."

For some reason, Nickle was a little disappointed with the graduation ceremony, which entailed McDwindle coming up to each of the Dwarves and nodding while singing an odd song.

After graduating High School, McDwindle led the students to a large cafeteria where they were dished out portions of meat and small portions of vegetables. The conversations became more alive as the Dwarves gradually grew more comfortable with each other. The food was not as good as it was the night before, but it was still not too bad.

It was not long before Cynthia Mallet appeared, her face looking more contemptible than before. "On your feet! On your feet!"

The Dwarves stood up and pounded their chests.

The troll-like lady stepped to the center of the room. "Form a column! We've got to burn off that fat you just put on your bodies. I'm going to make you boys strong!"

The Dwarves were shuffled out of the cafeteria and back into the vast field where they were before. Then they began running. It was not long before one of the Dwarves lost his lunch. The rest curved around the retching Dwarf and continued on. Cynthia led them on a small trail that ran up a hill. With each step they took, the hill seemed to get bigger. After an hour, they finally reached the top, much to everyone's relief.

A few of the Dwarves collapsed on the grass, gasping for breath.

Cynthia stood over one of the poor boys, staring him down. "What you doing, restin'? Did I say you could take a break! Get your body up before I break you in two." She picked the kid up by one of his arms and flung him to his feet. "Follow me." She marched them through a rock archway and into a circular arena.

The arena was like nothing Nickle had ever seen. It had ladders and ropes everywhere, large tunnels that dug deep into the earth and seemingly disappeared, and huge wild bushes that twisted and turned with unnatural life. There were makeshift buildings and gigantic towers that stretched out at odd angles, huge spiked walls and fiery pits.

"Welcome to Grindlemire, the famous Tortugan obstacle course. You boys might be able to grow a beard, but until you complete this course, you won't be considered a Dwarf. Here you'll face your worst fears, fight your darkest secrets. There are magical forces so powerful that it will turn the bravest Dwarf pale. Each day, the obstacle course rearranges itself; each day, you'll find a new challenge. Now line up, let's see how your Cohort compares to the Dwarf girls I sent through here this morning. You there! What's your name?"

"Nickle Brickle'Bee, Ma'am."

"You first."

Nickle pointed at himself. "Me?"

"Did I stutter? Get in there before I throw you in. Whoever can get to the other side of the course gets a free day."

Nickle took the obstacle course at a run. The first thing he encountered was a rope that swung over a filthy looking lake. *"This isn't so bad."* He leaped for the rope, caught it, and was halfway to the other side before the rope started biting him. The pain was not nearly as bad as the shock. He let go of the rope and fell headfirst into the filthy water below.

Cynthia cleared her throat. "The rope was cursed with a biting Hex. What Nickle failed to do was properly resist the magic. You have to open your mind to the world around you. Your enemy is not going to warn you that they've set a trap. You've got to feel it, sense it. Magic leaves a trace behind, almost like a smell. It'll itch the back of your neck and send a shiver down your spine. Once you've detected it, you must resist it. Next."

A slender but eager Dwarf volunteered. Like Nickle, he took the rope swing at a run. He successfully made it past the biting rope but was quickly knocked off the next platform by a swinging log.

"And sometimes your opponent won't even use magic. Sometimes you just need to dodge a big thing that's coming at you. Who's next?"

A muscular Dwarf raised his hand as he charged forward. He made it past the biting rope, dodged beneath the swinging log, and leaped over a pit of fire. But the next obstacle was a soccer ball-shaped creature that had a large nose and even larger ears. The creature stared at the Dwarf with beady black eyes, daring him to make the first move.

As the Dwarf ran to the left, the animal conjured a fireball that hit him square in the chest.

Cynthia smiled. "Ah, a Hobgoblin. They're excellent at Alteration magic and devilishly tricky. Of course, it's not a real one. If it were, we'd be burying that Dwarf later tonight. All the opponents you face here are based on creatures found in the real world. They are the pinnacle of Dwarf innovation, but that don't mean they won't hesitate to light you up."

Before Cynthia even asked who was "next," Jason stepped forward. With a yell, he ran at the rope, grabbed it in mid-jump, and flipped backwards onto the other side. He then slid under the log and leaped over the burning pit. The whole thing was so smooth it almost seemed scripted.

"He's a cocky one, isn't he?" Cynthia whispered.

As he approached the Hobgoblin, he pulled something out from his pocket and flung it forward, which exploded into a fantastical flame that sent the creature flying backward. He then entered into a mess of swinging sticks. Somehow, either by magic or skill, Jason made it past them. He then leaped through a hole that was continually changing sizes and onto a moving platform.

A few of the other Dwarves clapped. Cynthia frowned.

While on the moving platform, a dozen stone statues charged at Jason with their fists raised. He was able to use Runes to stop a few of them, but the rest he had to dodge. On and on, Jason went, passing each obstacle as if it were nothing. When he was almost to the finish line, however, a mix of exploding birds caught him off guard and sent him plummeting into the filthy water below.

Cynthia grinned. "Not a bad run—for a Tenderfoot. Although I didn't give him permission to use Runic magic, he did at least make it close to the end."

Some of the Dwarves began to applaud before they were interrupted by Cynthia. "Stop that. Stop that. The rest of you get in line. Just because one of you maggots makes it close to the end, does not mean the rest of you get it easy. It's my job to get you Dwarves ready for combat, and I won't slack until I do. Now, who's next?"

Chapter 9

Dwarf Bout

The first thing Nickle heard every morning was the low growl of Cynthia's voice. After a few days, he was sure that no alarm clock was ever more effective, ever more commanding than her gruff tone. At times she yelled with so much force, he found himself leaping out of bed so that he could stand at attention that much quicker. Once the Dwarves were all in line, Cynthia would have them run laps around a track until they were heaving for breath—sometimes longer. Then came breakfast, which went by way too fast to consider it much of a break. From breakfast, they were either sent to a massive gym, which had weights the size of television sets, or they were marched up to the infamous Grindlemire obstacle course.

On the first day of lifting weights, Nickle put a modest ten pounds on each side of his barbell. He was tempted just to try bench pressing the barbell, but he thought it would make him look weak. He did a repetition of the weight with no problem. So he added more weight. This time he put twenty-five pounds on each side. He tried it again, and it was just as easy as before. More and more weight was stacked on, each set seemed just as easy as the last. Soon he was bench pressing just over four hundred pounds, which had him shaking his head in disbelief. He kept grabbing the weights and hefting them, just to make sure they had not suddenly turned to styrofoam.

For a few brief moments, Nickle thought he was a superhero. As he looked around, however, he realized that everyone else was lifting even more weight than he was. After Nickle finished, Jason took a turn on the weight bench. It only took him a few sets before he passed up Nickle's max, a few more before he passed up everyone else. By the end of his final set, Jason was benching just under seven hundred pounds. As he grunted with the strain, a group of Dwarves surrounded him, cheering him on.

The cheering was cut short by Cynthia's booming voice.

"What's this crap! You're supposed to be building muscle up, not building each other up."

After gym, they almost always were marched to the obstacle course on the familiar long and narrow path, which seemed to stretch out farther each time they did. The obstacle course was as tricky each day as it was different. The harder Nickle tried to get through, the worse he seemed to become. After a week of training, Cynthia began keeping score of who was doing well and who was not. By the end of the month, Nickle was ranked dead last.

It was not that Nickle was bad at controlling magic—he actually was better at it than most. But he had a hard time controlling the magical attacking elements while dodging the traps that came at him. His inability to do two things at once always stalled him for a second too long.

One day, after seeing him fall for the third time in a row, Cynthia walked towards Nickle. "You've got to focus! When you're out in the real world, and more than one thing is attacking you at once, you've got to be able to deal with them both."

Nickle nodded.

"Let's try an experiment, shall we? I want you to tap your head and rub your stomach."

Nickle swallowed. "Right now?"

"Yes, you slimy pup. Of course, right now."

Nickle began to obey but quickly found himself tapping both his stomach and his head. He narrowed his eyes, trying to force his hands to make opposite motions. He succeeded in changing the tapping of one hand to rubbing, but then his other hand stopped moving altogether. It took him a few more awkward moments of concentration before he could do it right.

"Interesting," Cynthia huffed.

"What is?"

"You might have a Dwarf body, but your brain has been hardwired like a Human."

"What?"

"Your brain is not like a Dwarf. Dwarves are natural multi-taskers. If I asked any of the other Dwarves to do the same thing, they'd have no problem. That is one of the basic tests they should have put you through to determine if you're a Dwarf."

"Well, how do Humans make up for it?"

Cynthia pulled him out of the soggy water. "They have quicker reflexes. We Dwarves can do two things at once, but Humans can do one thing faster. I want you to practice rubbing your stomach and tapping your head every day while you're here. Is that understood?"

"Yes, ma'am."

As Cynthia ordered, Nickle began practicing the drill for the next several weeks. It did not help much, even though Nickle did do it with the greatest dedication. He was seen tapping his head so often that some of the Dwarves began calling him "Tap Man," which did not make sense to either Nickle or Jason, but much to Nickle's dismay, the nickname stuck.

One thing Nickle did learn, however, was how to take a beating. It only took him a few laps on the obstacle course to realize that Dwarves had tougher skin and bones than Humans. A few times when he was struck, he was sure he would open his eyes to find himself in the next life. But every time, he was somewhat dismayed to find himself still in Tortugan. He also noticed that the pain he thought he would feel, never came. Even his worst injuries did not cause him much discomfort. This resilience proved essential on the treacherous obstacle course, but even more valuable with their next segment of training—axe wielding.

Dwarves did not wield the puny axes Piddlers often used to intimidate small trees, and for good reason too. Instead, they used massive axes that were thick enough to cut a person in half just by dropping it on them. The axes were meticulously crafted with Runes running the whole length of the weapon. There were hundreds of styles of axes; each one had a different name. A Dwarf would never call something just an "ax"—that would be embarrassing. Instead, they had a system that was so exact it could describe an axe down to every detail.

As Nickle picked up his first axe, the Runes alongside it glowed a bright red for half a moment. The axe was heavier than Nickle expected, despite him purposely selecting the smallest one available.

Jason leaned over to Nickle. "Looks like you've got a twenty-four thumb, double-sided, brake back design with the added cannon-ball bottom. It's an older model, but it still has self-adjusting counterbalances and auto-Rune release."

Nickle arched his eyebrows. "What?"

"You picked a good one."

"Line up, you turds!" Cynthia yelled. "Today, we're gonna begin our axe training. There's no better weapon than a Dwarf axe. Last year, I had one of the Fallen Dwarves ask me why we had to use an axe if there were guns available. Hah. I about threw the poor Tenderfoot out of my class. A well-crafted axe that is endued with Runes of power is the most formidable weapon a Dwarf can carry. Not only will the Runes grant the wielder strength, but they also absorb magical attacks and allow you to cast counter magic. The blade of a Dwarf axe is self-sharpening and self-maintaining. When a Dwarf axe is in the hands of a powerful Son of Hurn or Daughter of Lucretia, even the most powerful Elf Arcons second guess themselves.

"Now, line up. Before I teach you how to activate the Runes in your axes, you'll first learn to fight with one. Contrary to popular belief, an axe is not a clumsy weapon used to bludgeon through battle. It's a graceful tool, one that takes years to master. Over the next few weeks, you'll be learning the basic defense and attack postures. You'll be learning how to hold your blade and how to throw it.

"Now grip the top of your axe and let your arm run the length of your weapon. Where your elbow is now is where you will hold the axe. Eventually, you'll only be wielding your blade with one hand, but to ensure you get the motion right, I want you to practice with two. To begin, we'll cover basic defense postures. Watch my movement and then repeat."

Wielding the axe seemed natural to many of the Dwarves— but to Nickle, it did not. He would have cut his legs off a dozen times had they not been using practice axes, which turned rubbery as soon they came too close to flesh. The techniques were all one fluid motion and required the use of the body's momentum as well as the weight of the axe. The way Cynthia described it, the axe was the most majestic and graceful weapon—and when she was wielding one, it truly was.

Nickle was not the worst one with the axe, much to his relief. There was another kid named Danny, who was so eager to be good with the weapon, he did not have the patience to learn the techniques. As the days progressed, his movement became more and more choppy—so choppy, in fact, it looked like he was being electrocuted as he practiced.

After two months of training, however, the Dwarves began to master the blade. To Jason, the weapon became so natural that it was like an extension of his arm. He earned the praise of everyone that saw him using it, including Cynthia. Armed with this new weapon, the Dwarves were once again sent through the obstacle course. Having an axe greatly helped Nickle, who used the blade more to absorb attacks than to deal them; this allowed him to focus on the actual obstacles. Despite having a weapon, the obstacle course was still challenging since it was continually adapting to the Dwarves' skill level. Only Jason showed any promise of completing the course, and even he was struggling with it.

After three months of training with the axe, the Dwarves began their training in Runic magic. Nickle was excited to learn magic. He thought he would be good at it because, frankly, he was horrible at everything else. First, Cynthia taught the Dwarves how to activate the Runes on their practice axes. This task required absolute concentration and the correct pronunciation of the Rune.

Nickle's axe had three core Runes inscribed in it: the first was for strength, which would renew the wielder's energy as well as double their power; the second was a Fire Rune that could be used to shoot various projectiles or engulf the blade in flames; and the third was a defensive Rune that would cover his skin in a faint protective glow. Since the Runes were deeply inscribed in the blade, they were reusable, but it took a while for them to recharge. The Runes inscribed in the axes were as diverse as the Dwarves that carried them. Some axes had the power to shoot out large rocks, while others could make the earth shake, and still, others that could shoot out blasts of wind or bursts of steam. According to Cynthia, a real battle-ax had about ten core Runes and five minor ones. Dwarf armor, on the other hand, usually had six core Runes and two minor ones. The inscriptions in a set of Tines had a much quicker recharge time and could be devastating to anyone that stood against a Dwarf. A new popular trend was to inscribe Runes onto the shields the Dwarves carried. Shield Runes, however, were usually harder to activate and even more challenging to aim. For the most part, the Dwarves practiced with square shields that were barren of Runes.

Once Nickle and the others learned how to use the Runes on their axes, Cynthia began to teach them how to make Runes themselves. This training was a great relief to Nickle since it involved sitting in a classroom for several hours a day. Each Dwarf was given a book of Runes, which was about as thick as a dictionary, and an unlimited supply of large sheets of paper. They were also given thin, half-dollar sized metal disks.

The Dwarves began by tracing a Wind Rune onto large sheets of paper using thick paintbrushes. The Runes had to match the pictures in the book exactly. They spent hours tracing the Rune, hours longer learning the correct pronunciation. After Cynthia was satisfied with their progress, they began tracing the Runes onto the circular discs. Writing on a disc was different than paper because it required a great deal of concentration. If a Dwarf did not maintain focus while working, the Rune would simply not show up. The larger the Rune was, the stronger the spell. The proportions also affected the strength and type of spell: If one line in the Rune was more extensive than another, it might cause the spell to misfire or shoot off in the wrong direction. The most brilliant of Dwarves, called Golden Calligraphers, were able to manipulate the Runes just enough to get the exact result needed. Many of the Runes looked almost identical, but the subtle differences could completely change the spell. Several of the spells were a combination of multiple Runes. Even the pronunciation of the word shifted the effectiveness of the spell. If one sounded slow and sluggish, the spell would creep along like a snail traveling uphill. If a Dwarf's tone sounded angry, the Rune often exploded before it could take shape.

Nickle would have enjoyed the time he spent drawing the Runes had it not been for Cynthia's unrelenting corrections. She insisted that they held their brushes in an awkward position—even if one could do it better in another way. She spent her time slowly walking around the classroom, glaring at anyone that was hunching their shoulders or not concentrating hard enough.

After the Wind Rune, they began mastering an Earth Rune. The symbol for earth was easier than wind since the lines were thicker and boxier. It was not long before each one of them could create perfectly-etched Earth Runes. When coupled with the right word of power the Earth Rune would shoot a pillar of dirt straight in the air. Often times, when Cynthia was not looking, the Dwarves would compete to see who could stand on their Rune the longest as it propelled them into the air. Jason always won.

The Dwarves were given a leather belt called a Balteus or a Rune belt, which had a dozen small cylinders to hold their Runes. When Nickle first saw one, it reminded him of the change holders that Piddlers often used in banks or grocery stores. Each cylinder had a spot to place a stack of Runes in the top, and a small slot where they could be taken out individually at the bottom. Most of the belts were large enough to hold about two hundred Runes, but some of the chubbier Dwarves had belts big enough to hold up to four hundred.

One day, after learning nearly a dozen Runic spells, Cynthia gathered the Dwarves together in a large, octagonal room that had decorative Dwarf armor along each wall. Above the Dwarf Tines were dozens of odd and interesting looking axes. The floor had a black octagon painted in the very center of the room.

Cynthia grinned. "This is the Arena. Today will be the first day you use Runic magic in combat. You will be using the Runes you've etched, so if they don't work, it's your own fault. For those who don't know, this is called a Dwarf Bout—or as some kids call it, a slugfest. You'll start thirty paces from each other with your axes holstered on your backs. You are free to use axes as well as Runes. No shields will be used in this bout. So who's first? How about you, Nickle?"

Nickle swallowed.

"Nickle will face…McBrian."

McBrian was a burly Dwarf that had the sides of his head shaved; the rest of his hair was braided into a long ponytail. Next to Jason, he was the strongest one in the class. His arms bulged out like they had soccer balls stuffed in them.

Jason approached Nickle and whispered in his ear. "Keep him at bay with your Runes. If he gets too close, I don't think you'll last long. I saw him etching a mix of earth and air Runes, so he might try blowing dirt in your face. He probably didn't even do them right, but if he does throw one at you, block with a water shield Rune—that should stop it cold."

Nickle took a deep breath.

Jason patted Nickle on the back. "You'll do fine."

"All right," Cynthia roared, "Strap your axes on your backs and come to the center of the room. You'll have three, two-minute rounds. If a kill shot is made, the victory goes to whoever struck the blow.

Otherwise, I'll keep track of the points, and the first to accumulate fifty points wins. The point system is complex, so we won't get into that right now, but the best thing a fighter can do is inflict as much pain as possible on their opponent. A shield will stop any projectiles from leaving the arena, so don't worry about hitting the crowd. None of you know any Runes that can kill your opponent, and your armor will protect you from anything too life-threatening. Understood?"

Nickle nodded. McBrian grinned.

Cynthia continued. "Both of you take positions at opposite ends of the room. You must remember to stay within the black octagon or you'll be considered out of bounds and will lose points. Per mandate 717, there cannot be any eye-gouging, scratching, or biting. Ready…begin!"

Like a bull that had broken loose of its pen, McBrian charged at Nickle, his large feet thudding as he went. When he was halfway across the room, he grabbed the axe from his back and began to swing it wildly.

Nickle retrieved a Rune from his belt. He meant to grab a Fire Rune, but instead, he grabbed an Earth Shield. He said the wrong incantation and threw it at his opponent. It hit McBrian square in the chest, but the Rune only gave a small pop and fizzled. The next moment, McBrian swung his axe right into Nickle's side. Despite the padding that suddenly appeared on the end of the axe, and the thick training armor he was wearing, the impact was so strong, it sent Nickle sailing through the air like a Frisbee.

"Minus five points Nickle!" Cynthia barked. "That was almost a kill shot, but you're not getting out of it that easy. Get back in there."

Nickle stood up and blinked his eyes. He took in another long breath before he charged back into the ring. McBrian was waiting for him. The towering hulk took another swing with his axe, but Nickle tucked and rolled, barely dodging the blade. He used the momentum to gain his feet and get behind McBrian, who swung his weapon enthusiastically through the air. The large Dwarf charged forward and brought his blade down on Nickle. At the last moment, Nickle was able to free his axe. The weapons rang as they connected.

McBrian went on the offensive, swinging his weapon so quickly that Nickle could only step back in defense. Twice, Nickle tried to circle around his opponent, but both times, he was quickly blocked. The large Dwarf drove Nickle further back until he was on the other end of the arena.

Nickle was forced to defend himself wildly. He took a hit to the arm, another to the leg. He was hit two more times as he grabbed a Rune from his side. He was not sure what he had in his hand, but he whispered an incantation and threw it at the feet of his opponent. Instantly, a geyser of air erupted beneath McBrian's legs, shooting him up in the air like a leaf in a windstorm. The large Dwarf flipped backward while simultaneously activating one of the core Runes of his axe. As he came down, he slammed his weapon into the ground, which sent a shock wave rippling through the floor until it was just beneath his opponent. Nickle's feet quickly became jelly as the world all around him shook.

"Concentrate, Nickle!" Jason screamed. "Clear your head! Resist his magic."

Nickle obeyed quickly. He focused his mind until the trembling Earth had little effect on him. While he was distracted with the quake, however, McBrian ran forward and swung his weapon right into Nickle's arm. The Dwarf was sent sprawling across the floor. A moment later, McBrian swung again, this time hitting Nickle in the knee.

"Come on, Nickle," Cynthia yelled. "You're falling behind."

Nickle shook his head, almost as if to disagree with Cynthia. She wanted him to score more points, but Nickle was just looking to survive. He lifted his axe in the air, blocking a blow aimed for his head, and then rolled out of bounds to avoid another attack meant for his belly.

"Minus five points again!" Cynthia roared.

Nickle stood up and gave an apologetic smile. He then stepped back in the arena only to be hit back out again.

Cynthia gritted her teeth. "At this rate, you'll be at negative fifty before McBrian can *score* fifty. Use your strengths. Use your strengths."

Nickle swallowed. *"Use my strengths. Use my strengths. What strengths? I don't have any strengths."*

"Keep him at bay!" Jason said from the sidelines.

Nickle drew out a Fire Rune and stepped back inside the ring. Just as his opponent swung at him, he held up the disc and used it to deflect his opponent's weapon. The result was immediate as the Rune exploded and sent McBrian's axe flipping through the air until it stuck in one of the walls. A few of the watching Dwarves applauded.

Now that his opponent did not have a weapon, Nickle had the advantage, but, before he could exploit it, Cynthia's loud voice interrupted.

"That's round one. Both of you go to your corner. Good job, McBrian."

Nickle had not noticed before, but he was seething for breath. He sat down on a little stool and rubbed his hands through his hair. Despite all of the cardio they had been doing the last several months, despite all of the training, he was winded. He took a deep breath and wiped the sweat from his brow.

Jason ran to Nickle's corner. "You've got some nice moves out there."

Nickle arched his eyebrows. "What are you talking about? I'm getting killed. If we were using real axes, I would've been cut down the first ten seconds."

"True. True. But he's not even trying to use Runes."

This observation, as true as it was in the first round, did not apply to the second. McBrian must have received an earful from Cynthia about using his Runes because, in the next round, that seemed like the only thing he did. Nickle spent most of his time in the air, flying back and forth between the explosions that were amply thrown at him. The only respite he received was when McBrian's Runes did not work. During these times, Nickle grabbed whatever Rune he could and attacked. Many of the spells were absorbed by McBrian's broad ax—the rest seemed to have little effect. The most success Nickle had in the second round was when he made a half dozen columns of dirt that he could hide behind. It was not long, however, before McBrian began slicing the pillars and sending them spilling out across the floor. Just as the last pillar was cut in two, Cynthia called an end to the second round.

Jason returned to Nickle's corner and began massaging his shoulders. "That a boy. Way to stay on top of him. For a few seconds, I thought you had him."

"Are you even watching the fight?"

"Yeah, you're doing great."

Nickle guffawed.

"Focus...focus...it's all about focus. Pretend like you've already lost, pretend like it's all over. If you do, you'll have nothing to lose. You're giving this fight too much importance. This doesn't mean anything. A week from now, after the bruises are gone, you won't even remember most of the details of the fight."

"Yeah, probably because of brain trauma."

While they talked, Cynthia cleaned the arena by activating a massive Rune on one of the walls that eliminated all of the debris in the middle. After she was done, she looked at the two fighters in turn. "All right. The score is forty-seven for McBrian and negative two for Nickle. Three more hits and McBrian wins."

"You got this guy—"

"I got this guy?" Nickle asked. "Did you not just hear the score—"

"—BEGIN!" Cynthia yelled.

Nickle gritted his teeth and narrowed his eyes towards his lumbering opponent. He cleared his mind as he stepped forward. Instead of reaching for a Rune, he charged his opponent with his axe. McBrian was shocked by this sudden aggression, but not for long. The two opponents went into a mad flurry of attacks and blocks. Nickle was surprisingly holding his own until he was hit in the calf, which sent him to the floor. McBrian moved in for the kill, but Nickle scooted backward, trying to stall the inevitable.

"*Focus...focus,*" Nickle thought. He began reaching for a Rune but then stopped. He narrowed his eyes, raising his hands towards his opponent. A warmth began to trickle through his body that felt like the first rays of the sun melting the morning frost. He dropped his axe, and brought his hands together. As he did, the heat increased in his fingers.

McBrian noticed the sudden change. He hesitated only for a moment before swinging his axe straight for Nickle's neck. Just before the blade reached flesh, however, Nickle's hands exploded into a beam of white light, hitting McBrian right in the chest. The large Dwarf flew across the arena until his body slammed against the opposite wall, where he collapsed to the ground, unconscious.

Adrenaline shot through Nickle. He stood up with his hands in the air, a grin spread wide across his face. But to his surprise, no one was cheering. In fact, no one was even looking.

Unbeknownst to the two fighters in the middle, Cynthia and everyone in the class were all turned the other way. When Nickle was first hit in the calf, Edward Thunderhoof entered the room, drawing the gaze of everyone except the two fighters in the middle. The Dwarves pounded their chests and inclined their heads as the large Cennarian entered.

"Cynthia, you're needed at once," Edward said with a rushed tone. "The Faeries are threatening to blackout EarthWorks. All trained Dwarves of the Silver Army are to suit up and prepare for battle."

Cynthia's face turned a shade of white that none of the Dwarves had ever seen before. "We're going to war against the Faeries?"

"I don't think it will come to that. We're only needed to provide crowd control. The Tri'Ark is in negotiations with the Faeries as we speak."

Her face relaxed ever so slightly. "All right. I'll be there, Ed." At that exact moment, as the class watched Edward salute and leave, McBrian could be seen flying in the background, hit by the beam of white light Nickle had released from his hands. Just as the large Dwarf struck the far wall, Cynthia turned around and faced the class "All right. The rest of the day will be a free day."

"A free day?" One of the Dwarves asked.

"Yes...," She said as her temper began to return to her, "...and don't think you'll ever have another one. So, enjoy it!" With this, she stomped off and slammed the door behind her.

Chapter 10

Joshua Brickle'Bee

"Did you see what I did?" Nickle said excitedly.

Jason nodded. "Yeah, you disarmed McBrian in the first round, avoided him in the second, and—"

"No, I mean at the end. Did you see what happened?"

"Edward Thunderhoof came in and interrupted the fight."

"Yeah, but McBrian and I didn't know that. We kept fighting. And then my hands started getting warm, and I felt something rising up my spine. Then, just as McBrian was about to finish me, I shot out a beam of light that hit him right in the chest and sent him flying through the air—he's probably still unconscious. Maybe we should check on him."

Jason arched his eyebrows. "What? That's impossible. That sounds like Elven magic. You must have been using a Rune and mixed up the incantation."

"No, I didn't. I didn't even have a Rune in my hand."

"Well then, either you're lying to me, or you're the first Dwarf ever to do Elven magic without some sort of totem or relic."

"I can do Elven magic?"

Jason shook his head. "Actually, I think you're lying."

"But I—"

Jason nodded and began walking towards the Administrative building. "Ok, I believe you, but let's stop talking and start doing something. We've been stuck in Tortugan so long I'm beginning to forget what the real world looks like. We need to do something fun."

Nickle quickly caught up to Jason's side. "What if we go to a movie?"

Jason laughed. "Movie? That's such a Piddler thing to say. Nobody besides kids go to the movies in EarthWorks. I've never understood Piddlers' fascination with movies: It's like paying someone for the opportunity to be bored for two hours. I can't imagine sitting in front of a screen for that long, watching other people live the adventure that you could be living."

"Where do people go then?"

"The Library."

Now it was Nickle's turn to scoff. "The Library? I mean, I enjoy reading a good book now and then, but to go to a library on a Friday night seems—"

"Do you remember when we first came here? When we read those Piddler books on that useless junk—Trig-something and Geo-metro-something else?"

"Yeah, of course I do. You kept getting in trouble for not paying attention. Why does that matter?"

"Books in EarthWorks don't just tell the story, they allow you to live it. Just like the textbooks, it feels like you get sucked into them. But unlike the characters in the book, you can't die. Sometimes you can even affect the ending of the book, depending on how stubborn the author was when he wrote it."

Nickle's mind began racing with possibilities. "Really? Where are we going, by the way? I've never been on this side of the camp."

"We're going to pick up our money."

"We're getting paid to be here?"

"Of course. You didn't think this was volunteer work, did you? Now, don't be disappointed by how much you get. A lot of our gold dust is being saved to pay for our Dwarf armor. And I can't wait for that day to come."

"Why do you want your Tines so much?"

"Are you kidding? Dwarf armor is the coolest. We practice with some beat up and broken-down gear in Tortugan, so you probably don't have any idea what Dwarf armor really is. Girls won't give you the time of day without it. And when we finally have our personalized Rune empowered and reinforced armor, we'll be nearly invincible. No one in their right mind messes with a Dwarf dressed in full battle Tines."

They entered into a large, stoic building that was etched with powerful stone figurines. Jason had apparently been here before because, despite the dimly lit rooms, he found his way quickly. They talked to a Dwarf named Snuffy, who kept sneezing, and were promptly given pay. Nickle received a completely new medallion while Jason pulled out his old medallion and had gold added to it. After they finished collecting the gold dust, they ran back to their barracks and changed into their formal Silver Army attire.

Nickle had never tried on his formal uniform and he had a difficult time getting it on. He put on a white shirt and then a light-yellow leather jacket that did not have a collar. The uniform was lined with silver buttons that complemented the badges on his arms and chest. Next, he pulled on a set of tan pants with a black seam on the side that magically adjusted. It took him twice as long to get dressed as Jason, but when he did, he was surprised at what he saw. He had not spent much time in front of a mirror at camp Tortugan—there was no need or time—but now, as he stared at his reflection, he barely recognized himself. His arms were thick and muscular, his eyes sharp and alert. He let his beard grow in—although it was still short and well-trimmed according to camp protocol—but it was more than he had ever been allowed to grow before. He honestly did not recognize himself.

"Let's get going, Nickle," Jason said, "before all the good books are taken."

Nickle turned to face Jason. "What happened to your beard?"

Jason grinned. "I improved upon it." Instead of the shabby facial hair all the Tenderfoots grew, Jason now sported a beard that had intricate symbols and designs cut into it. It very much resembled the sprawling drawings that were seen on so many Dwarf buildings.

"So...what do we need to bring?"

"Just your best pickup line and your medallion."

"Pick-up line?"

"Yeah, there'll be Dwarf ladies—and maybe Elves."

"I've never seen an Elf girl—or even an Elf for that matter."

Jason winked and led Nickle out of the barracks. They traveled quickly to the edge of Tortugan where they hailed a Taxi-Lator. Once onboard, it did not take long before they were in the Heart of EarthWorks, whipping through the city.

Jason had been right about The Library—it was packed. Long lines started at the entrance and poured out in every direction. Loud music and lights were bursting out of the building, almost like it was some sort of club. A few workers were attempting to make sense of the chaos, but they seemed overwhelmed by the crowd around them. The Library was the largest Nickle had ever seen. Two gigantic creatures were at the entrance, glaring down at everything before them. It became abundantly clear that these creatures were there in case the line turned into a mob.

Nickle pointed. "What are those?"

Jason slapped Nickle's hand down. "Don't point. Those are Rinacons—one of the toughest creatures ever to grace the Earth. They've got the lower body of a rhinoceros and the upper body of a giant. They're powerful beasts that are almost impossible to stop. Never make one mad."

Nickle could not help but stare as he passed the giant creatures. They were massive, taller than two stories. Their arms were riddled with muscles that were continually being flexed. With each enormous step the creatures took, Nickle could feel the ground shaking.

Once they made it past the main entrance, Jason leaned over to Nickle. "They're not too bright—however—which is the reason they're usually nothing more than bodyguards or bouncers." After a few moments of silence, Jason continued, "So, what book do you want to read?"

"I don't have any idea."

"Well, if you have a vivid imagination, you do. How about a taste of Tolkien? I'm thinking when the Orcs are raiding the castle—that's a good one to get you started."

"Minas Tirith?"

"Yeah, that's the one. Do you know how to man a catapult?"

Not long after, Nickle found himself buying tickets to *The Lord of the Rings*—the book. After a Cennarian lady took their gold dust, they were led to room number five, which was filled with squishy bean bags. The small room was crowded with all shapes and types of people and creatures—most of them were young. After engaging in awkward conversation with a few of them, Jason grabbed a book from a cart.

Nickle was about to grab one too but Jason stopped him. "If you want to be in the book together, we've got to read the same book."

"Oh," Nickle replied, "that makes sense." With their book in hand, they found a comfortable set of bean bags and sat down.

Nickle turned the book in his hands. "What do you do?"

Jason grinned. "Just start reading—and then, fight like there's no tomorrow."

After finding the right page, they both began reading. It was not long before the words started to swim off the page, almost as if they had suddenly become fish. Then they began to drip down from the book and onto the floor, where they stayed for a moment before starting to stretch and expand. The room rippled like a pond. When the room finally settled, they were no longer in The Library. Nickle felt his breath slip from his lungs as he stared out from one of the walls of Minas Tirith. Thousands of Orcs were marching up to the gate, armed with wicked-looking swords and mismatched armor. He looked down at himself, amazed at what he saw. He was now wearing thick Dwarf armor that had intricate designs all over it.

Jason shoved Nickle to the side. "Boulder!"

Suddenly, the wall they were standing on exploded as it was struck with a massive rock. Debris and dirt scattered through the air, leaving nothing but a cloud of smoke behind.

Jason pulled Nickle off the ground. "You about wrote your own ending."

"You said you couldn't die!"

"Yeah, you can't really die, but if you die in the book, it pulls you back to reality. The longer you stay alive, the more of the story you get to see unfold. Now get up." Jason pointed towards a far wall. "Let's man that catapult."

Nickle nodded and began following Jason. They passed foot soldiers and archers, massive pots of boiling oil and stockpiles of stone. They reached the catapult and ducked behind a wall just as a host of arrows passed overhead.

Jason rolled over to a stack of rocks and began pushing one into a sling. "Help me out with these rocks—they're heavier than they look." Nickle crawled over to Jason's side. Between the two of them, they were able to push a massive stone into a large gurney that they used to lift the rock onto the far end of the catapult. Once loaded, Jason grinned mischievously before he pulled on the release. The large boulder was airborne for several seconds before it struck the ground, sending orc bodies and debris in every direction.

"Good shot," Nickle whispered.

Jason slapped Nickle on the back. "Yeah, let's see if we can hit that orc carrying the big banner."

"Are these things that accurate?"

"Depends on who's using them."

They spent the next several minutes loading and reloading the catapult. Each time they released a gigantic rock, Nickle felt a rush of adrenaline flush through his body. Jason was good with the catapult—almost too good. He could put the boulders on just about any target he wanted. After several more shots, one of the enemy's projectiles, clipped the top of their catapult, making it useless. They both grabbed bows and began firing at enemies as fast as they could spot them. It was not long before the Orcs broke through the first gate, and Nickle and Jason were forced into hand-to-hand combat. They were able to cut down a good amount of Orcs before Nickle took an arrow to the back and was sent spiraling out of the book. Jason survived quite a bit longer but was finally forced out of the novel by a horde of wicked-looking Orcs carrying long spears.

Nickle could not believe how much time had passed in the book. It seemed like only ten minutes had gone by, but as he looked at a clock in The Library, he realized he had been there for close to an hour.

After Jason finished reading, the two Dwarves snuck into room 24, which was reading *Jurassic Park*. Between Velociraptors, massive Tyrannosaurus Rexes, and Pterodactyls, they spent most of their time running. They were able to get the power back on, but they found themselves cornered by a pack of Velociraptors. They made a good defense, taking down three of the creatures with a pair of axes, but they were quickly flanked by more of the vicious creatures and forced out of the pages of the book.

The next book they read was *Gladiators of the Naumachia,* where they spent most of their time training and fighting as gladiators. After a few bouts, they found themselves amid a Naumachia on Roman warships, surrounded by opposing forces. They sent a good number of opponents into the water below but were finally forced out of the book by a talented archer that took them both down.

Next, they stepped into the world of *Moby Dick,* where they were both commanders of ships. They did not last long in this book before they were both sunk by the massive white titan that appeared so suddenly that neither one could react.

They went from book to book, experiencing the best scenes

of everything they had read. They took a break in the afternoon to eat at Meaters before they returned to their reading. By six o'clock, Nickle was too exhausted to read another book. The two boys found themselves in a circular room in the middle of The Library that had hundreds of soft couches. They collapsed on separate couches and talked about their adventures from each book. It was not long, however, before Jason saw a sign flash, "*Star Wars, Episode 12*—Now Reading." Nickle declined to go, but Jason headed off towards room 104 with a rather large contingent of nerdy-looking Humans.

Nickle felt awkward sitting in the massive domed room by himself. He could see people of all ages and types running around excitedly, carrying an odd array of snacks and food in their hands. At the other end of the large room, there was an equally impressive tunnel that stretched on into the darkness. Only a few people were walking in and out of the tunnel, each one carrying a hefty book or bag.

He stood up and approached the room, eyeing it with caution. When he finally entered, he was greeted by a transparent man who smiled grimly. The man was dressed in a large toga that dragged tentatively across the ground. Nickle was not sure if it was just his imagination, but the man seemed to be floating a few inches off the floor.

Nickle swallowed. "Are you a ghost?"

"No. Not exactly—more like the shadow of a ghost."

"A shadow?"

The man nodded slowly. "When a Human dies that is so passionate and powerful, their ghost often leaves a Shadow behind. I am the Shadow of Hectorillian Brannon—the inventor of the toothpick, but you can call me Hector."

"So, are you real?"

"Yes—as real as any emotion."

"What happened to your ghost?"

"He passed on to the next life and left behind a great legacy. And as long as people remember him, I will live on for eternity. I am fueled by those memories."

Nickle arched his eyebrows. "How old are you?"

"No one can be sure."

"And what do you do here?"

"I am a Researcher," the man nodded again slowly. "Ask me

what you need, and I will find the book you seek."

"Oh," Nickle replied. "So, this is like a real library."

The floating man rolled his eyes. "This is the only library. Those books out there are cheap tricks of Piddler-born magicians. Through this doorway and down these halls is where you'll find real adventure—real power."

"What do you have in here? Textbooks? Maps?"

"Everything ever written. Do you want to see what you got on a fourth-grade spelling test? Do you want to see the pictures you drew when you were a child?"

"You can't have everything."

Hector shrugged. "Ok, not everything, but most things, unless it's protected by enchantments or deemed top secret by the Tri'Ark."

"So, you seriously have pictures I drew when I was a kid?"

The man gestured inside. "Only the pictures that created some sort of deep emotional reaction. For some kids, we have almost everything they ever made; for others, we have very little. It depends on the child, young Nickle Brickle'Bee. Enter the true part of The Library and see for yourself."

Nickle obeyed, but slowly. Once he passed through a magnificent archway made of stone and ferocious gargoyles, he entered into a room that he knew was like no other room he had ever seen. There were rows of books, stacked onto shelves that were six or seven stories tall. The room was so expansive that it seemed possible to fit a whole town inside. Along the walls were curving decorations that changed continuously as Nickle talked.

The old Shadow led Nickle to an ornately designed chair and table. Nickle took a seat. After a moment of silence, the Dwarf spoke. "How did you know my name?"

"I know a great many things about you—some of which I can share, most of which I cannot."

"Do you know why I'm here?"

"I know why you think you're here."

Nickle scoffed. "That doesn't make sense. Wouldn't the reason why I'm here and why I think I'm here be the same?"

"No."

"Well, I just wanted to see what you have over here."

The old man sighed deeply. "That's the reason you think you

are here."

"Well, I have no other reason to be here besides that."

"Are you sure? Remember, this room has almost everything ever written. Are you sure you can't think of something you might want to know?"

Instantly, a conversation popped into Nickle's mind. It was something Thornhead had said, something that had turned his stomach. "Maybe there is. How can I find it with all these books?"

"I can find it. You just have to tell me what you need."

Nickle paused to gather his thoughts. "There was a man that told me that my father had turned Troll. What does that mean?"

Hector vanished. A moment later, three massive books appeared in front of Nickle. One of them was opened and laid across the table.

"What is this—"

"—The answer to your question."

Nickle glanced down at the worn pages:

"Dwarves have been known to turn Troll on rare occasions. The cause of this transition is unknown, but greed is certainly a key factor in the change. One who has turned Troll will neglect family and friends, leaving them for a life of solitude. Often they will end up on the surface, tormenting panic-stricken Piddlers with noises in the night. Like all trolls, they like dark and damp places. A favorite spot is under bridges or in swamps. As the transition progresses, the Dwarf will lose all sense of civility and memories of their former life. They will become fueled by their lust of gold until it becomes their only clear thought. Despite the loss of cognition, they surprisingly have been shown to increase in magical power. Some hypothesize that Trolls are immortal since no Troll has ever been found that has died of old age...."

Nickle narrowed his eyes. "Is that why I'm an orphan? Because my father turned Troll?" As soon as Nickle spoke, the three books disappeared, and a stack of newspapers replaced them. One of them had a picture of a massive Dwarf on the front with a sharp jaw. Nickle scanned the page until he found a date. "This is dated over two hundred years ago." He looked at the ghostly old man but, after he gave no response, Nickle turned his attention back to the paper.

"Joshua Brickle'Bee was found to have turned Troll earlier this week, reports Thornhead Back'Break, Acting Chief Warlord of the Silver Army. According to the Cogs of Hurn, "Everything is being done for his recovery, but as of yet, no cure has been discovered for Troll." The beloved Joshua was a renowned Dwarf made famous by his epic defeat of Sea Gargantics, his diplomacy with the Faeries, and in his help in capturing the Demon Lord. Although the specifics of his turning are a mystery, authorities hope to have more answers as the investigation continues. As far as the Scathians can tell, the source of conflict might have been over the recent disappearance of his pregnant wife...."

Nickle rubbed his hands through his hair as he stared long and hard at the photo in the paper. The longer he stared, the more the photo blurred and shook. It was not long before the room around him swirled, and he felt pulled into the picture. He was hoping to see his father but was sadly disappointed to find himself at the scene of the investigation. Humans and Dwarves were walking in and out of a small room, all of them rummaging through broken pieces of furniture or shattered pieces of glass. He tried talking to one of the investigators, but the man did not seem to be able to hear him.

He walked around the room, looking at the damage that had been left behind. Something or someone had trashed the place, leaving nothing intact. There were massive claw marks spread throughout the home, most of them around the front door.

As Nickle was turning to exit the house so he could examine the damage on the outside, a Dwarf was simultaneously entering. It was Thornhead. The Dwarf looked scared, maybe even a little angry. His hair and garb were disheveled, almost as if he had just woken up. His eyes were bloodshot and his cheeks were sagging. Thornhead went from room to room, shouting out Joshua's name in frustration.

Nickle swallowed.

Just as suddenly as he was pulled into the picture, he felt himself being yanked out. He shook his head and stood up. He was back in The Library, the old transparent man floating by his side, a slight smile on his face.

"My father helped capture the Demon Lord? Who exactly is the Demon Lord?"

The Shadow disappeared and reappeared with another newspaper. On the front was a large picture of a man. At the top of the paper, in a massive font, were the words, "Kara'Kala Proclaimed Emperor." Nickle was sure of two things about this man: One, he had never seen him before in his life, and two, he somehow knew who he was. He was more muscular than an average human and quite a bit taller, but besides those two traits, he did not seem much different than any other Human Nickle had seen. There was one thing that did catch Nickle's attention—the color of the man's eyes. His eyes were blue around the center of the pupil, but as they progressed to the edge of the eye, they suddenly became an emerald green—just like Nickle's. Time slowed as he stared at the man. For a moment, Nickle could have sworn the man could see him—he could have sworn he saw a look of curiosity on his face—but that moment quickly passed.

"Who is that man? The man with eyes like me?"

The Shadow gave a slight nod with his head. "Now, that's the reason you're here." Hector disappeared for a moment before he reappeared with three stacks of books. The books were all sorts of sizes and colors; some looked old and worn while others were brand new. Nickle looked down to discover a thick book before him, one that had a red binding and gold letters. It was opened to a page with a picture of the man with multi-colored eyes.

Nickle stared long and hard at the photo. "Who is he?"

"Read," Hector answered.

The young Dwarf cleared his throat.

"Kara'Kala Shivell is a powerful Arcon that established and led the Insular Movement. He is largely credited for being the founder of EarthWorks and for establishing the Tri'Ark. He quickly became Supreme Judge and led EarthWorks into a prosperous age. His climb to power, however, began to disturb others—especially the Elves, who saw his Insular Movement as a vie for power. In response, Kara'Kala established the Royal Police, whose sole purpose was to root out all those that opposed him. No one is quite sure when, but around this time, Kara'Kala performed the Crossing, a powerful incantation that turns a Human into an immortal Demon. Hundreds of Kara'Kala's

119

supporters followed suit, turning themselves into the powerful and immortal creatures of times past. With his red followers, Kara'Kala formed a secret group known as the Demon Brood. After hundreds of deaths and disappearances, three of the most powerful wizards from the primary races gathered together to form the Triumvirate, which opposed all things of the Demon Brood. Civil war broke out: The side of Kara'Kala was called the Royals, the side that supported the Triumvirate was known as the Populi. After several months of open warfare, victory seemed all but lost for the Populi. In the battle of Three Stones, the Triumvirate was able to lure Kara'Kala out into the open, where they quickly discovered that the Demon Lord was indestructible. By some unknown force or by some wicked spell, Kara'Kala had gained invincibility—a feat that has never been accomplished or duplicated. The members of the Triumvirate, however, were able to subdue the Demon long enough for burning chains to be shackled around his arms and legs. The FireWall was erected shortly thereafter and is currently the holding cell for Kara'Kala and all of his Demon followers...."

Nickle let out a long sigh. "He's still alive."

"Yes," Hector replied. "And powerful."

"I've seen where they keep them—the track of the Tube travels right through their prison."

"Yes," Hector nodded, "it does. I imagine that's an intentional reminder to all those who would seek power above all else."

The Dwarf looked up into Hector's face and narrowed his eyes. "What does Kara'Kala have to do with my father? If my father died two hundred years ago, how could my mother be pregnant for that long? How long are Dwarves usually pregnant?"

Instantly another book appeared. At the top of the first page, the word "Dwarf" was inscribed in long golden letters. Nickle read the words below.

"A Dwarf woman typically is pregnant for eighteen months, but some records indicate they can carry a child for up to twenty-four months. The longest Dwarf pregnancy was reported as being twenty-seven months, but skeptics have brought new evidence to light that discredits this claim. During the pregnancy, a Dwarf woman will tend to feel stronger and..."

Nickle pulled his face away from the book. "This doesn't make sense. How could my mother have been pregnant with me for two-hundred years?"

Hector leaned forward with a generous smile on his face. "Excellent question, but I'm sorry, young Brickle'Bee, this section of The Library is now closing. You'll have to come back another time. I believe your friend is waiting for you by the entrance."

Chapter 11

The Demon Brood

"I'm not saying that he's wrong, Nickle. I'm just saying that every Shadow that works in The Library is a bit odd," Jason explained after they had reached their barracks that night. "They all pretend to know a ton of stuff about the future, but that's only so people revere and remember them. If people forget about them, they disappear—so they've got a real motive to act as if they know something. One time, a Shadow tried to convince me that I'd be a famous warrior one day. Hah, I'm sure they say that to everyone."

Nickle shook his head. "But he knew my name—"

"Probably looked it up in The Library."

"What do you know about the Demon Brood?"

"Oh, boy. Is that what that old man was telling you? The Brood is gone—all locked up in their fiery prison. You saw it when we were riding in the Tube down here; they're locked behind the FireWall. They don't have a chance of ever escaping and good thing too; they about destroyed the world two hundred years ago—"

"My father disappeared shortly after the Demon Lord was captured. I think the Brood might have had something to do with him turning Troll."

"Your father turned Troll?"

"Well, that's what the newspaper said. It said he turned Troll after Kara'Kala was imprisoned, which doesn't seem to make sense."

Jason shook his head. "There's no way your father would turn Troll if he had a wife and kids. Only old-timers that have lost everyone they love turn Troll—even then it's rare."

"Exactly!" Nickle nodded quickly. "Maybe it's a bogus story. Maybe my father is still out there. Like you said, Dwarves live over six thousand years; he could still be alive." He turned around and headed for the door. "We've got to get back to The Library—"

Jason caught up to Nickle and rested his hands on his shoulders. "We can't. We've got lights out in half an hour. We'll be in big trouble if we're not in our bunks."

Nickle slowed his walk but he did not stop. "What? That doesn't sound like you; usually, rules mean nothing to you. We've got to get over there."

"Hey, even I have my limits. We could be in serious trouble if we went missing. We'll get over there sometime, but we can't do it tonight. Maybe next week—maybe then we'll have a chance to sneak away."

Nickle lowered his head. "You're right."

It was not long before they were back in bed, waiting for the lights to turn off. Even after lights out, Nickle could not sleep. He kept imagining the face of his father—a father that he did not even know. Sometimes he would picture his father wrenching in pain as he turned into a Troll; other times, he envisioned him surrounded by fiery Demons and forced to go into hiding. The more he thought about it, the less the story made sense.

"*Nickle Brickle'Bee*," a voice hissed from across the room.

The Dwarf stirred in his bed and looked around. Besides the blackness of the room and the outlines of a few bunk beds, he could see nothing. "Is that you, Jason?"

"*No.*"

He turned around, scanning the room even more intently for an intruder.

"Who are you?"

"*A friend.*"

Nickle suddenly realized that the voice he heard was not an audible one—at least, not one that anyone else in the room could hear. Someone was whispering in his head, like a little bug that had crawled inside his ear.

"Where are you?"

Suddenly, a man appeared at the edge of Nickle's bed. He held perfectly still, almost as if movement would cause him considerable discomfort. He was head to toe in blue plate mail that was ornately decorated. Around his neck was a blue cape that looked black in the darkness of the room. A nasty, purpled scar dripped down his left eye until it reached his chin. Nickle armed himself with his pillow and scooted away as far as he could.

"What are you going to do with that—pound me into the ground?"

Suddenly, Nickle recognized the voice. "Locke?"

"Yes," the man replied.

"What are you doing here? I don't think Humans are allowed in Tortugan after hours."

"I'm no Human—not anymore."

Nickle leaned forward. "You're a Scathian. But what do you want with me?"

The man laughed. "So, you do remember meeting me before. Well, we need to talk. Come with me. It takes a great deal of concentration to mute our conversation from everyone's ears, and I don't have the energy to keep it up for much longer."

Nickle swallowed. "Where are we going?"

"Just outside," Locke replied as he climbed down to the ground. Nickle quickly followed. He felt a mix of excitement as well as awe for the giant warrior. Since first meeting Locke, when he had been summoned to the Cogs of Hurn, Nickle had heard many stories about Scathians and their mind control powers. If only half the stories were true, Locke was sure to be an unstoppable force on the battlefield.

The two stepped outside the barracks and crept towards a darker spot on the grounds. Around the camp were a few hovering Fire Runes, which provided some light, but it was only along major paths and thoroughfares. The majority of Tortugan was pitch black. When they finally stepped into the darkness, both of them spoke at once.

"So, you're the child—"

"Jason has told me all about Scathians—"

Locke gestured to Nickle to continue, and so he did. "You guys are like legends. I hear you can change people's minds and manipulate their thoughts. They say you guys practice endlessly with the sword and that you don't sleep or eat for weeks. Is that true?"

Locke nodded. "Yes—some of it—but there's a lot to our order that's shrouded in mystery."

"How many are in your order?"

"That's one of the mysteries."

Nickle scratched his head. "Are you reading my thoughts right now?"

"No."

An awkward moment passed before Nickle continued. "What about now?"

"Still no."

"Man," Nickle grinned, "if I could read people's thoughts, I think I'd be doing it all the time. That would be incredible to hear what other people thought of me. Jason isn't going to believe that you suddenly appeared here tonight. He barely believed me when I told him about the first time we met."

Locke kneeled next to Nickle. "Mind reading is complicated. The keener the mind, the harder it is to read. But that's not why I'm here. I've been waiting for you for a long time. You were harder to locate than anyone I've ever met."

"Well, I've spent most of my time on the surface."

"I'm sure I was the first to find you, but I will not be the last. Your life is an odd one. Two of the Human factions know you are down here—maybe the other three know as well."

"Why would someone be looking for me? I'm barely a Dwarf fourth class."

"I don't know. I don't think anyone does just yet."

"What are you talking about?"

Locke frowned. "I think that people might want to find you for different reasons. You've been marked—you know that, don't you? No Dwarf has ever had multi-colored eyes like yours—everyone thought that was impossible. That particular mix of color does happen to Humans on occasion when one of the parents is an Elf."

"Why does eye color matter?"

"Eyes are the window to the soul. The last person to have eyes like yours—"

"—was Kara'Kala, the Demon Lord."

Locke arched his eyebrows. "You've picked up quite a bit with your little time down here."

"And why would you want to find me?"

"An old man prophesied that you'd come. He said I should find you, and find you I have."

"An old man? How do you know I'm the right one?"

"I'm sure you are—you've got to be. I looked into your file

and, despite it being heavily classified, I was able to quickly find out that none of it makes any sense. You're only fourteen, and yet your mother was pregnant with you two hundred years ago."

"I know. I just found out myself."

"I've also discovered something that I don't believe anyone else knows. Before your mother died, she was living with the Faeries—which is something that no Elf, Human, or Dwarf has ever been allowed to do. If you want to discover the truth, you need to visit Titania—the Faerie Queen. She's the only one that can tell you what befell your mother."

"The Faeries? Won't they kill me?"

"Maybe, but I don't think so—not after they cared for your mother for so long. Why would they care for her while she was pregnant and have no affection for the baby that she carried? They might even recognize you. I'll be watching over you, making sure that the other Human factions don't interfere with your life. But you need to speak to the Faerie Queen."

"That sounds insane."

"Insane or not, it's the only way to fit the pieces of the puzzle together. In our world, knowledge can be more powerful than the strongest spell. Now, keep your wits about you—you'll need them. Stay hidden; stay safe."

Locke began to walk off, but Nickle interrupted him. "How will I contact you? How can I even trust you?"

The armored Scathian turned his head back slightly towards Nickle. "I'll know when you're trying to contact me."

Moments later, the warrior was gone, leaving Nickle with nothing but a confused look on his face. After a while, the Dwarf returned to his bunk where he shifted at least a dozen times before he finally fell asleep.

***

Nickle did not have very many clear thoughts for the next few weeks. Whenever he was taking a break or sitting down for a meal, his eyes would drift up to the roof while he tried to piece together everything that he had recently learned. Jason did not offer much advice about the situation except, "definitely do not visit the Faeries—they will tear your skin off your body." Despite this constant distraction, Nickle actually did better in his training.

Training gradually became less physical and more technical. They spent most of their time in class, learning various offensive and defensive Runes. Nickle was able to do most of them, but he was best with a Sight Rune. It enabled him to stick a Rune against a wall and to view what was going on behind it through another Rune—almost like a video camera. The Sight Rune was a little painful, however, because one of the Runes had to suction cup itself onto your eyeball for it to work.

After a few more weeks of training, Nickle finally had the chance to escape to The Library. Jason had made it through the obstacle course on his thirtieth attempt—a feat that had not been done by a Dwarf for five hundred years—and was allowed to take a day off along with another person of his choice. The two Dwarves excitedly scurried towards their barracks, talking about Jason's near impossible triumph over of the obstacle course.

"So, where do you want to go?" Jason asked with a grin.

"The Library," Nickle replied, "of course."

Jason leaped up in the air. "Yes, I knew you'd say that." But then suddenly, Jason's excitement ebbed. "Wait, what part of The Library?"

"The side that has real books."

Jason rolled his eyes. "Come on. A strange guy shows up in the middle of the night, telling you to kill yourself by visiting the Faeries, and you're going to do more research on it?"

Nickle patted Jason on the shoulder. "I appreciate you selecting me to have a free day off, but there's nothing else I'd rather do than figure this out. You have to admit, a Scathian showing up in the middle of the night is more than just odd. I've got to piece this together. I've got to find out what happened to my parents. They might still be alive for all we know. Wonder if they're still living with the Faeries, and I could see them any time I wanted?"

"What if the Scathian is wrong? What if he talked to the wrong kid?"

"Well, that's one thing I've got to find out. I'm not going to just run off to the Faeries, screaming 'here I am, here I am.' I don't know anything about Locke—maybe he's the bad guy. I can't help but think, however, that my parents' disappearance is somehow linked with the Demon Lord."

"How could it be? Your parents disappeared after the Demon Lord was captured and thrown behind the FireWall."

"I don't know... call it a hunch, but I've got to find out."

"Fine, we'll go to the Archives."

"Thanks. I appreciate it."

"But you're paying for the Taxi-Lator ride…and for lunch… and for incidentals."

Within thirty minutes, they found themselves in the massive entrance to the Archives. Hector was not there. In his place, there was another, mysterious-looking Shadow that acted twice as all-knowing as Hector did.

They began with a book entitled *The Demon Brood—The Disaster of Kara'Kala*. The book was filled with horrific pictures of Demons and the like, all of them with fiery red eyes and spikes that shot out of their shoulders and back. Under each image was a name and description of the Demon. Jason read out loud:

Moloch: The Demon Prince of Envy. Formerly, he was known as Justin SouthHeart, but he quickly took on the name Moloch after his changing. This once leading apprentice of the famous Elven Arcon Shallin, fell prey to the persuasive antics of Kara'Kala. Before his transformation, Justin was known for his endless envying of others. It was this path that led him down….

Belial: Demon of Destruction. Formerly, he was known as Jithilian the Wise. He was recruited early on by Kara'Kala and was one of the principle powers within the Royal Police. When Belial changed form the rage that was contained in him transformed him into a massive beast. He was one of the few Demons to have a Centaur-like body. He is extremely dangerous, even to other Demons around him. After his transformation, his primary thoughts became that of destruction….

Chemos: Demon of Swords. Formerly, he was known as Yuri Sible. This once bright student of the Harbordeen Academy graduated top of his class. He studied with the Scathians for a while and became a Master of the sword. During the rigorous routine of the Scathians, the Demon Lord made frequent visits to Yuri. After disappearing for a year, he came back as a powerful Demon. His transformation left him with an odd skin pigmentation that made him appear like he had vines wrapped around his body....

Jason shook his head. "The list goes on and on. How many people did Kara'Kala deceive?"

Nickle looked over Jason's shoulder. "What was he trying to accomplish?"

Jason flipped towards the beginning of the book to a chapter entitled "The Beginning." He cleared his throat before he continued.

"Kara'Kala Shivell was a visionary. Born to an Elf Father and a Human mother, he was endued with a powerful mix of magic. This odd blend resulted in a unique eye pigmentation. Usually, Elf and Human half-breeds have little to no magical talent, but Kara'Kala proved a rare exception. He went to the best surface school, where he received the highest honors. His magical powers gave him much sway in the Council of Magic, which was eventually abolished by Kara'Kala's command. During the early years of his life, he began touring the world, gaining support for his "Insular Doctrine," a doctrine that demanded the complete separation of the Piddler world from the magical one. By Kara'Kala's direction, the Dwarves were commissioned to dig down to the center of the Earth, where magic is the strongest, and establish EarthWorks—one of the first completely Piddler-free cities in the world...."

Jason skipped a few pages:

"More disturbing than the Royal Police was the number of spies Kara'Kala employed. Even to this day, it is difficult to estimate how many people the Demon Lord controlled. During the Dismal Days, few could be trusted; fewer still could be counted upon as reliable allies.

During this time, powerful sorcerers began to produce ample evidence that the Earth had started to die. The Triumvirate blamed

Kara'Kala, who, in turn, blamed it on the Piddler's pollution. After Kara'Kala consolidated his power by forming the Demon Brood, he then proclaimed himself Emperor for Life over EarthWorks."

Jason let out a long sigh. "It seems he just wanted power. I don't even think he knew your dad existed."

"That doesn't add up." Nickle scribbled his father's name on a piece of paper and handed it to the Shadow that was helping them. "Here. Find whatever you can about this person." Moments later, thirty books were piled up on the table. "Thank you."

Nickle grabbed one book, Jason another. Between the two of them, they were able to make good time through the stack of books. Many of the newspapers in EarthWorks preferred to publish their information in books, rather than on large pieces of free-floating paper, as the Piddlers did on the surface. This allowed the news agencies only to deliver one book each year as opposed to a daily newspaper. As more news stories developed throughout the year, the books would fill up with more information until they were full. Once full, the newspaper would start the publication of another book.

Nickle sighed as he read each article, which all came to the same conclusion: Joshua Brickle'Bee had turned Troll. Most of them were even worded the same, almost as if it had been copy-and-pasted. Once they were halfway through the books, Nickle had the Shadow retrieve more books—this time, he had handed the Shadow a piece of paper with the name Elinda Brickle'Bee on it. The ghost returned with a small stack of books. Like before, the articles were almost identical.

"How's this possible?" Nickle asked with frustration after he put down a book the size of his palm. "How can it be possible that the articles are all exactly the same? Why have the same material in thirty-plus books? Most of those articles come from competing newspapers. How can one newspaper have almost identical articles as a competing newspaper? Don't they have plagiarism laws or something?"

"Well, let's do an experiment," Jason replied. "Why don't we try looking for my parents: Mr. James and Jessica Burntworth. They also died mysteriously, and the information would have been reported in a similar manner." Jason wrote the names of his parents and handed it to the Shadow, who, in turn, brought back a stack of forty books.

They began rummaging through the books, scanning them for

the Burntworths. Every article they came across, however, was completely different. Even some of the articles posted in the same newspaper had contrasting views. With each page and paragraph Nickle read, he became more confident that the information about his parents had been tampered with.

"This is how the information should look," Nickle pointed towards the array of books in front of him. "Someone replaced the real articles with this copy-and-pasted rubbish." He grabbed a pencil and began scribbling on a small piece of paper.

"What are you looking up now?"

"My father again."

"We already went through all of it—it's all the same."

Nickle handed it to the Shadow who rolled his pale eyes before he sped off. When the Shadow returned, however, he only brought one book with him.

"What's this?" Nickle asked. "Last time I put this same name down, you brought more than thirty books back."

"No," the Shadow corrected in his airy voice. "You put a different name than before. You might have spelled it wrong."

Nickle took the piece of paper from the Shadow and studied it. "I didn't spell my name wrong. You must have read it wrong."

"Well," Jason said, "I need a break. Why don't we go get something to eat?"

Nickle scratched his head and opened the book, scanning it for his father's name. It took him a few moments to find it, but when he finally did, adrenaline whipped through his body. "Jason! Look at this. There's a whole article about my father that's different."

"What? How's that possible?"

Nickle held up the book. "Since the newspaper misspelled my father's name, it didn't get changed."

"Well, lad, what does it say?"

Nickle cleared his throat.

"Joshua Breckle'Bee was praised by the Tri'Ark for his triumphant diplomatic skills with the Gnomes. For the last one thousand years, Gnomes have kept to themselves after their King was accidentally sat upon by Elishna—the High Elven Goddess. The offense was so grave that the Gnomes swore off any contact with

131

anyone but the Leprechauns. Joshua Breckle'Bee has been able to break down these barriers with his tremendous skill in the Quintillian Games. Gnomes are an invaluable asset to relic making because they alone can perform the Chillian spell—a powerful incantation that endues any object with an internal source of power. Despite years of research and development, no other wizard has been able to replicate the Gnome's magic. But, thanks to Joshua Breckle'Bee, we don't have to…."

"That's the answer," Nickle whispered.

"What are you talking about?"

Nickle rubbed his chin. "My parents' disappearance must have had something to do with the Gnomes."

Chapter 12

The Final Course

After six months of solid training, the Tenderfoots were nearing graduation. They had changed since that first day in Tortugan. Their arms were thick and strong, stiffened by the unrelenting exercise regimen. Their confidence was bolstered along with their various skills. They now knew something worth knowing. Only one challenge was left—the successful completion of the final Grindlemire course. For this final gauntlet, the obstacles had been made the most difficult yet. The one good thing about this last and final task was that they were to enter the course in groups of four. If any in the group failed to make it through, however, the whole group was forced to repeat the last two months of training.

Nickle and Jason joined up with two odd-shaped Dwarves—a skinny one named Forex, and another named Hendrix, who looked like a misshaped potato. Despite their appearances, they were both skilled Dwarves. Nickle felt fortunate to be placed in a talented group, and he thought everyone else in the group felt the same way. That is, until he overheard Forex trying to convince Jason to drop Nickle from their team.

"He's the worst student in the Cohort," Forex hissed.

"Not by my judgment," Jason replied.

"And he's got those freaky eyes—just like Kara'Kala. I don't trust him. If he's on the team, I won't be."

"Then join someone else's team."

But Forex's threat was hollow. Dozens of Dwarves would have loved to be on Jason's team, even if that meant they had to be grouped with Nickle. Despite Forex's numerous attempts to negotiate Nickle off the team, Jason simply would not stand for it. When Forex persisted, Jason threatened to remove Forex from the group.

During the last week of camp Tortugan, the small group drilled primarily alone. Jason instantly became the unofficial leader and began a series of strenuous drills that eclipsed all their previous training. Fighting in a group had its advantages, as Nickle quickly found out. For one, it was a lot easier to spot attackers. For another, everyone brought a unique talent to the table: Hendrix could take a solid hit and hardly be fazed; Forex was excellent at defensive magic, which usually consisted of Wind or Earth Runes; Jason was good at everything; and Nickle was excellent at complimenting the other three as they went to work. It's not that Nickle did not try as hard as the others; in fact, he put in twice as much effort, but he would always crack under pressure. The only real benefit that he brought to the group was his ability to act as bait. For some reason, Nickle was always singled out by their opponents and became the object of their attack.

For practice, the Dwarves would often stage mock wars against other groups. By the end of the week, it was Nickle and Jason's group that was the most respected—mostly because of Jason.

On the day of the final test, the Dwarves padded up in their second-hand armor, grabbed their chipped axes, and lined up in front of the obstacle course for the last time. The arena had changed far more than it ever had before. It now looked like a massive abandoned castle that was covered with large gnarled vines that climbed around the crumbling stone. The only way in was a long drawbridge situated between two giant stone statues. Nickle was not the top of his class, but he could tell just by looking at them, that the figures were not just stone. He could sense magic wafting off their rocky exteriors.

The first group that was sent into the course puffed out their chests in confidence as they strode towards the gate. This boldness, however, quickly evaporated as the statues stirred with life. After a few confused screams of terror, the group made a haphazard run across the drawbridge and into the castle.

"Cowards," Cynthia Mallet hissed.

This became the pattern for the next several groups. The stone statues were tough, but they were slow, and once the Dwarves were able to get past them, they would have a clear shot to the entrance.

"Your group is up, Jason Burntworth," Cynthia yelled.

Jason grinned. "All right, boys. Let's take down those statues!"

The other three roared with approval as they approached the entrance.

Nickle waited until they were out of Cynthia's earshot before asking, "You were just saying that to impress Cynthia, right? We're not really going to try and take down those statues, right? I mean, they're impervious to our Runes. I saw one of the Dwarves hit a statue square in the chest with a Hellion Rune and it did nothing—and that's the strongest Fire Rune we've learned so far."

"Ah, Nickle, I meant what I said," Jason winked. "We're going to take them down."

Forex flanked Jason. "Maybe, for once, Nickle is right. We've still got the whole obstacle course to prove our skill; let's not wear ourselves thin."

Jason began to pick up speed. "Just keep your distance until I can make them angry. Once they're mad, be ready with your Rope Runes." With that, the young Dwarf ran straight towards one of the statues, his axe shining with light. Whether it was out of surprise or just their slow reflexes, the figures did not move until Jason was at the feet of one of them. Immediately, the quick Dwarf slammed his axe into the ground, sending a shockwave that stirred both the statues to life. A moment later, Jason became the target of the monsters' rage. The Dwarf dodged left and right. After ducking under a horrific swing, he ran up the side of one of the statues and flipped back in the air, slicing it in the leg as he went. To Nickle's surprise, the statue groaned in pain.

This only intensified the statues' determination. They pounded the ground with their fists, swinging wildly at Jason. The ground quickly became a mesh of craters and loose rock. Jason leaped between the two of them, slicing out chunks of stone each time he did.

Nickle was so in awe at Jason's skill, he almost missed the cue from Forex to jump in. While Jason danced in the middle of the stone creatures, the other three began to circle the statues, shooting rope out of Runes that they had smashed in their hands. The figures were so angry at Jason that they did not notice the mess of brown web that was slowly weaving around them. Nickle was able to run around the creatures six times before they were so tangled in cord that they could not move. The stone statues were powerless to do anything but yell in frustration.

The waiting crowd erupted in applause as the four Dwarves slowly began to make their way across the drawbridge towards the entrance. Jason had his arms in the air, almost as if he had just saved the world from certain destruction.

"Man, Jason," Nickle whispered. "How do you think up this stuff?"

"Those things were based off of Rock Golems—strong but slow in more ways than one. I knew we could take them the moment I saw how slow their reflexes were."

Jason was the first to step inside the castle, closely followed by Nickle. The first room they entered was misty and dark. They could hear rats squeaking below them.

"If you sense magic," Jason said, "don't keep it to yourself." They reached a hall that split off into two directions. Jason took the lead and went to the right. They came to a room that had been torn to shreds by someone or something. Half the roof was missing, which allowed a solid beam of moonlight to illuminate their surroundings. This seemed odd because when they entered the castle, it had been daylight—and that was less than two minutes ago. The air was tense as the Dwarves fanned out into the room. They could feel and hear their feet bumping into large pieces of broken furniture.

"Whatever was here," Forex hissed, "it was something big. The Dwarves in front of us must have scared it off—"

Jason raised his hand in the air and closed his eyes. He lowered his head towards the ground, straining his ears. "Did you hear that?"

Nickle swallowed. "It's faint, but I can sense it. What is it?

Jason took a deep breath. "It's all over the room."

"I don't sense anything," Hendrix said.

Jason's eyes opened wide as he grabbed a Wind Rune from his belt. "SPRITES!" As soon as he yelled, the room filled with hundreds of bat-like creatures, each of them had white, shining eyes and inch-long claws. The little fiends formed into an arrow that headed straight towards Jason. Just before impact, the Dwarf exploded his Wind Rune into the floor, sending hundreds of the little creatures thudding against the walls and roof.

The Sprites did not take long to recover. They regrouped and headed for Nickle, who ducked under the wave of the flying creatures. Hendrix stepped forward and batted a dozen of the small beasts out of the air with the side of his axe.

"Ice!" Nickle screamed. "They can't stand the cold." As he

spoke, he reached for a Rune, but before he could activate it, one of the creatures sliced his unarmored forearm. The wound pulsed with pain but, thankfully, it was not deep.

Jason ran up to Nickle's side, chopping down a few of the creatures. "Stay alert, Nickle. They'll tear you to pieces if you don't."

From the corner of Nickle's vision, he could see a swarm of the creatures charging straight for them. He pulled Jason to the side just as Forex shot an Ice Rune at the Sprites. The creatures sputtered in the cold blast that greeted them, forcing them in all directions. The other three Dwarves began to mimic Forex's actions and pulled out their own Ice Runes from their belts. Moments later, the floor was covered with an inch of ice and the Sprites had vanished from sight.

"Good job, Forex," Jason grinned. "You too, Nickle. Come on, let's get moving before they warm back up."

They traveled down a long hallway and entered into a kitchen with a marble floor. They moved deeper into the castle, the tension thickening with each room they passed. Leaving the kitchen, they entered a massive library filled with nothing but old books, broken furniture, and…giant spiders. At first, the spiders were nothing more than a nuisance, but the deeper they went, the larger and more aggressive the insects became. Hendrix and Jason proved the most valuable as they set about hacking through the creatures. Despite the mound of bodies the Dwarves left in their wake, the spiders seemed relentless as they poured out of holes in the walls. Jason finally started throwing Hellion Runes at the beasts, which effectively drove them off—but only for a moment. It was not long before they were surrounded by spiders almost as tall as they were. With everyone pulling out Hellion Runes from their belts, the spiders stalled in their attack—but they did not retreat.

"What do we do?" Forex asked Jason. "You've studied these creatures."

"I can tell you how they suck the blood out of their victims," Jason yelled back. "Does that help?"

"Mix your Runes," Nickle hissed to the others. "Use wind and water."

Jason grinned. "That's not a bad idea, Nickle." He pulled out a couple of Runes, smashed them together, and began to shoot a torrent of rain towards the eight-legged creatures in front of them. The spiders retreated before the water, slinking back into their holes.

"That a boy Nickle; way to keep your head."

With the other three mimicking Jason's actions, they soon cleared the rest of the spiders out of the room. After the creatures were gone, they ran into a dozen Pest'Lins—foul, grey creatures with sturdy running legs and protruding teeth. The Pest'Lins wore mismatched armored that complemented their rusty weapons. Their ears were long and gnarled like weathered branches, and their heads were bald like onions. A quick skirmish later, the Dwarves were able to escape to the next room, their adrenaline shooting up their body every time they heard the floor squeak. They made good time through the castle and reached the halfway point far faster than any of them expected. Sometimes they could hear the shouts of the other Dwarves in the distance, but they never ran into any of them.

The four Dwarves entered a massive, pillared room that had gargoyles perched along the walls. As they made their way through the hall, the gargoyles shed their stone skins and came swooping down. There were only four of them, and not very big ones either, but their large talons kept the Dwarves ducking for cover for several minutes. Jason finally cut one down, which scared off the other three.

The challenges of the obstacle course continued to assault them: They were almost caught up in quicksand, but Forex was able to provide an Earth Rune that freed them almost instantly; then they ran headlong into an Ogre den, but the creatures never awoke from their slumber—much to Jason's disappointment; then they walked into a large, blue room crowded with Shadows who all did their best to confuse the Dwarves with wild information. They fought a dozen more creatures before finally reaching a massive pit with a hundred-foot drop. At the bottom of the pit was a lake of lava that continued to splash against the rock walls. Despite the distance, they could feel the heat wafting up to them as they peered over the edge.

Anchored in the lava were a series of thin pillars that had large, flat rocks stacked on top of them. The flat stones formed a disconnected bridge that spanned the distance.

Jason kneeled as he studied the scene. "I think this is the last obstacle of the course; as soon as we all get to the other side, we're Scot-Free. We're going to have to go two at a time. Although it might look like they are, I doubt those platforms are attached to the stone pillars that are holding them up. If one stands too long on one side, I think it will tip over into the lava. We'll have to have two people on a stone at the same time, both on opposite ends to keep it balanced."

"How are we going to make the jump between stones?" Hendrix asked.

"We're going to have to activate the Strength Runes in our armor," Jason answered. "That should give us more than enough strength to jump the distance—but be sure not to jump over it. Of course, we're going to have to wait a while for the strength Runes to recharge between each jump, but—"

"Archers!" Nickle pointed to an outcropping of stone that was high above them. A dozen Skeletons appeared, armed with crooked looking bows and makeshift arrows. One of them released an arrow aimed straight for Jason. The Dwarf blocked it with his axe, and then returned a rock projectile at the bony opponents. The shot was a perfect hit and smashed two of the Skeletons to pieces, sending fractured bones over the edge and down into the lava. As soon as the first two fell, however, four more appeared in their place.

"They're coming from behind too!" Nickle yelled. The others turned around to see several dozen Skeletons coming to life from out of the ground and the surrounding walls.

"GO!" Jason yelled at Hendrix.

The potato-shaped Dwarf activated his strength Rune and launched himself into the air. With so much adrenaline pumping through his body, he misjudged the distance and jumped too far. In midair, he quickly activated a Rune in his axe and slammed the blade into the stone just before he disappeared into the lava below. This saved his life momentarily, but soon the flat rock began to tip his direction, making it increasingly more challenging to hang on.

"You're up, Forex!" Jason yelled.

As quickly as Jason spoke, Forex obeyed and vaulted himself in the air and out to the flat rock, which slowed the tipping of the large stone but did not stop it. It was not until Hendrix pulled himself up a few moments later that the stone balanced itself. The large Dwarf looked longingly at his axe, which was still stuck deep in the stone tablet.

"Nickle, you start using your Runes to take out the archers. I'll fight them off our flank. As soon as Hendrix and Forex get to the next stone, I want you to bound out there as quickly as you can—I don't know how long I can hold them back."

Nickle put down his axe and began pulling out Rune after Rune from his belt. It only took a few moments between each throw to find his next target. The exploding Runes sent rocks and Skeletons flying everywhere. He soon ran out of Hellion Runes and switched to a Wind Rune, which he smashed into his hand and sent twisting forward.

Jason charged headlong into the mass of Skeletons that were attacking their flank. The bony creatures were armed with a mix of rusty swords and butcher knives—a few had shields and spears. He sliced one of them across the legs, another he chopped in the arm. A third and fourth, he exploded with a Disintegrating Rune—which he was technically not supposed to know yet.

One of the creatures was able to break through Jason's defense and sliced him across the belly. The armor absorbed the blow, but it left an enormous dent behind. He stumbled backward, a look of disbelief now on his face. He looked up, his eyes narrowing. "So, you think you've got some skill, eh? Come on!"

A moment later, Hendrix and Forex's strength Runes recharged, and they, in turn, were able to reach the next flat stone.

"Come on, Nickle!" Forex yelled. "We'll cover you while you make the jump!"

Nickle swallowed as he peered over the edge. He had never quite mastered the Strength Rune and now seemed like a horrible time to practice. The fall alone would kill him, not to mention the lava. He shook his head and shelved his fear. With his jaw clenched, he activated the Strength Rune on his chest and leaped into the air. His aim was a little off, but he was able to balance the stone again by walking towards the middle.

Jason grinned. "I'll be there in a moment, Nickle! Hang on!" The Dwarf activated his axe and sent a wave of fire that swept forward impressively. Despite its showy appearance, the wall of flames did little more than anger the Skeletons.

"Oh, crap."

Jason turned and ran. The Skeletons picked up pursuit. Just as one of the bony fingers was reaching for his shoulder, Jason activated his Strength Rune and leaped into the air. A few tense moments passed before he landed right on top of Nickle—their armor clanged as their bodies hit and rolled to one side. Their combined weight tipped the large rock towards the lava below, forcing them to struggle wildly for a grip. Jason was able to grab a Rune and stick it against the rock, giving him a firm hold. But Nickle was only able to find a small crack for his fingers. As the rock tipped more and more, Nickle knew his grip would not last.

"Catch!" Hendrix yelled. The large Dwarf activated a Rope Rune and shot a long cord towards Nickle just as he lost his grip completely. For a few tense moments, Nickle's body fell through the air. He grabbed wildly for the rope—it was only inches from his fingers. Just as he was about to outdistance the end of the cord, he snatched it out of the air. As the cord tightened from the tension, it sent Nickle swinging to the side.

Even though he was still high above the lava, the warmth cascaded over his body, making his forehead instantly turn to sweat. He could tell that the armor was absorbing most of the radiating heat, but he was not sure how long that would last. With one hand on the rope, he used his other to grab an Ice Rune from his belt. Once he whispered the magical incantation, he attached it to the center of his armor. As soon as he did, he felt a cold sensation trickle down from his chest to his legs and out to his arms.

Jason's situation became increasingly more dangerous as the flat rock he was on was almost perpendicular to the ground. The next moment, the stone slid free from the pillar and headed right towards Nickle who had just begun climbing up the rope. Nickle had no option other than to close his eyes and wait as the massive rock came hurtling towards him.

Jason grabbed a Rune from his side, fixed it into his axe, and then slammed the weapon into the rock platform. The powerful combination exploded the rock in two, sending shards of debris in every direction.

"NICKLE!" Jason yelled.

Nickle opened his eyes just in time to see that instead of a massive rock flying towards him, it was only Jason. Their bodies collided and twisted. Jason's grip slipped, but Nickle grasped his friend's arm and held him fast. Moments later, the chunks of rock splashed into the lava, making two large waves that crashed into the sides of the pit.

Hendrix's strength began to give under the burden of both Nickle and Jason. At the same time, the extra weight started to tip the stone platform on which Hendrix and Forex stood. It would only be moments before their stone tablet would be sent pitching to the side— moments before all of them would end up in the lava below. Forex had taken an arrow in the arm and could do nothing more than use Defensive Runes to protect Hendrix.

Jason laughed. "Well, Nickle, you dirty dog, it was a good run anyway. Two more months of Tortugan won't be so bad. We'll know all the answers this next time around."

Nickle did not hear his friend. Instead, he gritted his teeth and narrowed his vision. He could feel a warmth begin to swell inside of him. A faint light circled his eyes as he focused his thoughts. "Hold onto the rope, Jason! I need one of my hands free." A sudden power exploded in Nickle's body, almost like a lightning bolt that shocked him to the core. The light began to pulse from his right hand and collect into a small ball of energy. As the seconds passed, more light collected until it was so blinding that Jason could not see.

Just as Hendrix and Forex were about to fall into the lava below, Nickle shot the light into the far rock wall. Instantly the beam cut through the rock as if it was nothing more than a slab of butter. A massive portion of the stone split and tipped forward, splashing into the lava below. As it fell, it collided into the other stone pillars, tipping them forward like a set of dominoes. As Hendrix and Forex's pillar was hit, they were pushed forward until they could jump safely to the other side.

"Hang on!" Hendrix shouted as he activated a Strength Rune in his armor. "We'll get you up here!" With the added strength from the Rune and his massive biceps, Hendrix began to pull Nickle and Jason back to the top. The pillars began cracking and breaking into large shards of stone, which fell straight for the two Dwarves below. Nickle was hit in the arm by a large stone. Pain rippled through his body and instantly pulsed from the wound. More pieces of rock fell, these ones even larger than the first.

"Hurry!" Forex yelled at Hendrix. "Pull with everything you've got!"

They were almost at the top when a massive knife-like boulder broke loose and slid sideways, cutting the rope. Jason saw it coming moments before it happened. He attached a Wind Rune to the bottom of his boot and grabbed Nickle by the shoulder. Just as the rope was cut, Jason activated the Wind Rune, which sent the two Dwarves flying wildly upwards. They crashed into Forex and Hendrix, who were both peering over the edge. As soon as they all reached the other side, the Skeleton warriors shuffled away. The stone pillars also righted themselves, resetting for the next group of unlucky Dwarves.

The four of them rolled across the ground, seething for breath. They laid there for a long time in silence. Like a cold shower on a hot day, a sudden relief wafted over Nickle's body.

Jason laughed. "Dang...I mean, dang. That was close."

After several long moments, Forex propped himself on his elbow. "What was that beam of light? I couldn't see where it came from?"

"That looked like Elf magic or even Faery magic," Hendrix said.

Nickle looked at Jason, and Jason back at Nickle.

"It..." Nickle began, but Jason cut him off, "It was a Steam Rune. The distance and the heat from the lava must have made it look different."

"A Steam Rune...," Forex began to say but Jason cut him off.

"Come on, we better find Cynthia before she thinks of some reason to disqualify us."

Chapter 13

The Elf Sector

Three days later, the Dwarves were lined up on the parade grounds, dressed in their formal Silver Army attire. They stood at attention while a host of important members of the Cogs of Hurn and the Tri'Ark scurried up a small stage and took their places on large plush seats. Cynthia Mallet looked disappointed, almost as if she had not expected so many Dwarves to make it through her training. Apart from Nickle and Jason's Cohort, there were several hundred more Dwarves. Nickle was surprised by how few of the Dwarves he recognized. He glanced over to see how many girl Dwarves were graduating—just over half of their entire class. He had seldom seen the girl Dwarves training since they were on the other side of the camp, but when he did, he had a hard time looking away.

The thing that attracted the most attention, however, were the massive Dwarf Lords that sat in front, each wearing a unique set of brilliantly colored Dwarf Tines. When Nickle first saw Dwarf armor, he thought it was pretty cool looking; but now, after drilling with second rate practice armor, he knew exactly what real Dwarf Tines could do. Nickle almost began drooling as he longingly stared at each set of armor. It would be twenty-five years before he could earn his Tines, maybe even longer. *"Twenty-five years—that seems like half a lifetime away."* He looked at Jason's longing face and instantly knew that he was thinking the same thing.

Once everyone arrived, Edward Thunderhoof trotted up to the front. The large Cennarian looked even more prominent on stage. "As the liaison between the Tri'Ark and the Silver Army, I've been asked to direct this graduation. I would also like to recognize the presence of Thornhead Back'Break, the illustrious and bold leader of the Silver Army. It's good to see so many of you Dwarves here too, even better to see that you're all alive. Besides a few broken arms and bandages, you've made it through your first year of training unharmed. So, it's with great pleasure that I welcome you into the Silver Army!"

A roar of approval erupted from the crowd.

Edward continued. "After the formal ceremonies, you'll sit down with me or another counselor to help you decide upon a career path. This will be the first step of many. You may not get the position you want or the job that is the most exciting, but I suggest whatever your assignment is that you leap into it will all of your heart. The people of EarthWorks work as a collective unit—a single body that focuses on the prosperity of the future...."

Nickle whispered out of the corner of his mouth. "Jason, that's it. We need to make sure that we're assigned something to do with the Gnomes."

"What?" Jason hissed.

"That's how we can find out what happened."

"You're obsessed."

Nickle gave a light laugh. "Yes, maybe. You want in?"

"Of course I do. Wherever you go, you seem to attract trouble. And trouble is just the sort of thing I'm looking for."

"Good."

Edward Thunderhoof gestured dramatically to one of the Dwarf Lords behind him. "I want to now turn the time over to our visitor—the Elected Chief Warlord of the Silver Army, Thornhead Back'Break. He seldom attends graduation, so when he does, we like to give him all the time he wants to speak."

The whole audience roared with applause as the massive Thornhead stood and walked to the center of the stage. The Dwarf was wearing gold and silver armor that shined when he walked. It was so perfectly constructed and seamlessly put together that it seemed more alive than the Dwarf who wore it. In his thundering voice, Thornhead gave a war cry that echoed throughout the parade grounds.

The crowd mimicked the yell.

"Welcome, lads and lasses, to the first day of a life worth living..."

The large Dwarf went on and on about the might and power of the Dwarves—about how they were the true keepers of the Earth. He then went into a ballad of battle stories, where he described in great detail the overwhelming odds Dwarves had faced. He explained how pollution from the Piddlers was killing the world, and that once again, Dwarves were being called upon to save the Earth from destruction. In between each transition of subjects, the crowd roared its unanimous approval. If there was one thing to be said about Thornhead, it was that he knew how to give a speech.

When Thornhead finally concluded, the mass of Dwarves cheered for a long time after. The ceremony concluded with Edward Thunderhoof and Cynthia Mallet calling out names and handing out battle axes to the graduating Dwarves. When Nickle hefted his blade, he was surprised by the craftsmanship that went into it. It was ornately decorated with gold lines that formed into Six powerful Runes and three minor ones. It was far more deadly than the little practice blades they had used before, far more dangerous than anything Nickle had ever held. He also noticed that each blade was different and had been tailored to a graduate's specific talents. In large gold letters, Nickle's full name was inscribed on the handle. It even had his middle name—Bree. "Bree…my middle name is Bree? What was my mom thinking?"

The last person to receive their axe was Jason Burntworth. Before Edward handed him the blade, the Cennarian announced to the crowd that Jason had been selected as the Novus Dwarf—the number one student of their graduating class. The crowd cheered as Jason received an axe made with the finest skill. The blade was massive and looked sharp enough to slice through stone; it had four major Runes that were inscribed into it and six minor ones, each glowed with lethal power.

After a final cheer, someone threw a Rune into the air that exploded into a thousand tiny stars that zoomed up and around the parade grounds. Nickle watched the little stars speed off until they finally faded.

As Jason returned to his seat, he tugged on Nickle's arm. "Come on. If we have any hope of getting the Gnome Detail, then we need to be first in line."

They pushed through the crowd and headed straight for a mess of tables that had several small, official-looking Dwarves seated behind them. As the two Dwarves approached, however, both their faces fell—the Gnome Detail required a year of battle experience.

Jason gritted his teeth. "We don't qualify."

Nickle shook his head. "There has to be a way to join—"

"If it isn't Nickle Brickle'Bee and his fierce friend," a voice said from behind.

Nickle slowly turned around. "Thornhead, sir."

Both Dwarves instantly pounded their chests as they snapped to attention.

"Drop the formalities, lads," Thornhead said as he hit Nickle in the arm. "So what Detail are you boys interested in?"

"We want to be on the Gnome Detail," Nickle said boldly.

Jason stepped between Nickle and Thornhead. "Yeah, but it appears we can't join because we lack the experience. We didn't know that until now, but I'm sure we can find something else. Come on, Nickle."

Nickle locked eyes with Thornhead and took a deep breath. "Jason and I got top marks in our last obstacle course. I think we can handle our own in the Gnome Detail." A deathly silence fell across the parade grounds.

Thornhead narrowed his eyes. "Our relations with the Gnomes have not been good for the last two hundred years. We need battle-seasoned soldiers to deal with them—not wet behind the ear Tenderfoots. The Gnome division is not a picnic; war may break out any day between the Dwarves and the Gnomes."

"Yes, you're right—" Jason began, but Nickle interrupted.

"I've been reading up on Gnomes and know more about them than any Dwarf here, and Jason is the top of the class. Between the two of us, I'm sure we would be a valuable asset to the Gnome Detail—if we're given a chance, sir."

Thornhead nodded. "Now, I see the fire in your eyes that was missing when I first met you. If I approve your placement in the Gnome Detail and it comes back to burn me—"

"No, sir. I'll obey all orders without question," Nickle answered. "...and Jason here is one of the most obedient Dwarves ever to pick up an ax."

Jason suddenly became very serious, almost as if he was trying to play the role of something he knew nothing about.

Thornhead's face became even more stern, like a rock suddenly stricken with rigor mortis. The tension mounted with each passing second. Finally, the large Dwarf broke out into a laugh. "All right, you're in. But, I want you to report directly to me if anything goes awry, is that understood? Directly to me—no one else."

Nickle and Jason both saluted.

"Good," Thornhead said as he nodded. "You should receive your official orders by tomorrow. As soon as you do, report to Thomas Noondrag. He'll be regrouping with his Cohort on the southeast landing port of Tortugan; he'll drop you off at Camp Tulla. You'll be reporting to a Dwarf named Hampshire Cleaver."

"Yes, sir."

Thornhead winked. "I need a few Dwarves I can trust in the Gnome Detail. Don't let me down, lads."

***

"Maybe I misjudged him," Nickle said after they had left the parade grounds. "He seemed so uptight when I first met him that I thought it'd be impossible to convince him to let us join the Gnome Detail."

Jason nodded with agreement. "I don't know what he sees in you, but I've heard he has punched Dwarves for asking him for favors like that. I can't believe it worked. I thought you were going to lose your life—at the very least, a few teeth. Thornhead is the kind of guy that sees everything in black and white. He's always exactly obedient. Did you notice how perfectly shiny his armor was? Did you not see how carefully he arranged his Rune belt around his waist? To him, rules and orders are like religion. He *never* breaks or bends the rules."

"He did this time," Nickle answered.

"I can't even believe he let us graduate—especially after that stunt you pulled in the obstacle course. Maybe he doesn't know about it yet."

"What?"

"You know what I am talking about. The white light that you shot out from your hands. That's the second time you've done that. Where did it come from?"

Nickle shrugged his shoulders. "I've no idea…it just sort of erupted out of me."

Jason shook his head. "Don't tell anyone; don't even hint at it. Hopefully, that can stay between you and me. Forex seemed skeptical that it was a Rune, but not skeptical enough to tell anyone about it."

"Why does it matter?"

"That's not Dwarf magic. That's something else. Can you conjure light anytime you want to? Can you conjure light right now? Do you know how to control it?"

Nickle shook his head. "I told you; it just sort of came out of me."

"Exactly. And according to the Tri'Ark, that makes you dangerous. Until you know how to control it, I suggest we don't tell anyone else about it."

Nickle lowered his head. "What will they do to me if they find out?"

Jason swallowed. "I have no idea, but I'm sure you don't want to find out. Anyway, forget about it—forget about the whole obstacle course. There's a good chance no one will ever find out about what happened. Forget about it. Come on, cheer up. We just graduated. We need to celebrate."

"Celebrate?"

"Oh," Jason said with a wicked grin, "I know where we need to go to set your mind at ease: Belmont. It's a gigantic building just on the border of the Human and Elf sector. I've got an old Human buddy that still puts me on the VIP list. They've got it all there, from candy cider—an Elven concoction that Humans have never been able to imitate—to four different levels of dance floors, to massive magic arcades, to axe throwing competitions. There's a room that's called the Sphere, where gravity keeps switching on and off until you don't know which way is up. Another room has a buffet so big that you'll be winded by the time you reach the end of it. The food is excellent. The arcades are fantastic. And there'll be Elf girls."

"Are Elves pretty or something?"

Jason threw his head back dramatically and laughed. "You don't know what pretty is until you've seen one of them. One time, I almost kissed one."

"Almost?"

"Her boyfriend knocked me over the head when I wasn't looking, and I spent the next several minutes acting like a doormat as people stepped over me."

Nickle nodded. "What about the graduation dance? I saw dozens of pretty Dwarf girls. We could just stay here—that's what everyone else is going to do."

"Oh, come on, Nickle. There won't be Elf girls at the graduation dance."

Nickle gave half a grin. "All right, if you think it'll be fun. I'm in."

"Yeah, that's the spirit, lad. Let's get Forex and Hendrix to come too."

It only took a few minutes to find the other two Dwarves, a few more minutes to convince them to come. Within a half-hour, the four Dwarves were cramped in a Taxi-Lator, heading for Belmont. The Taxi-Lator dropped them off a few blocks short of their destination.

"Hey," Jason said to the Hawk'Head driver. "We still have a ways to walk from here."

"I'z not going in there," the Hawk'Head squeaked. "Not safe for anyone but Elves."

"You're insane," Jason answered. "The Elf Sector is the safest area in the whole of EarthWorks."

"Not for my kind—"

"—Since you didn't take us all the way, you don't get all your pay. You can forget about the tip."

The Hawk'Heak shrieked. "You made promise...you can't break."

"I promised you a tip, but you promised to take me to Belmont—"

"It's all right," Nickle said as he pulled out his money medallion. "We can walk from here."

Jason gritted his teeth but did not say anything else.

Once the Taxi-Lator zoomed off, the Dwarves began following Jason at a very close distance. This part of EarthWorks was different than anything Nickle had ever seen. Every building was made of a combination of wood and precious stone. Many of the wood pillars had flowers or leaves carved into them with such precision that they seemed alive. Nickle even tried to smell one—just to see if it was real. Nothing but the rich smell of freshly cut wood greeted his nose. The streets were also cleaner—almost too clean—and they were not crowded. Despite it being early in the evening, they hardly passed anyone on the road. Those that they did walk past wore regal clothes that shimmered brilliantly in the fading light.

Nickle could feel the stares that followed them. Whenever he turned around to see who might be watching, however, he saw nothing but a sudden ruffle of shades or blinds. They finally entered the Elven Quarter, which was very similar to the street that they had come from except it was even more ornate. The Elves loved to make long elegant buildings with broad windows. The style reminded Nickle of a Swedish home he had seen in a National Geographic magazine. The streets changed from solid pavement to a smooth and evenly placed cobblestone.

Nickle glanced left and right, hoping to catch his first glimpse of an Elf. But despite his neck cramping from the effort, he could not see anyone in the street. When he did see a face or a figure, it was too far in the distance to make out clearly. He began to think that he would never see one when suddenly, out of a sizeable mansion with a metal fence, a tall skinny Elf stepped outside.

The Elf had sharp, keen eyes and a face that was free of wrinkles. Despite his youthful appearance, he walked as if he was old. His eyes were a pale emerald green that shined as brilliantly as if they had been polished. He looked exactly like Nickle thought an Elf would, with pointed ears, narrow features, and skin that seemed to slightly glow. The tall Elf walked slowly, almost as if it did not matter when or even if he reached his destination. He was only a few steps out of his house when he spotted the Dwarves passing by. The Elf pulled his head back suddenly, almost as if the Dwarves had brought with them a rotten smell, and he had just caught a whiff of it.

In a high pitched and heavily accented voice, the Elf spoke, "What are you Dwarves doing in front of my house? What are you doing here?"

Nickle was about to turn and talk to the Elf, but Jason spoke first. "We're walking by—old Elf. Do you have a problem with that? Or should we stop and stay?" Jason's voice had taken on a brute tone that Nickle had only heard him use once before.

The Elf took a step back. His face paled as he struggled to speak. "I…I…" As the Dwarves disappeared around the corner of the house, they could hear the Elf shouting, "I'm going to call the

Praetorian if you come by my property again! Do you hear me! I'm going to call the Praetorian Guard!"

Jason almost yelled back, but Nickle caught his arm. "What are the Praetorian?"

Jason craned his neck in the Elf's direction for a while before he turned back around. "Those are the Elven police—they're more like thugs if you ask me. In the Elven Quarter, they have a completely separate police force, army, and court system. They rarely help out if EarthWorks needs assistance, and yet, they're always asking for assistance when they've got a problem. And just because they pretty much own every building in EarthWorks, the Tri'Ark always complies. The Silver Army has been dispatched here hundreds of times to help out with some 'desperate' crisis, or to chase some fugitive, but I've never—not once—seen a Praetorian policing the streets of EarthWorks. I hate Elves."

"Is that why I never see them in the other sectors of EarthWorks?" Nickle asked.

"That," Jason replied, "and the fact that they know how to teleport—which is a spell they've kept to themselves for the last several thousand years. Pretty much all the traffic congestion in EarthWorks could be cleared up if the Elves shared a few insights on how to teleport. But no, it's 'magic that Dwarves can't handle.' Every Arcon in the Praetorian Guard can teleport. They pretty much can appear almost instantly anywhere they want, but still, they don't help out with much. Despite the fact that we have to travel for hours on our Dwarf Warships to get anywhere, we're usually the first to respond, and then Humans—eventually. Just because they're wealthy, Elves think that they don't have any responsibility."

Forex nodded. "Yeah, they stink of money—everything does in the Elf sector. If it weren't for the Elf girls, I'd never come here."

"Yeah," Jason answered. "If it weren't for the girls, I'd say they are worthless."

Nickle shrugged his shoulders. "What makes Elf girls so special? Are they really cool or something?"

"Who? Elf girls?" Jason laughed. "No, they're as mean and demanding as a girl can get. None of them have ever worked a day in their life. You'd be hard-pressed to find one that wakes up before noon. Daddy's medallion pays for everything they've never needed. Spoiled brats—every last one of them. I've heard that ninety-percent of all of EarthWorks' resources are used up by the Elves—but they're only five percent of the population."

"So," Nickle said slowly. "Why are we going to try to flirt with them?"

Jason rolled his eyes. "Because they're hot."

Nickle shook his head but did not answer.

They finally reached Belmont, which was starkly different than the structures all around them. The building had massive pillars that shifted colors in sync with the beat of the music playing inside. The music itself was different than anything Nickle had heard before: Instead of a loud bass—like most Dwarf music—the Elvish tunes consisted of mystical airy flute sounds mixed with a modern tempo.

At the front door, there were two Elves, fully armed and armored in thin plate mail. From their backs poked the pearl hilts of curved swords. They both had sharp jaws, narrow eyes, and a long strip of blond hair that was braided on one side. As the Dwarves stepped closer, the larger of the two held up his hand.

"What are you doing here—little Dwarves?"

Jason's face tightened. "We're coming to pay Belmont a visit. We've got gold dust—we should be good."

"Policy change," the Elf continued. "You must be on the guest list to enter."

"Well," Jason said with an even response, "we're on the guest list—and I'd appreciate it if you dropped your tone. We're members of the Silver Army and dang important ones at that. I doubt your policy excludes members of the Silver Army."

The Elf narrowed his eyes. "Depends on who it is. What's your name—Dwarf?"

"My name is Jason Burntworth, and these are my friends."

The Elf picked up a piece of parchment from off a small table. With his long, bony finger, he wrote "Jason Burntworth" onto the paper and waited for a few moments for the name to fade away. It was not long before Jason's name reappeared with a checkmark next to it. The Elf inhaled slowly. "Looks like…you're on the list."

Jason nodded. "Yes, of course, we are. Did you even doubt us for a second? I'm good friends with Arillian, one of the investors of this place."

The Elf forced a smile and pulled the door open. "Proceed…Dwarves."

Once inside, the Dwarves were directed to a large podium that had two annoyed-looking Elves behind it.

"Wow," Forex whispered as he studied the billboard behind one of the Elves. "Sixty-five grams just for the entrance fee? You've got some rich blood, Jason."

"Come on," Jason answered. "We're celebrating. Relax."

As they paid, a beautiful Elf girl attached bracelets around their thick forearms. Hendrix's forearm was so thick, she had to attach two of the bracelets together so it would stay on.

Jason grinned roguishly at the Elf girl while she placed the bracelet around his wrist. "So, do you come here often?"

The Elf girl rolled her eyes. "I manage this place, Dwarf."

Jason swallowed. "Yeah, so…then the answer is yes."

"You're going to have to leave your Rune Belts at the door."

Jason winked. "That would give us another chance to talk when we come by to pick them up—"

The Elf folded her arms as she shouted. "Next!"

"Well," Jason said in one last attempt. "I'll see you…later."

She ignored Jason completely as she warmly greeted the next customers—a group of pale-faced but well-dressed Humans. The four Dwarves passed through a large arched hallway and into a massive spherical room. When Nickle first entered the room, his head began to spin. There were young Elves and regally dressed Humans dancing everywhere, including along the walls and ceiling. The music pulsed from a ball that floated precisely in the middle.

With a grin on his face, Jason nodded to the other Dwarves. "Make some room, lads. I'm going to show you how it's done." With this, he gave a yell and charged onto the dance floor. The other three Dwarves stared as Jason began to dance in a way that seemed completely disconnected from the music.

Forex frowned. "Well, I'm going to check out the buffet. I'm sick of eating cafeteria food."

Hendrix nodded. "I'll go with you."

Forex glanced towards Nickle. "You coming?"

"Nah, I'm going to stay behind and make sure Jason doesn't get into any trouble."

"Watch your back."

Nickle nodded as the other two left. He stood there, watching the people dance in the middle. The longer he stood and stared, the more awkward he felt. After two Elves accidentally bumped into him, Nickle decided to move. He sat down at a table and was promptly greeted by a server—a Human girl that had so much makeup on it was hard to tell what she really looked like. All the servers appeared to be Humans.

"What can I get you?"

Nickle cleared his throat. "What about candy cider?"

"What? Little Dwarf, you're going to have to speak up."

"Candy cider."

The girl nodded and walked away. Moments later, from the center of the table, a large tall glass of candy cider appeared. Nickle gingerly pulled the drink closer and took a sip. Instantly, a wave of flavor tickled his tongue and shocked his whole body. It tasted like a mix of chocolate and vanilla chased by a citrus flavor. It was not long before he downed his first drink and was ordering another.

After finishing a second glass of candy cider, Nickle decided to go exploring. He passed through a room that was pitch black. He did not understand how people could be dancing in the room without lights, that is, until one of the employees handed him a pair of glasses. As he put them on, the room instantly turned into a crazy display of color. He felt a little nauseous staring at the multicolored space, so he decidedly took the glasses off and handed them back to the employee.

The next room was full of magical arcades, which were a lot different than the arcades Piddlers played on the surface. Instead of just using a screen and a set of buttons, the players felt like they were sucked inside the game and forced to face dozens of deadly obstacles. Nickle tried a zombie hunting game and then a desert adventure game, but he was not good at either. He spent some time at the arcades, watching some of the other players, but he felt too self-conscious to play any game for too long. So he continued on to a large wooden room that had axe throwing targets that moved in every direction.

Nickle quickly became the undisputed champion as he dominated everyone that competed. One particularly competitive Human refused to give up until he won at least one match against Nickle. The stack of losses mounded up for the Human until Nickle finally quit out of sheer boredom.

He found another dance floor that was filled with bubbles that were like mini-television screens. The music here was different, almost too different to dance to. Most of the other people were just sitting around, laughing and talking. He left a few minutes later and was about to go looking for Jason when he ran into Forex and a very pale Hendrix.

Nickle smiled. "How was the buffet?"

"Good," Forex answered. "But Hendrix was allergic to something in the pasta and broke out in hives. We're going back to the barracks. You coming?"

Nickle shook his head. "No, I better stick with Jason. He's probably almost ready to go anyway."

"All right," Forex said, "we'll see you back in Tortugan."

Nickle had been wrong, however. Jason was not even close to being ready to leave. Even after Nickle had eaten his fill at the buffet, thrown some more axes, became quite good at a racing game, and drank another pitcher of candy cider, Jason was still on the dance floor.

"All right, Nickle," Jason said after Nickle started to gesture towards the door. "Give me half an hour more, and then we can go." But that half-hour quickly turned into an hour, and then two. Finally, when there were only twenty or so customers left, the manager of Belmont announced that they would be closing.

Exhausted by his several attempts to persuade Jason to leave, Nickle had fallen fast asleep on a table. Jason had to prod Nickle awake with his finger. "Hey, we better go. They're closing down."

Nickle lifted his head, a straw wrapper stuck to his face. "What time is it?"

"It's too late to stay here."

Jason pulled Nickle to his feet, and the two Dwarves exited Belmont. They were greeted by a thick darkness that had settled over EarthWorks. The only light came from small spheres hovering a few feet above the ground. Jason leaped up onto a wall and laughed. "Hah. Now that was a night!"

Nickle gave a half-hearted grin. "Did you meet someone you liked?"

"Elf girls are so beautiful."

Nickle shrugged his shoulders. "They're all right."

"All right…all right? How can you say that?"

"I don't know…Dwarf girls seem just as pretty—plus, they don't have the attitude or wear nearly as much makeup."

Jason did a backflip off the wall. "You don't know what you're talking about."

Nickle shrugged his shoulders. "Maybe."

They walked on in silence until they reached a street that was even more dimly lit than the one before. Apart from a few stray cats, everything seemed devoid of life.

"I think we should be able to catch a Taxi-Lator at the next turn—" Jason started to say but then stopped mid-sentence.

"What's wrong?"

Jason hit the ground, pulling Nickle down with him.

Nickle frowned. "What is it? What do you see?"

"It's blood," Jason whispered. "Vamps. I think I smell Vamps."

Nickle took a whiff of the air. "I don't smell anything—"

"Get up," a raspy voice called from down an alley. "We know you're there."

Jason slowly stood, pulling a Rune from his belt as he did. "We don't want any trouble. We're just passing through."

"Well," the voice hissed. "If you didn't want any trouble, then what are you doing on our turf?"

"This is a public street; this is no one's turf—"

A tall and extremely pale-faced Elf walked out from the shadows. He wore a long black coat with a flipped-up collar. His eyes were green but had large, pronounced blood vessels spidering through them. His fingernails were sharp like daggers, his stance was cocky. While the two Dwarves were distracted by the Elf in front of them, four more crept in from behind.

The tall Elf stretched out his neck. "You have no idea the trouble you just got yourself into."

Jason threw his head back and laughed. "I was about to say the same thing to you. We're both Dwarves in the Silver Army reporting back from an important assignment. If there's even the slightest delay in our arrival, Thornhead will unleash a dozen fully armored Dwarves to find out why. You Vamps might be quicker than us, but that won't matter when our friends show up."

Now it was the Elf's turn to laugh. "You're a smart kid. Very good. But I don't think you were on a special mission—unless that mission included you hanging out at Belmont all night and flirting with girls that are so out of your league."

"You want money," Jason removed his money medallion from around his neck. "Here, take anything you want." While he handed it to one of the Elves, the Dwarf secretly attached a Hellion Rune onto the back of it. Only Nickle was able to see the quick exchange.

The lead Elf nodded. "That's a good place to start but—"

Jason pushed Nickle to the ground. "Get down!"

Suddenly, the Rune exploded into a massive fireball that sent the Elves flying backward. The explosion stunned the attackers, giving the two Dwarves a chance to make a run for it. They took off, heading towards a street that had hovering balls of light. The Vamps recovered quickly, however, and began moving so fast that their legs blurred as they charged, hissing as they went. As they ran, they leaped over fences and along the sides of walls, flipped off planter boxes and garbage cans. They were so agile, so stealthy, it was impossible to keep an eye on all of them.

One of the Vamps grabbed Jason by the throat and lifted him into the air. "And you Dwarves think you're so strong…"

Another Vamp came up and seized Jason around the waist. "You pathetic coward—" The Vamp's words were cut short as he was interrupted by an explosion of ice that hit him square in the chest. Nickle threw another Rune at the Elf that caused a set of roots to suddenly shoot out of the ground and wrap around anything that was close by.

Then, out of the darkness, a white light was sent hurtling towards Nickle. He fell to the ground just as the searing projectile streaked past him. Two more beams followed but he was able to roll out of their way. He activated a Defensive Rune just before a third beam hit him in the chest. The Rune absorbed the majority of the blow, but Nickle still received a good portion of it. He flipped backward and into the side of a building.

Jason punched one of his captors in the face, sending the pale-faced welp rolling across the ground. With both his hands free, he was able to pull out Rune after Rune and fling them in every direction.

Another beam of light exploded out of the darkness, aimed straight at Nickle's head, but Jason tossed two Earth Runes at the last moment, instantly making pillars of dirt that absorbed the beam. Dirt and debris erupted into the air, creating a thick cloud of dust.

Jason rushed towards Nickle's side. "Are you all right? Can you run?"

Nickle winced in pain. "They must have hit me with a Paralyzing spell or something. I deflected most of it, but my legs don't work."

"All right," Jason murmured. "The strength in your legs will return, but it will take some time. If only we had some Dwarf Armor, then we could show these Vamps what's up. Stay down. I'll draw them off. Once they're after me, find a place to hide and lay low until your legs return to normal."

Nickle shook his head. "Just get out of here. I can handle myself."

"Save the brave talk for when we get back to the barracks." With this, Jason tossed six Earth Runes into the middle of the street, each one quickly forming into large pillars of dirt. As the last one formed, the Dwarf threw three Hellion bombs into the mix and then tucked and rolled. The effect was a deafening explosion that sprayed dirt in every direction. Instantly, the air was filled with a thick cloud of dust that covered the street.

Jason laughed. "You Vamps might have speed, but where's your talent!" Just as he spoke, three beams of light came streaking towards him, one of them missing him only by inches. With that, Jason took off in the opposite direction, throwing Runes behind him as he did.

Nickle listened as Jason and the Elves disappeared through the cloud of dirt. He had to sit there for a while, waiting for his legs to regain their strength. It was another minute before Jason's cocky voice faded entirely into the night. Nickle rubbed his legs, hoping to force life back into them. *"Jason needs me."* Feeling finally returned to his toes and then spread up to his ankles and shins. After he could feel his knees again, he propped himself against a building. Painfully, he began to walk down the street, away from the dust cloud. He had not gone more than twenty feet when he heard something behind him move.

Without waiting to see who or what it was, Nickle crouched down against one of the walls of an Elven home. Through the thick blanket of dirt, he could see a figure approaching. The individual was tall and thin, had long nails and a dark coat. Nickle considered running, but with his legs not working properly, it did not seem like a real option. He looked around for any other escape. To his right was a small dog door leading into the backyard of an Elven house. He hesitated only for a moment before he began pushing himself through. Halfway in, however, he found himself stuck—unable to pull himself through or push himself back out. He could hear the Vamp's footsteps getting closer, hear the creature's troubled breathing and the clicking of its fingernails. It would only be moments before he was discovered. With one last effort, he raked his hands into the grass and pulled himself the rest of the way through.

The Vamp stopped walking and looked around, straining his keen eyes in the dark. The pale-faced creature tightened its fists as he took in a deep breath. Nickle grabbed a Rune. *"Did he see me? Is he just distracting me while the attackers come from somewhere else?"* Nickle looked around. It was a few long, tense moments before the Vamp let out a wild shriek and vanished into the night.

Chapter 14

Sharlindrian Avish MeithDwin

Nickle lay back on the grass and let out a long sigh. He closed his eyes as he waited for his legs to regain their full strength. He laid there for the better portion of an hour before he could stand and look around. As he stood, lights suddenly appeared, revealing a massive garden filled with hundreds of colorful flowers. It was a faint blue light that seemed to be coming from underneath large mushrooms. Everything was so ornately decorated that it looked like a picture from a magazine. As Nickle walked, more mushrooms activated, giving him just enough light to avoid stepping on any of the plants.

He thought it unwise to leave through the small door that he came in—just in case the Vamp was waiting for him outside. Instead, he walked around, looking for a gate that led back to the street. The yard stretched out for dozens of yards and had no end in sight. His legs were still a little numb, forcing him to limp. As he walked, he passed a gigantic fountain that shot water ten feet into the air which led to an ornate waterfall that collected into a pool with orange fish.

Nickle shook his head. "How in the world can a flower garden this big be in the middle of EarthWorks?"

"Are you sure you're supposed to be here?"

Nickle ducked behind a statue of a bull and peered around the legs. Besides a few lighted mushrooms, he could barely see anything. He shifted left and then right, trying to catch a glimpse of the person that had spoken. After a few long moments, Nickle began to think that it must have been his imagination. He stuck his hand out in the open and then pulled it back. He did it again—this time taking more time—but again, nothing happened. Slowly, he stood up, using the statue in front of him for balance. He looked around, waiting for something to happen, but nothing did. He let out a sigh of relief.

That is when the attack came.

161

A beam of white light suddenly hit him square in the chest and sent him flipping backward. He landed fifteen feet from where he had been, his back against a stone wall. Despite the shot knocking him off his feet, he recovered quickly and drew out a set of Runes. Another burst of light was hurtled towards him, but this time he was ready. He crushed a Defensive Rune in his hand and rolled to the left. The white light was sliced in half by a green smoke that shot out of his Rune.

Again, the unseen assailant took a shot, but again, Nickle was able to block it. He returned fire, throwing a Hellion Rune that exploded into a wall of flames, engulfing a large tree. With the light from the fire, Nickle could finally see his Elven opponent, dressed in a grey cloak which had partially caught fire.

The Elf cursed before going back on the offensive, lighting up the air with dozens of beams of light. Nickle ducked behind a statue of a wizened old man with a cane. A moment later, nothing remained except the cane as a beam of light obliterated the statue. Nickle took refuge behind a square tablet, but this too exploded.

Nickle hugged the ground and rolled into a dry ditch, his mind racing with frantic thoughts. He grabbed several Sight Runes from his belt—which were the only ones he had left, and held them tight in his hand. *"Why didn't I refill my belt?"* Nickle's own thoughts answered his question. *"Because I didn't think I'd be attacked by Vamps. Because Jason said it would be "fun" to go to Belmont—not life-threatening."* With a sudden intake of breath, he stood up and began to run around the flower garden as fast as his small legs would allow. His opponent quickly picked up the pursuit, shooting beam after beam of light after him. Every few feet, Nickle stuck a Sight Rune on a critical point in the garden.

After he had completely circled his opponent, he hid inside a big bush that was somewhat hollow on the inside. With his Sight Runes in place, Nickle took out another Rune from his belt. After whispering an incantation and sticking the Rune to his eye, he could see the garden—even more importantly, he could see his opponent. By whispering another incantation, he was able to switch his sight to night vision, which gave him an advantage he was sure his opponent did not have.

He watched as his opponent went on the hunt. Now that he could see better in the dark, he was surprised that the Elf was not tall—only about Nickle's height. The Elf was also thin and had skinny white arms that tentatively poked out of the large grey cloak. The Dwarf had to keep switching views between his Sight Runes to keep track of his opponent. Slowly, the Elf made its way around the garden until it was standing right in front of Nickle's hiding spot.

"*This is it,*" the Dwarf thought.

As the Elf turned its back towards Nickle, the Dwarf leaped through the bushes and tackled it. The Dwarf easily overpowered and forced his opponent to the ground, knocking off its hood as he did. From under the grey cloak, a long wisp of white hair whipped out and a set of soft green eyes looked up.

Nickle frowned. "You're a girl."

"And you're a bright little dirt-digger, aren't you?"

"What are you doing here?"

"What am I doing here? What am I doing here? I live here. Get off of me."

Nickle narrowed his eyes. "Why were you trying to kill me?"

"Kill you? If I wanted you dead, you would be."

"Why were you attacking me?"

"Why do you think?"

"Because you're an Elf."

"No," the Elf corrected quickly, "because you're on my property—and it's not permitted for anything but Elves and Faeries to enter here. You have broken the law, and you must be punished. I can't believe you even made it in here—there are Hexes that should have sizzled your skin the moment you hopped over my fence. Now, let me up or I'll melt your skin myself."

"No," Nickle said as he shook his head. "If I let you up, we would begin fighting all over again. Look, I'm just hiding here from one of your Elf friends—a Vamp or whatever you call him—so I need to stay here just a little bit longer, all right?"

The girl's expression changed. "A Vampire? Where? Here?"

"No, not in here—that's why I'm here. Wait, that's what Vamp means—Vampire?"

The girl rolled her eyes. "Oh, out of all the grubby little dirt-diggers, I happen to run into a stupid one. What? Don't you know anything about anything? You don't know what a Vampire is?"

"Yes, of course, I do—I just didn't know they really existed. But they looked like Elves—Elves with some serious hangnails and freaky eyes."

"They are Elves, but they've Crossed over. Elves are the only ones that can become Vampires, and that's only by choice. There's a whole process to it. Now, let me up before I rip you in two."

"If you could rip me in two, you would've already done it. And I'm not going to let you up if you keep threatening me. Listen, I'm sorry for trashing your garden, I really am. In fact, if you show me the exit, I'll be happy to leave you in peace."

The Elf scoffed. "Everyone knows that a dirt-digger's word isn't worth anything. Your whole race is a bunch of drunken brawlers that do nothing more than pick fights."

"Maybe," Nickle replied. "But if you call me a dirt-digger one more time, I'm going to spit in your face. How would you like it if I called you an arrogant, lazy brat?"

The Elf narrowed her eyes. "You don't know anything about me. Look at this place. You think I could earn enough gold dust to own a place like this if I were lazy? I bet it's twenty times bigger than any home you've ever lived in. Everyone loves me. Everyone thinks I'm adorable. You don't know anything."

"Yes," Nickle nodded, "I can see why they would think you're so adorable. If you had a set of button eyes and a tag attached to your body, you might pass for a beanie baby."

"A what?"

Nickle swallowed. "They don't have those down here?"

"Are you crazy?"

"Listen," Nickle whispered, "if you promise not to go ballistic again, I'll let you up. I don't want to destroy your garden. I want to get out of here just as much as you want me to go. I'm only trying to leave—"

"—All right," the Elf hissed, "let me up."

"You have to promise."

"I promise. Now let me up."

Nickle let out a loud sigh as he stood up. "Now, just remember—you promised."

The Elf narrowed her eyes. "Yes, I think I remember—"

"What's your name?"

She began to dust herself off. "What does it matter to you?"

Nickle shrugged his shoulders. "It's hard to trust someone if you don't know their name."

The Elf stood. "What's your name?"

"Nickle Brickle'Bee. And yours—"

"None of your business. Now let me show you the way out."

"Sure, yeah. I tell you my name, but you don't even have the decency to tell me yours—that makes sense. Just point the way, and I'm gone."

"Good," the Elf replied. "Follow me."

Nickle obeyed a little too eagerly and accidentally ran into the Elf as she stepped forward.

She tripped but caught herself before she fell. "Watch where you're going."

"Sorry," Nickle whispered. "It's dark out here."

The Elf walked quickly towards the darkest part of the garden. They passed under two archways and through a large bush that was shaped like a fish. "What is a Dwarf doing in the Elf Quarter anyway? I've never once seen a Dwarf here alone. On the rare occasion that Dwarves are here, it's usually because they're policing the streets and looking for some deranged Demon—not raiding the private gardens of Elves."

Nickle shook his head. "We went to Belmont."

"And they let you in—"

"—Yes, of course they did. I've got some influential and very powerful friends…" He thought of Jason while he mentioned the words "powerful friends," and he had a hard time sticking to the bluff. "But I can't say I liked it much, or that I like the Elf Quarter. Belmont was overpriced and understaffed. There were too many fur coats wrapped around arrogant rich kids. I don't know if I found it more ironic that Humans were dressing like Elves or that Elves were trying to act like Humans. The whole scene was flipped on its head. Then after that, we were jumped by a half a dozen red-eyed Vampires— which, until moments ago, I thought only existed in legend."

"They did," the Elf answered.

"What? What do you mean?"

"Vampires had disappeared for centuries. No one, not even the wisest of Elves knew where they went. But now they're back—and their numbers are increasing."

"Increasing? What do you mean?"

The girl turned around, her silver hair whipping the air. "More Elves are crossing over. The whole Elf quarter is talking about it, talking about the gangs that run rampant in the streets. It used to be safe enough to walk from one end of the Elf quarter to the other, but now it's too dangerous to even step out at night."

Nickle rubbed the bruise that was forming on his chest. "You seem to be able to handle yourself."

The Elf smiled ever so slightly. "What is that? A joke?"

"No. Honestly, I thought you were one of them."

"What do you know? You're just a kid."

"Hey, I was just commissioned in the Silver Army—"

The Elf poked Nickle in the chest. "How old are you then?"

"Fourteen, maybe fifteen."

She rolled her eyes. "You don't even remember when you were born?"

"I was very young at the time—so of course I don't remember. How old are you?"

"Twenty-five."

Nickle's eyes widened. "Twenty-five? You're almost twice as old as me."

"And almost twice as smart."

The Dwarf shook his head. "How's that possible? We look almost the same age; you're even shorter than me."

"Elves don't mature as fast as Humans, and not nearly as fast as Dwarves."

"So, if you're twenty-five, what are you doing cooped up in this place? Do you get to leave on occasion?"

The Elf's lips tightened as she whispered something under her breath. A doorway suddenly appeared in the wall and swung open, leaving a path that led to the street. "I'd appreciate it if you would leave now."

Nickle flushed with a sudden pang of guilt. "I didn't mean to make you mad—I was just surprised. Listen, I'm sorry for trashing your garden; I feel really bad about that."

"Just go."

"I can pay you for the damages."

The Elf laughed. "What will you pay me with? A collection of dirt clods?"

Nickle stepped forward until he reached the doorway. "Suit yourself. I was just trying to help." He was halfway out when the Elf grabbed his shoulder.

"Wait. There's one thing you can do for me."

Nickle turned around, his hair flipping through the air, almost as if he was some rogue in a romantic film. "Yes. What's that?"

"Can you take out my trash?"

"What?"

"Don't tell me Dwarves don't use trash cans."

"Why don't you take it out yourself—or at least have some maid do it for you?"

"My father does not allow the staff to take out the trash, nor will he let me obliterate it with magic. He says I need to develop a work ethic."

Nickle shook his head and turned back towards the garden. "By taking out the trash? What is that going to teach you?"

The Elf nodded curtly. "Yeah, I know. Tell me about it. It's filthy."

Nickle rolled his eyes. "Fine. Where is it?"

"Oh, I don't need it taken out right now—just every Tuesday night."

"Well, I might be able to make it next Tuesday, but—"

The Elf narrowed her eyes. "—Good. Meet me in the garden at eight—and don't be late or I'll report this whole thing to your supervisor."

Nickle shrugged. "It was your magic that destroyed everything—except for the one tree that caught on fire. That one was on me—" As Nickle spoke the door, slowly began closing on him. "Wait. I'm not coming if you don't at least tell me your name."

"Sharlindrian Avish MeithDwin…"

"Wow, that's a big—"

But before the Dwarf could utter another word, Nickle found himself talking to a closed door. A sudden flash of anger washed over him. He stared long and hard at the wood door, hoping that it would open again. But it never did. Finally, after a long sigh, he turned around and headed down the street.

It was another hour before Nickle walked into the barracks, his feet dragging behind him. His whole body felt like a dishrag that had been wrung dry. Every muscle in his arms and legs protested as he climbed up to his top bunk.

Jason was there waiting for him, a grin fixed to his face. "You made it. I only saw four of them after me and I think there were five in total. I was worried that one of them had stayed behind. I can't believe you made it."

Nickle rolled over the last step and flopped onto the bed. "Yeah, barely. My legs took a while before they'd move, and then I ran into this crazy little Elf girl who wants me to start taking out her trash. What happened to you?"

"I took off down the road, exploding as many Runes as I could. After a few blocks, the noise woke up enough people that the Vamps began to worry about being caught—or something. After a while, the bloodsuckers gave up on the pursuit. I had to dodge some Praetorian Guards, but I was finally able to make my way here. I was just about to head back to look for you."

"Well, thanks," Nickle nodded. "You really put it all on the line for me back there—of course, if it weren't for you, I wouldn't have gone to Belmont in the first place and those Vamps would have never jumped me. So, thanks, sort of."

"Well, you're welcome, sort of."

Chapter 15

Camp Tulla

The next morning, Jason and Nickle received their official orders. They had been assigned to a Cohort in the TorMunger clan, which was known for its axe throwing. It took them a few hours on a cramped Dwarf Warship before they arrived at Camp Tulla. It was pathetically small and depressing. There were eight primary buildings, all of which were spaced out in an octagonal pattern. The buildings were more functional than ornate, except for one building that was circled with massive marble pillars. This building appeared to be the headquarters of the operation. The rest of the camp was disheveled and run down, much like the Dwarves that lived there. The Dwarves looked dirty and grizzled, their eyes vacant and worn. Many of them had burn marks that streaked across their armor—a few of them even had their beards completely singed off. There was garbage everywhere, including in the small streets, which themselves were in disrepair. A wood fence circled the landscape but only made it halfway around before it collapsed into a pile of firewood. Rusty tools and equipment were left out haphazardly, as if they were relics of some horrible memory that their owners were eager to leave forgotten.

"Just remember," Jason said, "this was your idea."

Nickle swallowed.

Jason gestured to the main building. "We better report to our commanding officer."

Nickle nodded, throwing his rucksack of clothes and gear over his shoulder. "You're right."

Jason did the same, and they set off towards the other end of the camp. As they did, the large Dwarf Warship groaned with movement. The two Dwarves turned around and watched the ship slowly beginning to take off. Everything felt so much more permanent now that the Dwarf Warship was disappearing down a long tunnel that headed in the direction of EarthWorks.

"I'm about ready to request a transfer," Jason said, only half joking.

Nickle laughed. "It's not so bad." As they turned around, a rag-tag group of Dwarves slowly began to appear as they deboarded a Worm. "What happened to them?"

The Dwarves looked as if they had been in pitch battle. There were fresh burn marks across their arms and armor. One Dwarf in particular looked up at Jason and Nickle, meeting eyes with them for the briefest of moments. The Dwarf then looked away, either out of exhaustion or contempt.

"Yeah, things are starting to look brighter by the moment," Jason replied.

Nickle and Jason entered the large building with caution, as if they were entering a bear cave. The inside was just as broken down and dirty as the rest of the camp. A trail of dirt went from the entrance into every room, like the tracks of a train.

They approached a Dwarf who was fast asleep. His deep breaths curled his beard as he dreamed.

"Excuse me," Jason said.

The Dwarf did not stir.

Then a door slammed behind them, creating a noise so loud that it shook the dust from the chandelier above. The sleeping Dwarf shot to attention, pounding his chest in a salute.

Jason and Nickle crisply returned the salute. Despite the sleepy Dwarf's uniform being covered in dirt, they were able to recognize the insignia of a First Class Pivot, which was four ranks higher than a Tenderfoot.

"I'm not sleeping," the Dwarf said quickly. When the Dwarf noticed that only Jason and Nickle were standing in front of him, the tension in his body disappeared. He slumped back into his chair, his eyes drooping. "Ah, it's just you two. You must be the new recruits." He studied the two boys, a slight smile spread across his face. "I feel sorry for you lads. Not a great day for you two to show up."

Nickle swallowed. Jason opened his mouth to ask a question, but the other Dwarf did not give him a chance to speak.

"My name is Timithen Underbrook, First Class Pivot in the Silver Army." The Dwarf saluted again, this time with much less enthusiasm. "For Honor and Glory…and all such. Today is just not a good day to meet the Centurion. Of course, it's nothing you two did. We're on high alert. Everyone here is pulling a triple shift, myself included. Most of us haven't seen a bed for three days—so everyone is a little on edge."

"We can come back if there's a better time," Jason suggested.

"No, no. A boiling pot will continue to boil as long as the flames persist. And I don't think this flame will go out anytime soon. Just keep your head up and your temper in check, and you'll do fine…probably." First Class Pivot Underbrook gestured to the door that had previously been slammed shut. "Through there. He's waiting for you."

Nickle and Jason saluted. "For Honor and Glory."

Underbrook only laughed as he kicked his feet back up onto the desk.

Leaving their rucksacks at the door, they entered into the room, first Nickle and then Jason. They immediately saluted and stood at attention, their eyes locking onto the far wall. They remained in that position for several minutes. Using his peripheral vision, Nickle could get a sense of a very messy office. Papers were stacked to odd heights and in distorted piles throughout the room. There was a wall of plaques and trophies to their right, but they were dust-covered and seemingly forgotten. There was only one other Dwarf in the room, and he was busy reading something from a stone tablet.

Finally, the Dwarf stood, his expression stoic and stern. He was a mighty Dwarf, and his presence demanded immediate respect. "I requested new battle Tines for my warriors, and they send me second-hand gear from Tortugan. I ask for increased funding, and they cut my budget. I beg for two Cohorts, and they send me two Tenderfoots."

Nickle swallowed.

"What in the name of Hurn are you two doing here?"

Nickle's nerves got the better of him and he suddenly burst out. "For Honor and Glory."

An awkward silence fell over the room.

Finally, the Dwarf laughed. It was faint at first but then grew in strength. Soon the Dwarf was laughing so forcefully that the other two began to fear that he had gone crazy.

"Ahh," the commanding Dwarf said at last, "to be a young Tenderfoot again and have faith in your leadership. Brings me back to when I first started in the Silver Army. At ease, Tenderfoots. Standing like that, you two look like stuffed animals mounted on a wall."

Jason and Nickle shifted into parade rest.

"I'm Centurion Hampshire Cleaver," the Dwarf said. He then nodded to Nickle, "The last Dwarf to hold this post was your father. He was a fool, as all of us here, as am I. Gnomes are temperamental at best, manic at worst. Since your father turned Troll and left the rest of us to rot here in Camp Tulla, the Gnomes are just shy of an all-out revolution. The best we can do is keep track of their movements. They want nothing to do with us—nothing to do with this Cohort. Worse still, since we're closer to the surface, their magic is stronger and ours is weaker."

Hampshire sat down, his hands slamming into the desk. "Thornhead thinks he can break me—first by not sending me funding and second by not sending me warriors. How long have you two been out of Tortugan?"

"Two days," Jason replied.

"And it's your first year at Tortugan?" Hampshire asked.

"Yes, sir," Jason replied. "We're ready for battle."

Hampshire shook his head. "Blasted Tri'Ark. Blasted Cogs of Hurn. Blasted old Thornhead. He thinks he can finally get rid of me. Well, I won't fall for his trap. I hope you boys like sitting around and doing nothing because that's all you two will do here."

"What about the Gnomes?" Nickle asked.

"You two won't ever see a Gnome while I'm in command," Hampshire replied. "I'm not going to risk the lives of two untested Tenderfoots and ruin my reputation."

"But…" Nickle stammered. "We've been assigned here."

"So, you have," Hampshire replied coldly, "and here's where you'll stay."

Nickle's mind was working furiously, grasping at any possible response. "But we've been assigned to the Gnomes."

Hampshire's face shifted into an ugly frown. "Don't test me, boy. For the sake of your father, I haven't chucked you out a window just yet."

Nickle took a deep breath.

Hampshire lowered his voice to a growl. "Besides, you two wouldn't last a day out there. These creatures are devilishly tricky and so easy to offend. They won't kill us—not yet anyway—but they also won't hesitate to singe our armor. If we fight back, it will ruin everything we've been trying to build—not that it matters. This whole project is a waste of time. Thornhead knows it—that's why he doesn't send any real assistance—and now I know it. Just keep your heads down lads, and I'll see what I can do about getting you a transfer out of here."

Nickle's face went red.

Noticing Nickle's complexion, Jason took over the conversation. "Well, sir. Thank you. We better go find our bunks. Come on, Nickle." They both saluted and turned. Nickle gritted his teeth before following Jason out the door.

Nickle felt his heart pounding against his chest as he walked away from the building. Jason eyed his friend tentatively as they approached the barracks. As they entered, their senses were instantly assaulted by the smell of body odor and unwashed sheets. They stumbled over gear as they found some available bunks. Nickle threw his rucksack onto the bed and slumped down. His eyes drifted to the ceiling high above.

"At least you're not on the top bunk anymore," Jason said with a wink.

"We've got to think of something," Nickle replied.

"We'll figure something out."

"We're so close. There's got to be something we can do. I've got to talk to the Gnomes—at least for a few minutes. There has to be a way we can change Hampshire's mind."

"Hampshire is a broken Dwarf," Jason replied. "Did you see all those awards on the wall? He used to be somebody—that's probably how he got the post in the first place—but he hasn't been able to do anything with it. Did you see how eager he was to have success here? I bet he'd sell his own mother's Tines if it meant he could broker a peace treaty with the Gnomes. He's nothing short of desperate, and desperation very easily becomes recklessness."

"I just feel like I'm so close to finding out something important. If I could just have ten minutes with a Gnome—"

"I don't think they'll be spending any time talking to a Dwarf for any reason. If you had ten minutes with a Gnome, that'd be ten minutes they'd have to attack you."

"My father won them over somehow," Nickle replied. "They must have trusted him."

"That doesn't much matter," Jason replied, "Hampshire isn't going to let either one of us visit the Gnomes. He seemed pretty convinced that both of us are a liability and not an asset. This whole camp is a liability. Look at this place, all falling apart. The morale here is about as thin and frail as a paper window. One good tussle with the Gnomes and the camp might completely come apart. No one here cares about the Gnomes; they don't even care about their camp."

Nickle nodded. "You're right—they don't. But that gives me an idea."

Chapter 16

The Race of the Pigs

The next morning Nickle and Jason awoke before any of the others and headed to the kitchen. It was a wreck, like every other room in Camp Tulla, but it was still well-stocked. The Dwarves stationed at Camp Tulla never had time to cook a meal, let alone clean up after one. The trash was heaped up until it was almost touching the ceiling. The dishes were all out on the counter, each one covered with layers of food so thick that they were substantially heavier than they should have been.

"So, this is your idea?" Jason asked.

"Not all of it," Nickle replied, "but yeah."

Jason set about cleaning, Nickle cooking. Nickle did not know how to use magic for cooking, and so he defaulted to the only way he knew how—by hand. By the time most Dwarves started waking up, they were greeted with a smell they barely recognized. Nickle was not a good cook, but he did not have to be to draw a crowd. Before long, the complete Cohort appeared, curious expressions fixed to their faces. Jason had cleaned enough trays, plates, and silverware to accommodate the horde of Dwarves.

A line formed, trays were acquired, and food was distributed. For the first time in months, perhaps years, the Dwarves were able to devour strips of cooked bacon, eggs, toast, and orange juice while still being at Camp Tulla. Surprisingly, the most popular item turned out to be camel's eye, which none of the other Dwarves had ever tried. The Dwarves were so focused on eating, there was hardly any conversation. But soon, as stomachs were filled, the levity began. Several Dwarves began flexing their bellies to show off the food they had eaten. For the first time since arriving, Nickle began to hear genuine laughter.

The laughter steadily grew until the whole camp was alive with the noise. One robust Dwarf suddenly jumped onto a table, his hands hugging his round belly. "I want to propose a toast to the ol' Lord of the Gnomes! Here's to Reckle Berry! The Gnome that brought us all together!"

The room filled with a chorus of laughter and boos.

"Sit down, you ol' clod," one of the Dwarves yelled.

Another Dwarf stood up, raising a glass to the air. "Instead, let's toast the fine pig that gave his life for breakfast!"

This had the whole mess hall cheering.

Then Hampshire appeared, his face set with a frown. The noise vanished in an instant as all eyes fell upon their commanding officer. All Dwarves stood, pounding their chest in a salute.

The Centurion walked around the room, first with anger, and then with curiosity. It seemed apparent that he had come running from his bunk, thinking there was some trouble he needed to sort out. But instead of finding a problem, he was relieved to find only laughter.

"What's all this?" demanded Hampshire.

No one answered for a spell. Finally, a large Dwarf with an unusually high-pitched voice answered. "It's breakfast."

As quickly as the laughter had left, it now returned in full force. Nickle was not sure what was so funny, whether it was the Dwarf's high-pitched voice or that he had simply stated the obvious. In the end, he decided it was most likely because the Dwarves had not laughed for so long, that it felt good to do it now.

Hampshire smiled as he scanned the room. When he finally spotted Nickle and Jason behind the serving counter, he was able to complete the picture. Then Hampshire locked eyes with Nickle and shook his head, as if to say, "Thanks for breakfast, lad, but you still don't get to visit the Gnomes."

By the time Nickle and Jason finished cleaning up after breakfast, most of the Dwarves had padded up in armor and started their patrols, leaving the two Tenderfoots to their own devices.

"Well," Jason said. "I hope that wasn't the entire plan, because we're still here and all the Dwarves are out there."

"We still have some work to do," Nickle answered.

With this, they set off to clean the camp. First, they picked up the trash, and then the neglected and rusty tools. It was a monumental task that required more perspiration the longer they persisted. Nickle used Wind Runes to corral much of the debris into a corner, while

Jason made it disappear with Fire Runes. Once the outside was complete, they turned their attention to the insides of the buildings.

By the time the Cohort had returned from their patrols, they had found two things they did not expect: First, Camp Tulla was devoid of any garbage, and second, dinner was waiting for them. The Dwarves were not nearly as lively as they had been during breakfast, but they were grateful. It had been another wretched day of Gnome ambushes, as evidenced by their battered armor.

Once again, Hampshire spotted Nickle at dinner, and once again, he shook his head. Each day Nickle and Jason arose with the same dutiful energy. They spent every waking moment cooking and cleaning. But each time Hampshire saw Nickle, the result was the same. He would resolutely shake his head.

On the fifth day, Jason woke up, his back aching from overuse, and spilled out of his bed. As he looked around, he realized that Nickle was the only other one left in the barracks.

Nickle grinned as he saw Jason stir. "Man, how did you sleep through all that noise?"

"Where is everyone?" Jason asked.

"They geared up and moved out half an hour ago," Nickle replied. "I don't know how in the world you didn't hear it all."

"It's all the chores you've been having me do," Jason answered. "By the end of each day, I'm so exhausted I could sleep on my feet."

"Things aren't changing," Nickle said.

Jason rubbed the sleep from his eyes. "Did you really think by doing a few chores Hampshire would change his mind? Hampshire is just trying to preserve his career at this point—that's the only thing he's thinking about."

"I just thought that if he could see how much better we made the camp," Nickle replied, "that perhaps he'd see us as something more than just Tenderfoots."

"Well, I don't think—," Jason was interrupted by a sharp squealing.

"What was that?" Nickle asked.

Jason grabbed his axe and ran for the door, Nickle was not far behind. Bright light greeted them as they stepped out and scanned their surroundings. Another squeal erupted to their left, drawing their attention. The source of the noise was immediately apparent. Two pigs had somehow appeared and tangled themselves up in a rope. The pigs pulled in opposite directions, apparently trying to break free.

"Where did they come from?" Nickle asked.

"Come on, Nickle," Jason said, "let's see if we can run 'em down."

"I've never seen pigs in the camp before—at least not ones that hadn't already been turned into bacon," Nickle replied.

But Jason did not hear. He was already sprinting in the direction of the animals. As Jason approached, the pigs who, only moments before, were pulling against each other, now decidedly ran in unison away from Jason. The Dwarf had been one of the fastest at Tortugan, but he was no match for the pigs.

"Come on, Nickle," Jason said with a grin. "These are racing pigs! A hundred grams of gold dust to the one that can catch them!"

Nickle joined the pursuit, tripping over a broken fence post before he got too far. He rightened himself and continued on in a dead sprint. The creatures soon outdistanced him, the rope that was caught around their necks whipping in the wind.

"We've got to charge them at the same time," Jason said. "You come from their right; I'll come up from the left."

This plan, as brilliant as it sounded, soon failed as the pigs escaped right through the middle. Nickle lunged for the rope, barely catching a part of it that was tangled into a knot. Even though Nickle had the rope, the pigs did not stop—if anything, they began to pull harder. Nickle ate a dirt sandwich as he was dragged behind them.

"That's it, Nickle!" Jason yelled. "Hang on."

Nickle was trying to do just the opposite. He had decided to let go almost as soon as he grabbed the rope, but his hand had become twisted in a slip knot that was made all that much tighter the more the two pigs pulled. Nickle hit a rock, and his body bounced up like a rubber ball.

Jason could not help but laugh.

"I can't get my hand free!" Nickle yelled.

"Hold on," Jason replied. "I've got this." But instead of running towards Nickle, he ran in the opposite direction. For a few brief seconds, Nickle thought this would lead to his eventual death. He felt embarrassed by the thought of it—even more embarrassed as he pictured how the speaker at his funeral would have to explain how he had met his demise.

Then Jason appeared, not from behind, but now in front. In his hands, he held two Runes, which he smashed together, creating an instant spray of ice. The pigs banked left and away, but they were not quick enough to avoid being caught up in sleet.

Nickle rolled to a stop, his chest heaving for breath. The pigs struggled, but their hoofs had frozen to the ground. He pulled himself to his knees and wiped his mouth, pulling a long strand of grass from the back of his throat. "Those are not normal pigs."

"No," Jason said excitedly. "These are racing pigs."

"No such thing," Nickle replied.

"And yet, here they are."

"Where did they come from?"

"One of the Dwarves must be keeping them close by. I wonder how they got out of their pen."

Nickle spat out a dirt clod. "Who races pigs?"

Jason did not answer, however. He was now grinning so broadly that all his teeth were visible. "I just had the best idea I've ever had."

It took a few minutes to work out the dynamics of this new idea, a few minutes more to make the contraption. But within half an hour, Jason stood back, his hands folded across his chest.

"Are you sure you want to claim this as the best idea that you've ever hand?" Nickle said with some skepticism.

"Let me show you how this is done," Jason said.

While the two pigs had been frozen in place, the young Dwarves had removed the rope and turned it into a harness. They then took the harness and attached it to a small, four-wheeled cart that Nickle had discovered a few days prior while cleaning one of the storage sheds. The contraption now looked like an ill-conceived chariot.

Jason stood on the wagon, his hands grabbing the improvised reins. One whip on the back of the pigs, and they were off, pulling the cart with a fury. Jason kept his balance at first but was sent spinning off into a wood fence as he tried to turn. The fence disappeared as well as Jason's body. It took a minute for him to recover, and several more before they were able to chase down the pigs again. Jason tried again, this time, he brought a small anchor with him that he could drop into the ground if he fell off. That way, Jason reasoned, the pigs would be easier to catch next time since the anchor would dig into the dirt and slow them down. Jason lasted a little longer this time, but he lost his footing as the wagon hit a rock and sent him pitching into the sky.

Nickle could not help but laugh.

Jason stood and dusted himself off. "Well, ain't you just full of the giggles. Why don't you give it a shot?"

Nickle frowned. "They already dragged me through the dirt. I'm not going to do that again."

"Come on, Nickle," Jason grinned. "It's only fair that I get to see you try it."

"How does that make any sense?"

"Come onnnn…come onnnnnn…"

Nickle shook his head, "You keep saying that like it's a convincing argument."

"Come onnnnnnn…," Jason drawled.

Nickle threw up his hands. "Fine, I'll give it a go."

"Lean back at first," Jason advised. "Otherwise, you'll fall off just as they bolt."

"Spare me the lecture," Nickle answered. He took to the cart, his hands wrapping around the reins. "How do I get these things going?"

"Hang on!" Jason yelled as he slapped one of the pigs in the rear. Immediately the pigs shot off, pulling the cart in a mad dash. Despite leaning back, Nickle almost lost his footing. He steadied himself and focused, his eyes narrowing into slits. His hair whipped in the wind as the pigs barreled on straight for one of the buildings. He pulled hard on one of the reins, hoping the pigs would get the message. Either they were just as eager to avoid colliding into the building, or they had responded to Nickle's touch, but the cart veered away from the structure. A ripple of adrenaline pulsed through his veins, forcing him to smile.

He pulled on the other rein forcing the pigs in the opposite direction. They obeyed, and soon the cart was swinging to the right. The wagon hit a piece of wood and took to the air. A moment later, it landed again, and so did Nickle. His body was completely in sync with the cart.

Jason yelled something, but Nickle was too distracted to hear exactly what it was. He assumed his friend was egging him on. But he had been wrong. A second later, Hampshire suddenly appeared, stepping right into the cart's path. Nickle pulled the pigs hard to the left, sending the cart careening to the side. The same fence that Jason had previously knocked down with his body, now became a ramp. Nickle and the cart went airborne as they sailed through the air and into Hampshire's office window.

The wreckage was not nearly as startling as the deafening sound. Glass sprayed into Hampshire's office along with chunks of wood from the cart. The cart went halfway through before it wedged to a stop. Nickle's head continued on, hitting the top of the window, knocking him to the side. His vision went fuzzy as he was caught up in the reins. He was not sure if he passed out, but the next moment, it appeared as if Hampshire was right in front of him and upside down.

Nickle squinted, trying to force his mind to focus. "*Why is Hampshire standing on the ceiling?*"

"Get that fool down from there," Hampshire said to a few Dwarves. Nickle was cut free, his body placed upright. He suddenly realized that Hampshire had not been upside down, but that he had been. He almost collapsed, but two sturdy Dwarves held him upright by the arms.

Initially, Nickle thought the Dwarves had pulled him free from the cart to make sure he was all right. But then Hampshire slapped him in the face, dispelling that notion.

"Are you awake, lad?" Hampshire said. He slapped Nickle again. It was not a vicious blow, but it did have a sobering effect.

Hampshire raised his hand again, but Nickle caught it. "I'm awake. I'm awake." He blinked again, his eyes finally able to focus.

"Good," Hampshire said with a grin. "The rest of you, leave my office." Once alone, Hampshire gestured for Nickle to sit. It was a solemn moment, Nickle knew. This little stunt might have just cost him his commission in the Silver Army. He might have just earned a one-way ticket to the surface. But he had a hard time keeping a straight face, mostly because a pig was still suspended in the air, held up by its makeshift harness, slowly spinning around as the other two talked. The pig was only inches from Hampshire's head, who now was sitting comfortably at his desk.

"What was that?" Hampshire asked.

Nickle was first confused by the question. His mind began to replay the events that led him to drive a cart pulled by pigs through his commanding officer's window. After considering his words, he began to speak. "It...it was...an odd sort of...event...series of events really...that just sort of snowballed into—"

"—Just stop," Hampshire said. "I was watching the whole thing from the beginning. What I want to hear, though, is how badly do you want to see the Gnomes?"

Nickle straightened. "What do you mean? Am I still in trouble?"

"No," Hampshire replied. "Well, I mean, you'll have to clean up the mess, of course, and I'm going to dock your pay for the repairs of the window. But what I'm interested in knowing is how badly do you want to see the Gnomes?"

"Very much so."

"Why?" Hampshire asked.

Nickle took a deep breath before answering. "I think they might know something about my parents' disappearance. And, I'd do anything to find out what it is."

"Would you now?" Hampshire said, his eyebrows furrowed in thought.

"I want to know what happened to my father and mother. I don't believe my father turned Troll."

"Are you sure you're willing to pay the price for that knowledge?"

"That's the only reason I'm here," Nickle replied.

"You know you look just like your father," Hampshire replied. "Same furrowed brow, same perfect hair. He was a little wider around the chest, but not by much. He was a powerful warrior—I hear you're not."

"Did you know him?"

Hampshire nodded. "He was a better Dwarf than me. Better than most. I liked him, most of the time. He could be a little cocky on occasion. But that's usually what happens when someone wins as many awards as he did."

Hampshire shifted in his chair to look at his dusty wall of plaques and trophies. "Listen, lad. Let me level with you. I want out of this Cohort. I've been here for two hundred years, and I'm a bit ready for a change of scenery. I'd do just about anything to go, but Thornhead told me he wouldn't make that happen unless I make peace with the Gnomes. But you also want something—to learn more about your father from those tiny creatures. What if I told you there's a way that both of us can get what we want?"

"I'd be very interested."

"It's risky, but in this life, anything worth achieving comes with at least a little risk. Are you game?"

"I'd do anything to find out what happened to my father."

Hampshire leaned back in his chair, his fingers steepled. He took several long moments before finally making a decision. "Report to the armorer and gear up with the finest Tines you can find. You and Jason get your wish. In half an hour, we're going to pay the Gnomes a visit."

Chapter 17

The Gnomes of Tiran 'Og

As they boarded the Worm thirty-two minutes later, Nickle felt his stomach churn. It was not the fact that his last experience on a Worm ended so badly that troubled him, nor was it the fact that the armor he wore felt bulky and poorly maintained. Something else was making his heart race. He was feeling an emotion he did not wholly understand.

He began tightening and then slackening his grip on his axe, but no matter how hard he squeezed, the tension in his body did not slip away. Soon, very soon, he would be meeting the same Gnomes that knew and trusted his father. Nickle took a deep breath, *"Don't mess this up. You can't mess this up."*

Despite the Worm jolting even more than Nickle's first trip, he did not vomit. It was not long before the Dwarf Cohort marched out of the Worm in a tight formation. It was not even a complete Cohort as only thirty-two Dwarves were present. All the Dwarves were alert and spent much of their time scanning their surroundings. They were marching in an odd-shaped tunnel filled with black trees that hung from the ceiling like cobwebs. Along the walls and ceiling, there were thousands of baseball-sized holes that had little doors at the end of them. The doors had been painted with vibrant colors, but neglect and age had faded them until they were almost as black as the trees around them. Nickle happened to glance to the right and see a little graveyard that seemed a perfect complement to the depressing landscape.

As they marched, Hampshire called out to his troops. "Halt. Present arms." Suddenly the sound of armor and weapons stopped. The Dwarves growled as they held their weapons at the ready. The Centurion paced in front of his troops. "Jason and Nickle, with me. Let's see if you're as lucky as your father. The rest of you are to remain here until I get back—but keep your eyes open. We can't afford another disaster like last week."

Nickle broke out of the formation and joined Hampshire's side. Jason was only a second behind.

The Centurion sighed as he studied the two young and inexperienced Dwarves. It seemed he was starting to have second thoughts on whatever scheme he had developed. "I'm only allowed two escorts to this affair. So, if anything goes bad, well, you two will have to do."

Nickle did not hesitate. "Yes, sir. We appreciate your confidence, sir."

Hampshire grumbled. "It's more out of desperation than confidence. But you two must obey me no matter what I ask. These Gnomes have as many customs as Dwarves have axes. If you make one mistake, you could undo everything. Understood?"

"Yes, sir," the two Dwarves echoed.

"Good. Now follow me. We have an audience with King UnderBridge—the ruler of the UnderBridge Clan. Make sure to be respectful and treat each Gnome as an equal. If you don't know what to say, just mumble something under your breath and smile. Most of the Gnomes don't understand our language, so it should be easy for you to avoid talking. Remember, you two are nothing more than escorts—nothing more." The other two Dwarves nodded. "Good. Now swallow these Runes." The Dwarf handed them each a Rune that was about the size of a nickel.

Nickle took the small token and stared at it. "Swallow?"

"Do we get some water to wash it down?" Jason added.

Hampshire narrowed his eyes. "Put it in your mouth before I send you both packing. If you want to stay with me, you're going to have to swallow those Runes."

Nickle nodded briskly and popped the Rune into his mouth. He moved his tongue around, trying to work up enough saliva to swallow it. Finally, he closed his eyes and forced it down. It slowly slid down his throat, scratching the sides as it went. The Rune hit his stomach like a weight. He instantly felt nauseous.

"Don't let it come back up," Hampshire said, "those things are costly and I don't think your paycheck can take another hit today. Now let's go." With this, the large Dwarf began walking down the tunnel. With each step he took, his body shrank a foot. Before long, he was only five inches tall.

Jason and Nickle stared in amazement as the Dwarf almost disappeared before them. But then suddenly, as they watched, Hampshire, along with the large tunnel they were in, seemed to get bigger and bigger. The change happened in jerking motions, almost like a car that is running out of gas. It took a few moments before Nickle finally realized that Hampshire was not getting bigger again, but that he and Jason were actually becoming smaller. He looked at his hands and feet, expecting some dramatic disproportion to his features, but everything appeared normal. He looked over to his side to see Jason with a puzzled expression on his face.

Hampshire approached the two Dwarves. "The only thing that's changed is your size. Now let's go before we're late."

The two young Dwarves nodded and fell in behind Hampshire. They walked quickly but cautiously to a massive set of doors that were fixed deep into the side of the tunnel. According to Nickle's former height, the doors might have seemed ordinary—maybe even a little small—but now they stretched up like a mountain. As soon as they were within a few feet of the doors, they began to open, slowly at first but quickly picking up speed.

Standing before them were a dozen Gnomes—the tallest of which was about five and a half inches. They wore shelled armor that was exquisitely crafted from pinecones and bark. On the top of each of their heads sat a dark red cap that drooped down to their necks. Their spears were made of pine needles; their swords were fashioned from insect legs. Slung to their backs were round shields made of leaves that had been stretched tight. From out of their hair poked long ears that ended in a sharp point. The men had beards that were precisely cut and meticulously maintained.

Despite himself, Jason scoffed at the armor.

Hampshire gave Jason a warning look before he stepped towards the Gnomes, his arms spread wide. "Ah, pleasant people of Tiran 'Og. I come here today as your servant, excited to celebrate the birth of Reckle Berry's new son." The Dwarf then bowed so low his beard nearly touched the ground. Jason and Nickle mimicked Hampshire's gesture.

A small, fat Gnome broke out of the group and walked towards Hampshire. This Gnome was dressed differently than the warriors behind him. He wore a pointy green hat and had a long shabby beard that shot out of his chin. His clothes seemed to be entirely made of leaves that had been sown together with grass. Despite the brittle material, the clothes seemed just as hardy as any Nickle had ever seen—maybe even more durable.

The Green Capped Gnome bowed even lower than Hampshire. When he came up again, he had a grin as wide as his face. "Welcome, noble Dwarf Centurion Hampshire. We have eagerly awaited your arrival. This day is a momentous occasion, one that will burn into the memories of our children for generations. Boysenberry, King of the Fair Folk, eagerly awaits your arrival. Please, follow me." As the little Gnome finished speaking, the Red Caps rushed in and circled the Dwarves. Nickle and Jason instantly hefted their axes, but Hampshire gestured for them to put them down. Everything they possessed that could even remotely be called a weapon—including their Dwarf armor—was taken from them. They were given a set of clothes to wear made from leaves.

As Nickle changed in a private room, he kept imagining the leafy clothes flaking away as he walked until he was left completely naked. This concern, however, was quickly resolved as he put the clothes on. They felt and looked like leaves—they even smelled like leaves—but the Gnomes had done something to them to make them stronger, more resilient. He felt as comfortable wearing his leafy clothes as anything he had ever worn.

After they were dressed, the troop of Gnomes marched them through the immense golden doors and into the famous city of Tiran 'Og. The room they entered was pillared with trees and rocks that had been painstakingly carved. Huge, shimmering crystals hung from the ceiling. Off to the right, a massive fountain hissed out clouds of steam and jets of water. There were hundreds of Gnomes in every direction, all of them topped off with either a droopy red cap or a pointy green one. The Gnomes seemed to consist of all levels of society: Some of them were dressed in eloquent butterfly wings that had been carefully stitched together, while others wore an off-color mix of mushrooms and shrubs that were covered in dirt. It quickly became apparent that the Green Caps were not as wealthy as the more confident and commanding Red Caps.

As they walked, the hall filled with whispers that continued to echo long after they had moved on. They exited the large room and entered into an expansive hallway that was lined with Red Caps, each armed with large cleaving spears made from beetle pincers. Everywhere they looked, there were various doors decorated with exotic plants. The air smelled like honey and roasted peanuts. Before they could exit the hallway, they were ushered into a smaller, holding room, where they waited for the next few minutes.

While they waited, Nickle approached a small yellow sign that he had seen hung up on almost every wall. The writing was written in rough and spotty Gnomish. Nickle could not read it at first, but the more he stared at it, the more it began to make sense to him until he could read the whole thing:

GNOME RULES WHEN DEALING WITH PIDDLERS

1. A GNOME CAN NEVER LEAVE A HUMAN'S PRESENCE UNLESS THAT PIDDLER BREAKS EYE CONTACT.

2. GNOMES CAN NEVER TAKE ANYTHING FROM PIDDLERS UNLESS SOMETHING OF EQAUL VALUE IS LEFT BEHIND.

3. GNOMES CAN NEVER SPEAK TO A PIDDLER EXCEPT ON AN OVERCAST DAY.

4. GNOMES CAN NEVER HELP A PIDDLER UNLESS THE PIDDLER'S NAME IS KNOWN.

5. IF A PIDDLER KNOWS YOUR NAME, YOU MUST ANSWER THEM TRUTHFULLY.

6. GNOMES CANNOT PLAY TRICKS ON PIDDLERS UNLESS IT IS COMMONLY AGREED THAT THE PRANK IS TOO GOOD TO PASS UP.

7. GNOMES CANNOT TAKE AND HIDE THE KEYS OF PIDDLERS SINCE THIS IS A PRANK THAT IS SO OVERUSED BY THE LEPRECHAUNS, IT IS NO LONGER FUNNY.

As Nickle read, he could hear the names of dozens of Gnomes that were being presented before the court. The names all seemed to derive from berries or fruits. Finally, Hampshire's name was called, and the Dwarves entered into a massive circular room lined with decorative cobblestones that changed colors as they walked. Every type of flower that Nickle had ever seen, or had even known about, could be found lining the walls of the room. The flowers stretched up and around the room, almost as if the structure was dependent on the foliage for support. The air was filled with hundreds of fragrances that came at them in sweet waves. Among the plants were bees that busily went from flower to flower, watering and pruning.

As they approached the center of the room, Nickle could see a massive bird's nest that stretched up a good distance above his head. Weaved in and out of the nest was a mix of scarfs that gave it a colorful hue. They walked around the mess of twigs and scarfs until they reached the other side. As they did, a silence fell over the room.

Hampshire turned slightly towards the two other Dwarves. "Stay back and keep your heads down."

Hampshire continued on to two thrones. One of them seemed to be a continuation of the walls around them and was built from a tight mesh of green flowers. The other was constructed of coarse rock and animal bones that had been dyed red. Upon each throne sat a Gnome with sharp eyes. Like their thrones, each Gnome was as different as the sun and the moon. The Gnome seated on the flowery throne was dressed with a mix of wildflowers and butterfly wings that were seamlessly pieced together. The other wore thick-shelled armor made from rose thorns and was topped off with a crown fashioned from the skull of some animal. As Hampshire walked closer, he quickly became the focus of everyone's gaze.

The King on the flowery throne stood up and smiled broadly. "Welcome Dwarf Lords, Builders of EarthWorks, Keepers of the Old Treasures. Hampshire, it's pleasant to see you on this already pleasant day. We thank Mother Earth for your safe journey here and your regal presence—"

"Regal presence!" interrupted the Gnome Lord on the red throne. "This Dwarf is the same Dwarf that led the attack on one of our outposts not two weeks ago. Who invited a Dwarf to my son's birthing ceremony?"

The Green Capped King stirred on his throne, his expression slightly annoyed. "I did. As you should have—as is demanded by our customs."

"He's a Tri'Ark spy, sent to butter us up and force us into slavery," the Red Cap Lord replied. "These bearded swine have long since neglected Mother Earth and sold their souls for her treasures."

"Reckle Berry!" the other King yelled. "Do not appraise our guests with less respect than you appraise yourself. We're from the Clan of UnderBridge, the oldest clan of Gnomes."

"Hah, Boysenberry," Reckle replied. "You don't know what Dwarves are capable of. I've seen the worst they can bring; I know what they can do. I don't treat guests like dogs unless they are dogs. You've tricked me into permitting these Dwarves to come here this night, but I'll not again be deceived by the Tri'Ark or the petty Dwarves they use as puppets. I remember well the misery they have brought to this people, and I have made a sacred oath never to let it happen again."

"And I hope that you don't—that's your job—but this night is one of celebration, not one of finding fault. They are here as our guests, and under the law, they will be protected."

"Then protected they shall be," Reckle hissed. "But just because I won't kill them this night, does not mean I'll forget or forgive their sins. We are the UnderBridge clan, and we were the ones that freed the Gnomes from the captivity of the Tri'Ark. No other clan came to our aid. We did not depend on the Gypsum Gnomes and their fruit-filled gardens, nor the White Wingers and their host of domesticated birds; the Underlings were busy helping Piddlers, and the BlackBerries were too disorganized and disheveled to lend a hand. Where were the Grinning Cappers, and the Strawberries? Where were the Laughing Gippers and the Yellow Jakes? Make no mistake, we must be on guard because our enemy of old now entreats us as a new guest. And when this guest finally becomes our enemy, it will be the Clan of Underbridge that will stand against them."

The room filled with applause that was so loud it shook several of the wallflowers to life.

Boysenberry clenched his jaw. "Thank you for your stirring...speech, Reckle Berry. But let us forget our differences; let us put aside the ills of the past." Before Reckle Berry could reply, Boysenberry clapped his hands. "Green Caps, bring in the tables and chairs. Let's not forget the reason we're here: To celebrate the birth of Reckle Berry's first child."

When Boysenberry finished, the space filled with movement as hundreds of Green Caps began scurrying around the room, eagerly carrying all types of furniture and articles of food. Within moments, the audience hall turned into a banquet hall. Thousands of sea-shell plates were set on the table along with pine needle forks and spoons. A flourish of cups fastened from nuts appeared next.

Nickle and Jason found themselves forced into two plush chairs. The cushions melded around their bodies and quickly became the most comfortable thing either of them had ever sat upon. The four nutshell cups in front of each of them were filled with various juices and ciders.

Each Green Cap server carried a slender skewer that held various cooked vegetables. Whenever someone wanted a particular food, they simply had to put one finger to the side of their head and nod towards the server. Nickle and Jason did not understand the process at first, but the sweet smell that filled the room quickly encouraged them to learn. Soon, they were so adept at ordering, they required two extra plates to hold their collection of food. None of the items the servers brought were meat—although some of it tasted just like it. There were mounds of roasted mushrooms and cucumbers, stacks of buttered squash and roasted asparagus, troves of roasted tomatoes, fried green beans, and buttery bread. Some of the mushrooms tasted so much like steak that, with their eyes closed, neither Jason nor Nickle could tell it was a fungus. There were dozens of different mushrooms to try, each with a distinct flavor. Sometimes the servers would bring out fresh, grilled pineapple that was so tender and juicy it left one's face dripping with satisfaction. The food was so tantalizing, Nickle quickly forgot that he was not hungry and stuffed his body with everything he thought it could hold.

Hampshire had been assigned a chair close to the two Gnome leaders and away from the other two Dwarves—which turned out to be a stroke of good fortune for Jason and Nickle. The two boys were so eager to eat that all the civility they had ever possessed was seemingly put on hold. They quickly had competing grease stains on their faces and drips of food down their chests. Despite their wretched appearances, they seemed to fit right in with the lively Gnomes that dined all around them.

About halfway through the meal, music started to flow from the flowers. The notes were soft and delicate, almost as if they were carried by a gentle wind. The tune was different than anything that either of the Dwarves had ever heard. It began so naturally, so lofty, that it seemed to lift the listeners out of their seats. But it soon became so passionate and invigorating that Nickle could not help but imagine himself in the midst of combat, fighting for his life against all odds. As the music tempo quickened, several dozen Gnomes stood up and began to dance. The dance was formal and structured, with several couples lining up and weaving around each other. Many times, the dancers in the middle would form various shapes of flowers or plants that shifted during the dance. As the music progressed, so did the complexity and difficulty of the dance.

Just before noon, Reckle Berry stood up, knocking over a nutshell filled with a fruity wine. The drink spilled out and splashed across the floor, drenching a small furry caterpillar that was apparently a common pet in Tiran 'Og. The Gnome Lord dramatically raised his hand to the sky. "Today, we celebrate the birth of my son—the firstborn of the line of Berry. Let the ceremony begin!"

A cloaked Gnome suddenly appeared in the middle of the court. In one hand, he carried a single seed; in the other, he held a glowing sphere. Just as the Gnome began to speak, the lights dimmed. "Gnomes and Gnames, gentlemen and gentlewomen, honored Kings and Queens, and...Dwarves. Our history is an ancient one, one that bends back before time even existed. When the first hawk was formed from the hand of Freyr, it built a nest—just as great and grand as the nest we have built here. In the nest, the hawk laid two eggs, one a brilliant blue, the other a vibrant green. During that time, the Great Fire that was caused by the Dwarves was scorching the land, burning everything in its path. As the flames passed, the great Hawk covered her eggs, protecting them with her life. Despite her great sacrifice, only one egg survived the blaze. As the Hawk died, two tears dripped down her noble face and splashed against the egg. From these tears, the first Gnomes came to be. The Gnomes took the egg and kept it warm and safe, tending it until it finally hatched. From its depths, came all the creatures of the Earth. And that's why Gnomes are the only race that matters: We are the adopted parents of every living creature upon the Earth—including the Piddlers that walk about with foolish looks on their faces. It is in this tradition that we have built this nest to commemorate the firstborn of Reckle Berry—the Red Cap Lord."

The Gnomes burst into applause.

"And now," The Gnome screamed, "at the stroke of noon, Reckle's baby will take its first breath!"

Nickle looked down at his wrist, but he did not have a watch. He looked around the room, scanning the walls for a clock, but nothing seemed too promising. It must have been close to noon because the next moment, a Gnome yelled, "A BOY IS BORN!"

The Gnomes turned into a frenzied mob. Red and Green Caps were flung in every direction as Gnomes screamed in delight. One excited Gname grabbed Jason's head and kissed him on the cheek before he could protest. Reckle Berry ran down his throne and into the bird's nest. He disappeared for only a moment before he reappeared a second later, this time holding a little pink Gnome wrapped in olive leaves.

"My son is born!"

Again the crowd thundered with approval. "Brighten the lights! Let the Clan of UnderBridge see their future Red Cap Lord."

Certain flowers suddenly became as bright as the mid-day sun. As the lights went on, everyone fell to their knees. Whether it was because they were disoriented by the brightness of the light or they were trying to get a better look at the baby Gnome, Jason and Nickle kept their feet.

One of the Gnomes closest to Nickle tugged on the Dwarf's clothes and mumbled in slurring Gnomish, "Down on your knees. Down on your knees."

Nickle shook his head. "Sorry, I don't speak Gnome."

With all the Gnomes on the floor, the two Dwarves stood out like a set of roses in a garden of lilies. The dynamics of the room changed as Reckle Berry spotted the two Dwarves. First, Reckle felt surprise ripple through his body, and then anger, but then his emotions shifted to something he had never felt before. It was an emotion hard to describe to anyone that has never felt it. It is like when someone loses a favorite toy when they are young and then finds it later in life. A rush of memories overcame Reckle Berry like a sudden wave crashing against a rocky shore. The Red Cap Lord handed the baby to a servant behind him and whispered, "Take him to his mother." The Gnomes all looked up tentatively, hoping to see the cause of the interruption to the ceremony.

Reckle Berry stepped closer to Nickle—the expression on his face unreadable. He narrowed his eyes and sucked in a sharp breath, scrutinizing the Dwarf. Long moments passed before Nickle decided he better kneel.

He was halfway to the ground when Reckle Berry grabbed his shoulder and pulled him back up. "Is that you, Joshua?"

Nickle swallowed. "No…"

"But…I swear you're him. What happened to your eyes?"

"—My last name is Brickle'Bee, …but my first name is Nickle."

Reckle stared at the Dwarf for several moments. Slowly, a twist of rage began rising up his throat. The Red Cap Lord turned around and pointed a bent finger towards Hampshire. "What is this treachery? How dare you try to fool me! How dare you attempt your Tri'Ark tricks on me!"

Hampshire stood from his kneeled position and approached the Lord. "This is no treachery. This is my new aid, Nickle Brickle'Bee, son of Joshua Brickle'Bee. I know it is hard to believe, Reckle Berry, but it's as true as I'm standing here. I saw the reports of his lineage myself."

Reckle Berry spat on the ground. "You had me fooled for a moment, Dwarf, but I will not remain the fool. Joshua died—and you Dwarves dishonored his memory by saying he turned Troll. This is not his son—he couldn't be."

Nickle stepped forward, his gaze steady. "I am the son of Joshua." Several hundred Gomes gasped. As if the room had suddenly filled with snakes, a thousand Gnomes began to whisper. All eyes fell onto Nickle. The Dwarf felt a panic trickle down his throat and settle in his stomach. He took a deep breath and let it out slowly. "Although I have never met him, I am the son of Joshua Brickle'Bee."

Reckle laughed, a deep gut-wrenching laugh that filled the hall.

"Boy, you are nothing more than a Tri'Ark trick, sent down here to gain our trust so we'll sign your new peace treaty. Have you no honor for the memory of a great Dwarf? You don't have any idea who Joshua is, nor do you have any idea what he has done for us. He had so much talent and skill that if you were his son, you'd have at least a portion of it. But you look more like a frightened kitten—not the son of a great Dwarf Lord."

Nickle looked up, a flash of light in his eyes. "The same blood that ran through Joshua's veins now runs through mine. I am his son."

Hampshire stepped closer. "I have the papers here to prove it—"

Reckle Berry turned towards the voice. "Papers can be forged…and Dwarves can lie."

"What are you saying, oh great Lord?" Hampshire asked.

"Joshua was the only Dwarf to ever win with the chariot, and even if a portion of his magical talent passed down to you, you should be able to do just as well."

Nickle shook his head. "I don't know anything about chariots. And why does it matter who my father is anyway—"

Reckle stepped towards Hampshire. "—Because Dwarf, if you aren't Joshua's son, then we'll have proof of the Tri'Ark's treachery." The Gnome stepped closer to Hampshire. "It's usually a spineless Dwarf that comes to our gates to broker out a deal of peace, but today—if I may be so bold—let me make you Dwarves an offer. If this is truly the son of Joshua, then I challenge him to compete in the Quintillian Games."

The Gnomes and Gnames gasped as the challenge was issued. A dark-skinned Gnome yelled out to the court. "A challenge has been issued!"

"If this is truly the son of Joshua," Reckle Berry continued, "he would relish the chance—as his father did two hundred years ago."

"And why would we want him to do that?" replied Hampshire.

Reckle continued, an idea forming in his head. "If he wins, then I'm at fault, and I'll admit my poor judgment. But, if he loses, I want you Dwarves to leave our land and never return."

"That's a hefty wager," Hampshire said with a weak smile. "He may be Joshua's son, but he's still a Tenderfoot. He's barely graduated from his first year at Tortugan. He hardly knows anything about…well…anything."

"Then—Dwarf—let me make this a fair wager. If this supposed son of Joshua wins, I'll sign your peace treaty. I'll allow free trade between my people and the Tri'Ark."

Hampshire shook his head, sweat beading on the sides of his neck. "He's just a boy—"

"—That's my offer, Dwarf. You have one chance to acquire the thing you seek. Accept my challenge—or admit to me that this boy is another trick of the Tri'Ark. If you confess to me right now, before all these witnesses, that this boy has no connection to Joshua, I may let you live."

Hampshire met eyes with Reckle Berry. "But the boy has no training—no expertise with the chariot."

"Joshua trained for one month before the Games," Reckle replied. "I will postpone the Games so he can be trained."

"But who will train him?" Hampshire replied. "There's not a Dwarf that knows anything about the Quintillian Games."

"He will be trained by Thistle, the greatest Charioteer trainer in all of Tiran 'Og, and he will be allowed to use one of my own personal teams. Are there any more excuses you want to make, Dwarf?"

Hampshire swallowed, his face turning slightly pale. "Let me have a few words alone with the boy. You and I both know what this means, but Nickle does not."

"Losing your courage so quickly?" Reckle mocked. "You have one minute to discuss, another minute to decide."

Hampshire bowed low, "Thank you, oh great Lord, for your consideration." With this, he pulled Nickle back into the waiting room. Jason followed. Once inside, they looked around, making sure the place was empty.

"That's my plan, Nickle," Hampshire said. "It didn't happen exactly as I envisioned, but it'll work just as well."

"What's your plan?" Nickle replied.

"Your father is the only Dwarf to ever compete in the Quintillian Games. Not only that, but he won the first time he raced. Joshua was a fine spokesman, but without his skill at the chariot, he would have never been able to broker a peace treaty with the Gnomes."

"What are the Quintillian Games?" Jason asked.

"It's the only sport that Gnomes seem to enjoy," Hampshire replied. "It's chariot racing, and it can be a rather violent affair."

"This was your plan?" Jason said in disbelief.

"When I saw Jason driving those pigs around the camp, I recognized, the lad had talent. But when you drove the cart, Nickle, you were so much better."

"Hey," Jason protested.

Hampshire continued, undisturbed by the interruption. "I've only seen one other person handle a team of creatures like that, and that was your father. Your family seems to have some sort of connection with animals, or something that gives you an advantage at racing."

"Why didn't you tell me this before?" Nickle asked.

"Your surprise had to be genuine for us to pull this off," Hampshire replied.

"So, I just drive a team of pigs around a track?" Nickle asked.

"No, it's so much more than that," Hampshire said. "Listen, my boy. I've tried everything—everything I can think of to broker a peace treaty with the Gnomes. I've begged, threatened, pleaded, bribed, and persuaded. None of it works with Reckle Berry. I've even suggested they let me compete in the Quintillian games, but Reckle always has refused. This is not only our best shot; this is our only shot."

"How dangerous is this race?" Jason asked.

For the first time, Hampshire nervously took a step back. "I won't lie to you Dwarves. Death is a real possibility on the course. What's more, there may be a few Gnomes that try to target you specifically during the race."

"Death?" Jason arched his eyebrows. "Yeah, I think that's a hard pass."

Hampshire took in a deep breath.

Suddenly, there was a knock at the door. A muffled voice from the other side came through. "The Great Red Lord has ordered me to instruct you that you only have a minute left to decide."

Nickle turned around and looked down at the floor. It was several moments before he turned back around and headed for the door.

"Wait, what did you decide?" Hampshire asked. "Where are you going?"

"Probably headed for the exit," Jason suggested. "I know I would be."

Nickle opened the door in a rush, Hampshire and Jason following quickly behind. The hall was noisy as Nickle approached Reckle, his chin held high, but with each step he took, the clamor decreased. Soon it was deathly silent. Gnomes pulled back and away from Nickle as if he was infected with a disease.

Nickle took to the center of the hall, his chest inflated. "If I win, Reckle, then I only want one thing from you."

Reckle shifted his weight to his back foot, intrigued. "And what's that?"

"If I win, Reckle, the only thing I personally ask is that you be honest with me about my father."

Reckle frowned. He had not expected that response. He studied Nickle more closely now, as if he was really starting to consider if this was Joshua's son. Then in a whisper, he answered, "Agreed."

Nickle raised his voice so all the Gnomes could hear. "Then, I, Nickle Brickle'Bee, Tenderfoot in the Silver Army and son of Joshua Brickle'Bee, accept your challenge."

Chapter 18

Garbage Run

"What do you mean you don't want to go?" Nickle asked.

"I don't want to waste my precious time visiting an Elf girl," Jason replied, "...especially to take out her trash. It will take us several hours just to get there, and then several hours back. We'll return to camp late, and we've still got to wake up early tomorrow."

Nickle rolled his eyes as he entered the Taxi-Lator. "I can't believe you. Not even a week ago, you almost got us both killed so you could have the chance to dance with an Elf. Now, you get to meet one face to face, and you're dragging your feet."

"Yeah, but we're going to take out her trash."

Nickle nodded. "We might get some information out of her."

"Information? Are you kidding? The only thing she knows is that she's rich and we're not. She better be good looking, or I'm leaving early. We should be with the Gnomes, practicing with the chariot."

Nickle shook his head as the Taxi-Lator shot off into the sky. Several hours later, they were once again in the Elf Quarter. Nickle led the way with a pace that was quicker than a walk, but too slow to be considered a jog. His eyes darted from street to street as they went, scanning for possible Vamps.

After a while, Jason realized what he was doing and let out a loud scoff. "Don't worry about it, Nickle. It's only six. There's no way we'll see any Vamps right now."

"How do you know the time?"

"I swallow Time Runes once a week."

"What?"

"They're pricey, but it sure beats carrying a Piddler watch."

"How do they work?"

"Well, you just swallow one and for the next week, you always know what time it is."

Nickle nodded, but did not slow down his pace. The two Dwarves ended up becoming lost in a maze of Elf buildings. They would have asked for directions, but the Elves barely acknowledged their presence—let alone answer their questions. Jason even grabbed a few of them by the arm, but the Elves shrugged themselves free and continued on. The only ones that offered even the slightest bit of help were some Elf children playing a game involving hovering discs.

Finally, Nickle and Jason found themselves in front of the little dog door Nickle had used several days ago.

"This is how we get in there?" Jason asked.

"Yeah, I suppose," Nickle replied. "I don't know how I fit through there the first time. I guess having a Vamp on your tail is a good motivator."

"Why don't we just find the front door and knock."

Nickle shook his head. "What if someone else besides her answers the door? What if her dad answers? We could be arrested by the Praetorian Guard before we had a chance to explain ourselves. She'll be expecting me to come this way anyway."

"Well," Jason said as he gestured towards the door, "you first."

Nickle nodded. "Just do me a favor. If she's waiting on the other side to spring a trap on me, pull me out by my ankles."

"Will do."

With this, Nickle kneeled on the ground and let out all his breath. His head fit through easily, but his shoulders quickly became stuck. He wiggled back and forth, trying to force himself the rest of the way. The small dog door began to squeak from the movement. He was able to force one shoulder through, but the other resisted. It was not long before the awkward position began causing a numbness along his right arm. He kicked with his legs until his other shoulder was finally freed. With his upper torso through, however, he lost most of the leverage he had with his legs.

"Give me a push," Nickle said.

"Are you kidding?"

"Come on. I'm almost through."

Jason shook his head and began doing his best to shove Nickle the rest of the way. He had to stop a few times and act casual as a couple of Elves passed by. Finally, after both of the boys were heaving for breath, Nickle clawed himself to the other side.

Nickle stood up and dusted himself off. "All right, Jason. Now it's your turn."

"No way."

"What? Come on, let's go."

"That's where the pet goes in and out. There's no telling what drool or pee might be left behind. Go find the girl and get her to open the door."

"You chicken." Nickle turned away from the fence, took one step, and almost collided with Sharlindrian.

The Elf hissed. "Who is that?"

"That's Jason."

"And why is he here?"

Nickle shrugged his shoulders. "I thought he could help take out the trash. I assume there's a lot to carry if you didn't want to do it yourself."

The Elf folded her arms and turned away. "You wretched Dwarves. I can barely stand the sight of one of you…"

Nickle scoffed. "Well, if you let him in, we'll take out the trash twice as fast and be on our way. I would hate for your delicate eyes to be irritated by our sight for too long."

Sharlindrian whipped around. "Fine. But you're responsible for him. If he does something stupid, then you'll be the one in trouble." With this, she approached the wall, whispering something under her breath. A moment later, the wall shifted and sputtered, shaking as if it had caught a sudden cold. Like a door, it cracked and flipped open, revealing the roguish grin of Jason Burntworth, who seemed to think that somehow it was by his talent the wall had suddenly opened.

The Elf frowned as she studied the Dwarf; Jason's expression also seemed to change.

The two spoke in unison. "I know you."

Sharlindrian shook her head. "Of all the Dwarves you have to bring, you bring the cockiest one of them all."

Jason pointed at himself. "Me! Oh, please, don't even start—you treacherous snake."

"I'm the snake? I don't spend my time flirting with people that are already taken."

"How was I supposed to know?"

"You're a Dwarf—you're supposed to know that you're not

good enough for me."

Jason threw his hands up. "That's it. I'm outta here."

"Wait," Nickle stood between the two with a look of awe on his face, "how do you know each other?"

Jason crossed his arms. "Remember that Elf I was telling you about—the one that distracted me long enough for a group of thugs to knock me over the back of the head."

Sharlindrian rolled her eyes. "It was not a group of thugs; it was one Elf. And he did not knock you over the back of the head. It was a fair fight—one that you lost."

Jason broke eye contact while he rubbed the back of his neck. "I don't know what story you remember, lady, but that's crazy talk. I was only twelve at the time, untrained and unprepared..."

"That's really fascinating that you guys both know each other," Nickle said with a sarcastic tone, "but let's just do this thing and be on our way. You won't have to see us again—until the next time we take out your trash."

Sharlindrian and Jason stared at each other, neither one willing to back down. Finally, Jason let out a huge sigh. "Fine. He's right. Let's just take out your trash and be on our way—" As he spoke, he stepped out of the alley and onto the lawn. The moment he did, however, Jason's skin began to burn, almost like he was an ant caught under a magnifying glass. Violent pain shot through his body, forcing him to the floor. He tried to take a step back, but his legs buckled underneath him.

Nickle pulled out a Rune from his side and looked around for some unseen attacker. "What's happening to him? What are you doing to him? Sharlindrian, stop whatever you're doing!"

The Elf shook her head, caught in a daze. "It's not me...it's the Hex."

Jason's arms were starting to turn red. Moments later, they were crimson.

"Well," Nickle replied. "Stop it!"

Sharlindrian stepped forward and placed her elegant hands on Jason's forehead. This simple gesture abated the lightning pain that was shooting through his body, but it did not stop it. "We need to get him some honey! Nickle, grab his legs. I'll get his arms. I have some honey in the kitchen."

Nickle approached Jason and hefted him over his shoulder. "I'll carry him. You just lead the way."

Sharlindrian nodded and took off with Nickle close behind. It was not long before they entered a gigantic home that was exquisitely crafted. The floor was tiled with marble and covered with large plush rugs. Almost every room had a fireplace that was as tall as the space was wide. Massive wood columns stretched up and out to an elegantly carved ceiling.

Sharlindrian entered the kitchen and pointed to a far table. "Place him over there."

Nickle obeyed and gently placed Jason on the table, accidentally knocking over a few wooden bowls. Sharlindrian showed up a second later with a jar of honey. Without wasting a second, she opened Jason's mouth with one hand and poured honey with the other. In a somewhat anticlimactic fashion, the honey slowly slid into Jason's mouth. As soon as it hit his tongue, the heat from Jason's body disappeared. Despite the soothing effect the honey seemed to have, the Dwarf lost all consciousness.

"What happened?" Nickle asked. "Did you kill him?"

Sharlindrian shook her head. "He's fine—as fine as a Dwarf will ever be. He just needs a few minutes to recover, and then he will be as ugly as he was before."

"What happened back there?"

"It's the home. It has a powerful Hex on it. If anything that is not an Elf or Faerie enters the property, this is what happens to them. It's not fatal, even if they never receive honey. It just incapacitates them until they can be dealt with. If your Dwarf friend was any good at magic, he should've been able to counter the Hex."

"Why didn't you warn him?"

The Elf collapsed onto a fluffy chair. "It's not my fault. I didn't think it was working. I mean...look at you. You're on the property, and you're just fine. It should have crippled you just as much as it did Jared."

"His name is Jason."

"That's what I said."

Nickle shook his head and collapsed into a chair that was next to Sharlindrian, who promptly slid her chair away. The two stared at each other for an awkward moment, trying to guess what the other was thinking.

Finally, Sharlindrian spoke. "I didn't know...that Dwarves were so strong."

Nickle nodded. "And I didn't know Elves were so paranoid."

"Well, you would be too if..."

"If what?"

"If you heard half the rumors I do."

Nickle rolled his eyes. "I've never even seen another person on this property before. Who's telling you rumors?"

"You don't see anyone else here because no one else lives here. This is my house. I live here alone."

"Are you serious? This place is big enough to fit a whole football field inside."

"What's a football field?"

Nickle shook his head. "It's a...well, forget about it. You live here alone?"

"Well, wouldn't you live here if all this was yours?"

"Yes, maybe, but that still doesn't answer my question. Where are your parents?"

"I live on my own."

"Really," Nickle furrowed his eyebrows. "Answer me this then. What's up with the Hex? Why are you so paranoid? What could a wealthy Elf, such as yourself, have to fear?"

"The same thing every decent person with money fears—the escape of Kara'Kala."

Nickle took a deep breath. "He can't escape...he's trapped behind a wall of fire that's as tall as a football field is long."

"Again, with the football field. What is a football field?"

"It's nothing...just a measurement Piddlers use. But tell me, how could Kara'Kala be coming back? I mean, everyone turned against him."

"Not everyone—hardly anyone really. One thing that everyone tends to forget is that most people were for him, at least in the beginning. Even later on, people were never really against him. Some people hailed him as a hero—a warlord that was about to lead the attack against the Piddlers."

"If he was so great, why does everyone talk about how evil he was?"

Sharlindrian laughed. "Because no one wants to champion the

side that lost. History is written by the victors. Most people did not know how vile he was until he was imprisoned. Even then, it took years for people to come to grips with the idea that their champion was really a Demon. He was a fantastic speaker, both passionate and powerful. His words held you captive—almost as if they were magic. It was not until later that everyone discovered he was secretly ordering hits on his political opponents."

"He was ordering hits on people?"

"And now, there are whispers that his followers are increasing."

"How's that possible? His side lost."

Sharlindrian nodded. "Elves wouldn't be so cautious if it wasn't possible."

"Were the Vamps that attacked me and Jason part of Kara'Kala's forces?"

"Most likely not. The Vamps are a reaction to Kara'Kala's possible rise to power, not an effort to promote it. Of all the races, the Elves were the most opposed to Kara'Kala. To stop the evil of the Demon Lord, many Elves embraced the Order of Vampires so they would have increased speed and strength."

"That's crazy."

Sharlindrian nodded. "From what my father tells me, I hear that there's a secret movement that's trying to free Kara'Kala."

"The Demon Brood?"

"Every Demon in the Brood was arrested, but that doesn't mean all their supporters were. My father knows of a few Dwarves and Humans alike who support the old regime."

"There's a big difference between reminiscing on the days of Kara'Kala's rule and actively trying to free the Demon Lord."

"My father says that there are plenty of individuals who do both."

Nickle swallowed and stood up. "Well, we better be going."

"Wait," Sharlindrian squeaked, "you didn't take out my trash."

"Where is it?"

She stood and walked over to the other end of the kitchen, where she pointed towards a medium-sized bag of trash. "There it is."

"This is it?" Nickle asked.

Sharlindrian narrowed her eyes. "Yes. How much trash do you expect one person to make in a week?"

Nickle returned to the table, grabbed Jason by the belt, and threw the Dwarf onto his shoulder. "Hand me the bag. We better get going."

"Eh, I'm not going to touch it."

Nickle rolled his eyes, walked a few paces to the trash can, and with a great grunt, bent down until he could reach the bag. With only a little strain showing on his face, he stood.

Nickle smiled and nodded. "Thanks for the information. Can you point us towards the door?"

Chapter 19

The Great Track

The next day, Reckle Berry escorted Nickle, Jason, and Hampshire to a massive stadium at the heart of Tiran 'Og. Inside the stadium was a long system of tunnels that twisted around the audiences' seats in seemingly random directions. On the straightaways, the smaller tunnels joined together into one massive tube that stretched on until the next turn. The air above looked so much like the sky, Nickle had a hard time believing he was still underground.

Nickle could not help but speak. "How does the audience see anything if all the riders are in the tunnels?"

"That's such a Piddler thing to say," Reckle Berry jeered. "I can't believe you thought you could pass this half-breed off as Joshua's son."

Hampshire answered Nickle's question. "A few minutes before the race, magic will change the dirt tunnels, so they're as transparent as water."

"That way," Reckle continued, "everyone in Tiran 'Og will see you fall."

Nickle swallowed, and Reckle continued. "I'll be allowing you to use my own personal team of Hedge Hogs, which is one of the fastest teams that can be found between here and the surface. If you plan on using the excuse that 'you weren't given a good team,' you can forget about it. Every Gnome or Gname with a cap on their head knows these four critters by name. They have been made famous through the dozens of championships that I have won with them." The Red Lord walked briskly to the edge of the stadium and pointed towards two Red Caps. "Bring me the Four Fiends."

Nickle could not see them, but he could hear several Gnomes grunting as they attempted to force some unseen thing through something else. He could hear several animals growling in protest. A few Gnomes screamed in fear. At least once or twice, Nickle could have sworn he heard an animal snap its teeth. The noise grew louder as Reckle's chariot drew nearer. A set of doors opened, sending dust across the floor. Four of the biggest Hedge Hogs Nickle had ever seen stood in the entrance, each of them bearing a massive set of teeth. From almost every part of their body, thick needles poked out. Many of the needles had been sharpened until they resembled small blades. Two of the creatures were grey, one was black, the last one was a mix of the other three. Nickle tried to imagine what the Hedge Hogs would have looked like if he was still his original size, but the idea of it kept his head spinning.

Reckle Berry ran towards the creatures, embracing each one as if it were his child. The critters stopped baring their teeth as their master patted them on the head. Two of them began purring, a third one looked like it was smiling. Reckle Berry flipped around, his thorn armor bouncing menacingly as he did. He walked straight over to Nickle's face and gritted his teeth, much like the Hedge Hogs had done. "Are you sure you can handle my team—son of Joshua?"

Nickle matched the Gnome's gaze. "Sure…yeah…I'll give it a go."

"It's not too late to change your mind—if you admit that you are not really the son of Joshua."

"He is my father," Nickle replied evenly.

Reckle frowned. "Fine, use this ruse until you're killed by it. Do you know how many skilled riders were severely injured last year? Seventeen. Do you know how many years a rider trains before they are even allowed to enter the Quintillian Games? Ten. If you compete, the best you can hope for is to stay alive."

Nickle stepped forward to speak, but no reply came to his lips.

Reckle let out a low and bitter laugh. "In four weeks, you'll enter into the track and prove whether you're truly the son of Joshua." With this, the Red Cap Lord turned around and exited the arena, flanked by his royal escort.

"That Gnome is pretty high-strung," Jason said.

Moments later, the smallest Gnome Nickle had ever seen suddenly appeared from around the Hedge Hogs. "My name is Thistle, and I'll be teaching you everything you possibly can learn about something that can't really be taught."

Thistle was small and, much like his name suggested, he quickly became annoying. He began by having both Nickle and Jason run laps through the tunnels that wrapped around the arena. It seemed pointless—especially since Nickle would be riding and not running in the race. It was only after Thistle was thoroughly convinced that Nickle knew every bump and turn on the track that he was allowed near the animals.

"First," Thistle said. "We have to see if the Hogs will take kindly to you. If they don't, then there's no point in teaching you how to drive a chariot because none of the critters will let you." Nickle was then given a bottle of flowery perfume and instructed to put it on liberally before he groomed the Hogs each day. The aroma allowed Nickle to get close, but it did not seem to endear the creatures to him. It was not until the Dwarf was finally allowed to feed them that he made any progress. Much to Thistle's surprise, the Hedge Hogs took to the Dwarf rather quickly.

Despite having been bitten by the thorny creatures several times, Nickle rather enjoyed them. Each of them had a distinctly different personality. First, there was Amaryllis—the prideful one. She was twice as fierce and stubborn as the other three combined. Her burly nature made her ideal for the outside position of the chariot where, Thistle claimed, other Charioteers are most likely to attack. Amaryllis was big and black, had longer than normal spikes, and a massive set of teeth—of which Nickle could attest. Next was Azalea—the passionate one. She was by far the fastest and was harnessed in the middle of the chariot, where she could set the pace for the others to follow. Then came Arbutus and Arbullian, identical twins that not only looked alike, but also ran alike. Usually, one Arbu twin was placed on the outside, while the other was placed two spots over. Despite the separation between them, the twins were so connected, they were able to run in sync, which helped the team to be as smooth as a swan gliding through water.

Each of the Hedge Hogs had a golden harness strapped around their bodies that was connected to a metal bar that ran under their bellies. The bar was then connected to a beam that was hooked to a golden colored chariot. The chariot was made from a coconut that had been eloquently carved. A set of golden olive leaves were fastened to the rim and sides of the chariot, giving it a regal appearance. The whole thing was controlled by two thick reins made from spell hardened grass that was attached to each of the Hedge Hogs. When all four were harnessed together, ready to run the track, Nickle felt a ripple of adrenaline race through his body.

After three days of training, Thistle began explaining the fundamentals of driving the team. It was more difficult than it looked, especially since the track was so twisted and confusing. Along the turns, gravity did not seem to exist, and the drivers were able to drive along the walls and ceiling with no difficulty. Once leaving the turns, however, a driver had to be sure to no longer be on the walls or ceiling as gravity returned. The course was hazardous and expansive. Roots of all colors and sizes would periodically appear, blocking the path ahead. Sometimes other creatures were set loose on the track but, as Nickle was constantly assured, that was only in preliminary games— not in the championship race he would be competing in.

Eventually, Nickle was allowed to enter the chariot. The first time he whipped the Hedge Hogs forward, however, he was thrown completely out of the chariot. It took seven Gnomes over ten minutes to chase down the creatures and return them to the starting line. As the Gnomes were bringing the chariot around, Nickle was still shaking off the dust from his arms and legs.

Thistle shook his head as he approached the Dwarf. "These critters are a lot faster than you think, a lot faster than any Hedge Hog Piddlers might have owned. They have been bred for speed for the last seven thousand years. You can't whip them forward and expect to stay on if you're not balancing your weight properly. Hang on to the bar. Lean forward."

Nickle frowned as he whispered. "Now, he tells me."

"Come on," Thistle said. "Get back up there. This time I'll come with you."

The Dwarf grunted, but he did not protest as the two of them stepped on to the chariot. No sooner had Nickle latched his right hand on to the railing did the team of Hogs take off in a sudden burst of speed. Nickle's face was immediately flapping in the wind, like a flag that had been unfurled during a windstorm.

As they went, Thistle yelled out instructions to Nickle. "You need to trust your team. You're nothing more than a rudder on a boat. All you need to do is point them in the right direction."

A set of black roots that looked like hairy spider legs suddenly appeared in front of them. Nickle immediately reacted by veering to the right—barely dodging the roots. Thistle grinned.

They rode on and on, circling through the track until they passed through every tunnel at least once. Nickle noticed that the large tubes were usually more direct, but they also had a greater array of roots and obstacles.

Thistle glanced back at the Dwarf. "The roots will be nothing compared to the threat of the other riders. It's illegal to use weapons or magic on another Charioteer, but everyone does. I don't suggest you play dirty, however; you'll be more closely scrutinized than anyone else. Gnomes will be looking for a reason to disqualify you."

Nickle nodded.

"All right, boyou," Thistle said, "now it's time to start going at racing speeds."

"What do I do?"

"Slap the reins down onto the backs of the Hogs," Thistle replied. Nickle obeyed and the animals surged forward. The Dwarf smiled at the dump of adrenaline that hit his bloodstream.

Thistle nodded. "That's it. You want some tension in the reins, but not too much. If you need to turn, gently pull on the side that you want to turn. The harder you pull, the harder you'll turn."

Nickle grinned. "And how do I go faster?"

Thistle gave a quick gaffe. "You just might be the son of Joshua. If you whip the reins down on their backs several times in a row, they'll break into an all-out gallop. But I don't think you're—"

Nickle snapped the reins down in quick succession. "Let's see what they can do." He whipped the reins down hard until the Hedge Hogs were at full speed. They entered a small tunnel, the large wheels of the chariot echoed as they did. Nickle felt something come alive in him, a warmth that quickly spread throughout his body. His eyes sharpened on the tunnel before him, gauging the turns and angles that were to come. They whipped around a turn, and for a moment, one wheel came off the ground.

"Easy," Thistle yelled. "Any fool can drive the straightaways, but it takes a great driver to manage the turns."

"I can do this," Nickle whispered.

A sudden root sprang from the ground. Nickle maneuvered

the chariot to the left and glided along the wall. Another root sprouted and Nickle was forced to veer so hard to the right, they ended up on the ceiling. The change in gravity made Nickle's head spin, but it did not put a second of hesitation into his movements. *"I have to get good at this. I have to earn Reckle's trust."* He drove the chariot back to the floor just before they exited the tunnel and entered a long straightaway. Jason cheered them on as they passed by.

Thistle pointed ahead of them. "Be careful in the small tunnels because it's easy to lose track of which way is up. The small tunnels will make you go faster, but they are certainly more dangerous. I'd stick to the medium-sized tunnels."

Nickle would have obeyed, but Thistle's advice came too late. They plunged into a small tunnel that sent them spiraling like a corkscrew.

"Slow down," Thistle growled.

Nickle pulled back on the reins, but the Hogs barely responded.

"Slow down!" Thistle repeated.

Nickle nodded but, before he could yank the reins harder, a sudden bump in the track shot them out of control. The chariot flipped to its side, spilling Thistle and Nickle out. Nickle was able to hang on to the side of the chariot; the Gnome was able to hang on to Nickle's boot. The chariot dragged the two through the dirt, spraying dust in their faces like water from a sprinkler. They hit a root, and the chariot vaulted into the air. When it landed again, Nickle's grip slipped. He was able to grab a bottom brace of the chariot, but with the weight of Thistle still on his leg, Nickle's hands were quickly losing their grip.

"Let go!" Thistle yelled.

"Are you insane?"

Thistle shook his head. "Let go before both of us are ground into dust!"

Nickle closed his eyes. A moment later, he released his grip on the chariot. They began to roll around like a couple balls of lint caught in a dryer. Nickle ended up on the other side of the track, his arm tucked disjointedly underneath him. Thistle ended up on top of Nickle's back, almost as if he had used the Dwarf as a surfboard.

Nickle shook his head. "Let go? Why did you want me to let go?"

Thistle grinned broadly, a piece of dirt hung loosely from his shabby beard. "I think that's enough practice for one day. Don't worry about the chariot; I'll have the others retrieve it. Impressive stuff, boyou."

"Impressive stuff?"

"Yeah. I have no major injuries, the chariot's not damaged, and you still have a head on your shoulders. To me, that seems like the end of a good practice." The squat Gnome stood up and dusted himself off. "I'll see you tomorrow, Nickle…Brickle'Bee."

The next day was very similar to the day before. They drilled on and on, practicing all sorts of maneuvers with the chariot. Nickle had a natural affinity towards driving, but he was clumsy when it came to dodging the roots that sprang from the ground. He was also not good at maintaining a racing speed that did not completely exhaust the Hogs in the first few laps.

The days quickly turned into a week, and then the weeks into a month. Before Nickle had much confidence in anything he was doing, he found himself dressing up for a regal festival that was set to take place the night before the Quintillian Games. Nickle half wondered if this would be the last social event he would ever attend.

Chapter 20

The Island of 'Og

To say Nickle felt he was out of his element was an understatement. The clothes he now wore starkly contrasted with his more conservative earthy Dwarf attire. He was now wearing a mix of red, yellow, and orange that was so vibrant the colors looked alive. The red in his clothes came from dye made from cherries, the yellow from sunflowers, and the orange came from orange peels. Nickle usually preferred to blend into the crowd rather than stand out in it—especially in places and among people he did not really understand. Now, with this skittle-colored attire, he did not think that melding into the crowd would be a possibility.

His one consolation was that, since Jason was assisting in the chariot race, he too had been forced into a similar, brightly colored outfit. Unlike Nickle, however, Jason rather enjoyed his new set of clothes. No matter what room or hallway he found himself in, whether it was small, dark, damp, or dirty, Jason somehow managed to find a full-body mirror where he could give himself a roguish wink before walking on. He also kept sniffing his clothes, like some hound on the hunt, enjoying the sweet scent that wafted up and tickled his nose.

The two Dwarves exited their changing rooms and entered a hallway that was so long that it seemingly had no end. Along the walls, large murals made of thousands of flowers and plants, scurried up until they reached the ceiling far overhead. Even though the hallway was crowded, they made good time as they walked, since Gnomes were practically tripping over themselves to get out of the way of the Charioteers. The Gnomes they passed wore clothes that were a conservative mushroom brown or a watered-down barnyard red. Most of them donned polite, but distant smiles—a few of the Gnames curtsied.

With each passing second, Nickle could feel a knot in his throat tightening like a drum. Even though moments where Nickle was the center of attention were rare, he hated them with a passion that people usually reserve for lifelong enemies. With each glaring eye that fell on him, with each respectful smile and grin he received, he felt his nerves seizing control of his body. By the time he reached the main entrance to where he was supposed to go, his brow was brimming with sweat. The worst part about the whole affair was his hands: He did not know what to do with them. He had suddenly become painfully aware of the awkwardness in his hands and arms, almost as if they had just appeared on his body, and for the first time, he was learning how to use them. He kept folding and unfolding his arms until Jason finally jabbed him in the ribs.

Just inside the archway, Nickle and Jason found themselves at the end of a long line of Gnomes that spiraled down several marble steps and onto an ornate dock. Many of the Gnomes had impatient but excited expressions on their faces as they waited for a ship to dock and take them aboard. At first glance, the vessels on the lake were so numerous and went so many directions, it seemed like they did not have a clear destination. It only took Nickle a few moments of staring off into the distance to realize the end destination of each of the crafts was a massive golden-brown tree that filled the vast cavern. Despite it being a good distance from him, Nickle was entirely overwhelmed by the sheer size of the tree. Even with his normal Dwarf size and stature, the tree would have dwarfed him. He had seen documentaries on massive trees before, seen photos of the supposed "largest" tree in the world, but this monstrosity completely surpassed anything he had seen. It was a magical tree that seemed just as alive as every Gnome around him. From each leaf beamed a blue luminescent light that sparkled through the cavern and skipped across the water. Even though there was no breeze, the tree seemed to sway ever so slightly, almost as if it was breathing.

A high-pitched voice interrupted Nickle's thoughts. "You no wait in line. You Charioteer, right?"

Nickle turned to face the Gname, a distant and lofty expression still attached to her face. "What?"

She was a short, well-groomed Gname. She had a large set of pointy ears that upheld an even larger and pointier green cap. "You…Charioteer?"

Jason stepped forward. "Yeah, he's a Charioteer. And I'm with him."

The Gname nodded importantly and pointed her chin towards the dock. "You no wait in line. Right to front you go."

Jason did not need to be told twice. He immediately broke from the line and headed down the steps, Nickle awkwardly followed behind. Within moments, they were on the dock, walking past the crowd of Gnomes. The Gnomes, almost on cue, opened up the line and waited while Nickle and Jason walked by. They would have made it on the next ship but a large Gnome dressed in white and yellow flowers blocked their path.

The figure turned around, a menacing grimace on his face. The Gnome was huge, about six inches tall. "So, you must be the litl' Dwarfy that is racing?"

Jason nodded and tightened his jaw. "And what of it?"

"Your presence offends me. You dirt-diggers offend this place."

Even though the slight was meant for Nickle, Jason was the one that stepped forward.

"Easy there flower-power, we're not looking for any problems."

The Gnome glared at the Dwarves, frowning with so much disdain that his face looked like a melting candle. "For someone who isn't looking for problems, you two certainly seem to find them." The creature's English was broken and sharp.

Nickle studied the Gnome. "You're dressed in bright colors. Will we be competing together tomorrow? What animals will you be driving?"

The Gnome guffawed. "Competing, no, for I don't consider you competition. If you want to know which chariot I am driving, look for me at the front of the race, for that is where I'll be. You'll have to squint your eyes because I'll be so far ahead."

Nickle half smiled. "What's your name, sir?"

"My name is LuckLock, the Champion Charioteer of the Grinning Cappers." And just to prove he was part of the Grinning Cappers, his face split into a wide, wicked-looking grin.

Nickle bowed his head slightly, "My name is—"

"—not worth knowing," The Gnome interrupted. "Listen,

Dwarfy, this is our land, this is our home. If you think for a second you can parade in here, ordering us all to fall in line, you are *dead* wrong. And after tomorrow, you'll just be *dead*. Just like your father..." Everything the Gnome had said until now had meant nothing to Nickle. He had heard plenty of Gnomes insult him over the last few weeks, but none of that had ever phased him. But with the mention of Nickle's father, the Gnome had traversed into a subject that cut him to the core.

The Dwarf locked eyes with the much taller opponent. Despite the Gnome's size, Nickle knew he was much stronger, and with his training, he was pretty sure it would be a fair fight. He didn't know if it was the Dwarf blood in him, but he just could not back down. He leaned forward and clenched his fists. Something inside of Nickle was pushing for a fight. It was like a little switch had gone off in his head. Any fear or apprehension he had only moments before suddenly evaporated.

Nickle let out a stream of air through his gritted teeth. "No Dwarf should have to hear insults about their father, especially when he has done nothing to deserve it. A Dwarf's father is as sacred as his honor, and you journey dangerously close to starting a fight I don't think you can finish."

"Yeah, flower tower," Jason yelled, "shut your crooked mouth before—"

But he did not have time to finish his sentence before the Gnome rushed in, swinging a fist aimed straight for Jason's head. The movement was so quick and unexpected that it should have easily landed on the Dwarf's cheek, but then with incredible speed, a figure lunged towards LuckLock, knocking the Gnome into a marble handrail. The impact was so horrific that LuckLock flipped backward over the rail and plummeted several inches down into the liquid below. With an explosion of water, the Gnome disappeared from sight.

Jason had to blink twice before he realized who the figure was that saved him from a good punch. "Nickle?"

Nickle himself seemed surprised by what he had done. He looked at his hands just to make sure that he was indeed still himself.

Jason approached his friend, slapping him on the back. "Where was that speed in Tortugan? You've been holding back on me all this time."

A thick silence fell over the crowd. The only noise came from far off Gnomes, who had not witnessed the conflict. Nickle did not seem aware of his surroundings. He stood stone-faced, staring down at LuckLock, who had now managed to resurface and was slowly paddling towards the shore.

Jason's voice turned from amusement to fear as he looked at the Gnomes surrounding them. "Come on, Nickle. It looks like LuckLock had some friends in the crowd."

Nickle ignored him. His jaw was still taut, his fists still clenched.

Jason grabbed the Dwarf by the shoulder. "Come on, Nickle. We better keep moving."

Nickle turned around, suddenly embarrassed by his violent behavior. He had never snapped like that before. Even Jason had been surprised, which was more than difficult to do. Every Gnome in sight had stopped what they had been doing and now stared openly at Nickle, their eyes seemingly burning a hole of guilt in the Dwarf's chest. Several of them had raw anger in their expressions. Instinctively, Nickle grabbed for his Rune belt, but of course, it was not around his waist. He had never been allowed to carry it into Tiran 'Og, despite his many complaints.

"Sorry," he mumbled to the Gnomes.

This feeble apology did not seem to satiate the crowd, all of whom were staring at Nickle as if he had just shattered some sacred relic. Even though his eyes could not see any trace of it, Nickle could feel magic being used, feel the hair on the back of his neck standing up. He knew little about Gnome magic, but he did know it could be deadly. There was a good reason Dwarves were not allowed to sign up for a Gnome Detail without combat experience—and this was it. He knew it would only be a matter of seconds before he would have some sort of burning projectile hurtled towards his chest. With Dwarf armor, the Gnome's projectiles would bounce harmlessly off—at least for a while anyway—but now, with nothing more than fancy Gnome clothes protecting him, who knew how deadly each shot would be.

"Nickle," Jason whispered. "I think we'll have to swim for it. There's no way we can take on all of these Gnomes."

Nickle nodded. "Right. You ready?"

"Stand back! Stand back!" A sharp, crisp voice split the air.

"Out of my way! Out of my way! By order of the King of Tiran 'Og, Boysenberry the Bright, I command you to make way. I'm on official business."

The two Dwarves did not see where the voice was coming from, but they knew it was getting closer. As the voice approached, Nickle expected to see the owner of it, but somehow, the Gnome stayed out of his vision. Moments later, Nickle knew why. A tiny Gnome appeared, dressed in regal gold. The Gnome was so small, he could have easily been mistaken for a child, had it not been for his long white beard and his regal clothing.

"Thistle?" Nickle asked.

"Yes," Thistle replied. "Who did you expect? The Queen of the Faeries?" Thistle, however, did not give any time for a response; instead, he turned his attention back to the crowd. "These people are guests. Have you forgotten what that word means in Tiran 'Og—that ancient word that was indeed created by the Gnomes. Weren't we once guests here in Tiran 'Og ourselves?"

"But he attacked a Gnome!" cried a random voice in the crowd.

"Did he attack a Gnome, or did a Gnome attack him?" Thistle replied. The crowd became a sea of murmurs that waxed and waned as the moments passed. "They are under our protection, and by the laws of Tiran 'Og, they will not be harmed. I have been sent by the King to escort them to the island of 'Og. Come on Dwarves, follow me. Everyone else, make way."

Thistle led the way to the edge of the crowd, but two large Gnomes were standing there who did not look too eager to let the Dwarves just slip away.

Thistle stopped a few paces short of these two Gnomes. "Make way. If I have to say it again, I'll blaze a hole in both of your chests."

This final phrase seemed to have the effect Thistle had been looking for. The crowd parted, leaving a clear path to one of the boats. Thistle slowly walked down the dock, eyeing each of the Gnomes carefully as he passed. He hopped into a small boat, gesturing for the two Dwarves to do the same. Moments later they followed, somewhat haphazardly. They both jumped in at the same time, precariously rocking the ship.

Thistle only shook his head in annoyance. After the boat

settled, the little Gnome looked up at the mast, staring intently at something far above. Out of thin air, a bird appeared, burning bright with fire. It was a large bird, almost the size of a Gnome. It had dark black eyes and feathers that turned into flames.

"What is that?" Jason asked.

"The best Alteration magic has to offer—that's a Phoenix," Thistle said. With that, the Phoenix began to pull the ship by a magical cord. The vessel lurched forward into the direction of the distant island of 'Og.

Nickle sat down on a wood bench that spanned the width of the ship. "How does Alteration magic work? I know the Cennarians use it, as well as many of the creatures in the Beast Quarter."

Thistle shrugged his shoulders. "Actually, that's a common misconception. The Cennarians use Transformation magic, which looks similar, but is vastly different. Cennarians transform things into other things with their magic, like changing air currents into a fiery bird projectile. Our magic is much more powerful. You wouldn't understand. You're a Dwarf, how could you?"

"They can see the magical patterns in normal day stuff," Jason said, "and then they simply adjust the pattern until they get the result they're looking for."

Thistle shook his head. "It's not that easy—"

"Maybe not, but it's not nearly as complicated as you make it out to be."

Thistle frowned. "Leave it to a Dwarf to oversimplify the fabric of Mother Nature. Everything around us has patterns, including the sky, the air we breathe, the food we taste. All of it leaves traces of Mother Nature in them—almost like a signature. It looks like…like…" Thistle's eyes became very distant, "…well, like something you can't imagine, like a colorful tapestry…but it's everywhere you look. You have to be trained to see it just as much as you have to be trained to swim. Some of these patterns can be changed, others can be broken. Mother Nature has to let you change the patterns; she has to let go of her control to allow you to control her. It isn't something you can just do whenever you want, or for whatever purpose. If you aren't in tune with Mother Nature, you won't even be able to see the patterns—let alone change them. Air is the easiest to change—that's what I used to conjure the Phoenix."

"How do you get in tune with Mother Nature?"

"Now, you're asking for answers you really would not understand."

Jason rolled his eyes but did not protest.

Once they reached the island, Thistle jumped on the land, towing a rope attached to the boat over his shoulder. The ship bumped gently against the sandy shore. Nickle noticed that they had not been taken to the large dock that was on the other side of the island. Thistle was either trying to help them avoid problems, or he was too embarrassed to be seen helping the Dwarves.

When Nickle jumped to the shore, he gave Thistle a slight nod. "Thank you for everything. Thank you for getting us out of that mess back there. Most of all, thank you for taking the time to train me with the chariot."

Thistle frowned. "Those were my orders; I had no choice in the matter."

"Still—"

"—I had no choice," Thistle interrupted. "Now listen up and listen good. The only way you two can avoid any trouble tonight is to stay on the edge of the party. There are too many hotheaded Charioteers who would love to introduce their fists to your faces. And yes, I know how tough you both think you are, and yes, I'm sure you'd do fine in a brawl, but if you hit one Gnome, you're bound to find a dozen more that will charge in and hit you in the back. If there's one thing to be said about Gnomes, we stick together—much like you Dwarves. As long as you stay away from Gnomes wearing colors, you shouldn't have a problem. If you stay on the edge of the party, everyone there will hail you as a celebrity and will be offering to get you drinks the entire night."

Thistle led them up several stairs towards the base of the gigantic Mother Tree. Before long, they could hear the sound of a fiddle cutting through the air. The music was so vibrant and fast-paced one could only imagine the kind of party the Gnomes were having. The closer they drew to the noise, the quicker their hearts beat into their chests. Thistle led the way down several stone steps and into a circular tunnel that led a dozen or so inches into the earth. The tunnel opened up into a massive room that went several stories down from where they stood. Gnomes were everywhere, dancing and shouting, eating and drinking, smiling and laughing with intoxicating vigor. Jason was instantly pulled into the crowd by a Gname dressed up like a flower.

Another Gname attempted to pull Nickle to the dance floor, but the Dwarf was too quick. Instead, he pretended that his sandals needed immediate attention.

Thistle laughed. "Not much for crowds are you boyou. Me neither. Come with me, I'll buy you a Honey Nectar."

Nickle smiled, unsure if he should be grateful. When he tasted the Honey Nectar, which was given to him in a flower that had been shaped into a glass, he was grateful. The Honey Nectar was phenomenal, and he proved it by emptying three flowers of it.

Hundreds of Green Cap Gnomes scurried around the massive room, carrying with them an assortment of fruits and vegetables that smelled divine. Nickle was not sure if he was hungry or not, so he took it upon himself to find out. It only took him three bites of a piece of squash for him to realize he was starving. A Green Cap that was wearing shoes way too big for his feet stumbled towards their table with a mix of roasted vegetables. Nickle thought nothing of the large shoes until he saw several more Gnomes who were also stumbling in their tracks.

Nickle took a few bites of a green pepper. "Tell me, Thistle, why do so many of your people wear shoes that don't seem to fit?"

"That's because they're young, too young to fill an adult's shoes. When a Gnome is born, they're given shoes that are too big for their feet. As they grow into that first pair, they are given another pair that's too big. This goes on and on until they grow into their final adult pair."

"How long does that take?"

"Usually, one hundred and twenty years."

"That's a long time to be tripping in your shoes."

"It keeps them humble."

The two ate and ate until their bellies could hold no more. Nickle pressed Thistle for details of Joshua Brickle'Bee, but the Gnome seemed strangely silent on the subject. This was not odd, however, since most Gnomes did not enjoy reminiscing on the past.

"Why is that?" Nickle asked.

"What's that?"

"Why do Gnomes generally avoid talking about anything that

happened more than a week ago?"

"Well," Thistle said through a hiccup. "Part of the reason we don't, is we can't. Most Gnomes perform an Alteration spell on themselves at least once a week that helps them forget the past. They don't forget everything, of course, but it makes everything a little more foggy. It's harder to remember names that way, but people are much nicer to each other if they don't remember the foul things they've done."

The more questions Nickle asked about the Fair Folk, the more distant and preoccupied Thistle became. Finally, the Gnome slapped the table and stood up, which made him only slightly taller than when he was sitting down. "Come with me, boyou. There's something I've got to show you."

Nickle swallowed. "What about Jason?"

"He'll be fine—as long as he stays in this area."

"That's what I'm worried about...," Nickle whispered. Despite his reservations, the Dwarf followed the Gnome through a small tunnel that led to the surface.

Thistle frowned as they walked. "I did know your father. Not as well as Reckle did, but I did spend a few weeks with him, teaching him techniques on the chariot. He was very talented."

"What do you know about my father? Do you know what he was working on when he died?"

Thistle gave a light laugh. "So, you don't think your father turned Troll, eh?"

"No," Nickle shook his head, "that doesn't make any sense."

"No, it doesn't," Thistle replied, "and no matter how many petitions, and envoys Reckle sent to the Tri'Ark, pleading to widen the investigation, the Tri'Ark insisted that Joshua had turned troll. It was a cover-up, and every Gnome knows it. That's why Gnomes either love you, or they hate you, Nickle. On the one hand, you are the son of Joshua Brickle'Bee, the only person from the Tri' Ark the Gnomes ever trusted; on the other hand, you're an agent of the Tri'Ark, a government that the Gnomes have never trusted."

"So, you think I'm the son of Joshua Brickle'Bee?"

"Of course I do."

"Thistle, answer me honestly, what was my father working on? What did he know about the Gnomes that got him killed?"

"That, my boy, is as mysterious to me as was your father's death. Reckle is the only one that will know what Joshua was doing. Those two were the best of friends; they did everything together. If anyone knows anything, Reckle does."

"He hasn't said more than a few sentences to me since he challenged me to the Quintillian Games. How am I supposed to get him to trust me?"

Thistle sighed. "You have to earn Reckle's trust, not expect it. He's a kind, gentle old soul, one that is passionate about protecting his people. He thinks in the old ways, where honor and respect are all that is needed to strike up a bargain. And you must also consider that he has his people to rule and control. If he openly embraced you as the son of Joshua, it might create divisions among our people."

"What can I do then?"

"I don't think there's anything you can, boyou. But never mind that now, we've come to the place I wanted to show you."

Nickle looked around, surprised to find himself on top of a pearl white bridge. The top of the bridge was made of lush grass that was an extension of the land around them, and so at first, it was difficult to tell they were even on a bridge. The Dwarf looked over the white railing towards a swirling torrent of water below. It was a lake of sorts, shaped like an eye. The water on the outside of the eye was turning clockwise while in the middle it turned counter-clockwise. Nickle could feel the magic pulsing all around him, feel his skin tingling with a numb sensation.

"What is this place?"

"This is the ancient bridge of Fanqueen—the forgetting bridge. The bridge spans the distance over a well of water, which is said to be the source of all magic on Earth. The bridge was first built to protect the well from being tainted by naïve travelers. The day after it was completed, ancient words appeared in the wood, carved deep into its framework. The craftsmanship is so fine that there's little possibility that a Gnome could have done it—or any creature for that matter."

Nickle placed a hand on the pearl white banister. "It's warm."

"It's more than warm," Thistle replied. "It's alive. This is a sacred place to the Gnomes, one that we will defend with our lives to the last Gnome. But that's not why I brought you here. There's a reason we call this the forgetting bridge." Thistle made a quick motion with his hands, altering the air around his fingers. For a split second, Nickle thought he could see the threads of air he was manipulating. A sheet of paper suddenly appeared.

"Nickle," Thistle said, "I have to ask you for your forgiveness."

"What? Why?"

Thistle looked down. "All this time, I've been training you to compete in the Quintillian Games. It's because of me that you think you have a chance to win, but, you don't."

"Am I not good enough?"

"You're talented, extremely talented. I'd say you'd give your father a good challenge. But there are some here that hate the Tri'Ark with a passion that has never been seen among the Gnomes. There are some here that will cheat; there are some here that will kill if that means they can sever ties with the Tri'Ark. LuckLock is just one example of possibly millions of others who want you dead. If you ride tomorrow, I'm afraid it will be for the last time. The only way you can possibly survive is to be last. It's better to be dead last than to be first and end up dead." Nickle noticed that as Thistle spoke, words appeared on the piece of parchment that the Gnome held.

Nickle shook his head. "I don't understand…"

"I've deceived you, boyou," Thistle said, "and that's why I ask for your forgiveness. You're not in an easy position, and I put you there. If you ride in the race tomorrow, you will end up dead; if you don't, the Dwarves will likely punish you in some horrible way that I don't want to imagine. You could have walked away when the challenge had first been issued, but it was my training that gave you hope that you could win."

Nickle put his hand on the little Gnome's shoulder. "You did nothing but train me. There's no evil in that."

"Then, do I have your forgiveness?"

"Yes," Nickle replied.

"Then take this sheet of paper and drop it over the bridge."

Nickle moved slowly at first, unsure of what precisely the Gnome meant. He grabbed the sheet of paper, looking at it ever so briefly. It held the exact words of their conversation penned in golden ink. He then held it over the edge of the bridge and let it go. It softly floated down towards the water, twisting and turning as it went. As it floated, it began to shift forms, turning into drops of water. It splashed into the waves below, shimmering once with a golden hue before disappearing completely.

"Did it turn into water?" Thistle asked.

Nickle turned around, surprised to see the Gnome had taken a large step back from the railing. "Yes."

The Gnome let out a long sigh. "Ah, good. That means your forgiveness was genuine."

"Of course, it was. I forgive you. Don't even think about it for a second longer—it's water under the bridge."

Thistle nodded. "You're a good soul. And I will miss you."

"I'm not dead yet," Nickle replied.

"But you will be soon."

Nickle gave an awkward laugh, unsure if Thistle meant this as a joke or not.

"We had better get back to the party before your friend finds trouble."

"Yeah," Nickle replied, "yeah, we better."

Chapter 21

The Chariot Race

The first thing he put on was a padding made from a sunflower, which still smelled faintly of the plant it once was. Next came a heavy set of Gnome armor made of rose branches. Nickle pounded a fist against his chest as the armor was situated into place. He was surprised at how strong the armor felt—it was almost as well-crafted as Dwarf Tines. He was given greaves and a multi-colored kilt for his legs and a large pair of sandals for his feet. He was not sure what the sandals were made of, but they instantly cushioned his toes as he slipped them on. Next, a red sash was tied around his waist, followed by two thick shoulder guards made of beetle heads that were snapped onto his breastplate. He then was given arm bracelets made of dragonfly wings and a set of thin gloves made from lizard skins.

As he finished strapping the gloves to his hands, he felt a sudden rush of nerves. He took a deep breath, and then another, but it did little to calm him. His feet sounded like weights as he stepped across a stone floor and into the open arena. As soon as he entered, the crowd erupted with noise. Hundreds of Gnomes cheered while several thousands began to boo.

Nickle looked around, awed by the presence of so many spectators. The massive arena had ample seating—Thistle had once said that it fit just over a million spectators—but the stadium was so packed that the audience looked squished. Despite the cramped conditions, everyone was on their feet, shouting as if they were being paid to do it. From the ceiling of the arena, which looked like a perfectly blue sky, massive banners were unfurled, each one illuminating the name of one of the Charioteers. Nickle noticed that a small contingent of Dwarves had been allowed to attend. They had a pitiful banner stretched out between them with the name "Nickel Brickle'Buy" spelled out across it.

As the crowd roared with noise, a large voice erupted out of nowhere. "Presenting, Nickle Brickle'Bee—the alleged son of Joshua Brickle'Bee, who was the first and only Dwarf ever to survive the track. He weighs in at six ounces, stands a short four and three-quarter inches, and will be driving Hedge Hogs. Please welcome Nickle Brickle'Bee!"

Nickle approached his team of Hedge Hogs, where Jason was waiting for him. As the two friends looked at each other, Jason tried to force a smile but only succeeded in a grimace.

They both spoke at once but then stopped to let the other talk. After a few moments of silence, Nickle finally whispered, "Hope it goes better than practice."

Jason punched his friend in the arm. "What are you talking about? You've managed to stay on your game all last week. You're driving just as well as any of them."

"It's not the driving that has me nervous; it's the crowd of chariots that will be on the track. I'm not used to racing against other teams."

"Who, them? Don't worry about them—"

The announcer continued, but this time in Gnomish. Nickle could only understand a few words. "Toolin danter: Dandwin Rivertwist—hijoe de Raton Rivertwist. Panny poser seven ounces, twillin six inches. Hellion montando Ratons."

As this announcement finished, a Gnome entered the track through a small side door. The Gnome was covered in armor made from maple leaves. He had uncommonly long, pointed ears and a nose that jutted out like the end of a ship. His eyes were small, black, and shifty and his movements were quick and jerky. After walking around with his arms in the air for a few moments, he leaped onto a chariot that was pulled by four very large rats.

Thistle patted Nickle on the shoulder. "There you are, boyou. I see you've managed to dress properly."

Nickle swallowed. "I didn't know Rats were in the race."

"Oh, yes," Thistle replied. "Rats have good acceleration, but they don't have as much endurance. They're notorious for cheating, so keep your distance from them."

Next, the announcer introduced a small Gname called Squeaks Lowfire. She was dressed in armor made of twigs and topped off with a hat made from one solid leaf. Once the crowd ebbed in their cheering, Squeaks walked over to a chariot harnessed to a team of Squirrels.

Thistle nodded. "Squirrels have the quickest acceleration and can maintain a rigorous pace. Their little bodies, however, are often pushed around by the other critters."

The next Gname presented was named Brownburra, and she had a chariot pulled by Hamsters. She was quickly followed by a large Gnome named Green Worm, whose chariot was pulled by Moles. The more contestants that appeared, the drier Nickle's throat became.

Then LuckLock BaneBirth, the champion of the Grinning Cappers, appeared. He made a dramatic entrance as he pointed a crooked finger towards Nickle and shouted, "You're dead Dwarf! Do you hear me! Dead."

Next, a Gnome entered who drove a team of small Rabbits, then one that drove Chinchillas. There were all sorts of creatures used for the race, some that Nickle did not readily recognize: there were five teams of Ferrets, seven teams of Gerbils, four teams of Guinea Pigs, three teams of Hedge Hogs and a few dozen teams of Squirrels, Hamsters, Rabbits, Rats, and Moles.

Suddenly, almost as if someone had hit a mute button, silence fell across the track. Nickle looked around, scanning the area for the cause of the abrupt change. The arena felt oddly empty without the noise filling it up. Moments later, a small thundering clap began to ripple through the audience. It was first scattered and offbeat, but it was not long before it became a deafening noise that filled the air. The cheer caught momentum, and soon, not a Gnome or Gname in the audience stood idle. The sound became so loud that the words of the announcer were drowned out.

Then a Gnome dressed in black armor entered the arena and the audience went manic. The Gnome's head was topped off by the red skull of a creature with massive fangs. His armor was bulky and thick, having been made from black lobster shells. On his feet were boots that were shaped like daggers. The audience cheered on and on as the Gnome approached a black chariot that had seemingly appeared out of thin air.

Nickle did not know the name of the creatures harnessed to the chariot, he did not even know what species they were, but he knew they had to be deadly. He could only stare with his mouth half open, gaping at the spectacle before him.

Thistle reached up and shut Nickle's mouth with his hand. "Piddlers call them Frilled Lizards, but I imagine these are quite a bit different than the ones you have on the surface."

Nickle shook his head. "I didn't know anything like that existed."

"They're fast—faster than anything else in the race—and deadly too. They have a flap of skin connected to their necks that they use to make themselves look bigger; their teeth are deadly sharp, and poisonous. The venom will kill you within an hour, maybe even sooner if your adrenaline is going."

Jason narrowed his eyes. "What's a creature like that doing in the Quintillian Games?"

"It's going to win," Thistle replied, "that's what it's doing. Lord Reckle is the only one that can compete with Lizards because he is the only one that has been able to train them to run as a team. If you've ever valued my advice, listen to it now: Stay away from Reckle and his Lizards."

Nickle swallowed. "Lord Reckle is driving those Frilled Lizards?"

"Yeah, you didn't think he would miss his own party, did you?"

"He's the Lord. Why would he be competing?"

"Because, well, he's almost guaranteed to win; he's won the last seven years. Nothing can beat those Frilled Lizards. No one even comes close."

Nickle slammed a red helmet on his head. "Now you tell me. Not only am I going up against a Lord, but also one that is unbeatable."

"You've got real heart, boyou," Thistle said, "but don't let that fool you. Not even Joshua Brickle'Bee could race alongside those Frilled Lizards. Just remember what we talked about last night."

"Why did you wait until now to tell me?"

The announcer interrupted. "Monta Chariotes."

Thistle clapped his hands together. "I didn't want to scare you. Listen, you've got some natural skill, so let that keep you alive. Remember, shoot for last place, boyou." The little Gnome turned around and walked away, waving gleefully to the crowd as he did.

Jason patted Nickle on the back. "Here comes our old friend

Hampshire. I think he's going to offer you some real encouragement."

Just as Jason finished speaking, Hampshire saluted by pounding on his chest. "Nickle, this is your time; this is your moment. Prove your worth to the Silver Army. If you win, you'll be looking at a nice promotion."

"And if I lose?"

"You…will be transferred somewhere else where I don't have to see the sight of you again. Let's not focus on that. So…good luck, lad. May the Armor of Hurn protect you."

"Right back atcha."

With this, Hampshire saluted again and left.

"Not a very good motivational speaker, is he?" Nickle said.

Jason's face changed. "Listen, Thistle's right. This whole thing is mad. Just because your father was good at this, they expect you to have some talent. This whole game has been fixed from the beginning. Reckle Berry is going to win."

Nickle stepped onto his chariot and gripped the reins. "So you think I should shoot for last?"

Jason pulled his head back. "Last? No, don't shoot for last. Shoot for something in the middle. That way, you can at least say you gave it all you could, but you aren't putting yourself in too much danger. I'm serious about that, Nickle. This is as real as it gets. You put your life on the line, and you might lose it. And for what? The possibility of the Gnome's trade embargo being lifted? The possibility of you getting a promotion?"

"I've been thinking about this, Jason. If I win, or even if I just do well, I could earn Reckle's respect. If I can do that, then he will answer the questions I have about my father. Reckle is the key to the puzzle, and for the first time, I've got a chance to put it all together."

Jason shook his head. "You won't be putting anything together if you end up in pieces. Just stay alive, Nickle—"

The announcer began speaking again.

"I've got to line up," Nickle yelled.

Jason nodded as he began walking backwards towards the outside of the track. "Good luck." He finally turned around and took his place with the group of Dwarves in the stands. As Jason melded into the crowd, the ground began to rumble as teams of chariots lined up. Nickle was assigned to the very back of the long procession, where he was joined by several newer Charioteers. The track was wide enough to accommodate twenty chariots shoulder to shoulder with ten chariots in each row. As the animals moved towards their assigned starting positions, a few of them began to hiss and growl at the critters around them. One of the Rat teams became so impetuous, a Gnome "Watcher"—who was some sort of referee—had to join the throng and separate the creatures. Nickle's Hedge Hogs snapped at a few opponents, but his team was able to reach their assigned area without much trouble.

Once the chariots were in position, silence fell across the track.

The announcer's voice came back—this time, he was counting down.

Nickle did not understand the numbers, but he did understand the word "go."

"Cleve, Stoomp, Ono…Ett."

The ground thundered as one hundred riders simultaneously whipped their teams forward. Confusion and chaos set in as dirt was kicked up. To Nickle's right, a group of Squirrels ran into a set of Guinea Pigs. Squeals followed as one of the Squirrels latched its jaws into the side of the lead Pig. Both drivers tried to maintain control, but the animals ignored their drivers completely.

Just in front of Nickle, a team of Rabbits caught up to and bit the hindquarters of some unsuspecting Gnome who was driving a team of Weasels. The driver fell off and was almost trampled by Gophers. Without a driver, the Weasels banked hard to the right and flipped over a chariot of Hamsters.

Dust and debris were kicked up as team after team collided with each other. Each collision sent a ripple of excitement through the crowd that would either turn into a wave of applause or a bout of booing. Nickle was forced to whip his team to the left and then quickly to the right to avoid colliding with several other chariots. At one point, he had turned so sharply one of his chariot wheels momentarily tipped off the ground.

Crack.

A chariot directly in front of Nickle ran head-on into a team of Rats that had somehow been turned around and were running the wrong way. Both chariots exploded into shards, sending their drivers flying high above the action. Nickle swerved left, barely dodging one of the unfortunate Charioteers who was now desperately running for his life. Nickle's chariot lurched into the air as it hit the shattered remains of one of the chariots. A moment later, he broke out of the tangle of riders and into the clear. As the dirt and debris faded, he could see dozens of racers in front of him—far in front of him.

Nickle slowed the Hedge Hogs down to a trot, which was just fast enough to keep him in last place. A few other Charioteers passed him, screeching insults as they did.

"I'm in last now—if I can just stay back here, I'll be fine," Nickle said. He trotted on for a while, staring at the horde of chariots that were shrinking in the distance. "Just like always—I'm last." These words triggered an image of himself in the orphanage. As other kids were adopted, he remained—he was always last. Then he thought of Tortugan and how he would have never been able to graduate had it not been for Jason—and even then, he was last in his class. This thought turned into another, which finally turned into his father. *"Joshua Brickle'Bee—he was the last Dwarf to run this race. I'll never know what happened to him if I don't win—I'll never know how he really died."*

Nickle whipped the Hedge Hogs so hard and so suddenly that the creatures leaped forward, barreling towards the other Charioteers like a bullet shooting from a gun. With the large open space between himself and the other riders, Nickle was able to quickly gain speed. He reached his first opponent just as the mob of riders entered the tunnels. The majority of the Charioteers took the large tunnel, but Nickle swerved into a smaller one on the right side. He often took this tunnel while he trained, and he was hoping that few Charioteers knew about it.

He was going so fast around the turn that his wheels squealed in protest. The walls of the tunnel whipped passed him as he encouraged his team on. Rounding a corner, he almost collided into the rear of a slower moving opponent. He tried passing on the left, but the Charioteer veered in front of him, nearly clipping one of his Hedge Hogs in the head. The same thing happened when he tried to pass the rider on the right.

Nickle let out a deep sigh and narrowed his eyes. As quickly as he could, he steered his team along the far wall, driving them further and further up it. Soon, they were on the ceiling of the tunnel—their opponent just below them. As soon as the rider realized Nickle was trying to pass him from above, he quickly steered his chariot up the wall and towards Nickle.

It looked like they were going to collide, but Nickle turned away from the rider and traveled back down the opposite wall. The pursuit continued, making their movement look like a corkscrew as the Charioteer chased Nickle around the tunnel. The longer they traveled, the more blurry their movements became. The other Charioteer, however, soon forgot exactly which wall was the floor and which was the ceiling. As they entered the large straightaway, Nickle was on the track, while the other Charioteer, who was still on the top of the tunnel, ran out of road. Like a weight dropped from a building, the rider crashed into the ground, his chariot exploding on impact.

Nickle could not help himself—he grinned. His grin persisted even longer when he realized that his speed in the tunnel had enabled him to pass a good portion of the other chariots. In the long straight tunnel, however, Nickle found that his Hedge Hogs were not as quick as most of the other animals. Slowly, Charioteers began passing Nickle, grinning madly as they did. One of the unfortunate drivers was so distracted with the grin on his face that he did not see a root that had suddenly appeared in front of him. The chariot split in two—half of the vehicle continued with the critters, the other half, along with the Charioteer, were sent rolling in the dust.

Nickle was passed by three other chariots before they finally entered another turn. Once again, the Dwarf selected a smaller, more dangerous tunnel. He took the turn so quickly his wheels squealed louder than ever before. By the time he shot out of the turn and onto the straightaway, he only had three opponents ahead of him. As he passed the starting line, he was greeted by a mix of applause and boos.

Jason stood up on his feet. "That's it, Nickle! Turn up the heat. Only nine more laps to go!"

Once again, on the straightaway, Nickle lost ground, but once again, he was able to make up for it on the sharp turns. Despite the ground he gained, he could not catch up with the leaders. Lap after lap passed—still nothing changed.

It was not until the sixth lap that Nickle finally had his chance.

One of the contenders for first place—a large Gname dressed in Acorn armor—attempted to pass Reckle Berry, who still held the lead. Reckle immediately countered the movement by swinging his black Frilled Lizards into action. The Lizards swarmed in like a pack of snakes, hissing and clawing at their opponent. The contender pulled back just in time to save her team from being sliced to pieces.

This gave the next contender a chance to break for first. Another Gnome dressed in green and driving a team of squirrels whipped his critters forward. This attempt, as noble as it seemed, soon turned into a disaster as Reckle's Frilled Lizards opened their fanned heads and rushed in. The lead Squirrel was bitten in the leg, another one was cut across the chest. The Squirrels collapsed to the ground, taking their driver with them. The Gnome Lord pulled into the lead again—but this time, Nickle was not far behind.

Reckle laughed as he looked back and saw Nickle. "You must be a talented Dwarf to have survived this long but be sure to keep your distance. I will not stop my Lizards from tearing those Hedge Hogs apart just because I own them."

Nickle ignored the taunt but, despite himself, he pulled in safely behind Reckle. He stayed there for a moment, waiting for an opening. Then without warning, another chariot rammed into him. The impact was so sudden that the Dwarf did not have time to prepare for it. His left wheel made a sickening crack but luckily did not break. Nickle looked over and saw a furious looking Gnome dressed in animal bones and driving a team of Weasels.

Nickle pointed at himself. "I'm not even in first. Reckle is the one you want to ram!"

Despite this, the Gnome swerved in again—but this time, Nickle was ready. He pulled hard on the reins, slowing down his team so they were in line with his opponent. A moment later, a Weasel squealed as its flesh was stabbed by the spines of the outer HedgeHog. As Nickle pulled back from the collision, he could see a few drops of blood still on the back of Amaryllis. With the lead Weasel injured, the Gnome's team was forced to slow down. As soon as the Weasels melted into the distance behind them, another team appeared on the opposite side of Nickle, attempting to ram him against a wall. Luckily, the Dwarf was able to escape by entering the next turn.

Nickle whipped his team on but not as fast as before. The Hedge Hogs' bodies were starting to show signs of exhaustion. They had beads of sweat dripping from their brows and onto their long noses. Foam as thick as root beer froth was seeping from Arbutus' mouth; Arbullian did not look much better. Nickle knew he only had one good push left in them.

As he left the turn, he caught air on a jump and almost landed squarely on Reckle Berry and his team. The Gnome Lord made a rash maneuver that saved him from being squashed, but also sent him off track. Another contender attempted to take the lead, but once again, Reckle's Frilled Lizards rushed in and turned the chariot into a dusty mess.

Instead of pushing for the lead, Nickle pulled back a safe distance. Just as he did, however, a Gnome in pinecone armor pulled up next to Nickle. The two Charioteers exchanged hard stares. It was LuckLock, the large Gnome that had insulted him the night before. The Gnome was driving a team of Weasels. A moment later, LuckLock pulled out a spiked ball that had a long chain attached to it. The driver began to swing the chain high above his head.

Nickle swallowed. *"Is that a ball-and-chain flail? How was that permitted onto the course?"*

The weapon struck Nickle's chariot and punctured a hole in the side of it, sending a chunk of coconut shell that rolled across the track. LuckLock grinned. Nickle frowned. Again, the flail was whipped forward—this time aimed right at Nickle. The Dwarf took a hit to his left arm, denting his armor. Pain shot through his body. Despite the armor absorbing most of the blow, one of the spikes had pierced his skin and sent blood dripping down his arm.

He doubted that he could take another hit and survive. Just as his opponent went in to finish him, Nickle swerved to the left, his chariot ramming into LuckLock. The force of the impact sent the Gnome pitching to the edge of his chariot. He almost recovered, but then the flail got caught in one of his wheels. The effect was immediate: The chariot disappeared in a cloud of dirt and debris while the critters were sent rolling across the ground.

Jason grinned. "You got this, Nickle! Two more laps left—make them count!"

Nickle passed the starting line and entered into his final laps. He had not noticed before, but a large part of the crowd was cheering for him now. *"I could win. It's only me and Reckle left."* Nickle had been slowed by LuckLock, but Reckle had some problems as well. A team of two chariots had swarmed in on him, attempting to squeeze him into submission. It was not long before the Gnome Lord had sent the two opponents crashing into the side of the track, but it had cost him precious time.

Nickle pulled in close to Reckle but did not try to pass him on the straightaway. As they approached the next turn the Dwarf aimed his chariot for one of the smaller, more familiar tunnels, where he thought he could gain the advantage over the Gnome Lord; but, before he could, Reckle slowed his team down and cut him off, forcing the Dwarf to follow him into one of the mid-sized tunnels. The sound of the hissing Frilled Lizards echoed ominously as they both entered.

Nickle narrowed his eyes. *"Now is my chance."* He whipped his team to the left, and then the right, each time he was cut off. He drove his team along the wall until he was on the ceiling. Once there, he pushed his team harder and harder, forcing them on. As the turn was just about to end, Nickle maneuvered his chariot down the wall and back onto the floor—right in front of Reckle. Nickle was in the lead. The audience roared as the two chariots broke out of the tunnel and onto the straightaway.

Reckle cursed. "Enjoy the taste of being first, because you won't have it for long!"

Nickle weaved back and forth, trying to avoid the Lizards that were already snapping at him. The sight of the Dwarf's bloody shoulder put the Frilled Lizards into a frenzy. The scaly creatures hissed and spurned, sometimes even spitting as they tried to catch up. Just as they were approaching the starting line, one of the Lizards leaped forward and clamped its twisted jaw onto Nickle's wounded shoulder. A sizzling pain rocketed through Nickle's body that turned his breathing into gasps. The Dwarf fell backward, his head hitting the ground. He would have completely fallen out of the chariot had it not been for his left foot, which had somehow become entangled in the reins. With Nickle being dragged behind his chariot, Reckle whipped his Lizards forward and passed the Dwarf.

The pain in Nickle's shoulder was so intense that it forced every other thought out of his head. It pulsated like a drum, pounding up his shoulder and throughout his body. He lost vision in one eye and almost blacked out completely.

"It's the poison." His breath became wheezy and short. As his head bumped against the dirt below, he thought of quitting, thought

237

of kicking his leg free, and simply letting his body roll across the dirt until it came to a stop. *"It's over. The poison will kill me if I don't get help. I'm sorry, father."* But then something changed, something from deep within. It was the thought of his father that seemed to spark the warmth that began to flow over him. It was a warmth that began in his heart and spread out across his body, filling him completely. Although he could not see it, it felt like a white light that ignited in his chest. *"I can do this. I can win."* He took in a sudden breath and opened both eyes wide, forcing his vision to return. *"I have to win."* With this one thought pulsating through his head, he reached for the railing in front of him, grunting with effort as he pulled himself up.

Once he was level, he took another deep breath and narrowed his eyes. *"This is still my race."* His left arm was completely useless and hung limply from his body like a dishrag. He grabbed the reins with his other arm, ignoring the pain burning through his left shoulder. Using his one good arm, he pulled his sash from around his waist and stuffed it into the hole in his armor. This, at the very least, seemed to decrease the bleeding. Despite Nickle being dragged on his back for a good portion of the straightaway, the Hedge Hogs had maintained their pace and were not far behind. After the next turn, Nickle was once again on Reckle's heels.

The Gnome Lord beamed with an admiring grin.

Nickle nodded curtly.

The two fought for position on the straightaway, but Nickle's team of Hogs were too tired to make any real attempt to pass Reckle. The chariots entered the same tunnel in the final turn. Reckle began driving wildly, weaving his chariot back and forth to prevent Nickle from passing.

The Dwarf veered his team up the side of the wall and then onto the ceiling. He whipped the Hogs hard, mustering every last ounce of speed he could. Slowly, they began to pass Reckle, who was still directly below them.

Reckle shook his head. "Are you mad? As soon as this tunnel opens up again, you'll have no more road up there on the ceiling. You're going to have to come down from there sometime, and when you do, I'll be waiting for you."

Nickle said nothing. Slowly, his team pulled into the lead. He could see the end of the tunnel approaching, see the light from the large straightaway. He only had a few moments before he would be completely out of road. At the last second, he veered his chariot sharply to the right, sending it careening towards Reckle and his team of Lizards. The Lizards snapped with anticipation as Nickle's body came hurtling towards them.

Just before impact, Nickle yanked hard on the reins, slowing his team of Hogs down. This sudden reduction of speed lined up the Lizards perfectly with the spikes of the Hedge Hogs. It all happened so fast that Reckle had no time to react. The lead Lizard squealed in pain as a dozen of Amaryllis' spines pierced the creature's body. The next moment, the two chariots broke from the tunnel and entered the final straightaway.

The Charioteers urged their teams on, whipping them as hard as they could. They ran parallel to each other, each gaining the advantage one moment, but then losing it the next.

A few dozen paces before the finish line, the wounded Frilled Lizard suddenly collapsed from pain, sending up a wave of dust. Nickle pulled into the lead. A second later, he passed through the finish line. The audience roared with applause, screaming so loudly that the announcer was drowned out completely.

A Dwarf had won. Nickle had won.

He slowed his chariot, raising his one good hand in the air. Once he stopped, he took two steps towards the waiting crowd, a wide grin on his face. *"I won."* But then, the roar of the audience faded into the distance. He blinked several times, trying to focus his vision. Blackness began to close in on him. He collapsed. The world blurred and faded until finally, it disappeared completely.

Chapter 22

A City of Old

Nickle stirred slightly—his head was pounding. It felt like someone had hit it for an hour straight with a large club. He tried opening his eyes but was greeted with only darkness. His head hurt. As he tried to sit up, a gruff voice stopped him.

"Take it easy, Nickle. I know you're tough, but even you need a rest after something like that. Your strength will return, but you must give it time."

"Who's there?"

The voice laughed. Moments later, a light flickered on.

Nickle's eyes widened at the face that greeted him. "Thornhead Back'Break, what are you doing here?" He began to rise, but the thick hands of the Elected Chief Warlord stopped him.

"Great accomplishments deserve great rewards. You, lad, are something else—just like your father."

"You heard what happened?"

"Yeah, of course I did—I was in the stands cheering you on. I didn't want you to be more nervous than you were already, so I didn't bother telling you. But I saw it all from the beginning to the end. You like to live on the edge, don't you, lad?"

Nickle shook his head. "My only thought was of survival."

"And you would have survived just fine if you had stayed in the back. There's a lot more to you than what I first supposed, lad."

"Thank you, sir. I never got to thank you properly for assigning me to the Gnome Detail."

"Hah. It's I who needs to thank you. Look what you've done. Hundreds of Dwarves working tirelessly around the clock for over two hundred years could not accomplish what you did in the space of half an hour. Reckle is going to rescind his trade embargo with the Tri'Ark. Gnomes can now be employed again. You've changed everything;

you've made everything possible."

"What's so important about the Gnomes?"

"They can manufacture a sustainable source of light. Everything you see here in Tiran 'Og is powered by Gnome switches. Gnomes are the key to weaning ourselves off the company Faerie Light. Only Gnomes know how to cast the Chillian spell—a powerful incantation that gives an object an internal power source. The Tri'Ark has spent millions of kilos of gold dust trying to replicate their magic, but it was all in vain. A few attempts have been successful, but the magic is so complicated, so detail-oriented, that only Gnomes can reproduce it effectively. I'm sure you've heard about the trouble with the Faeries. They keep threatening to turn the lights out on us for good, but now, after a little bit of time, it won't matter if they do."

"How many Gnome switches can a Gnome make in a day?"

"Each Gnome can make about one switch a month. As I said, they're extremely complex, but for each one they make, we have another Dwarf room that's not dependent on the Faeries. Much of Tortugan is powered by Chillian spells—thanks to your father."

"Sounds expensive."

"It is indeed. Your father saw all this coming. He knew our dependency on Faerie power would eventually lead to war—that's why he fought so hard to win the Gnomes over to our side. If he hadn't turned Troll, we would be a lot further along by now."

Nickle frowned.

Back'Break shook his head. "Your father was a good Dwarf—despite how things ended up for him. Suffice it to say, the past is not nearly as important as the future. Now just get some rest. You'll need it to handle the responsibilities of your new promotion."

"Promotion?"

"Yes, you've been selected to be the Tri'Ark's official Ambassador to the Gnomes. It's quite an honor, since it's something way beyond precedent. We had to bend a few rules to get you in, so I hope you're up to the task."

Nickle swallowed hard. He felt a sudden rush to his head. "How did you appoint me so quickly?"

"I had it all lined up," Thornhead said with a wink. "I'd assumed you'd follow in your father's footsteps and win. Jason will also be promoted, if that makes you feel any better. You two will be touring the Gnome kingdoms, rallying support for our great cause. But don't worry about that right now—that's the last thing you need to think about. Get some rest." Thornhead stood, grinned, and left Nickle in the dark room.

Nickle slumped back onto his pillow. He was glad that Thornhead left. He did not know why, but the large Dwarf Warlord intimidated him like no one ever had before. He let out a long, exasperated sigh.

"You all right?" asked a voice from the darkness.

Nickle sat up, startled by the sudden presence of someone stepping close to his bed. "Jason?"

But it was not Jason's face that moved into the light—it was Reckle Berry.

"What are you doing here, hiding in the corner of the room?" Nickle said with less tact than he would have liked.

Reckle Berry stepped from the shadows and took the seat that Thornhead had occupied moments before. "So, you be the son of Joshua Brickle'Bee. I can barely believe my own eyes." Despite Reckle still wearing his black lobster armor, despite his regal presence and commanding demeanor, he seemed changed. If it weren't for the unmistakable and unyielding eyes, Nickle would have thought that someone completely different was sitting next to him. The Gnome Lord looked tired and worn, like an antique shoehorn. His face was just as serious as when Nickle first met him, but somehow, he was different.

"I'm glad to see you're alive, boyou," Reckle said.

Nickle bowed his head low and pounded his chest in a salute.

"Even in your victory, you're just as humble as he was," Reckle said. "You're not subject to our laws and customs as an Ambassador. You have immunity here."

Nickle smiled.

"And what do you think of the Tri'Ark?"

"It's as good as any government, I suppose."

"Do you know they once sided with Kara'Kala?"

"I heard a portion of them were—"

"—I trust you Nickle," Reckle said quickly. "And I trust many of the Dwarves in your ranks, but there are a good many in the Tri'Ark that would gladly free Kara'Kala from his prison. He promised freedom, and he delivered. Before he came to power, many of the magical races were close to extinction—including the Dwarves. The Piddlers were dominating the landscape, forcing all magical creatures from their natural homes. It was Kara'Kala that united us; it was Kara'Kala that formed the Tri'Ark."

"I don't understand. Was he good or bad?"

"He was both. Who knows how long he was evil—perhaps from the beginning—but his streak of good didn't seem to last very long. Once he pronounced himself Emperor, he changed. At that time, few could be trusted, even fewer were willing to do anything about it. Your father was the only Dwarf I have ever fully trusted with my life—and in case you haven't figured it out, he never turned Troll."

Nickle swallowed.

Reckle continued. "This world is on the brink of destruction—I can feel it just as much as I can feel my own heartbeat. In truth, my people are starving."

"There isn't enough food?"

"It's not food that feeds a Gnome, although that's needed, it's magic that keeps us alive. The same is true for all creatures—even Piddlers—but some beings are more affected by it than others. I feel broken inside, like a twig that has long since been snapped off a tree. Your father was one of the first to champion the idea that the Earth is dying. He was the one that took the news before the Tri'Ark."

"My father?"

"Yes. He knew something important, something that got him killed. Unfortunately, death is usually the price of being a good man during an evil time."

"What did he know?"

"I don't know what he knew, but I do know he left something for you to find. In the cursed city of Gillian, you will find it. Your father was once a great Dwarf Lord, ruler of the city of Gillian, but now nothing but cursed ruins remain."

"Have you been there?"

"None of the Fair Folk can go there—the curse is too strong. But here, take this." Reckle slowly pulled a crumpled sheet of paper out of his pocket. The paper had been folded and unfolded so many times there were permanent creases that spidered all over it. The sheet was yellowed and stained with drops of blood.

"This should help you find what you're looking for."

Chapter 23

The Cursed City of Gillian

After three days, Nickle's new position was promptly made official by Thornhead Back'Break. He rather enjoyed his duties as an Ambassador, mostly because of the excellent food he received everywhere he went. He typically spent his time traveling between Gnome kingdoms, giving speeches along the way. Even though he was never good at speaking, or even wanted to be good at it, his statements were always met with tumultuous applause. Occasionally, Jason would take charge of the speech giving because he was much more apt at it. Sometimes he spoke with so much passion, so much force that the Gnomes would clap for several minutes after he was done.

As per Thornhead's instructions, Nickle and Jason told the Gnomes about the jobs being offered by the Tri'Ark. They told them of the community that the Tri'Ark was attempting to build and the wealth and power they had already consolidated. On occasion, a few Gnomes would spurn Nickle, telling him that he was as much a liar as any in EarthWorks. The first time that happened, Nickle was somewhat taken aback. The further they traveled from Tiran 'Og, the more adamant and abundant the Gnome protestors became. One old Gnome—who must have been as old as the sun—went into a trance and prophesized of the destruction this new "openness" would bring.

After this occasion, Nickle decided to send other Dwarves to give speeches while he and Jason focused on facilitating the new Gnome employees. Despite any opposition, over a million Gnomes were employed in the first week. The next week yielded a number even higher. The two Dwarves were quickly inundated with paperwork and forms, which had to be magically inputted into stone tablets that transferred the information to the Tri'Ark Archives.

The work was long and tedious but, fortunately for Nickle and Jason, they did not have to do most of it. Both the Dwarves had been assigned two legions under their command, which was unprecedented and highly against Silver Army regulation. No Tenderfoot, not even in the worst season of war, had ever been placed in charge of two Legions. This raised more than a few eyebrows of prominent Dwarves and Humans alike. Whenever Nickle or Jason were publicly criticized for their promotions, however, it was always Thornhead Back'Break or Edward Thunderhoof that came to their defense. Eventually, the shock and murmurs died, leaving nothing but a few gossiping whispers that lingered behind.

Despite Nickle's additional responsibilities, despite the fact that he was more busy now than at any other point in his life, he could not get his mind off what the Gnome Lord had said. He found himself repeating the name "Gillian" throughout the day. From what little information Nickle could discover about the city, Gillian was a Dwarf settlement built near the surface, just below the state of Virginia. Besides finding out that it was established by Hammer Shonwald and Joshua Brickle'Bee, Nickle unearthed little else. The records he found were smudged, almost as if someone had taken a dirty eraser to them.

He tried for weeks to get away from his duties, but each occasion he requested time off, Thornhead would adamantly deny the request, saying "that if you left—even for a few days—everything might be undone."

The days turned to weeks and the weeks to months. Each day that passed by added angst to Nickle's already anxious mood. At least once per day, he felt the urge to leave so strongly that he would begin packing a few items for the trip. His sense of duty and obedience, however, prevented him from following through with his plans.

Surprisingly, the one thing that Nickle began looking forward to were the weekly visits from Sharlindrian, who would stop by the camp and demand to see Nickle. The guards would let her in without question, saluting the Elf as if she was some high ranking general. It was not her personality that Nickle looked forward to, or the fact that all the other Dwarves turned green with envy when she came by, it was the information she always brought. After only a week of research, she was able to figure out the location of the city of Gillian and the best way to get there. She also had figured out how Nickle could steal away for a few days without being noticed.

"It says, right here," Sharlindrian said one day in her all-knowing voice, "that Dwarves in the Silver Army may request days off, but it must be approved by their commanding officer."

"Yes," Nickle replied. "Exactly, and since I report directly to Thornhead Back'Break, he always shoots me down."

Sharlindrian arched one of her eyebrows. "But, much further down in the articles of the Silver Army, it says that around the holiday of Burnaday, which is the celebration of fathers, a Dwarf can take two days of leave without asking for permission, providing that they find a replacement and that their father once honorably served in the Silver Army."

"Wow, that's brilliant," Nickle said. "By the way, where did you find the articles of the Silver Army? That's supposed to be under lock and key—"

Sharlindrian only smiled in reply.

The week before Burnaday dragged on, even for Jason, who normally complained about the week going by too fast. But, eventually, Nickle found himself packing a small rucksack with some food and a few changes of clothes.

Jason walked into their shared quarters as Nickle packed. "I can't believe you're going. Our first few days off, and you want to spend it looking for a cursed city."

"Why don't you come?"

Jason shook his head. "I'm not going to a cursed city. These new jobs pay great, but we're so busy we never get to buy anything. I've already got three gold medallions that are too heavy to carry around my neck. I need to waste some money on something frivolous."

"Aren't you the least bit curious to figure out what my father was working on? Or to figure out what's going on down here. Two hundred years ago, our parents were in the middle of a war—a war that they almost lost. Don't you care about that?"

"No, not really. I would have been more interested in going if we were breaking the rules in doing so. Now that we have permission, the thrill just isn't there. And I don't think it's smart you're going alone either."

Nickle shoved the last shirt into his pack. "I'm not."

"Who's going with you?"

"Sharlindrian."

"The Elf girl?"

247

Nickle nodded. "Well, too bad you can't go. I'll bring you back a souvenir."

"The Elf girl is going?"

"Yeah, and a friend of hers is coming as well. Take care, Jason. I'll be back in a few days."

"Wait. You know, I think you're right. I'm a little curious to find out about the...stuff you were talking about. Give me a second to pack a bag."

"I can't wait. The Taxi-Lator just arrived."

"It'll only take me five minutes."

"Sorry."

Jason frowned. "I'll pay for the Taxi-Lator, you just make sure he waits."

With a broad grin on his face, Nickle left the room.

The two Dwarves were up in the air a few minutes later, zooming towards EarthWorks. The trip took several hours, but it went by quickly. Before long, they picked up Sharlindrian and went speeding off in the opposite direction. They arrived at the Tube platform, where they took a small Tube that shot them towards the surface. After eleven stops, they exited the Tube and began on foot. During the trip, Nickle and Jason tried to engage the Elf in conversation, but for the most part, she pretended like she did not even know the Dwarves.

By the time they exited the Tube, Jason was red-faced and grumpy. He grabbed Nickle and pulled him out of earshot. "Great plan you have for vacation—spending time with an Elf that thinks we're as interesting as a piece of gum stuck to her boot. And where is this friend you said she was bringing?"

Nickle patted the Dwarf on the shoulder. "I'm that friend, Jason. All I said was a friend of hers would be coming; I didn't say it would be another Elf."

Jason shook his head. "Pretty good trick, Nickle."

"Come on, Jason. You're the toughest Dwarf I know. If anyone can get us through a cursed city, it's you. I need you here—at least to help me build up the nerve to enter."

"Well," Jason said, "you probably wouldn't last five minutes without me."

"You're probably right."

"What are you two dirt-diggers doing?" Sharlindrian asked.

"We've got to get a move on if we hope to get there before it gets late."

Jason rolled his eyes as he whispered. "Who appointed her the leader?"

The three of them walked away from the tracks of the Tube and down a tunnel with smooth walls. The ground beneath had once been well cared for, but neglect had settled in and covered everything with pale weeds. The further they traveled from the Tube, the darker the tunnel became.

"Great," Jason hissed. "Are we supposed to feel our way there?"

Sharlindrian scoffed. "Aren't Dwarves supposed to have excellent vision in the dark?"

"Yeah, better than Elves and Humans anyway, but we can't see anything if its pitch black."

"What would you two Dwarves do without me?"

"Probably have a lot more fun," Jason whispered.

Sharlindrian pulled something from her purse. After whispering a quick incantation, a bright light shot out of the object, piercing the darkness far down the tunnel. "Follow me."

"What's that?"

Sharlindrian did not answer for a while, almost as if she was enjoying the silence. "These are moon rocks. Elf magic. You wouldn't understand."

"Well, thank you for saving us the explanation," Jason huffed.

The three walked deeper into the dark beyond. An hour later, they arrived at an intersection of tunnels—most of them smaller than the tunnel they had just come from. Sharlindrian only hesitated a moment before she chose one to the far left. They continued on, resting only briefly every so often to take a few drinks of water. The longer they went, the more Jason complained. He went into a long story about what he could have been doing instead. Initially, the stories seemed somewhat plausible, but as they went along, the tales became more and more exaggerated. Eventually, Jason was trying to convince Nickle that if they had stayed behind, they probably would have been elected to the Tri'Ark Council.

It was not until Sharlindrian raised an elegant hand in the air before he stopped talking. "This is it, Dwarves."

Nickle arched his eyebrows. "This just looks like the end of the tunnel."

"This *is* the end of the tunnel, but it's also the beginning of the city of Gillian."

Nickle's heart leaped.

Jason frowned. "Oh, you silly Elf. There's no city here. You just took us down the wrong tunnel."

"Did I?" Sharlindrian replied. "Ask Nickle if I did."

Nickle felt a chill run through his spine. It spread up his back and through his chest. A tingling sensation followed. He looked at his hands.

"Nickle?" Jason asked.

Nickle swallowed. "She's right, Jason. This is the place. I can feel it."

Sharlindrian smiled knowingly. "It's ancient Dwarf magic at work."

"How do we get in?"

Sharlindrian took a deep breath. "Only those who once belonged to the city can enter; only those who once lived here know the way in."

Nickle shook his head. "I was still in my mom's belly when I was last here."

"But that was enough for you to make a connection. You are the key, Nickle."

"All right—"

Jason stepped in front of Nickle. "Wait, wait. Aren't we forgetting something? This is a cursed city—a *cursed* city. I've never been to a cursed city. I don't even know what a city does to deserve a cursing, but we have to ask ourselves if we really, really want to go in there."

"Thank you for coming all this way, but you don't have to go," Nickle said.

"Oh, great," Jason replied. "Now that you say that, I'll look like a coward if I don't go. Come on. This has been a fun field trip, but let's get out of here—I'll pay for the Taxi-Lator back. What do you say, Nickle?"

Nickle turned his attention towards the Elf. "What do you think we can expect in there?"

She shook her head. "Beyond that wall, everything is dying but can never truly be dead. Even things like time and gravity are affected. You must be quick to travel in, and even quicker to get out. You'll feel the dying effect as well, feel it draining on your soul and eating at your skin. It will consume you, but it will never kill you. If you stay in there too long, you will become part of it. You won't have to worry about light because the city will reflect the light of times past; it might be dim in places, but it will never truly be dark."

Nickle swallowed. "How do we know if we've stayed too long?"

"If you're not able to leave."

"Wow, that's sure helpful," Jason whispered. "We won't know if we're in trouble unless we're already in trouble."

"Be careful."

"What?" Jason scoffed. "You're not going in there?"

"Sorry," Sharlindrian shrugged. "Fair Folk can't pass into cursed areas."

"Elves aren't Fair Folk—Fair Folk are things like Faeries and Gnomes. You could go in there if you wanted."

"Well," Sharlindrian said, "yeah, I guess so, but I don't want to."

Jason shook his head. "All brave and bad when you're on your own property but—"

The earth suddenly cracked beneath them, sending a shock through the tunnel walls. Unbeknownst to the other two, Nickle had walked forward and placed his hand on a massive rock. The ground continued to rumble and roar until the wall split right where his hand was. The crack widened and shifted, opening up like a sliding door.

Nickle stepped through the entrance, his face set with determination. "You coming?"

Jason let out a loud breath as he stepped forward. "I kinda have to now."

As soon as the two Dwarves entered, the massive stone began shutting. When the door finally closed, it made a loud thud that startled Jason. The Dwarf turned around, pale-faced. "So, I've seen enough. What about you?"

"Don't worry, Jason. Reckle gave me some advice and I think we can beat this. The curse will try to manipulate your thoughts until you can't remember who you really are and what you're doing. It feeds on fear, or at least that's what Reckle says in his note. Stay calm and when things get scary, just imagine you're eating a big bowl of ice cream."

"Ice cream?"

"Or whatever brings a smile to your face."

Jason grinned. "One time, I accidentally kicked a Gnome when I was walking. It was horrible and funny all at the same time."

Nickle frowned. "You never told me that—"

The Dwarf was interrupted by a loud shriek that echoed through the tunnel.

"What was that?" Jason asked.

"Do you really want to find out?"

Jason shook his head. "No. Not really."

"Then, let's keep moving."

They walked deeper into the tunnel, passing the occasional stone building or fence. The structures were magnificent in size, stretching up to the top of the tunnel. They had all sorts of designs and pictures sprawled out along them. Most of the pictographs were faded, some of them were utterly unrecognizable. The images shifted and whirled almost as if they were made of water rather than stone.

Jason pointed at one of them. "I think I see myself up there on the wall. Yeah, look. It's me, holding up a spear in one hand."

"Jason," Nickle whispered back. "Focus on something else. Think of the first day you found out you were a Dwarf."

"That was actually a horrible day. I was suspended from school because the teacher thought I exploded all of the toilets in the bathroom."

They passed through a large wall and entered the central portion of the city. The air was stiff and warm, almost as if the curse had not allowed it to circulate. To either side of them were dozens of buildings, each carved into the rock face. Nickle bent down, examining a round pearl that was on the ground. Just as he began to reach for it, another loud shriek echoed through the city. This time, both the Dwarves were startled by the noise. It was closer—more shrill. Nickle slowly pulled his hand away from the bead and looked around. The walls began to blur and fade. Finally, they disappeared completely.

They passed through a large wall and entered the central portion of the city. The air was stiff and warm, almost as if the curse had not allowed it to circulate. To either side of them were dozens of buildings, each carved into the rock face. Nickle bent down, examining a round pearl that was on the ground. Just as he began to reach for it, another loud shriek echoed through the city. This time, both the Dwarves were startled by the noise. It was closer—more shrill. Nickle slowly pulled his hand away from the bead and looked around.

"Didn't we already do that?" Nickle asked.

"Do what?"

Nickle let out a long breath. "We just passed through the city wall—and then we did it again, almost as if we had never really done it."

"Well," Jason said. "I don't remember passing through the city wall again but, you've already asked me that question—three times now."

"What are you talking about? That's the first time I've said anything like that."

"And that's the third time you've said *that*—exactly like that, every time."

Nickle swallowed. "Clear your mind. We're giving in to the fear. Focus on something different—something happier."

"Well, look at that," Jason pointed to a collection of rocks that were near one of the buildings. The stones were floating in mid-air, almost as if they were balloons half-filled will helium. Occasionally, one of the rocks would suddenly fall upwards and strike the ceiling; other times, they would hit the ground. It was almost like the stones could not decide exactly which way was up.

"We've got to keep moving," Nickle whispered. They walked on, passing wood carts and wells, a few gardens and small houses. The ground beneath them was made of cobblestone that kept changing in appearance: one minute, it looked cracked and worn; the next, it was brand new. Then, in a flash of light, they were suddenly on a set of stairs, climbing towards the top. Jason had a Rune in his hand, but Nickle could not remember him pulling it out.

"When did you pull out a Rune?" Nickle asked.

"You told me to," Jason replied.

"Runes won't do any good here."

There was a loud crack, and they were once again on the street. They entered a section of the city that was made by more discerning, talented hands. A colossal statue of a Dwarf stood in the middle of a stone forum, black water issuing from its mouth. Nickle had to take a second look at the figure because the first time he saw it, he could have sworn it was a statue of him. The second time he looked, however, it was the statue of an old Dwarf.

"How will we know where to go?" Jason asked.

"Reckle drew me a map."

Nickle entered a smaller forum, one that was lined with stores and merchant wagons. Something shrieked again. Like a shimmer of light across a lake, the scenery before them changed. The next moment, the forum was filled with Dwarves, each one laughing and smiling. Little children were playing a game with sticks next to a group of older Dwarves sitting on a set of chairs by a fire. Another group was situated in front of an ancient Dwarf who was telling a story. The forum was filled with color and music that flooded their ears and filled their bodies. The air hung thick with the smell of meat. A moment later, the scene disappeared, leaving only the ruined city of Gillian behind.

Nickle narrowed his eyes. "Did you see that?"

"The Trolls?"

"No, all the Dwarves."

Jason shook his head. "How come we don't see the same things?"

Nickle had no answer to give.

Jason let out a shaky breath. "How will we know where to go?"

"I already told you," Nickle said as he faced his friend, "Reckle gave me—" He would have finished his sentence, but Nickle realized there was no point—Jason was gone.

"Jason! Where are you?"

"I'm right here," Jason answered.

Nickle turned towards a voice that was behind him. "How did you get on the other side of me? You were on my right side just a minute ago."

"Nickle," Jason whispered. "You're starting to scare me. I've been walking on your left side since we entered the cavern. Now put that Rune away."

"I'm not holding a—" Nickle began to say, but he was interrupted as he looked down at his hand to discover that he was indeed holding a Rune. The Dwarf shook his head. "How is that possible?" When he looked up again, Jason had aged several thousand years; he had a beard that stretched down to the ground where it began to curl up.

Jason shook his head. "How will we know where to go?"

Nickle closed his eyes and rubbed his hands against them. *"Focus Nickle. Focus. Don't let the fear set in. Think. Think of what you're here to do. Your father. He's the reason you're here. He's probably the reason you're alive."* His mind latched on to the thought of his father, like a newborn infant does to its mother. When Nickle looked up again, Jason was back to normal—the only beard he had was the little stubble he had before.

Nickle laughed. "You're going to have to do better than that you wretched curse!"

The Dwarves continued down a long alleyway that ended in a flight of stairs. The walls suddenly rippled and spun, filling the air with vibrant and vivid colors. Slowly, the smell of roasting meat rose to Nickle's nose. He closed his eyes again, pushing all thoughts out of his head. The shriek came back, but Nickle could barely hear it. When he opened his eyes again, Jason's face had turned white.

"Pull out a Rune," Nickle whispered. "That will give you strength."

"But you just asked me why I had a Rune out. You said it wouldn't do any good here."

Nickle smiled. "Get a Rune in your hand. Somehow I forgot about this, but Reckle said that just by holding it, the curse would not have as much of an effect on you." Even as he said it, he knew it was not true. *"But, if Jason believes it will help,"* Nickle thought, *"maybe it will allow him to keep his cool."*

The Dwarf obeyed with a sudden jolt of speed. He raised a Rune in the air, readying himself for combat. His breathing quickened as his eyes darted around the city, scanning it for something that Nickle could not see. After a few tense moments, Jason's breathing slowed, and his hand relaxed ever so slightly.

He nodded. "You're right. It does help."

Nickle smiled again and continued up the stairs. When they reached the top, they were greeted by a set of massive doors made of pure gold. Despite the wear on the walls around them, the doors looked immaculate—not even the color had faded. Nickle pushed on the doors, which squeaked in protest. They stepped inside, expecting it to be dark, but they were more than relieved to see it was just as well-lit as the tunnel they had left.

"This is it," Nickle said. "This is my father's home."

"So, what are we looking for? What else did Reckle say?"

"That's where his advice ends. He didn't say anything else."

"What?" Jason squeaked. "What are we supposed to do now?"

"Whatever my father was investigating was important to him—probably the most important thing he ever did. I'm sure he kept notes on everything. Find his desk; that should have something in it."

Instantly, Jason set off like a blood-hound. He left the entrance and entered the kitchen. After finding nothing but knives, he went on to the next room and the next. After passing through another room, the Dwarves both simultaneously yelled.

"I found it."

In the corner of a bright room, decorated with gold olive leaves, they found a desk, which was built in almost a complete circle except for a cut out on one side. Jason jumped onto the desk, frantically swinging his hands in every direction. "Where is it? Where is it?" His voice had changed, almost as if it had suddenly gone hoarse.

Nickle approached from the opposite side of the room and clenched his jaw. "Calm down, Jason. We won't find anything if—"

Jason twisted around. "How will we know the way?"

"Easy. Big fella."

"What does the map tell you?"

Nickle smiled. "Jason, look at me. You need to calm down. Take another Rune from your belt."

Jason trembled and shook, his body shivering as if he was caught in a blizzard. He swallowed once, and then again. His face regained some color. "Hurry, Nickle. I don't know how much more of this place I can take. Please, hurry."

Nickle nodded. "We'll be out of here soon." He ran forward towards the desk and began pulling drawers out at random. Nothing but dust and debris greeted him. Anything that might have been valuable had either been carried away or taken by the curse. "Nothing. There's nothing here."

"What are you talking about?" Jason scoffed. "There's so many papers I can barely see the floor, let alone the desk. He must have something of value here. I've seen libraries that had fewer books than this. Your dad was a slob."

"There's nothing here—" Nickle began to say, but then inspiration hit him. "*It's the curse. The curse has eaten time and somehow reversed it—that's how he sees the papers and I don't.*"

Jason shivered again. "How will we know where to go, Nickle? What does the map tell you?"

Nickle ignored his friend for a moment and considered what he had to do. "*If I let the curse set in, I might be able to see what was on the desk in the past. But…what if I can't ever get back out? I can't believe I led Jason in here; I can't believe I'm here.*" He shook his head and closed his eyes. "*I can do this. Focus. I can do this.*" He let the fear swarm in on him, let it build up. He thought of the shrieking noise and the floating rocks, then the shape-shifting statue and the sudden flashbacks. "*What if I don't leave here ever again? What if I'm doomed to live here forever, trapped in the same place that killed my father's people?*"

When Nickle opened his eyes again, Jason was gone, and so was the gloomy scene. Bright lights and colors filled the room, almost as if it had been freshly refurbished. The Dwarf looked at the desk—it was shiny and clean. So clean in fact that a streak of light shivered across it.

He scratched his head. "Where are the papers that Jason talked about?" He pulled open a drawer only to reveal nothing. "*This is not the right time. I need to go deeper into the curse.*" Nickle let his eyes roll back into his head and the fears mound up. "*What if Jason betrays me? What if he is the one leading me into Gillian just to finish me off? Who is he working for? Why has he always been my friend? What does he gain from my friendship?*"

He opened his eyes again. The scene changed—this time, there were a few scattered documents and a half-empty plate of food. He went to the desk, looking at each sheet of paper that it held. "*Blueprints. Nothing but building blueprints.*" He closed his eyes. "*What if I'm no good as a Dwarf, and they send me back to the Pidders? What if Thornhead thinks me a fool and demotes me in front of the whole Silver Army? Maybe I don't belong here. What if I'm the reason my dad died? Was it my life he was trying to protect when he was killed? Or…did he just abandon me, transformed into a wretched Troll?*"

Nickle's eyes snapped open, revealing a room toppled over with papers. The colors had gone grey, almost black. It was dark, but not because there was not enough light. There was a gloomy feeling that settled in the room. He could hear voices from a hallway; some of them were talking about him.

Then the shriek returned. The noise was so loud, so close, that Nickle could have sworn it came from his own throat. The air became cold. He shivered. *"Focus, Nickle. The answer is here."* He began to rummage through the papers, picking up each one with more and more frantic movements. He saw all sorts of drawings, some of them were pictures of Runes, others were pictures of tunnels. *"Nothing. My father left nothing for me."* He picked up the next sheet, looked at it, and almost threw it away. But then a name caught his eye. *"Reckle?"* He pulled the sheet closer for inspection and read aloud. "Reckle must be told the truth about Brimming Borough."

Nickle looked through more sheets, now scanning for the name Brimming Borough. This time, the name appeared to be everywhere, but none of it seemed to make any sense. On one sheet of paper, Joshua had written, "Where is Brimming Borough?" and on another, he had written, "What are they making?" It took another minute before Nickle uncovered an old set of blueprints that were burned at the edges. He flattened the document on the desk, weighing the corners down with some ink wells to keep it open. "What is this place?"

As he looked through the blueprints, most of the rooms had standard labels like you would find in any government building, such as bathroom, and central office, but then Nickle read the words, "prison cells." As he stared at the document, he began to hear voices calling to him. At first, he thought it was his mind playing tricks, or perhaps the curse of the city, but soon, he began to hear pleas of help as if they were standing right next to him.

He felt overwhelmed by it, sickened by the noise. It became more intense—first pleading, then demanding. Nickle closed his eyes. More voices added to the mix, each one begging for relief.

"I'll save you," Nickle replied, his voice falling to a whisper. He studied the blueprint in earnest, taking note of a hasty location his father had penciled in towards the bottom. *"Where the food transportation pipes congregate before heading into EarthWorks."*

Nickle then noticed something odd. All the rooms in the upper chambers were gigantic as compared to the miniature prison cells in the lower levels. "How could anyone live in a cage that small?" Then in a horrible moment, his stomach became a ball of knots as he realized the answer. "Those cages are meant for the Gnomes."

Something flashed and then, Nickle was there, amid Brimming Borough, surrounded by thousands of Gnomes. The Fair Folk were grunting and sweating as they worked. A whip sounded in the distance and a cry of pain quickly followed. The room fluttered and twisted. Nickle stretched out his hand, trying to decide if he was trapped in a picture or if he was really in this room. But the noise and smells seemed too real. He covered his nose from the stench of body odor and blood.

The Gnomes all worked feverishly with small hammers and anvils. If they slackened, a Dwarf wearing an odd mask whipped them with a fiery rope. Right in front Nickle, a little Gnome fell to the ground, his legs buckling from strain. There were dozens of fresh whip marks across the little creature's back.

Nickle bent low and pulled the Gnome to his feet. He turned towards Nickle, obviously surprised by what he saw.

"Joshua?" The Gnome asked.

Nickle hesitated. "You can see me?"

The Gnome frowned. "Joshua. Look what you've done to us. Look at what they've forced us to build?"

Nickle shook his head. "It wasn't me."

The Gnome narrowed his eyes. "We loved you, Joshua. The Gnomes loved you. And look how you've dealt with us as if we're nothing more than the garbage that needs to be taken out."

Nickle frowned. "I'll set you free. I'll set all of you free." He stood up, shouting at the top of his lungs. "Come with me—all of you."

As Nickle finished speaking, the Gnomes hissed, cursing Nickle with every foul word they knew. They began to approach him, brandishing small picks and hammers. Nickle began to back away but quickly discovered that he was trapped.

"YOU BETRAYED US!" one of the Gnames screamed.

"We trusted you," an old Gnome hissed.

More Gnomes began to walk towards him, pouring out from the holes and cracks in the massive cavern. Nickle reached for a Rune, only to find out that his Rune belt was gone—so was his ax. He was unarmed and surrounded.

He raised his hands in defense. "I can change this…I can fix this."

These words seemed to have the opposite effect that Nickle wanted. The little creatures swarmed in, leaping towards him with blood in their eyes. Nickle held his ground for a few moments, but the sheer number of the creatures quickly forced him to the floor. They were biting him, tearing the flesh from his body. He could feel hundreds of burn-like injuries all over his skin.

He twisted violently, swinging his hands at his attackers. "I WILL CHANGE THIS!"

Far, far in the distance, between the pain and the yells from the Gnomes, Nickle could hear a voice calling him.

"Nickle! Wake up, Nickle!"

Chapter 24

Bottle of 1402 Burgundy

Nickle stirred but he did not awake completely. Then his thoughts came rushing back. "*The City of Gillian. The Curse. Where's Jason? The Gnomes!*" He took in a large breath as he sat up.

"Don't worry," said a voice in the dark. "You're no longer in Gillian."

"Jason?"

A light flicked on, revealing Jason's muscular frame. He looked different than usual, almost too different to be considered Jason. His face was pale, and his eyes were weary. Down one side of his face and neck were several deep cuts that looked fresh. He forced out a pathetic smile. "Yes, it's me."

"How did I get here? Where's Sharlindrian?"

"You've been here for the last several days," Jason said. "After you lost it completely, I had to carry you out. You gave me a pretty good fight, though. I would have left you behind had I not needed you to open the door again." He tried to laugh, but all that he could force out was a cackle. "Sharlindrian stayed for the first day—until the Healers came. Once they announced that you'd be fine, she left, mumbling to herself about her father being angry or something. Luckily, the rest of the Dwarves here seem satisfied with the story that you're sick."

"What happened to your face? Where did you get all the cuts on your throat?"

"You should know—you did it to me."

Nickle shook his head. "I'm…sorry, Jason. Sorry I got you into that mess."

Jason lowered his head into his hands. "We almost didn't make it out. I was almost completely gone myself when we stumbled out of that cursed city. Listen, Nickle, that was more than either one of us could handle. Not even experienced warriors who have long since earned their Tines venture into cursed cities."

"Well, thank you for going with me."

"We almost died in there."

Nickle shut his eyes for a moment. "Yeah, I know."

"Do you? Do you know how far gone you were? Do you know the things you were saying—the things you were prophesying?"

"I…I…I don't—"

"You about killed me. You grabbed a rock and waved it around, threatening to crack my skull if I stepped any closer."

"I don't remember any of that."

"It scared me."

"You're the toughest Dwarf I know—the first in our class."

Jason shook his head. "I won't do that again—I won't ever do anything like that again. I hope it was worth it." An odd silence filled the room as both Dwarves looked at the ground.

Finally, Jason stirred. A few moments later, he spoke. "So…what did you find out?"

Nickle slowly kicked his legs off the side of his bed. "There's a secret facility somewhere near EarthWorks. I think I might be able to find it. My father figured it out years ago, and he must have stopped it from happening."

"Stopped what?"

"The Gnomes have been enslaved. They're the secret to this entire puzzle—they always were. They're being sent off to work camps and forced to make something, something that they would not be making unless they had no other choice. I'm a fool. They've been enslaved—and you and I were the ones that made it happen."

"Who's sending them into slavery? What are you talking about?"

"The Tri'Ark—or at least someone in it. It can't be everyone in the Tri'Ark, or they wouldn't have bothered covering it up like they have. We haven't been recruiting Gnomes to build light switches but to be shipped out and forced into slavery."

Jason frowned. "I've seen some of the factories where the Gnomes work; they all seemed happy with their conditions to me—some of them even came up to me to say thanks."

"Those are the factories they showcase to everyone—those are the factories that they want others to see. But what about the others? Thousands of Gnomes were enslaved, so it must be a massive factory."

"The GreenHouse is big, and we've never been to that one."

"But I've seen Gnomes coming back from that one. If they were going to send Gnomes there to be enslaved, they wouldn't be allowed to return home. What about Yellow Vine?"

"No, I've seen a few Gnomes return from there."

Nickle began pacing the room. "What about Bright Road?"

"It's too far. It's clear on the opposite end of the world, near the surface, almost cut off completely from supplies. If a Gnome was sent out there, it'd be months before they would be allowed to come back."

"Yes, exactly," Nickle nodded. "Maybe we can call them?"

Jason shook his head. "You're in EarthWorks, not on the surface. There are no phones down here."

"There are pictures, though. We can look up the picture for Bright Road and communicate with them directly."

"No, we can't," Jason replied. "Remember that mistake we made a few weeks back, and we tried to reach out to them directly? The picture communications don't work with Bright Road because the factory is close to the surface where magic is weak. We had to dispatch a Dwarf courier to relay the message."

Nickle considered that for a moment. "So none of the Gnomes from Bright Road have been able to communicate through pictures with their families?"

"No."

"That's convenient," Nickle replied. "How many Gnomes have we sent there?"

Jason grabbed a stone tablet from a nearby desk. He traced his finger on it for a moment until it glowed with a blue light. After a while, the Dwarf answered. "Looks like...only two thousand."

"In total? I just sent two thousand there last week. That can't be right. You must be looking at last week's totals."

Jason shook his head. "No, I'm reading it right. It says two thousand in total."

"The week before that," Nickle replied, "we sent up four thousand, and the week before that, we sent up ten."

"It must reset every week."

"What if Bright Road is not clear across the world? What if it was closer to us than any of the other camps? What if Bright Road is actually Brimming Borough?"

"Then, no one would be missing those Gnomes for months."

"Exactly. But there must be another way they're funneling more Gnomes to Brimming Borough. I saw thousands of them—all of them with bleeding backs and broken spirits."

"How could you have seen them?" Jason asked. "It's not like you saw the past—you said your dad had stopped it before it even started. It's like you were seeing the present, but how's that possible? Gillian is nowhere near EarthWorks."

"I don't know," Nickle replied. "Could it have been the curse?"

"We don't know much about cursed cities," Jason replied, "because there aren't many people stupid enough to wander into them."

Nickle stared off in the distance. "It felt so real. I could feel the heat from their fires. I could smell the stink from their unwashed bodies."

Jason slid his finger along the stone tablet, which changed the tablet's color from blue to green. "Look at this. These are the numbers for each factory: Yellow Vine has three million Gnomes, two million of them active—"

"And what about the rest of them?"

"About half a million are on medical release, and the rest have either been terminated or on holiday."

Nickle rubbed his hands against his face. "They just started a few weeks ago and already they're on medical release? Or even holiday? And what holiday would that be? How do half a million Gnomes get fired that quickly? After we sent them off to their factories, someone must have swooped in and reassigned them—right under our noses. According to our records, everything looks fine, and it would too."

"Well, we better report it."

"Report it to who? Remember, it's someone within the Tri'Ark that's orchestrating this whole thing. We tell the wrong person, and our lives will end as quickly as our heroics. Remember…my father was killed for knowing the same thing we now know."

Jason shook his head. "Then how do we find out who started this whole charade?"

"We need to find out what they're making—and then we'll have some idea who's behind it all."

"How will that help?"

Nickle grabbed Jason's shoulders. "If we find out what they're making, then it'll be easy to figure out who benefits the most from it. The one who benefits the most has to be the one motivated to enslave millions of Gnomes."

"Are you suggesting we break into a government facility?"

"No, not us. But I know just the person for the job."

***

"Shemway Darkfiend," the skinny man corrected. "That's how my name is pronounced, and if you say it wrong again, I promise you'll regret it."

Jason frowned. "Don't try my patience, Thieftian. You're only here because Nickle wants you here. You're nothing more than a common thief who'd gladly steal from his own mum if it meant that you'd have an ounce more of gold dust to your name."

"And yet," Shemway hissed, "here I am, answering to a job offer...from you."

Jason narrowed his eyes. "Nickle wanted you here not me, you street rat—"

"—I'd put a little finesse on that tongue of yours, before someone cuts it out—"

Nickle suddenly entered the room, his hands laden down with books. The Dwarf grinned at Shemway and Jason in turn. The other two grimaced back.

"What?" Nickle asked.

Shemway's magnetically handsome face smiled for a brief moment, his brilliant teeth flashing like a stoplight. "I'm a busy person, one that does not enjoy the company of bearded children."

Jason stiffened but did not speak.

Shemway gave a low bow directed at Nickle. "How can I serve you, Ambassador?"

Nickle put the books down and stepped forward. With a thick

dirty hand, he slapped Shemway's arm, leaving a trail of dust behind. "So, you do remember me."

The Thieftian shifted uncomfortably while he pulled out a handkerchief from the folds of his clothes. "Yes, Nickle Brickle'Bee—fourth class Dwarf, who was recently promoted to be an Ambassador to the Gnomes. You graduated last in your class and were quickly assigned to the Gnome Detail because of your father's past success."

Nickle pulled his head back. "How did you know all of that?"

Shemway began dabbing at the dust on his clothes. "It was in the newspaper not long ago. Were your hands clean, by the way? You haven't been touching any sick animals as of late, have you?"

The Dwarf shook his head.

Shemway did the same. "Good. I just had this shirt washed."

"It's just dirt—"

Shemway nodded and began moving around the room, his hands behind his back like a professor. "I'll probably end up washing it anyway. Besides germing up my sleeve, what's the purpose of this summons?"

Nickle   stepped   forward.   "We   need   your   help." Jason cleared his throat.

Nickle took another step forward. "I mean, *I* need your help. And that's your job, right—to help new EarthWork citizens land on their feet?"

Shemway glanced around the room. "And so it is, but I hear that you're the youngest Ambassador ever appointed—and also the first one that's a fourth class Dwarf. I think you've landed on your feet well enough. What could I, a lowly administrator within the Tri'Ark, have to offer to such esteemed Dwarves—I'm, after all, a fourth class Human. Do you want to know how to catch the Tube to the surface? Do you want to know how to turn out the lights in your room?"

"I've figured all of that out—"

"Then I can be of no further assistance to you," Shemway said as he went for the door.

Nickle cut him off. "Come on. Why don't you stay awhile? We got you a bottle of Burgundy wine. I think the year is…1402."

"You don't have a 1402—" Shemway began to say, but he was interrupted by the light green bottle Nickle pulled from a cupboard.

The Dwarf grinned. "I hear it's your favorite."

"Touché, little Dwarf." The Thieftian eagerly accepted the glass of wine that was handed to him. He stirred it slightly, sniffing it with gentle care. "You've washed the glass since it was last used, I assume?" Nickle nodded. "Twice."

With this, the Thieftian drained the glass and set it back down on the table. His handsome face grinned as wide as a boy who had just returned from his first Halloween. "All right, Dwarf, you've got five minutes. I'm listening."

Nickle pulled his seat forward. "What I'm about to tell you can't leave this room. If it does—"

"—Then all of our lives will be in peril," Shemway finished. "Yes, I've heard this all before. Can I have another glass?"

Nickle complied, half filling the glass. The Thieftian looked disappointedly at the half-empty glass but drained it just the same.

The Dwarf continued. "We've discovered something, something about...."

"About what?"

"First, you've got to swear to not speak of this to anyone outside this room."

"Little Dwarf, please, I'm a low-level employee in the largest government organization in the world. Who would I tell? Who would care if I told them?"

Jason shook his head. "We can't trust him."

Nickle swallowed. "The Gnomes are being forced into slavery."

Shemway sat up abruptly, spraying wine across the room. "How do you know this? Who told you this?"

Nickle frowned. "Does that matter? Millions of Gnomes are suffering right now, being forced to do something that offends their very souls."

"How do you know what is in a Gnome's soul?"

"I know there would be no reason for them to be forced to do something if they were not willing to do it on their own. They're making something—maybe a weapon of some sort—that will affect you just as much as anyone else. You know how unstable the world is down here; in the wrong hands, a powerful weapon could upset everything."

"And what concern is that of mine?"

Nickle pulled his head back. "Did you not just hear what I said?

Millions of Gnomes have been forced into slavery, compelled to make something that might destroy EarthWorks or give rise to some evil power. That's why it concerns you."

Shemway helped himself to another glass of wine. "What do you want me to do about it?"

"I need you to find out what they are making?"

"And how much dust are you willing to pay?"

Jason stood up, knocking over a chair as he did. "Are you mad, Thieftian? Millions of Gnomes are out there suffering—"

Shemway's eyes turned to daggers. "—Suffering because of what you two did. Don't try to pass your guilt on to me. If I'm going to have my life on the line, it's going to be for a bag of gold—a big bag."

Nickle stood up and caught Jason's balled fist. "Why don't you go outside and wait. Just give us a few minutes."

Jason gritted his teeth and stared at the Thieftian for several moments longer. Finally, he left, slamming the door behind him as he did.

Shemway poured himself another glass of wine. "He's a little bit of a hothead, isn't he? But then again, most of you Dwarves are."

Nickle remained silent for a few moments. "If I pay you, will you be able to guarantee results? Can you guarantee that you'll be able to find the Gnomes and see what they're building?"

"The Gnomes are in Brimming Borough."

The Dwarf furrowed his brow. "How did you—"

"—As I said, Nickle, I'm the best at what I do. And because I'm feeling extremely generous today, I won't charge you for that bit of information I just gave you."

"I already knew that."

"Yeah, because I just told you."

Nickle furrowed his brow. "No, I knew that before you said anything."

Shemway leaned back on his chair and closed his eyes. "Did you now? Impressive, for a Dwarf. But do you know the amount of security that is in and around Brimming Borough? How many hundreds of guards are stationed in a camp not far from Brimming Borough, not to mention magical sensors and booby traps? That place is locked down tighter than the toughest clam."

"So, you're saying it's too tough for you to break into?"

"Don't put words into my mouth, Dwarf. I'm just saying that of all the places you could have picked to break into, you picked one of the most difficult. Very few know of its location, fewer still can find their way there on their own. The guards themselves have no idea where they are or when they will leave. No ordinary Thieftian could waltz in and live to tell about it. It's maddening just talking about even attempting such a feat—much less doing it. It's impossible—even for the best."

"Well, then, do you have the name of a Thieftian that will at least give it a try."

"No Thieftian will even think you're serious. Save yourself the time."

"I'll pay you ten kilos of gold."

Shemway's eyes widened ever so slightly. "The cost for the equipment alone will be more than that."

"Fifteen kilos."

"There's a slim chance of success if only fifteen kilos are involved."

"Twenty."

Shemway grinned handsomely. "Twenty-five and you have a deal—oh, and I get to keep the bottle of wine."

Chapter 25

Breaking into the Unbreakable

"*Are you ready?*" Nickle whispered.

Shemway's crackly voice replied. "Yes, but I'm not loving the idea of you two watching me through all of this."

"*Hey,*" Jason hissed, "*if you want to pull the plug right now, I'd be happy to take back our gold.*"

Nickle shook his head and mouthed the word, "No."

Jason grumbled. The young Dwarf had not been a fan of hiring the Thieftian; he had wanted to try and sneak in by himself. But when he found out how much gold the two Dwarves were paying the thief, he could not help but be in a permanently bad mood. It took all their combined money to front the bill, and still, they did not have enough. They had to borrow some money from a few other Dwarves to make up the difference, which was something Jason loathed more than anything. They had made good money as Ambassadors, better than most other Dwarves, but as quickly as a light turns off, their money had been spent. Jason doubted if he would ever have that kind of gold dust again.

Shemway laughed. "I've already spent most of your gold—but if you want to pull the plug, I'd be happy to give you the few grams that are left."

Jason turned as red as a tomato.

Nickle quickly replied. "*You're fine, Thieftian. We've already come too far not to go all the way. How far away will you be able to hear us?*"

"There's nowhere on this planet that I won't be able to hear you. The cream we placed on our lips and ears, comes from the earwax of a Blue Tip Water Faerie. As long as it doesn't dry out, I'll be able to hear you no matter what separates us."

"*How long does it take before it dries out?*"

"About an hour."

Earlier that day, Shemway had led the Dwarves through a series of maintenance pipes. The pipes were once used to transport food from one side of EarthWorks to the other, but new innovations had made the tubes useless as well as neglected. They reached a small room that had two dusty seats.

Nickle and Jason both carried Rune candles, which provided them enough light to see but not enough to fill the whole space. The candles were shaped like a Piddler candle except instead of a wick on top, they had a Fire Rune carved into it. They had been an expensive purchase, since only Golden Calligraphers were skilled enough to craft Fire Runes that burned slowly instead of bursting into flames. Jason had tried to save money and crafted his own candles, but the resulting explosion of fire singed off his eyebrows. As soon as the two Dwarves had set up, Shemway had taken off towards Brimming Borough.

Nickle squinted in the dim light. "These candles are crap."

"Now you know why Faerie Light is the Tri'Ark's company of choice," Jason answered. "Not only is it cheaper, but they make any room as bright as day. But on the flip side, these candles will last at least a year before they burn out—so I guess that's something."

Shemway frowned as he spoke through the Faerie balm. "That's why Thieftians never liked the idea of working with Faerie Light."

"That's because you prefer to rob people in the dark," Jason whispered.

"What's that, Dwarf?" Shemway asked.

Nickle cut in. *"So, if you run into any trouble, what do you want us to do?"*

"The only thing you can do—run away and tell someone taller."

Jason frowned.

The Thieftian had dressed in all black, from his head to his toes, and draped himself with a thin cloak. The black cloth released a hint of smoke, almost as if it had been endued with the essence of night. Attached to the Human's waist was a belt that was very similar to a Rune belt, having multiple slots and attachments. Instead of Runes, however, the belt was stocked with dozens of small vials, each one filled with a different colored potion. Shemway also had other things strapped to his body, most of them odd weapons and levers. Nickle and Jason added to the Thieftian's garb by padding him down with a mixture of Sight Runes—much to Shemway's annoyance.

"We'll be able to see what you see," Nickle explained. "We can watch your back—make sure that no one is sneaking up on you. Plus, we need to collect as much evidence as possible, and I'll be recording everything you see with a Memory Rune."

Shemway shook his handsome head as he spoke through the Faerie lip balm. "I can't believe the stuff I have to put up with—"

"*—After paying you twenty-five kilos of gold dust,*" Jason replied, "*I don't think you've had to put up with nearly enough.*"

Grumbling to himself, the Thieftian continued into the darkness.

Nickle stuck a Sight Rune to one of his eyes, which instantly made a sucking sound as it adjusted. A moment later, he could see out one of the Sight Runes they had attached to the Thieftian's head. Nickle switched the setting to night vision by whispering an incantation, which turned everything a reddish hue. "How does Shemway see in the dark?"

Jason also attached a Sight Rune to one of his eyes. "He's got Bunsin cream. I saw him putting it on before he left. It's a rare cream that, if applied to your eyelids, will give you sight in the darkness—as long as your eyes remain closed."

The more Nickle watched the Thieftian move in the darkness, the more odd the whole thing became. He could not quite figure out what was so strange about it, but it was almost too surreal to believe. The Thieftian was so quiet, so stealthy that he barely seemed to exist.

"It's called Bludin Fungus," Jason answered.

"What?" Nickle replied. "What is?"

"That's why he's noiseless. Thieftians are trained to be stealthy from the first day they're born—they're encouraged to steal so they can practice their stealth. But it's not until they start using Bludin Fungus that they become truly noiseless. It's a rare breed of fungus that feeds on noise. Only Thieftians know how to care for the fungus as well as apply it properly."

"For hating a group of people, you sure know a lot about them."

"Well," Jason stammered, "I never said they didn't have some cool potions."

Shemway Darkfiend was in his element. He loved the feel of

the darkness, the feeling of his heart pounding in his chest with adrenaline. His senses had been heightened by a sensory potion he had taken an hour earlier. The wall around him smelled like rust and decay. There was a rat scratching at something stuck in the floor several yards in front of him.

He slowed to a stop and looked around. *"This is the place."* With cat-like agility, he ran up one wall and leaped for a ladder that was high above him. He caught the last rung and silently pulled himself up.

"Wow...that was amazing," Nickle's voice transmitted through the Faerie lip balm.

"Can I expect a commentary every time I do something," Shemway mouthed back. "Stay alert and pay attention; only speak if you have something useful to say." With this, the Thieftian continued to pull himself up the ladder until he reached a hatch. He pulled a flask from his side and opened it, letting a clear but potent fragrance rise up and out of the trap above. As Shemway looked into the potion bottle, he could see through the mist that wafted up—much like a periscope. After a moment of scanning the surroundings and seeing it was clear, the Thieftian pushed the hatch open, revealing the inside of a much larger tunnel that was filled with hundreds of grey plants. He quickly corked his potion, pulled himself up, and silently set the hatch back down.

Shemway grinned. *"This is definitely it."*

In the distance, he could see a large, stone building with massive doors. The design and structure was definitely Dwarf, but the symbols of power that surrounded the building appeared to be Elvish. Shemway could tell that the light produced was not from Faerie Light, but lights made from well-placed Gnome switches. At the entrance were two of the biggest and ugliest Rinacons Shemway had ever seen. They were garbed in golden armor that was thick with Runes. One of them held an axe, the other held a spiked club.

Shemway nodded. "Typical perimeter defense, but they left the doors open—fools."

The Thieftian quickly moved forward, carefully brushing through the grey plants. He was just about to make his move for the front doors when a sudden sound of marching stopped him in his tracks. He lowered himself to the ground and pulled his cloak over his body, which instantly turned as gnarled and grey as the plants around him. From his dark hiding spot, he could see a column of Gnomes approaching the front entrance. The little creatures were beaten and broken; some of them still had blood dripping down their cheeks and faces. There were about four thousand Gnomes in total. A dozen Dwarves dressed in full battle armor escorted the Gnomes towards Brimming Borough. The Rinacons roared and spat as the little creatures approached—one of them yelling so loudly that it echoed several times before the noise finally died.

The Gnomes shuddered as they passed between the two blood-thirsty creatures and through the massive entrance. After the last chained Gnome disappeared, the enormous set of doors began shutting again.

Shemway grabbed a potion from his belt and popped off the lid, revealing a greenish smoke. He poured it on himself, dispersing the concoction with lightning speed. As the potion spread, it appeared to melt away his skin and clothes. Soon, Shemway was nothing more than an upper torso, the rest of him had disappeared. Moments later, he was gone completely; it was almost as if he had evaporated into thin air.

Nickle leaned forward. "Where did he go?"

Jason furrowed his brow. "He used Green Till. It's another secret Thieftian potion; in case you didn't already guess, it makes them momentarily invisible."

Shemway began running towards the large gate. Before he was halfway there, the massive doors were only three feet away from being closed. He picked up speed, jumped, and rolled, just barely making it through before the gigantic stone doors shut. The entrance groaned as heavy locks began clicking into place.

Shemway shook his head as he stepped forward. The inside of the building was hotter than it had been outside, despite an extensive series of ceiling fans. Even though it was hastily built, the builders knew what they were doing. The walls were several feet thick and enchanted with powerful Repulsion Runes.

Shemway stepped quickly until he reached a massive crevice that fell for hundreds, perhaps even thousands of feet. The blackness stretched for such a distance that not even his eyes covered in Bunsin cream could see the end of it. He silently stepped onto a catwalk that functioned like a drawbridge.

As he reached the other side, the Green Till began fading and his skin and clothes began to reappear. He suddenly felt his breath leave him. A massive black door stood in his way, ending any hope of him calmly walking through. Shemway put his ear to the door and listened. Moments later, he could hear water splashing, which confirmed his suspicions.

"What's wrong?" Nickle asked over the Faerie lip balm.

Shemway shook his head. "It's Asminian stone—the trickiest stone on Earth. This must have cost them a fortune."

"Well, you're a Thieftian," Jason said, *"why don't you pick the lock?"*

"Do you see a lock?" Shemway replied harshly. "The only way to open it is by putting in the correct Rune of power, which I don't have, and coupling it with the right words of power, which I don't know. It would be easier to blow a hole in the wall than to try to break through Asminian stone. I'll have to find another way."

"But you're on a catwalk over a crevice," Nickle said. *"There's no other way."*

"There's always another way," Shemway said as he pulled out a crossbow from his side and shot a small needle and thread into the wall. Before even waiting to see if the needle held, the Thieftian launched himself off the catwalk and into the air. With lightning-fast reflexes, Shemway leaped between the two walls of the crevice, occasionally balancing himself with the small needle and thread from the crossbow. He pressed on into the darkness. Every so often, he would push some button on the crossbow that would magically retract the needle. In those few moments, nothing but air and the Thieftian's agility stopped him from falling. Then Shemway would aim the needle and shoot it into the rock in front of him and swing on.

He flipped between the walls so quickly and with so much finesse that he often did not even need the needle and crossbow to keep him upright. He somehow seemed to spot every ledge in the rock, every crevice and handhold, and use it with the greatest effect. After several impressive moments, Shemway shot the needle into the rock above him and attached the crossbow to his utility belt, freeing up his hands.

He let himself gently swing to a stop and then put his ear against the rock. He could hear a loud, humming noise. He frowned and changed positions, moving more to his right. Again, he put his ear against the rock, and again he was disappointed by the humming noise that followed.

"Your little dirt-digger friends built this better than I thought," Shemway said. "They've got Repulsion Runes all along the walls."

"What do Repulsion Runes do? Can't you blow through them?" Nickle asked.

"Repulsion Runes deflect magical attacks, making them almost impossible to break through with a simple spell or potion. The only way through a Repulsion Rune is to attack it with a series of powerful spells. Even then, it would take a long time to break through—perhaps several hours, depending on how well the Rune was crafted. Piddler dynamite would be more effective than magic at this point. But there's always another way." The Thieftian whispered an incantation, and the little crossbow reeled in more string. Once he was several feet higher than before, the Thieftian again put his ear to the wall. But he was again disappointed by what he heard. This procedure persisted until Shemway reached the domed roof. Once there, he put his ear against it and listened. He could hear nothing.

"But you little Dwarves always forget to guard the roof," Shemway whispered.

He pulled another potion from his belt, this one was a black gooey substance that shimmered as Shemway began pouring it out on the rock roof. As soon as the goo hit the stone, it disappeared completely, like a cup of water poured into a lake.

"Is that going to melt the stone?" Nickle asked.

"No," Shemway said, "that would leave a nasty hole behind. This is actually a memory potion, one so strong that if a drop ever touched your forehead, it would erase everything anyone has ever told you. This batch is so powerful that it will force the stone to forget that it's supposed to be solid." The Thieftian then covered his head with a black hood and stood on the spot where he had poured the liquid. Then he waited. Long moments passed.

Jason opened his mouth to taunt the Thieftian, but before he could, Shemway began sinking into the stone. He sank slowly at first, but soon began to pick up speed. Moments later, he squeezed through the roof and dripped towards the ground below. Before he could fall too far, he suspended himself in the air by shooting his crossbow into the ceiling. He was in a large room, one that had been decorated with hexagonal pillars and large marble slabs. The room was far better constructed than everything else he had seen so far. A massive throne was positioned on the far end of the room, right below an equally large tapestry that depicted a picture of Kara'Kala—the Demon Lord.

Shemway narrowed his eyes as he caught sight of the tapestry. "Now, that's an interesting decoration."

He attached the crossbow to his lower back, which allowed him to face towards the floor. He waited for a moment, listening to the steps of some unseen guard. The footsteps came closer and closer until a Dwarf dressed in full battle Tines appeared. The armor looked ancient and evil, having dozens of odd Runes that neither Nickle nor Jason recognized. On his face was a helmet that looked more alive than any metal Nickle had ever seen. All sorts of metallic tentacles jutted out from the helmet, snaking from side to side. It looked like the face of a deep-sea creature that had long since become extinct.

Shemway swore. Without wasting a second, he released the cord on the crossbow and fell straight towards the Dwarf below. Just before contact, the Dwarf suddenly became aware of the danger he was in and turned to face the threat, armed with a massive axe. He shot a blazing white fireball at the Thieftian, who dodged it only by inches. A moment later, the two collided, sending both of them rolling across the floor. Shemway recovered quickly and grabbed a potion from his side, but the Dwarf moved just as fast and also grabbed the potion. Their struggle was brief as the two tugged on the bottle, trying to break the other's grip. But it was the glass that finally broke, sending shards in every direction. Instantly a black liquid filled the room, forming into a thick cloud.

Shemway disappeared into the blackness and ran as fast as he could in the opposite direction, all the while, white fire zipped past him. The walls to either side of the Thieftian exploded into shards of stone and debris, sending more smoke into the air. He jumped off a wall, dodging a red bolt of lightning that zigzagged into a wooden table.

"What is that thing?" Nickle asked.

"A Sumian Dwarf—one of the Hunters," Jason whispered. "They wear armor made from organic metal that can take other shapes. The armor heightens their senses to the point where it's impossible to get past them without being detected. Their sense of smell and sight are so far beyond anything natural that they are impossible to deceive. Once the armor is bonded with the Dwarf, it's difficult to get off without killing the poor fool that wears it. It becomes part of them, sucking its energy from the Dwarf's body—like a parasite on a host. Shemway is in real trouble."

The Thieftian continued to run, the Sumian Dwarf hot on his tail. Shemway entered a massive room that was smokey with heat. He was on a catwalk sixty feet above the ground floor. The room stretched out for hundreds of yards in every direction, dotted with thousands of Gnomes who were each wielding small hammers. Without a moment of hesitation, Shemway leaped off the catwalk and into the air, his clothes flapping as he fell. At the last moment, he threw a potion onto the floor that sent up an explosion of wind that slowed his fall. Once he hit the ground, he tucked, rolled, and caught his feet.

He glanced back up at the Sumian Dwarf, laughing to himself. "See if you can get down from that!"

The next moment, the Dwarf jumped from the catwalk and flipped through the air. His body slammed into the ground, sending an aftershock that shook the closest of Gnomes and kicked up a cloud of dust. When the dust cleared, the Dwarf stood, his Sumian armor seemingly unscathed by the impact.

"Crap," Shemway whispered.

The Thieftian set off running again. He flipped off a low table, dodging a horrific ball of flame. More projectiles followed, but each time his agility saved him. He ducked into a small tunnel, putting some distance between him and his pursuer. He was running so fast, he did not have time to stop himself before crashing into another Sumian Dwarf, this one carrying a massive hammer. Shemway lost his balance and landed on his side. A moment later, the Dwarf's hammer was coming towards him. He flipped back onto his feet, dodging the weapon at the last moment.

"All right," Shemway heckled, "let's see if he can handle this." He grabbed a potion from his side and punched the Dwarf in the chest. With the impact, the bottle broke in two and exploded into the Dwarf's armor. The blow sent the Sumian warrior flipping through the air and into a far wall, which cracked from the collision. The Dwarf stirred but did not get up.

Before Shemway could enjoy this small victory, two more

Sumians appeared. The Thieftian ducked under a swing and sidestepped another attack. The Dwarves pressed forward, forcing Shemway to run up a wall and flip backward. He then kicked one of the Dwarves in the face.

"*Wow,*" Jason said. "*You've got some mad skills.*"

Shemway narrowed his eyes. He grabbed two potions from his side and waved them threateningly at the opponents in front of him. "I'm a Thieftian of the highest order. If you want to escape alive, you'll turn back." As he spoke, Shemway pulled out a short sword from his back and poured one of the potions onto the blade.

One of the Dwarves growled, the other charged.

Shemway slammed the other potion into the sword, causing an explosion of light and fire. The flame wrapped itself around the blade, turning it crimson. Despite themselves, the Dwarves faltered in their attack.

"Now," Shemway jeered. "Go back the way you came from or—"

"*Behind you!*" Nickle yelled.

Shemway ducked just as a massive axe passed overhead. A third Sumian had crept up behind him, trapping Shemway in the tunnel. The Thieftian flipped backward and sliced the Sumian across the chest. The armor hissed and growled. The other two Dwarves rushed in, swinging wildly with their blades.

Shemway went on the offensive, attacking all opponents at once. He stabbed one in the leg and sliced the other across the arm. Still, the Sumians would not retreat. One of the Dwarves shot a ball of flame that struck Shemway right in the chest. The Thieftian's black armor absorbed the impact, saving his life, but the force of the blow sent him crashing into a wall several yards away.

He tried to stand but stumbled back down. The Dwarves ran forward, quickly closing the distance. But as they approached, their bodies began to slow down and their movement became choppy, like a toy that is running out of batteries.

Shemway grinned. "Hah. Did you really think you could best me—did you really think I would let myself get hit in the chest by your predictable fireball? Your pride just lost you this battle."

"He's brilliant," Jason whispered. "He must have thrown down an Artic Potion while he was hit in the chest. They would have easily detected and countered it had they not been so confident after hitting him with that Fire Rune. Shemway let himself get hit so they would run right into his trap."

The Sumians stopped moving altogether. Ice shards sprang up from the ground, wrapping around the Dwarves, and within moments, their bodies were surrounded by sleet.

Shemway tried to stand, but he fell back down. Using his blazing sword as a crutch, he pushed himself up to his feet. His head was spinning, his breath short. He stumbled out of the tunnel and back into the large room filled with Gnomes. The little creatures cheered and clapped their hands together, screaming with all the strength their small bodies could muster. Shemway enjoyed the attention—he even waved back at a few of the more enthusiastic Gnomes.

"Shemway!" Nickle yelled. *"I'm sure the alarm has been set off. You don't have much time before Brimming Borough is crawling with guards. You've got to find out what they're making and get out of there."*

The Thieftian nodded and continued, the Gnomes cheering as he went. He walked towards the center of the room, where a massive pillar surrounded by small spiraling stairs was located. Thousands of Gnomes covered the pillar like ants on an anthill. The Thieftian began running up the small steps, taking them two dozen at a time. As he reached the peak, he was blinded by the light that emanated from the top of it. Shemway shielded his eyes with a hand and peered past his fingers.

"What is it?" Nickle asked. *"What are they making?"*

The Thieftian squinted. "It's…a…a key."

A voice from the other side of the room interrupted. "In the name of the Silver Army, halt!"

Shemway frowned. "Well, Dwarves, it looks like I've got to go." The Thieftian grabbed the Sight Runes that were attached to his body and crushed them with his hands, severing the connection between the Dwarves and Shemway.

"Hello!" Nickle yelled. *"Shemway, we lost picture. Are you there? Can you hear us?"*

Chapter 26

Mobilization

Nickle paced the small room several times before he spoke. "He's trapped in there with no way out. Why did he break the Sight Runes?"

"He's a Thieftian," Jason replied. "If anyone can get out of that mess, he can."

"Why did the Gnomes just sit there? They weren't even trying to escape while Shemway was dealing with the guards."

"The chains they wear must be Hexed or something; I bet they can't even conjure up a puff of smoke, let alone escape."

"We need to do something."

"Like what? We still have no idea who's behind it all."

Nickle continued to pace as he spoke. "Why would they be making a key—a key to what? And what sort of key requires the effort of thousands of Gnomes?"

Jason shook his head. "I have no idea."

Nickle stopped in his tracks. "We don't have that much time. It sounds like the key is nearly finished—maybe it already is."

"What will happen to the Gnomes when it's finished?"

Nickle shook his head. "I can't imagine anything good. If just one of those Gnomes escapes, they could testify of what happened to them." Nickle paused in thought. Then his face turned grim. "They're going to exterminate the Gnomes to cover up their tracks. We've got to tell someone."

"Who?"

"Thornhead Back'Break—he told us we should report anything unusual to him, and this certainly qualifies. I imagine he'll be in Hurn. Come on."

Jason furrowed his brow. "But you said we couldn't trust anyone until we knew what they're making."

"We've got to tell someone or millions of Gnomes could be snuffed out by tomorrow."

Nickle and Jason quickly exited the long system of pipes and hiked out towards EarthWorks until they found a Taxi-Lator. It took them a half hour to arrive in Hurn. Nickle had not been back to the Dwarf city since his first day in EarthWorks. He remembered feeling a need to see everything—to immerse himself in his ancient heritage—but now that seemed like such a selfish idea.

Nickle had become accustomed to the worn down and dilapidated buildings that were found in the Dwarf outposts, and it was surprising to once again be surrounded by pristine structures. The Taxi-Lator fare was costly, and the two Dwarves had to use their last bit of gold dust to pay for the ride. They began their search in the largest, most official government buildings, but soon spread out from there. Occasionally, they would stop and ask for help, but everything they were told usually confused them more than it helped. Finally, after looking for over two hours, they ran headlong into Thornhead Back'Break—the Elected Chief Warlord of the four Dwarf Clans.

The massive Dwarf was dressed in brilliant armor that was filled with powerful and intricate Runes. Neither of the two Dwarves had seen Thornhead wear this particular suit of armor before, and it was evident that this was what he wore to battle. It was black and charred; several spots had large patches that had been repaired.

Nickle grabbed the Warlord's arm. "Sir, I need to speak to you."

"Sorry, lad, I'm right in the middle of something—"

"—This can't wait," Nickle said as he stretched to his full height and narrowed his eyes. "We have to talk to you now."

Thornhead pushed past. "Sorry, I wish I could but—"

"—It's about the Gnomes," Nickle hissed. "Give us five minutes to explain."

"The Gnomes?" Thornhead asked. "What about them?"

Nickle gestured towards an empty room. "Let's talk in there."

As soon as they entered the space, Nickle began shooting out words as fast as his tongue would let him. Occasionally Jason would jump in and "enhance" the story with the glorious details of his accomplishments. It took them over ten minutes to explain everything, but by the end of it, Thornhead looked pale.

The giant Dwarf turned away from the other two and looked

at the wall. "This is bad. Real bad. After all those years of building up relations with the Gnomes—after all that time of careful planning. Do you have any idea who's behind this?"

Jason quickly spoke. "No."

"And what about the Thieftian; where is he?"

"We have no idea."

Thornhead slammed his fist into a table so hard it split right down the middle. "We've got to fix this."

Nickle saluted. "Tell us what to do, Chief Warlord. We're at your service."

Thornhead whipped around, his jaw taut. "You need to tell the Gnomes everything, tell them of the work camps, tell them about the brutal treatment of their people. If we're to do something, we have to do it fast. We need to suspend all commerce between the Tri'Ark and the Gnomes, stop all personnel shipments in and out of Tiran 'Og. Nickle, you have to convince Reckle that you speak the truth."

"And what should I tell him?"

Thornhead sucked in a deep breath. "Tell him that his people have been tricked into slavery."

***

The two Dwarves left the room at a run. They exited the building and began hailing a Taxi-Lator when they suddenly realized that they had no money to pay for the ride.

Nickle grunted in frustration. "Now, what do we do? Why didn't we ask Thornhead for some gold dust? Do you know anyone close by that can lend us some money?"

"Shemway—he's got lots of money now," Jason grumpily answered.

Nickle shook his head. "Sharlindrian—she can help us."

Jason sighed. "I already know I'm not going to like this day much."

Just then, a Taxi-Lator stopped in front of them, its large doors opening with a pop. A Snake Head with large glasses hissed at them, "Where to?"

"The Elf Quarter," Nickle replied. "We'll pay double the fare once we get there."

Forty-five minutes later and after a near-death collision with another Taxi-Lator, they arrived a block away from Sharlindrian's home. Jason adamantly refused to approach the house; instead, he stayed in the Taxi-Lator and attempted to calm down the Snake Head, who went into a fit once he found out the Dwarves did not have the gold to pay.

Nickle sprinted to the house and knocked on the garden door. After a moment of waiting, Nickle lost all patience; he kicked the handle, but the solid wood did not budge. He was about to kick it again when Sharlindrian's pleasant Elf features appeared as the door suddenly opened.

The Dwarf was out of breath. "I… need… money."

"I think you have the wrong home. Social Services are several blocks from here."

"I'm…serious…"

It took several long minutes, all the while Nickle struggled for breath, before he could convince the Elf he would pay her back—with interest, of course. She disappeared behind the door and several moments later, reappeared carrying a medallion of gold.

She held the gold medallion just out of Nickle's reach. "Here, you can have this… but—"

"But?" Nickle asked. "But what?"

"But I want to come with you."

Frustration exploded in Nickle's chest and cascaded down his body. "*Doesn't this Elf understand? This is a matter of life and death. Lives hang in the balance here—millions of lives.*" The Dwarf nodded. "Fine, but we've got to hurry."

Sharlindrian nodded. "So, where are we going?"

Nickle gave a quick explanation over his shoulder as he sprinted towards the Taxi-Lator. He did not know if Sharlindrian understood what he said, but he did not care. Several times, he had to stop and wait while the Elf emptied a rock from her shoe or stopped to take a break. When they finally arrived, Jason was just getting up from the ground—the Taxi-Lator was gone.

"What happened?"

Jason shook his head. "He bit me and kicked me out."

Nickle rolled his eyes. "Of all the rotten luck. Why didn't you just hail another one?"

"We can try but Taxi-Lators don't often pass by the Elf sector." Sharlindrian pushed the two Dwarves to the side. "Let me help." With this, she took three steps forward and flipped her hair dramatically in the wind. Her soft skin seemed to glow in the Faerie light, making her appear even more beautiful.

Jason was about to scoff, but then four Taxi-Lators showed up.

Nickle shrugged his shoulders and boarded one of them; the other two immediately followed. They shot skyward and barreled towards Tiran 'Og. Nickle kept shaking his head, almost as if to convince himself that this whole thing was not his fault. There was an empty pit in his stomach, one that was becoming more painful the closer they got to Tiran 'Og. The long trip at least gave them a chance to explain to Sharlindrian everything that had happened. It took her a while to grasp the importance of the situation, even longer for her to show some sense of empathy. After three hours of riding in the bumpy Taxi-Lator, they arrived in a dramatic cloud of dirt.

"You better stay here, Sharlindrian," Nickle said.

"Then you better hurry," the Elf retorted.

Nickle swallowed the Shrinking Rune before he was even out of the Taxi-Lator. In retrospect, this proved a bad idea and actually slowed his progress more than it sped it up because as he shrank, the distance to the doors of Tiran 'Og dramatically increased. Jason ended up carrying Nickle the rest of the way and placing him at the foot of the eloquent Gnome entrance. Then he too swallowed a Shrinking Rune and joined Nickle's side.

The two Dwarves were well known in Tiran 'Og, and immediately they were warmly greeted by a set of guards. A chorus of "hellos" and friendly nods followed them as they quickly passed through the large gold doors and headed towards the main court. A Gnome had gone ahead of them to find Lord Reckle Berry, and by the time they arrived in the main hall, the Red Cap Lord and the Green Cap King of Tiran 'Og were present, perched on their thrones. Reckle looked grumpy as he sat on his regal chair, almost offended by this rude interruption. When he saw it was Nickle walking towards him, however, his expression immediately changed into a grin.

"Don't grin for me," Nickle said in a bold voice, "for this will not be a conversation that will have either of us smiling. Gather all of your people Reckle, at least as many as you can in the next few minutes, for I have news that affects your whole kingdom."

"Your presence already summons them," Reckle replied. "Many thousand are already coming, coming to see the great Nickle Brickle'Bee—son of Joshua Brickle'Bee. Now, tell me why the Ambassador to the Gnomes says a Gnome can't grin."

"Because," Nickle replied. "You and I have been tricked, fooled by some unknown enemy. I don't know who is responsible, but I will make it my mission in life to find who is."

Reckle's eyes narrowed. "Responsible for what? For the first time in over two hundred years, my people walk with a leap in their step."

"Oh, great Red Lord of the fair Gnomes of Tiran 'Og, I visited the home of my father—in the cursed city of Gillian. It was there that I found out why he disappeared; it was there I found out why I grew up not knowing him. Joshua was a friend to the Fair Folk of Tiran 'Og, and he died protecting millions of Gnomes from slavery. Someone within the Tri'Ark tried to enslave your people two hundred years ago—but thanks to my father, they failed. They tried again—but this time, they succeeded. Millions of the fair sons and daughters of Tiran 'Og have been put under the whip and forced to be slaves."

A gasp filled the room.

The Green Cap King of Tiran 'Og spoke. "What proof do you have of this?"

"My word is my proof," Nickle said quickly, "but if you don't believe me, I recorded everything with a Memory Rune." Nickle pulled a Rune from his pocket. "If any of you doubt what I say, place your forehead to this Rune, and you'll see for yourself. Your people are in bondage."

"How could this have happened?" Reckle screamed.

"How," Nickle shook his head, "I don't know, but what's important is that you now know. You still have friends on the inside of the Tri'Ark that are diligently working to bring those who are guilty to justice."

"And where are my people?"

"In a place called Brimming Borough. I don't know the exact location—even though I've been there. But it's in the area where the old food distribution pipes meet before heading into EarthWorks. According to our records, Brimming Borough is a factory that was never built. But it does exist. I've seen it. And they've been funneling off newly hired Gnomes to send to this factory and force them into slavery."

Reckle stood up, his face red with rage. "I trusted you—son of Joshua—and this is how I'm repaid, with blatant treachery."

Nickle sucked in a deep breath. "I'm still as trustworthy as I ever was before; I was deceived just as you, just as any of you. There is more at work here than just you or me."

Reckle spat on the ground. "The Tri'Ark is as corrupt as it was when Kara'Kala ruled as a tyrant. Well, I'm through picking up the scraps off the Tri'Ark table; I'm through with watching my people suffer. What say you, Gnomes of Tiran 'Og, are you with me?"

A sudden shout echoed through the large room. Nickle had not noticed it before, but the room had gradually been filled by Gnomes while they talked.

Nickle took a step forward. "Reckle, we've already begun sorting this out. It won't be much longer before an investigation begins, and the guilty party is discovered."

"And how long will that take!" Reckle said. "Twenty days—twenty years. By the time an investigation will gain any momentum, my people could be completely wiped out. You just told me that someone in the Tri'Ark has betrayed me, and then you say that this same Tri'Ark is going to save my people. They are a pit of snakes—a den of liars. Gnomes will not be part of something so filthy, so corrupt, that families are separated and destroyed. We are the ancient Gnomes of Tiran 'Og; we are the sacred keepers of the Earth! We may die, but it will not be with a whip at our backs. Red Caps prepare for war!"

The room once again filled with applause.

Nickle raised his hands in the air. "This is a battle you cannot win. I came here to inform you of the things that are already in motion to free your people."

"For the sake of Joshua, I will not cut your head off while you stand in my court. But let this be the new law that governs a Gnome: Any person or creature allied with the Tri'Ark will be considered an enemy to the Gnomes."

The Green Cap King stood. "Reckle, you don't have the

authority to make your own laws. We are an organized society, one governed by rules. As King, I have to be in agreement with every decision—"

"—The time for talk has ended," Reckle said, "now is the time for action, which is the portion of government I oversee, Boysenberry." The Gnome turned his gaze back towards Nickle. "You tell the Tri'Ark that we have assembled for battle, that we will not give up without a fight. We will be on the surface. They will know where I will be waiting for them. Tell them to bring our people, or be destroyed."

A voice shouted from the crowd. "Why don't we free our families? Let's march to Brimming Borough."

Reckle turned towards the voice. "We'd be walking into a trap. First, we need to break the will of our enemies. We will fight them on the surface, where our magic is the strongest and theirs is the weakest. After we have smashed the Tri'Ark, then we will free our people! I call upon all those who are loyal to Tiran 'Og to prepare for war!"

Chapter 27

Traitor

Jason tugged on Nickle's arm. "Time to go."

Nickle shook his head. "They're insane. They can't go up against the Tri'Ark."

Jason pulled hard on his friend's arm and whispered back. "True…true, but let's talk about it later when thousands of beady-eyed Gnomes aren't staring us down."

Finally, Nickle gave way to Jason's persistence, and the two Dwarves turned to go. Their quick pace eventually turned into an all-out run once they left the great hall. They reached the massive golden doors of Tiran 'Og faster than they ever had before. Once outside, they both swallowed Restorative Runes, which counter-acted the Shrinking Runes.

They walked briskly to Sharlindrian, who was surprised as they approached. "What happened?"

Nickle shook his head. "They're going to war—and no matter what I said, I couldn't stop them. I had no idea how fired up they would get. They're going to the surface to make a stand against the Tri'Ark."

Sharlindrian shook her head. "They won't stand a chance."

Jason nodded. "Yeah, but let's get out of here before they make an example out of us."

Sharlindrian nodded. "He's right. We need to go."

Nickle did not answer for a moment. Instead, he stared longingly at the entrance of Tiran 'Og. Finally, he spoke. "You're right. With any luck, Thornhead will have this all sorted out before we get back to Hurn."

The three of them entered into the Taxi-Lator and took off. Soon, Tiran 'Og disappeared from sight, and they began the long windy trip back to EarthWorks. They traveled in silence, all of them either too tired or pensive to speak. The hours flew steadily by.

Finally, Nickle sat in one of the cramped seats that pulled out from the Taxi'Lator wall. "I just wish there was more I could do—"

"—Do you feel that?" Jason asked.

"Yeah, what is that?" Nickle said as something tugged at his mind.

Jason narrowed his eyes. "I feel…an urge… to stop or wait…"

Sharlindrian nodded. "Yes…pull over."

The Beast Head looked back curiously. "Pull over here? We're in a tunnel. There won't be a platform for—"

"—Pull over!" Sharlindrian yelled.

The Beast Head suddenly swerved to the right, barely avoiding another Taxi-Lator that had suddenly appeared in front of them. Both vehicles slammed against the tunnel wall and slid to a stop. The Taxi-Lator lost power and gravity suddenly returned. Jason collapsed to the floor, followed quickly by Nickle and Sharlindrian. It was completely pitch black until Sharlindrian activated one of her moon rocks.

"What happened?" Nickle asked.

The door to their Taxi-Lator burst open. A Human with a scarred face stood just outside, scanning each of them in turn. He finally spoke. "Are you all right?"

Nickle looked up at the figure. "Locke? What are you doing here?"

"I came over here to ask you the same thing. Come on out of there. I'm sorry I had to enter your minds." He began pulling the passengers out of the Taxi-Lator one by one.

As Jason was pulled free, he suddenly frowned in thought. "That was you that told us to pull over? I felt it in my brain—almost like it was my own thoughts. Are you a Scathian?"

"Yes," Locke answered. "Very perceptive, but I'm afraid I don't have time to talk about it. I came here to see Nickle."

"Locke," Nickle whispered. "Something terrible has happened."

"I know," Locke replied. "Shemway told me everything."

Nickle raised his eyebrows. "Shemway? How did—"

"—Who do you think hired him in the first place?"

"Hired him?" Jason said. "We hired him; we paid him twenty-five kilos of gold dust."

Locke laughed, a deep belly laugh that filled the tunnel. "That dirty Thieftian tricked us both then. I paid him twice that much to break into Brimming Borough."

Jason shook his head. "Is he the one who's behind all of this? Is he the one that forced the Gnomes into slavery?"

Locke shook his head. "He's a Thieftian, nothing more. I'm just glad to see that you're all safe. You're getting too involved in matters that are too dangerous. Where have you been?"

"We're just returning from telling Reckle Berry about Brimming Borough, about the Tri'Ark's betrayal, about the millions of Gnomes forced into slavery."

"You did what?"

"I told him about what happened to the Gnomes. He was pretty upset. He mobilized the Gnome army and is leading them up to the surface."

"Of course he did. He had no other option. But what I don't understand, is where you're coming from now."

Nickle thought for a moment. "Tiran 'Og, of course."

"So, you haven't returned to EarthWorks since talking to Lord Reckle Berry?" Locke asked carefully.

"No. We're almost there though, so that's got to count for something."

Locke scratched his chin. "How's that possible? The Silver Army was mobilized over forty minutes ago. Thornhead himself told me that you had reported that Reckle Berry was heading up to the surface with his armies."

"I haven't returned to EarthWorks yet," Nickle replied. "I was delayed. I ran out of money and had to borrow some from an Elf."

Sharlindrian rolled her eyes. "I can hear you talking about me."

Locke rubbed his jaw and stepped away from the others. "That means…the Silver Army was mobilized before Thornhead even knew that the Gnomes were preparing for war."

"What?" Nickle replied.

Locke shook his head. "And now it all makes sense…."

"What does?" Nickle whispered. "Who's behind all of this?"

"Thornhead," Locke answered.

Jason scoffed. "The Elected Chief Warlord of the four Dwarf Clans a traitor? Please…."

The Scathian nodded a few times before speaking. "Nickle has been the key to Thornhead's plan from the beginning. Because of your father, he knew you would have the best chance of winning over the Gnomes. He knew that if anyone could open up trade again with the Fair Folk, it would be the son of the great Joshua Brickle'Bee. Nickle, when you were first sent to the Cogs of Hurn, what did they decide about your case?"

"That I wasn't enough of a Dwarf to stay. They voted against me being drafted into the Silver Army."

"And who changed their minds?"

"Thornhead."

"After you graduated from camp, who assigned you to work with the Gnomes?"

"Thornhead."

Jason shook his head. "No, we asked to be assigned to the Gnomes, not the other way around."

Locke nodded. "Yes, and yet it was against regulation for a Tenderfoot to be given such a high-profile assignment. Neither of you had enough experience or training. And I've never seen Thornhead break regulation, not even with his own sons and daughters."

"How did he know we would ask for the assignment then?" Jason asked.

"That day in The Library," Nickle replied. "Remember that book that showed up on the desk after the Shadow thought I had misspelled my own name? Well, I had spelled it correctly. Someone must have slipped the book to the Shadow so he'd bring it to me."

Locke nodded. "He knew you would win the chariot race if you thought you were fulfilling your father's legacy."

Sharlindrian folded her arms. "How in the world was he going to get away with all this? Eventually, someone would start looking for the Gnomes that had disappeared."

"Not if the Gnomes had been killed during an uprising," Locke said.

The gloomy tunnel became even more eerie as silence settled over the group.

Locke shook his head. "Nickle, who told you to go tell the Gnomes about their enslavement?"

"Thornhead."

"That's why he mobilized the Silver Army so quickly, so he can slaughter the Gnomes before the rest of the Tri'Ark army arrives. If there are no witnesses to the crime, then there's no proof. While Thornhead is fighting the Gnomes on the surface, he was probably planning on having a few Dwarves execute all the Gnomes in Brimming Borough. That way, he could say that there were two Gnome armies, not just one. And after he had successfully destroyed them both. He would have been hailed as a hero."

Nickle sucked in a deep breath. "He would slaughter thousands of Gnomes just so he could build a key? A key to what?"

"I'll tell you soon enough, but first, we must save the Gnomes. We need to split up: Jason Burntworth, I need you to try and catch up to the Silver Army and slow them down as much as you can. You should have some clout with the Dwarves because of your success as an Ambassador. Sharlindrian daughter of the MeithDwins, your father is a captain in the Praetorian Guard, is he not?"

"Yes," Sharlindrian frowned. "But how did you know?"

"I just read your mind."

Sharlindrian frowned. "I don't think you should be prying into the minds of others."

"My deepest apologies, but I have no time for drawn-out conversation. If you have any loyalty to your friends here, if you have any pity for the thousands of Gnomes and Dwarves that are about to lose their lives, I need you to talk to your father."

Sharlindrian frowned again. "My father? You want me to…talk to him…"

"You can do this. I know it has been awhile since he's talked to you, but he's still your father. Persuade him, if you can, to send out the Praetorian Guard. Even if just a few Elves teleport to the surface, that could slow Thornhead's advance. Can you do that?"

"He doesn't normally see me without an appointment. And he'll be furious with me for breaking protocol."

"Can you do that, Sharlindrian?"

"If you're so good at reading minds, why don't you go?"

Locke shook his head. "I need to meet with the Tri'Ark to convince them to mobilize the Human forces against the Silver Army. You two might be able to buy time, but unless enough soldiers are standing between Thornhead and the Gnomes, I don't think he'll stop."

"What about those in Brimming Borough?" Jason asked. "They're the ones in the greatest danger."

"The Thieftians are taking care of that," Locke replied.

"What about me?" Nickle asked.

Locke put a thick hand on the Dwarf's shoulder. "I want you to lay low until this is all over."

"What? I'm the one responsible for this mess. I should be the one out there taking the heat."

"You're too important to be caught up in this little mess," Locke said firmly. "There's a lot more at stake here than you realize. A million Gnomes may die this day, but the sun will still rise tomorrow without them."

"What?"

Locke shook his head. "I need you to find a safe place and lay low. You can't do any more than what you've already done." With this, the Scathian turned around and headed off towards his Taxi-Lator. The moment he disappeared, their Taxi-Lator suddenly sprang to life.

Nickle shook his head. "Lay low?"

Chapter 28

Tuatha de Danaan

Nickle's heart sank as Jason dropped him off in Hurn. *"Right now, at this very moment, a massive army of Dwarves are heading to the surface in their Warships."* He shook his head. *"There has to be something I can do, something more than what I've already done."* He looked up at the Taxi-Lators and hovering vehicles zooming overhead, pretending to be interested in how close they came to colliding into each other. He secretly hoped that Jason would turn around and come back for him—but as the minutes went by, so did the possibility of Jason returning.

He turned around and began roaming through the street. Like his body, his mind began to wander. He imagined the entire Silver Army, all dressed for battle, marching towards a massive Gnome force. *"The Gnomes will have the advantage in numbers—I imagine there will be a hundred Gnomes for every Dwarf—but the Silver Army is unstoppable."* He pictured hundreds of golden-colored, spiked Dwarf Warships traveling through the tunnels. He had no idea how fast the frigates could fly or how soon they would reach the Gnomes. *"The tunnels will be crowded—that will at least slow them down. The Gnomes will reach the surface first—hopefully they will have enough time to prepare a good defense."*

Nickle slumped down against a building. "Dad had this all figured out—he had stopped it before it had even begun. He must have known Thornhead's weakness, must have known how to stop him. Too bad he's gone. I'd give everything I own just to talk to him once—just once. And I wouldn't mind seeing my mother either, wherever she is." He stared off into the distance, trying to fight the emotion that was settling in his throat. *"Dad would know what to do."*

Then a thought floated to the front of Nickle's mind. At first, he brushed it off. But the more he began thinking about it, the more real the idea became.

"The Faeries know—they would have to know. They were with

my mother when she passed away—maybe they were with my father when he died too. Maybe he's not dead, and the Faeries know where he is. Perhaps they were even the ones who warned my father of Thornhead's treachery in the first place." Nickle stood and began marching towards a street corner. His steps slowed as Jason's voice popped in his mind, *"Faeries will kill anyone who sets foot in their forest."*

Nickle took a deep breath. "I have to do what I can. I have to do something."

The Dwarf boarded the next Taxi-Lator he could find, instructing the driver to head towards the Blackwoods. The Taxi-Lator driver looked Nickle over twice, gauging to see if he was barking mad, but eventually, after seeing the large gold medallion he had borrowed from Sharlindrian, he gave in and set a steady course for the kingdom of the Faeries."

***

Nickle was surprised at how quickly he had arrived at the Blackwoods. He had counted on a long trip that would have given him more time to think of a plan. But the only plan he could come up with was "don't get killed," which seemed like a good plan in itself, but wholly inadequate. The Taxi-Lator had dropped him off quite a distance from the edge of the Blackwoods, so he had to hike a ways to reach it.

He paused at the edge of the forest and stared deep into the woods. It was as dark as night and twice as eerie. Nickle could see no sign of life—no sign of anything besides old rotting trees. The only movement was the occasional shaking of a leaf, or the tremble of a branch, or the passing of a withered cobweb, which seemed odd because there was no wind.

Nickle swallowed. "This is it."

As he stepped into the woods, the light around him diminished. With each step deeper into the forest, the light dimmed even more, until finally, it disappeared completely. It became darker than anything he had ever experienced. Not even after several minutes of staring off into the distance did his eyes adjust; it was almost as if he had suddenly gone blind. His pace was slow, but he pushed on, using his hands to feel his way past trees and bushes. The deeper he went, the slimier everything became. The air also turned foul, like the rotting remains of some long-forgotten animal; it overpowered him at times, forcing him to gag and cough. He walked on for what seemed like hours, tripping over fallen logs and toe biting stones. The forest was mainly silent, but an occasional blood-curdling howl would send a shiver down Nickle's spine.

He stopped to take a break. As he sat, on what he hoped was a fallen tree, dark thoughts seeped into his head. *"I could be walking in circles."* Nickle looked around, stunned by his decision to venture into the Blackwoods. *"I'm lost. What am I doing here?"* He felt stupid for disobeying Locke's advice of "laying low," stupid for coming into the Blackwoods Forest. *"But what else can I do?"* He was lost and, as far as he was concerned, useless. *"If only I had a way to make light. If this is the supposed kingdom of the Faeries, then shouldn't there be more light here than anywhere else?"*

Then something interrupted Nickle's thoughts. It was only the sound of a stick breaking, a sound he would have completely ignored in most other situations. But now, without the use of his eyes and in a forest that was darker than a starless night, a stick breaking set off alarms in his head. He strained his ears—someone was whispering. He could hear it faintly at first, but then it moved in closer. More voices began to hiss, almost in unison. A few of them laughed.

Nickle cleared his throat. "Who's there?"

The only response was laughter.

"I am Nickle Brickle'Bee! And I've come to speak to the Faerie Queen Titania."

A sudden pain slashed Nickle across his leg, forcing him down to his knees. He felt the wound, felt the blood that began to drip. He stood back up. "I've come here to talk to Titania about my father and my mother."

The voices began to whisper again—this time, they were much louder and closer. The language sounded so sleepy and distant. Each voice echoed and faded as if it was trapped in a canyon and never could escape. Despite the strangeness of the noise, he preferred it over the absolute silence.

Almost as if the creatures could read Nickle's mind, the voices stopped.

The Dwarf felt four cuts across his body; blood instantly began to pour down his face and into his eyes. "You'll have to kill me where I stand before I retreat out of these woods. I'm here to speak to the Queen! I demand an audience with Titania."

The voices intensified, turning into chilling shrieks that pierced his ears. A hundred more attacks followed. Nickle felt stabs of pain all over his body; it was as if he was being chewed by dozens of little mouths. The Dwarf swatted his hands through the air, hitting a few of the creatures by pure random luck. He began to run, but without light, he had no idea where he was going. He tripped over a massive log and fell into a ditch. It offered momentary cover from the attacks, but soon there were so many creatures it did not matter.

He felt something tugging on his ear and something else pinching his knee. "I am the son of Joshua Brickle'Bee—"

Before he could finish speaking, something bit his lip and sent blood down his chin. He continued, pushing himself into a half-limp, half-run. The creatures followed close behind, whispering and laughing as they went, almost as if this was some childish game. One of them tripped him, and his stomach hit an exposed root, knocking the wind out of his chest. He turned around to face the horde of creatures charging at him, his fists swinging wildly. They seemed to take the gesture as an invitation instead of a threat and began flooding in on him. Pain filled his body like he had never felt before. His flesh was on fire, burning as thousands of vicious teeth bit into his skin.

Nickle mustered all of his strength for one last yell. "I am the son of Elinda Brickle'Bee, and I seek the counsel of the Faerie Queen!"

The pain stopped. A moment later, the forest exploded with light. It became so bright that Nickle was forced to cover his eyes. As he did, he noticed that there were no cuts or burns on his arms; there was no blood dripping down his body. He was perfectly fine—not a scratch on him.

"It is forbidden for outsiders to enter these woods," a voice thundered.

Nickle looked up, trying to find the source of the voice. The light was so bright he could see nothing but his own hand in front of him.

The Dwarf stood. "I'm not an outsider."

The voice broke into a wicked fit of laughter. "What are you, a changeling? Are you a Faerie in disguise?"

"I am Nickle Brickle'Bee, son of Elinda Brickle'Bee, and I have been here before—while my mother was pregnant with me. If you have any mercy for her, let it fall to me too. I only have a few questions to ask."

"And what pressing matter is of such dire importance; what new insight do you want that will dramatically change your life?"

"Please, Queen Titania, I only have a few questions," Nickle whispered.

"So quickly, you assume I am the Queen."

Nickle swallowed.

"I will tell you what—mortal—if you can answer a riddle, I will answer your questions. If you cannot, then I will have my Faeries eat you alive."

"And if I refuse to play your game?"

The voice became so loud that Nickle cowered to the ground. "Then I will give you a few seconds to leave my forest, unharmed. But never will you be allowed to enter here again; never will you be able to ask your questions. And if you ever set foot in the Blackwoods, by the mighty brow of Sisten, I will have my Faeries devour you like a wounded walrus caught in a pool of piranha."

"I've never really been good with riddles."

"Is that your choice?"

Nickle took a deep breath. "But I'm even worse at running away. I accept your challenge, Titania, Queen of the Faeries."

"You arrogant fool," the voice yelled. "In the last thousand years, only one person has answered my riddles correctly—only one of the tens of thousands that have tried."

"I have to do this," Nickle replied.

The voice suddenly became louder than it ever was before. "The choice has been made!" The lights went out. Nickle flipped around and reached for a Rune on his Rune belt. His lungs tightened as he realized his belt was gone. The absence of his belt, and the memory of the thousands of stings that covered his body, put hesitation in his movement.

The voice came back, this time it hissed like a snake. "Are you sure, Nickle, son of Elinda? Are you sure this is the place you want to die?"

Nickle swallowed. "I didn't come here to die. But because of me, there's a chance that millions of Gnomes will be murdered today. If I die in the attempt to save them, so be it. My father made that same sacrifice years ago, and I'd gladly do the same. Please speak your riddle, Queen of the Faeries. I accept your terms."

"Impressive, young Nickle. You speak as one with authority."

"I don't have much time. Oh, great and fair Queen of the Faeries, what is your riddle?"

The trees began to illuminate a crimson light as the Faerie Queen spoke. "What is so fragile that when you say its name, you break it—so discerning that it is impossible to fake? What is usually present in the midst of triumph, and yet often occurs during a moment of disappointment? What renders ears useless and makes mouths of little importance? What can fill a massive room in seconds, and disappear just as quickly? It can be everywhere at once and nowhere the next moment. Too much of it will drive you mad—too little will do the same."

Nickle swallowed. *"Crap...I have no idea."* He pulled his hands through his hair. "And how many guesses do I get? I'm pretty sure I heard someone mention the word three. I get three guesses, right?"

"You get one guess...and make it quickly."

Nickle began dicing up the phrases in his head, *"'What can be everywhere at once and nowhere the next moment.' Sounds a little like time—or maybe wind. 'It renders ears useless and makes mouths of little importance.' That could also be time. But what about the first phrase, 'What is so fragile that when you say its name, you break it.' If I say the word 'time,' does that break it? Does time break? Maybe when someone breaks a world record. But that doesn't make sense."*

"You're running out of *time,*" the Faerie Queen scoffed.

Nickle scratched his chin. *"Was that a clue? Man, I can't believe I agreed to this. I can't believe this is how my life is going to end—my body being slowly digested in the bellies of thousands of Faeries."*

"Do you need more *light?* Maybe that would help you think."

Nickle shook his head.

"Well, then, it seems that *silence* is your only answer."

"No, no," Nickle answered. "I have an answer...and it's a good one."

"What is it?"

Nickle stepped forward and stuck out his hand dramatically. "Is it wind?"

Silence fell throughout the woods.

Then something laughed, and then something else. Moments later, the whole forest filled with thousands of little voices that cackled with delight. Light filled the woods, and for the first time, Nickle could see clearly. He was in the middle of a perfectly circular grove of trees that stretched seemingly forever into the sky. The trees were so tightly knit together, it was difficult to see where one began and another ended. There were thousands of Faeries, each one with brilliantly colored clothes and wings. Some of them floated in the sky, others flew. There were so many sizes, colors, and shapes of Faeries that Nickle had a hard time picking them out individually.

The Faeries found him just as interesting and began to poke and prod his ears and face. One of them pinched his nose, but Nickle ignored the pain.

The Dwarf shook his head. "Was that the right answer?"

A voice from behind Nickle answered. "No, it was not."

He turned around and caught sight of the most perfect and brilliant person he had ever seen. She was small, only six inches in height. Her hair floated in the sky, almost as if she was underwater. From her face and body shined a white light that was as pleasant as the rising sun on a cold morning. Her eyes were wide and blue, but they often shifted to the color of green. From her back sprang two silk-like wings that kept her aloft. She giggled.

Nickle smiled and bowed low. "You must be Queen Titania."

"Aren't you a proper gentleman."

"I once failed to bow to the Lord of the Gnomes, and I paid dearly for it. I won't make the same mistake twice."

"You must be Nickle."

"Why aren't your Faeries eating me up?"

Titania raised her eyebrows. "Faeries don't eat people."

"But I've heard stories. There are hundreds of rumors about how Faeries eat people who wander into their woods. I really thought you were going to make a meal of me."

"The rumors keep people away."

"Yeah, they do," Nickle nodded. "People are scared of Faeries—I mean really scared."

"Few deserve to see *Tuatha de Danaan*; fewer still realize its importance."

"It's amazing."

"Yes," Titania nodded, "and it's the last place on Earth like it. It has become a refuge for Faeries and forgotten Fair Folk alike. The Tri'Ark keeps expanding, and our people are forced to keep retreating."

"I had no idea there were so many kinds of Faeries."

Titania pointed to a tall Faerie that had hair as long as its body. "That's called a Long-haired Pixy. You can tell she's a Pixy because of the trail of light she leaves as she flies." She then nodded towards a Faerie that had clothes that were made of leaves. "That is a Summer Sprite. Sprites have bat-like wings and leave a trail of dust behind that often makes the Tall-folk giggle."

Nickle gestured towards a creature shaped like a soccer ball that was slowly moving towards them. "What's that?"

"That's a Gruttle. They are slow-moving but hilarious. Watch."

Nickle watched the Gruttle timidly approach. It had fat cheeks that flapped as it moved and sorrowful looking eyes; its wings on its back had to work furiously to keep it in the air. When it was within a few feet of Nickle, the Gruttle suddenly sneezed. The sudden propulsion from its nose sent the creature spinning off course. Moments later, it crashed into the ground, sending up a puff of smoke.

Titania chuckled. "See…hilarious little creatures."

Nickle laughed in turn, although he was pretty sure it was caused by a Sprite that had just flown overhead rather than the collision of the Gruttle.

Titania began to fly around the large circular room, Nickle followed. "There are thousands of different kinds of Faeries, each one with their own set of unique cultures and customs. Here's a group of Shrimp-sized Jinglers. When they fly, their wings make a small bell sound. Over to your right is a Trick Tail Glider. Instead of flying, they glide to where they want to go. Be careful with them; they love to play pranks on travelers." Titania pointed high above. "There's a set of Spots. Spots shift color depending on their mood. Do you see that green one there? It's a Green Grubber Spot—they love to eat tomato leaves. They're often responsible for the little bite marks Piddlers find on their tomato plants."

Nickle began tallying the Faeries on his fingers. "So basically, there are the Sprites, Pixies, the Jinglers, and the Spots—"

Titania shrugged her shoulders. "There are a lot more species than that—that's just the beginning. You also have Sprittles, Sprouts, Thunder Caps, and the Flueren Dales. The Flueren Dales are the most numerous of any type of Faerie. Many of them still live on the surface, despite Piddler's insatiable appetite for destruction. The Flueren Dales look like flowers—sometimes they are indistinguishable from the flowers they protect, besides having wings, legs, and arms. Every time you look at a patch of flowers on the surface, you're probably looking at a few Flueren Dales too. They help the flowers grow and often sing windy songs to them at night. Your mother loved Flueren Dales."

Nickle nodded. "Titania, that's what I've come to find out from you that no one else seems to know. What happened to my parents? Where are they?"

Titania gestured towards an arched doorway. "Follow me, child, for this not a pleasant conversation." They entered a small room that had two normal-sized seats and a table. "Please, sit down."

Nickle pulled out a chair and began to sit but stopped halfway. He was no longer facing a six-inch tall Faerie Queen, but a person almost precisely his height. She was more beautiful than before and several times more radiant. She had on a silver dress that shimmered as she smiled.

Nickle suddenly felt very conscious of his sweaty back and his dirty fingers. "Titania?"

"Yes, Nickle," she replied. "Please sit down. This is how your mother and I would often spend our afternoons, talking about anything that crossed our minds. She was a very bright woman, much brighter than a typical Dwarf—if I may be so blunt. She was the only Dwarf I could talk to and not be beyond bored before the conversation even really started."

"What happened to her?"

"She died—here in *Tuatha de Danaan*—giving birth to you. It was a painless passing. That should at least give you some comfort. The last words she said were your name: Nickle Bree Brickle'Bee—that's how we knew what to name you."

"But if I'm only fourteen—"

"You're actually fifteen, and your birthday is on January 12th."

Nickle arched his eyebrows. "Really? I've never known my birthday. So, if I'm only fifteen, and my father went missing over two hundred years ago, that means my mom was pregnant with me all that time. How's that possible?"

"You're a very special Dwarf, and there was very powerful magic involved in your birth—magic that not even I, the Faerie Queen, understand completely. I don't know how you came to be. I don't know what happened to Elinda Brickle'Bee before she came here, begging for protection."

"Protection from what?"

"The supporters of the Demon Brood."

"Were they responsible for the murder of my father?"

Titania shook her head. "Your father was killed by Thornhead Back'Break several years after Kara'Kala was imprisoned in his fiery cell. Thornhead had long since been a silent supporter of Kara'Kala and was working on setting him free. Joshua, however, stopped him before he could."

"How did he stop him?"

"After the Gnomes had befriended the Tri'Ark, Thornhead forced a few hundred Gnomes into slavery, but before he could recruit more, Joshua discovered his evil plot. Your father was able to free the Gnomes, but as he was traveling back to EarthWorks to report to the Tri'Ark of the treachery, he was attacked by Thornhead and a group of Dwarves. It was a horrific battle, one that left Thornhead permanently scarred, but eventually, Joshua lost. But killing your father was Thornhead's undoing. Joshua was the one person who the Gnomes had trusted. After the mysterious events of Joshua's death and rumors of the Gnome enslavement leaked out, the Gnomes cut ties with the Tri'Ark."

"How long have you known this? Why didn't you tell someone? Why didn't you tell the Tri'Ark?"

In an instant, the Faerie Queen's features changed. She was no longer a smiling lady that enjoyed the pleasantries of life. She was now something different entirely—so different that Nickle pulled away from her. Her eyes narrowed into slits while at the same time, the light around her glowed more intensely. A raw power flowed through her veins and manifested itself in her now cold eyes. "Do not presume to judge me. I've only been able to piece this all together recently. Even still, I don't trust the Tri'Ark or their justice. I did not trust them when they were controlled by Kara'Kala, and I don't trust them now."

Nickle swallowed.

Her face shifted back into a pleasant smile. "But that's not why you're here…not directly anyway."

Nickle leaned forward. "The Fair Folk of Tiran 'Og are in trouble. Thornhead has finally succeeded in enslaving the Gnomes—much to my unwitting assistance. He is now headed to the surface with a massive Dwarf army, where he intends to slaughter the Gnomes to cover up the evidence of his actions. The rest of the Tri'Ark army has hopefully been mobilized, but they won't be there in time to sort out the details. The Gnomes will be dead soon…millions of them. You have to help me stop him."

"I can't interfere," Titania said.

"Certainly, you have a lot of power," Nickle pointed out to the mass of Faeries outside the room. "You've got millions of potential fighters out there."

Titania closed her eyes for a second, contemplating some scenario in her head. After a few moments, she shook the feeling off, and her eyes slowly opened again. "Now is not my time. I can do nothing for the Gnomes, but you can."

"Me?"

Titania leaned forward. "Challenge Thornhead to battle. Challenge him in front of his whole army—and he'll have to deal with you first before he can assault the Gnomes."

"I don't even have my Tines yet—"

"—But you've been trained with Dwarf armor, have you not?"

"Every Dwarf in the Silver Army has been trained with Tines, but I don't have a set of my own. Most Dwarves don't earn enough money to pay for their Tines for twenty-five years."

Titania smiled and stood. "Come with me. I have something to show you."

They walked quickly down a hallway and entered into a smaller room. Light filled the space as they entered. On a silver stand was a massive, perfectly crafted set of Dwarf Tines. It had large shoulder guards that were carved deep with spidery Runes. Attached to the back was a thick silver axe that shimmered as Nickle stepped forward.

Nickle touched the armor—a chill traveled from his fingers and down his spine. "This is amazing. Where did you get this?"

"It was your father's armor; it is the only thing your mother brought with her. It was forged by Limar, the Fire Thief. For generations, it was passed down to the firstborn of each family, and now it falls to you—even though you are not the firstborn. It was in bad shape, but I was able to get it repaired. I even made a few improvements of my own."

"But even if I have this armor, there's no way I'll be able to reach the surface in time. It took me a while to get here, even longer to find you. The Dwarves are probably unloading their troops on the surface as we speak."

Titania walked closer to the armor and smiled. "They are, as my Faeries tell me, and presently, nothing is standing in their way."

"Well, then, what can I do? I can't magically appear up there." Then inspiration hit Nickle. "Can you teleport me to the surface?"

"No," Titania answered. "But you can."

"Can what?"

"Have you ever performed magic that you did not understand?"

"Well...I...I..."

"Have you ever created light?"

"A few times, I shot a white fireball from my hands."

"As I said, Nickle, you're different. Only Faeries and Elves can naturally create that sort of magic. And only Faeries can make *true* light. You can create Faerie light."

"How do you know that?"

"When you were three, you suddenly vanished. It took us years to finally find you, but when we did, you were on the surface, living with a family of Piddlers. You seemed to like it better up there, so we let you stay. You had turned yourself into light and then back again— only Faeries can travel that way. Elves have a cheap imitation that is not nearly as safe or effective."

Nickle grabbed the breastplate and began situating it on his chest. "How do I do that? How do I change myself into light?"

"It should be easy because we are in *Tuatha de Danaan*—the source of all Faerie magic. Just think of your mother and I'll do the rest."

306

"Why don't you come with me? If you can't help me, at least watch what happens and make sure I don't do something stupid. Thornhead, is, after all, about to kill millions of the Fair Folk."

Titania helped tighten the breastplate. "We Faeries have our limits, and that is one of mine. I can't get involved in this conflict, not even at your request."

The Dwarf tightened one of his arm bracelets. "What if they are in the middle of the battle and they don't see me? I can't stop a whole army from charging by myself. What if they don't even notice me? I'm only one Dwarf."

Titania helped the Dwarf with the other arm brace. "That's one thing I can do for you—get their attention. After that, all you have to do is challenge Thornhead to combat."

Nickle swallowed. "He's a pretty tough guy—about as tough as they come. Are you sure I'm qualified for this—"

"—You'll find your armor has powerful Runes as well as a few of my own enhancements. Plus, you are used to living on the surface, and your magic will be comparatively much more potent than Thornhead's magic. You'll find that your armor will equal his skill. Don't forget to put on your Rune belt. It's on the table by the door."

Nickle sighed with relief. "Oh, that's great news. I was worried I'd lost that for good."

"Now focus, Nickle. Think of your mother, think of the time she spent here in *Tuatha de Danaan*. Imagine her voice; picture her face."

"Before I teleport, can I ask you one quick question that has been bugging me this whole time? What was the answer to your riddle, by the way?"

"*Silence.*"

Chapter 29

Dwarf Bout

"Form battle lines!" Thornhead screamed.

The Silver Army had just broken through the surface, and already the Dwarves were beginning to unload from massive Warships. Thousands of them poured out, their armor thundering as they marched. As the first line formed, they were reinforced by a second line, and then a third. The Dwarves seemed as numerous as the rocks beneath their feet. They flooded the field of battle and fell in to tight rectangular formations.

The Elected Chief Warlord of the Silver Army was wearing a set of black armor that was studded with horns. He looked at the Gnome army in front of him. It was the biggest collection of Fair Folk he had ever seen. He could distinguish banners of six different Gnome clans and two different groups of Leprechauns.

A Dwarf Warlord approached Thornhead's side. "Sir, we've got a count of the enemy forces. They're about eight million strong."

Thornhead nodded. "I will lead the main body of our forces into the middle, towards their Lord. I need you to bring the Warships around on their flank and unleash all your firepower—holding nothing in reserve. We'll meet in the middle after we've smashed through their lines.

"Excellent plan, sir."

"Ready your warriors."

"What about offering terms of surrender; we don't even know why they're rebelling."

Thornhead shook his head. "I don't trust those tricky creatures. It's better we charge in and catch them off guard. We can negotiate terms of peace once we've chopped off Reckle Berry's head and placed it on a tiny platter. Spare nothing until I halt the attack. This is the last time this race rebels against the Tri'Ark—this is the last time they come against us to war. I will make an example of them that will burn into the minds of everyone for a hundred years."

The other Dwarf shifted uncomfortably on one foot. "Sir, by order of the Tri'Ark, we must offer conditions of surrender—"

Thornhead turned to face the Dwarf, his hand raised in the air. "—Am I the one leading this army…or is it you?"

The Dwarf swallowed hard. "Sorry, sir. I misspoke."

Thornhead lowered his hand, but he did not take the edge out of his tone. "Fall back in line, soldier, and prepare to attack. Tonight, we feast over the dead bodies of our enemies. Tonight, we fight for the Honor and Glory of Hurn."

The clan leader slammed his chest. "For Honor and Glory."

As the Dwarf forces finished forming their battle lines, an odd silence fell over the field as the two sides stared at each other. The day was perfectly blue, not having a cloud in the sky. A few birds had been circling the area, but they seemed to sense the tension in the air and had long since left. Reckle Berry had chosen the battleground wisely. The Gnomes had situated themselves along the base of three hills, where they had entrenched themselves deep into the Earth. The rising sun was at their backs and would be in the faces of the oncoming Dwarves. The field between the Dwarf army and the Gnome encampment was long and filled with waist-high grass.

Thornhead scratched his jaw as his mind raced with thoughts. *"No doubt, there will be Gnomes hiding in the grass, waiting for unsuspecting Dwarves to fall into their traps. It will slow the army, but it will not stop it. We are stronger, but they have a better position. But none of that will matter once Reckle Berry is dead."*

The large Dwarf gripped his hammer and twisted the handle. "Lock your shields!" Thornhead said through the Rune Communicator attached to the side of his helmet. The Dwarves repositioned themselves. "Raise banners!" Several thousand standards were lifted high. "Forward march!"

A thunderous noise permeated the field as tens of thousands of Dwarves began to move forward, Thornhead at their lead. They entered the tall grass and pushed on. Moments later, a group of Dwarves screamed as they were engulfed in fireballs. They had hit the first nest of Gnomes. The fireballs slowed them, but it did not stop the heavily armored Dwarves.

Thornhead grinned as he pointed his large war hammer towards the entrenched enemy. "Double time!" Instantly the Dwarves broke into a jog.

More explosions of fire erupted from the waist-high grass. To Thornhead's right, a dozen Dwarves disappeared as the ground caved in. Large explosions followed as thousands of Gnomes leaped from their hiding places and began to wreak havoc with Alteration spells. The Dwarves countered with their Runic magic and sent hundreds of Gnomes flying in all directions.

Only a hundred yards separated the two armies when Thornhead gave his final command. "Charge!" The Silver Army broke into an all-out run. From the hillside, the Gnomes began launching massive bird-shaped projectiles that rained down on their opponents. Fireballs exploded all around them, sometimes engulfing a dozen warriors at once. Several Dwarves activated the Runes in their weapons and returned fire, shooting down the fiery birds long before they could do any damage.

Thornhead broke from the Dwarf column and sprinted towards the enemy. He was just starting to activate one of the Runes in his gigantic hammer when white lightning hit the ground twenty feet in front of him. The large Dwarf leaped for cover, barely dodging another thunderbolt that came streaking down. More lightning followed, striking the ground in quick succession. The explosions were so forceful and dramatic that the Dwarf army slowed their charge until they finally stopped. The Gnomes also stopped firing.

The pressure from the bolts sent a shockwave that shook the Earth and kicked up a wall of dust and debris. More lightning fell from the sky until it was so constant that it looked like one massive bolt. The air smelled scorched. The dirt beneath the bolts was blackened and smoking. Many of the closest Dwarves took cover—so did the Gnomes. The noise became louder and louder until only thunder could be heard for miles in all directions. The lightning twisted and turned, whipping with merciless power into the ground. Some of the closest rocks were reduced to gravel; anything that had been alive where the lightning struck, was now long past living.

Then, in an instant, it all ended. A sudden silence fell over the battlefield. A massive smoke cloud drifted up from the charred spot of Earth.

Thornhead looked up. Where the lightning had once been, a Dwarf now stood. His armor was a mix of red and black and studded with small rough nubs. He had no shield, but a massive, ornate axe strapped to his back. A thick helmet covered his head and eyes.

Thornhead shook his head. "It can't be...Joshua?"

Nickle flipped open the visor on his helmet. "All of you have been deceived by Thornhead. He's behind all of this madness. Lay down your weapons."

"No!" Thornhead replied. "This half-breed is a traitor. Don't listen to him."

"I'll gladly surrender, if you do the same, Thornhead. Throw down your weapons and we can all wait for official members of the Tri'Ark to sort this out."

"Not today, boy," Thornhead said, raising his hammer. "You'll have to kill me first."

Nickle slammed his visor back down and freed the axe from his back. A second later, a massive beam of steam hit Thornhead in the chest, sending the large Dwarf flipping backward in the air. His helmet was knocked loose and was lost in the tall grass. As the Warlord rolled, a rock split open his cheek, sending blood spilling down his chin.

Thornhead touched his face and growled as he saw the blood. "So, boy, you think you can take on a battle seasoned Warlord? Ambitious."

The Dwarf Lord pushed off the ground with his hammer and charged at his opponent. Nickle used an Air Rune to jet himself into the sky—Thornhead did the same, and a moment later, the two collided in mid-air, sending a horrific shockwave that rumbled the spectators far below. Thornhead flipped back and landed firmly. Using his momentum, he slammed an Earthquake Rune into the ground that shook the earth. Nickle cleared his mind, trying to withstand the magical quake. He was successful for a few moments, but the unrelenting shaking eventually broke his concentration, and he fell to the ground, his axe skidding from his grip and landing a foot away from his grasp. He had trained with Tremor Runes in Tortugan, but this was so much stronger.

Thornhead grinned as he approached his thrashing opponent. "What? Have you not learned about Earthquake Runes? Oh, that's right, you've only been in the Silver Army a year. You're barely a Tenderfoot. It does seem a little advanced for the likes of you."

Nickle stretched out his arm, reaching for his axe.

Thornhead slowly stepped forward, placing a large boot over Nickle's weapon. "And what do you think you're doing?"

Nickle grinned. "I'm distracting you while I grab a Rune from my belt." The next moment, a Hellion Rune exploded against Thornhead's armor, knocking the Dwarf onto his back. His armor absorbed most of the attack, but it left a gaping hole above his right breast. Despite the explosion, Thornhead recovered quickly.

The two Dwarves stood and cinched their weapons in their armored hands. They began to circle each other, gauging the other's strength. Thornhead went on the offensive, swinging his massive hammer with incredible speed. Nickle ducked and dodged, but a third swing clipped his right leg and sent him pitching to the side. The next moment, Thornhead shot a fireball from one of the Runes on his armor, hitting Nickle in the right shoulder. The Dwarf tumbled backward. He recovered just in time to dodge another fireball, this one several times larger than the one before.

The Warlord grinned. "You'd be a match for your father if he was still alive."

Nickle yelled and charged forward. His attacks were not nearly as powerful as Thornhead's, but they were precise. As their weapons met, large sparks shot in every direction. They were evenly matched for a few moments but, slowly, Nickle began to drive his opponent back. His skill, as well the brightness of his armor, seemed to increase the more he fought, and soon, Thornhead was fighting frantically to stave off the onslaught. Thornhead tripped in a Gnome hole and fell, dropping his hammer as he rolled. Once the Dwarf Lord was down, Nickle rushed in, swinging his large axe at his opponent's head.

It almost ended there, but at the last moment, Thornhead jumped up and grabbed two Runes from his belt. "Come on, boy! Did you think I'd just fall over dead!" He smashed the Runes together and whispered a few ancient words. The next moment, millions of pieces of fiery ash shot out like a tornado into Nickle's face. The young Dwarf stepped back, his body caught in the torrent of wind and flames. His armor initially resisted the small flames, but as the suit began heating up, Nickle could feel the burns spreading over his body.

He narrowed his eyes. *"Concentrate. Resist the magic."* He pushed the corners of his mind, forcing the small fiery ashes away from his skin. He could feel Thornhead's Rune wavering and weakening, but it did not break. Nickle grabbed a Water Rune from his belt and smashed it into his palms, which sent liquid exploding from his hands. He concentrated, forcing the water to mix in the air and extinguish the fire. Moments later, Thornhead's Rune broke, and the fiery whirlwind disappeared.

The Warlord clenched his jaw and narrowed his eyes. "Now, you die!" He grabbed a Rock Rune, crushed it in his hand, and began hurtling watermelon-sized boulders at Nickle. The Dwarf ducked under the first stone and sliced the second entirely in half. A third one hit him in the helmet, knocking it completely off. Another struck him in the leg and set him to his back. He rolled to his right side, barely dodging another rock that grazed his skull. He kept moving until he found a little cavity in the ground. The stones continued to zoom above, occasionally exploding into a cloud of dust as they hit the ground.

Nickle gritted his teeth. This whole situation suddenly seemed like a bad idea. *"I don't need to win. I just need to stall him—stall him long enough for the Tri'Ark to arrive."* Three more stones zoomed above, one of them bouncing dangerously close to his head. *"But what if they won't come for another hour—maybe they won't come at all. This could be it for me."* For the first time since being in the Silver Army, he felt fear deep in his belly. *"I hope the Faerie Queen was right—I hope there's something different about me."*

Nickle activated the Strength Rune in his chest and rolled up to his knees. A stone headed straight for his face, but he punched it out of the air, sending it spiraling off to the side. Another came at his chest, but he caught it and dropped it harmlessly to the ground.

"All right," Nickle whispered. "You might have the advantage in a straight fight, but let's see how you handle a little different setup." He stood and ran away from Thornhead, leaving his axe in the grass. While he went, he began pulling out Earth Runes and throwing them at the ground. As soon as they hit, the Runes exploded into massive columns of dirt that were nearly twenty feet tall. Before long, dozens of pillars stood between Thornhead and Nickle.

"You can't stop the inevitable," Thornhead yelled as he picked up his hammer. "Joshua thought he had stopped me, thought he had prevented me from ever succeeding. But you were the key to your father's demise! His own son!" The Dwarf Lord approached the first pillar and sliced it in half with his hammer, sending dirt clods rolling across the field. "If this is your great plan, boy, you might want to rethink it. You don't know what real combat is. You don't know anything about the heat of battle." He sliced the next pillar of dirt.

As Thornhead was speaking, Nickle went around sticking Sight Runes on key pillars. Before long, as he looked through the Sight Runes, he could see the Warlord slowly navigating the maze of dirt. Then, inspiration hit Nickle. *"It's me he's after. If I'm standing right in front of him, he won't be concerned with what's behind him. I have to time this perfectly."*

"Come on, Nickle!" Thornhead laughed. "Where's the fire you fought with before! Come out and face me like a Dwarf, or do I have to conjure a Wind Rune to blow your pitiful dirt pillars to the ground? Come out, boy. You can't hide forever!"

When Thornhead sliced through the next pillar, Nickle was waiting for him on the other side. The young Dwarf jumped up and punched Thornhead squarely in the nose. The movement was so quick that the Dwarf Lord could do nothing but stumble backward in surprise.

Nickle grinned. "Who's hiding?" With this, he turned and ran—Thornhead in hot pursuit. They ran through the maze of dirt pillars, Thornhead shouting curses all the way. Finally, Nickle ran out of room, trapped by his very own Earth Runes; the only exit was through Thornhead, who was now grinning enthusiastically.

Thornhead laughed. "Just like your father, trapped behind a wall of dirt."

"Wait," Nickle yelled, "before you kill me, at least tell me why you were forcing the Gnomes to make a key."

Thornhead shook his head. "If you can't figure it out, then you're too stupid to know. Now it ends, boy."

Nickle smiled. "Yes, it does."

As the Warlord prepared to swing his hammer, a set of Hellion Runes that Nickle had carefully placed as he retreated suddenly erupted. The explosion created a domino effect, toppling pillars of dirt. Thornhead turned around just in time to see a wave of earth flooding over him. A cloud of dust permeated the air, making it hard to breathe. One moment, Thornhead was there, grinning with victory; the next, he disappeared entirely under the dirt.

It took several moments for the dust to settle and the pillars of earth to stop toppling over. Nickle kicked the dirt off his boots as he slowly approached the mound. He stood there for a moment, a Rune in his right hand, waiting to see if the Dwarf Lord would somehow escape. He caught sight of Thornhead's large war hammer and fished it out of the dirt. Still, the Dwarf Lord did not emerge.

Then with a blood-curdling yell, Thornhead leaped out of the earth, a Strength Rune on his chest burning bright with use. "Die traitor—"

The Warlord's scream was cut short as Nickle knocked Thornhead over the back of the head with his own battle hammer. The Warlord crumpled to the ground, his body going limp as a dishrag.

The young Dwarf approached cautiously, raising the hammer in case this was some kind of trick. But Thornhead did not move. He was out cold. Nickle used the time wisely, stepping forward and wrapping a Rope Rune around the Warlord's hands. After the hands were bound, he unlatched Thornhead's armor. He could not completely remove it, but this would prevent the Warlord from using additional Runes.

As Nickle was finishing, Thornhead stirred, his eyes fluttering open. "Finish me, lad. You've beaten and broken me; it's your right to take your revenge. You owe it to your father."

Nickle frowned. "It would be fitting to finish you with your own weapon—"

"I'm ruined, boy," Thornhead wheezed. "End it here. I would have done the same for you. Take your revenge."

Nickle hefted the large war hammer. It would be so easy to strike him down. They were still surrounded by several dozen pillars and hidden from sight. But the moment passed and he let the head of the hammer fall to the ground. "No, that's not me. You'll pay for your crimes—not with a moment of pain—but with a lifetime of suffering. I don't know where Dwarves keep their criminals, but for your actions, I imagine you'll be there for a long time."

"You'll regret fighting me—you fourth class Dwarf!" Thornhead screamed. "I serve the Demon Lord—the one who will bring order to this land. Look around you, Nickle. EarthWorks is falling apart: the Cennarians are in rebellion, the Faeries won't honor their contracts, the Tri'Ark is full of thieves and spies—and Dwarves are fighting each other. I know you think he's evil, but that's because of who you've listened to. He's a good man, one that has the power to bring order to chaos. Has no one told you how efficient and orderly EarthWorks was when he was Emperor? It was a much better time— a glorious time. Now fear and panic run rampant in the streets. We are nothing but a shadow of what we were then. I know you don't believe me, but one day, you'll have to justify in your mind why you fight for a side that does not work together. There are others who will succeed where I have failed. Eventually, Kara'Kala will break free from his chains—eventually, he will rule EarthWorks again."

Nickle narrowed his multi-colored eyes and leaned closer. "And that's when the good people of EarthWorks will unite and tear him down."

Chapter 30

The Face in the Mirror

Nickle left Thornhead and limped out of the maze of dirt, carrying the Warlord's large hammer. As soon as he emerged, a troop of Dwarves and Gnomes began running towards him, their weapons held at the ready.

Nickle raised his hands in the air and stared at both sides in turn. "There will be no battle today. We've been tricked by Thornhead—he's betrayed us all."

The Dwarves stopped their charge but did not ease up on their weapons. A large Dwarf narrowed his eyes. "And what proof do you have of this, lad?"

Nickle took a deep breath. "The Gnomes in front of you are my proof—"

The Dwarf was interrupted by a low buzzing sound that slowly increased in volume. The next moment, the land began flashing like a set of cameras. With each flash, an Elf suddenly appeared, dressed from head to toe in intricate armor, which was a mix of pearl white and light olive green. They seemed to favor the sword, but Nickle also saw several carrying double-bladed staffs.

A large Dwarf approached the most important looking Elf, yelling at him before he was even close. "What are you doing here? We're in the middle of a battle!"

"Stand down, Dwarf."

The Dwarf puffed out his chest. "If you were going to teleport here, why didn't you flank the enemy!"

The Elf narrowed his eyes. "We're not here to fight with or against you. We've come to stop this battle. By order of the Tri'Ark, Thornhead Back'Break is under arrest." This statement was followed by an uproar from the Dwarves. "He'll be tried for crimes against EarthWorks and the Cogs of Hurn. Find him and arrest him. Where is the Dwarf they call Nickle Brickle'Bee?"

Nickle raised a weary arm—which was still smoking from combat. "I'm here."

The Elf approached the Dwarf as if he was something disgusting. "You're to come with me at once."

Nickle nodded. "But what about the battle?"

"There will be thousands of Elves teleporting here in minutes; they'll ensure the Dwarves and Gnomes don't kill each other. For now, your presence is requested."

"Who are you? Do I know you?"

"No, you don't, little dirt-digger," the Elf said without even looking at Nickle.

The voice and tone of the Elf seemed so familiar to Nickle, he was almost sure they had met before. "Are you Sharlindrian's father?"

The Elf's face went even tighter, but he did not answer. Nickle frowned. The two walked in silence until they reached the rear of the battlefield. They had to wait for nearly half an hour before a massive thorny Dwarf Warship appeared. As soon as the ship settled on the ground, a door fell open like a drawbridge.

"In there," the Elf insisted.

Nickle swallowed as he entered through a large set of heavily armored doors. The Warship looked much smaller on the inside. Nickle was taken to a center room where he immediately spotted a grinning Jason Burntworth.

Jason slapped Nickle on the arm. "How did you get to the surface so fast, you dirty dog?"

Nickle leaned in and whispered. "I'll have to tell you later—"

"Nickle Brickle'Bee," a familiar voice said, "is this your idea of laying low?"

The Dwarf turned around and spotted Locke. Despite his severe tone, the large Scathian was smiling.

Nickle nodded. "I had to try."

"I know you did; I just wish I would've been there to see it. The Elves have been teleporting to this Warship and updating us with everything that has been going on. Everyone is stunned by the little display you put on—so much so that they're not sure if you're really a Dwarf."

Nickle looked longingly at a chair that was a few yards away.

He had not noticed the pain from his wounds before, but as his adrenaline started to fade, he began to feel it now.

"Go ahead," Locke said. "Sit down."

"How did you know I wanted to sit?"

Locke laughed. "I don't have to read your mind to see you're exhausted. Go ahead, sit."

Nickle eagerly obeyed and carefully sat down on the chair. As he did, pain spidered up and down his body, especially in the leg where he was hit by one of the massive stones. He took a deep breath as he rubbed his hands through his hair.

"Where did you get the armor?" Jason asked.

"It was my father's—and now it's mine."

Jason grinned. "Look at you! You're only fourteen, and already you have your Tines."

"Fifteen. I just found out..."

"You amaze me, Nickle—you really do."

Locke pulled up a chair and sat down. "And me as well. Not very many could have stood against a Dwarf Warlord for long—much less beat him. You stopped a very evil man from doing a very evil thing."

"That's something I've been wondering. What was he forcing the Gnomes to make—" Suddenly Nickle's tongue stopped working. It was almost like the oxygen in the room had abruptly disappeared.

Locke's voice came to Nickle's mind as clear as if the Scathian was speaking out loud. *"Don't mention the key. There are many here who cannot be trusted."*

Nickle responded with his thoughts. *"But what does the key do? What does it open?"*

Locke's voice returned to Nickle's mind. *"You're a bright Dwarf. I'm sure you've already figured out what it was intended to be used for."*

"To free the Demon Lord."

"That's right. It's called the Eternal Key, and actually has never been completed before. It can unlock anything—even the most complicated enchantments. If it weren't for you, Nickle, we would be in a very different situation right now. The Demon Lord could very well have been freed. And that would be very bad."

"But you weren't alive when he was around the first time. How do you know?"

"I just know."

Jason suddenly stirred. "Why did it all of a sudden get quiet? We just stopped a massive army of Dwarves from squishing thousands of Gnomes into dust. We're heroes, Nickle. And girls love heroic guys. I bet they'll hold a banquet in your honor, maybe even give you your own holiday. Wouldn't that be something? Nickle Brickle'Bee Day— the only holiday that encourages you to pick a fight with your supervisor."

Locke grinned at Jason's enthusiasm. "I think it's best if we keep this quiet."

Jason's smile slipped. "What do you mean?"

"I'll handle it," Locke stated.

Nickle nodded, but he was barely listening now. He looked at Locke and forced his thoughts into words. *"Is there a room in here where I can be alone?"*

"The captain's quarters. It's right down the hall, the last door on the right. I'll make sure no one bothers you."

Nickle stood up. *"Thanks."*

"Where are you going?" Jason asked.

Locke put his hand on the Dwarf's shoulder. "Let him go. I'm sure he's exhausted."

Nickle headed down a long hallway. Pain still pulsed through his body, making it difficult for him to walk. He finally reached the captain's quarters and stepped inside. It was small but orderly. There was a desk, a bed, and a small circular window that overlooked the battlefield. Outside the window, Nickle could see thousands of Elves teleporting into the open space between the Gnome and Dwarf armies.

Nickle collapsed onto the bed and closed his eyes. He was tired, but his mind was too active to sleep. Only a year ago, he was a scrawny kid with weird eyes that was passed between foster homes. He could remember each family he stayed with vividly, remember the feeling of loneliness that had put him to sleep every night. He had not realized how much he needed a friend until he met Jason. *"There's no better friend than him. When we were in the city of Gillian, he put his life on the line when it really counted. He's the only reason I graduated from Tortugan and made it this far alive."* He then thought of everyone he had met. Their faces flashed before him with their most memorable expressions. He had met some wretched people, like Cynthia Mallet and Thornhead Back'Break, but he had met some really great people too, like Locke, Edward, and Reckle Berry.

In the past year, he had changed from who he once was. His arms had become stronger and thicker, his mind keener and quicker.

He had just done something that would have seemed impossible a year ago. He sat up and looked into a mirror that was sitting on a small desk. He studied his face for a long while, almost as if he was just meeting himself for the first time. Then he smiled—which is something he had never done in front of a mirror before.

Epilogue

Finally Home

Nickle entered his new apartment, a grin spread across his face. The furniture was in shambles, the walls were peeling, two of the windows had cracks in them. He took in a deep breath, filling his lungs with air. It was his air. Now that he was renting this place, he owned this air. This was his new place, and all of it belonged to him—well, him and his roommate, Jason.

He and Jason were no longer Tenderfoots, as indicated by the new insignia on their Silver Army attire. They were now Second-Class Bevels and did not have to reside at the barracks. It was a modest promotion, but reasonable, and so would not draw too much attention. It was the least the Cogs of Hurn could do after the two boys had saved millions of lives. With it came more freedom, a small pay increase, and more opportunities.

Jason followed in behind, knocking himself in the head as he entered the short doorway. "Ow, that hurt." He slipped further inside, unloading the boxes he carried onto a couch. The couch groaned before it broke on one side, sending the boxes tumbling to the floor.

With his arms free, Jason was able to take in his surroundings. There were cobwebs, but no spiders, a few broken shelves, a random book in one of the living room corners, and a stain on the floor that looked like it might be blood. It was probably cranberry juice, Jason decided.

"What do you think?" Jason asked.

"It's awesome," Nickle replied.

Jason folded his arms, inspecting the grandiose ceiling. "Didn't I tell you? We're big-time now, living in the heart of EarthWorks."

Nickle collapsed onto a dusty love seat and grinned.

Jason retrieved a stone tablet from the top of one of the boxes. "Check this out. You're gonna appreciate this."

Nickle took the tablet and read the article displayed on the screen out loud. "Thornhead Back'Break, the former Elected Chief Warlord of the Silver Army, was just sentenced to two thousand years of hard labor on the island of Patmose. Thornhead was arrested for his involvement in a plot to free Kara'Kala, the Demon Lord, who currently is sentenced to life and imprisoned behind the FireWall.

"To achieve his goal, Thornhead enslaved millions of Gnomes and forced them to make powerful weapons. Before the weapons were completed, however, Tri'Ark officials discovered some irregularities with the allocation of the Gnome workforce.

"Fearing that he might be caught, Thornhead enacted a bold plan to cover up any evidence of his crimes. He mustered the Silver Army and planned on murdering thousands of Gnomes. On the plains of Baldier, the Silver Army squared off with a host of Gnomes and Leprechauns, but before the two sides clashed, an unknown but talented Dwarf Warlord challenged Thornhead to combat. The battle stalled as the two Dwarves fought, giving time for the Human and Elven forces to arrive on the surface to diffuse the conflict."

"You'd think they'd at least give us an honorable mention," Jason said.

"I'm sure that's Locke's doing," Nickle replied. "But hey, they did give us some medals."

"Those tiny things. They even misspelled my name on the inscription.

"You're lucky. Sharlindrian didn't even get one."

"What am I supposed to do with that thing?"

"I bet you've got it in your back pocket right now, don't you?"

Jason frowned. "Well, you never know if you're going to run into a cute Elf girl that needs some convincing you're a heroic Dwarf."

Nickle laughed.

Then Jason suddenly grinned. "I get to pick my room first." Then he set off, heading down the hallway, Nickle on his heels. Jason turned into the first door on the right, ramming straight into it. He was knocked back into Nickle, who caught him just before he hit the floor.

"The handle's a little stiff."

"Well, give it another go," Nickle said. "This time, twist the doorknob before trying to run through the door."

"I did," Jason replied. He stepped closer, demonstrating in

slow motion. This time he successfully twisted the knob, but it also popped off. "Oh, dang. Not a big deal. That should be an easy fix." With the knob still in his hand, Jason entered his room. It was tiny, cramped, and musty. "Man, I've got big plans for this place. I'm going hang my axe on that far wall and maybe get a mini-fridge in here…."

Nickle only laughed as he continued on to his room. When he entered, he stopped at the threshold, his eyes taking in the scene. It was just as small as Jason's room, but more oddly shaped. As his eyes traced the walls, they fell upon a set of armor. It was his father's Tines.

"How did that get in here?" Nickle asked to the empty room. He approached the intricate armor, his eyes full of wonder. It had been cleaned and polished so well it could almost be used as a mirror.

"Before you do anything weird or start changing or something," a voice said from behind, "I want you to know you're not alone."

Nickle turned to the voice. It was Reckle Berry, Lord of Tiran 'Og. He was wearing a leaf jacket, pants made out of yellow flower petals, and a green, pointy cap. The Dwarf saluted and bowed low.

"You're not the Ambassador anymore," Reckle Berry said, "so there's no need to overdo it."

"You're dressed rather ordinary for a Gnome Lord."

"Sometimes, it's hard to sneak out of Tiran 'Og dressed as a Lord."

Nickle gestured to the armor. "Is this your doing?"

Reckle Berry smiled. It was an odd expression—a mix of joy and sadness. "Luckily, the Faerie Queen's magic protected it, so it wasn't beyond repair. When I first saw you fighting, I assumed your strategy was to beat the Dwarf Lord's fist with your face."

Nickle laughed. "That was the first Dwarf Lord I've ever fought."

Reckle Berry nodded. "Well, it's been completely repaired."

"I priced the repairs with a Dwarf Tine Singer, and it was beyond expensive. Who did you get to fix it?"

"Not a Dwarf, if that's what you're asking."

"Gnomes?"

"Yes, my boy," Reckle Berry responded. "Some of the best Gnomes and Gnames worked on your armor for a week—something that we have not done for a Dwarf for a thousand years. We even improved upon it with a few Chillian spells. I don't think there is another set of Dwarf armor quite like it."

"What do you mean?"

"Your Runes will recharge more quickly and can conjure light on command."

"I don't know how I can ever thank you."

Reckle Berry nodded. "I need to thank you. You saved my people."

"I'm glad it turned out the way it did."

"You're so much like Joshua. When I first met him, I had written off the Tri'Ark completely. But he was so relaxed, so different than every other Dwarf I'd dealt with. I remember one time, when he was invited to a Gnome banquet, they had given him clothes made from straw. Well, something had not been done quite right with Alteration magic and the material was made more flammable, not less. So, as I was being crowned the Lord, and as Joshua bent low in respect, he came a little too close to one of the sacred torches. In an instant, during one of the most important ceremonies we conduct on the island of 'Og, he turned into a ball of flames. Either from shock, or panic, no one knew what to do. Finally, Joshua leaped off the Fanqueen bridge and into the most holy waters of Tiran 'Og—which is the source of all magic. By Gnome law, anyone found in the water should be executed, but we only laughed. Joshua, could have chosen to be offended; he could have elected to accuse us of making an attempt on his life. But instead, he laughed along with us, as if he was part of the joke, not the butt of it. He was a noble Dwarf. It was on that day I decided to grant his one desire—to allow him to compete in the Quintillian Games."

"Thank you for sharing that with me. I know so little about my parents, it's always refreshing to hear about their past."

"He was a true friend, as are you. We need more people like that to fight against those like Thornhead. You know, there's more out there like him."

Nickle sighed. "Thornhead said there were. I can't imagine how anyone could fight for the Demon Lord, but Thornhead is proof that his supporters do exist. In any case, what will happen to your people now? Where will you go?"

"We'll stay in Tiran 'Og, at least until the decay of the Earth becomes more than we can bear. And after that, well, I don't know. We'll have to head to the surface, carving a home next to the Piddlers. And you? What do they have you doing now?"

Nickle shrugged. "We're no longer Ambassadors. Jason and I were both assigned to the Dwarf Enforcement Unit in EarthWorks. I'm still trying to decide if it's a punishment or not."

Reckle Berry walked to the door frame. "I'm sure you'll do fine. I better be going now. A Lord's duties never end. Watch your back, Nickle. There's more wrong with the Tri'Ark then there is right. Trust your friend Locke—he's better than most—"

Jason came rushing in, his face sporting a goofy grin.

As he passed the threshold, he kicked Reckle Berry like a soccer ball. "—Nickle, did you see the hookups for the Stone Screen we could get."

The Gnome Lord flew across the room, hitting the far wall. Luckily, Reckle Berry was quick to use his Alteration magic, which turned the wall rubbery.

Jason noticed the Gnome Lord for the first time. "How long has he been here?"

Reckle Berry was red-faced and rigid, his hands at his side. "Hello, Jason."

Jason nodded politely, completely unaware he had just punted the Lord of Tiran 'Og across the room.

"I better take my leave before Jason discovers a candy in his pocket and rushes back in here to share the good news."

"If you ever need me," Nickle called to his back, "just call.

"And me too," Jason added.

"Oh, and there is one more thing," Reckle Berry added. "I don't know what it is, but there's still something waiting for you in the city of Gillian. I appreciate you finding out about Thornhead's evil plot, but that is not what you were meant to find." Reckle Berry nodded once more before his body turned into a gust of wind, blowing out the door.

"What?" Nickle asked. "How'd he do that?"

"Alteration magic, Nickle," Jason replied. "What's wrong with him? Seemed a little grumpy."

"I wouldn't worry about it. What were you saying about the stone screen hookups?"

"We can get a 55-inch stone screen."

"Yeah, as soon as we can afford it."

Jason winked. "You know, they never stopped paying me my Ambassador's salary."

"Are you serious?"

"I probably should tell someone."

"Most definitely."

"But, we're not Tenderfoots anymore. We're Second Class Bevels, which means," Jason added dramatically, "we not only represent ourselves but the whole Silver Army as well."

Nickle nodded. "That's a good point."

"We wouldn't want to misrepresent the Silver Army with the state of our shabby apartment, would we?"

"Now that you put it that way," Nickle said, his hand stroking his chin. "It's almost essential we spend that money to refurbish the house. We just entertained a Gnome Lord after all."

"That's so weird," Jason said with a grin, "those were my thoughts exactly."

Just then, someone knocked on the front door. The two friends exchanged looks.

Jason began walking to the entrance. "You expecting anyone?"

"No," Nickle replied. "Maybe it's the neighbors and they brought over a house warming gift."

Jason threw open the door, a smile on his face. His expression changed upon seeing who it was. "Oh, it's you." He pushed open the door, allowing the person to enter.

Sharlindrian studied her surroundings. "I'm so sorry. I didn't know you guys had just been robbed."

Jason rolled his eyes as he collapsed onto the couch. This time, the opposite leg broke, making it level with the floor. The Dwarf ignored the noise and stared intently at his new stone tablet.

"Robbed?" Nickle asked. "If that were true, jokes on them. We've got nothing worth stealing. Come in. Sit down."

Sharlindrian smiled weakly. "Thank you, Nickle. I appreciate it, but I can't stay long. I just came to bring you this." She handed Nickle two tickets.

"What are these?" Nickle asked. "Tickets?"

"I thought you, Jason, and I could go together, as a celebration for our victory over Thornhead."

"Tickets to what?" Jason asked, his curiosity getting the better of him.

"To see The Harbingers," Sharlindrian replied.

Jason exploded out of his seat. "No way." He ran over to Nickle's side, snapping the golden stubs out of his hands. "These are tickets to The Harbingers. Are you serious? Do you know how expensive these are?"

"One of the members is a friend of mine."

"Well, I have no idea what you two are talking about," Nickle said.

Jason's eyes went so wide they almost exploded out of his head. "Are you serious? You've never heard of The Harbingers? This is fantastic."

"Will your dad let you hang out with us?" Nickle asked.

Sharlindrian bit her lip. "Well, in exchange for hanging out with you two on occasion, I've agreed to attend the Harbordeen Academy."

"You don't sound too excited."

Sharlindrian sighed. "Well, I'm not, but I've run out of excuses. So, at least I was able to get something out of the deal."

Nickle smiled. "Well, I'm sure you'll do fantastic."

"What a great way to start the year," Jason replied, his eyes still locked on to the two tickets. "This is going to be awesome."

Nickle stepped forward, looking at his two best friends in turn. "I'm sure it will be. This is shaping out to be the best year yet."

A Note from the Author

Sterling enjoys hearing from his readers. If you have any comments, thoughts, critiques, questions, and/or just want to say hello, please email him at isbnwriter@gmail.com. It may take some time for a response, but he tries to answer each email personally. Or, you can visit his website at sterlingnixon.com to learn about additional details of upcoming releases or pending projects.

If you enjoyed this novel and want to see more written by Sterling, please take the time to leave a review on Amazon. Your comments and support help out tremendously.

Other Books Written by Sterling Nixon

Historical Fiction:
Gladiators of the Naumachia

Dystopia Fiction:
Acadia
Titan
Charron

Young Adult Fiction:
Nickle Ricklee: In the Heart of EarthWorks
Nickle Brickle'Bee: In the Halls of Harbordeen
Nickle Brickle'Bee: In the Home of Atlantia
Nickle Brickle'Bee: In the Floating Isles of Balinbar

Made in the USA
Monee, IL
19 February 2022

91506567R00184